JEWEL OF THE KIMBERLEY

A STEELE OPS NOVEL

ERIN MOIRA O'HARA

Cover design by Fiona Jayde Media
Interior formatting by Author E.M.S.

ISBN: 978-0-9942469-2-9 (Print)
ISBN: 978-0-9942469-3-6 (EBook)

Jewel of the Kimberley is a work of fiction. Names, characters and incidents depicted in this book are the products of the author's imagination, or are used fictitiously. Any resemblance to actual events, organisations, or persons, living or dead, is entirely coincidental and beyond the intent of the author.

Published in the United States of America.

*Jewel of the Kimberley is dedicated to my father, Eric,
a true gentleman.*

Books by Erin Moira O'Hara

The Knight of Castle Kildare

Conspiracy in Emilia Romagna

Beat of the Jungle

Steele Ops Series

The Kalista Diamond

Precious Gems

Jewel of the Kimberley

The Amethyst Code

Bindarra Creek

Tempting Fate

Date with Destiny

A Twist of Fate

ACKNOWLEDGMENTS

Researching Jewel of the Kimberley has brought me into contact with some remarkable people and amazing experiences. I needed to know the mechanics of flying a helicopter. So, after a safety video and basic training, Skyline Helicopters gave me a flying lesson over the Port of Newcastle. It was fantastic.

My thanks to Master Mariner, David Phillips, who answered all my questions and arranged for me to board a coal freighter. Captain Rabi was very hospitable, taking the time to guide me over his ship. Broome's Port Authority and Tourist Association were also very helpful. One person I must acknowledge is a Seahawk pilot, who unfortunately I can't name. His help with my Black Hawk scenes has been fabulous.

Thanks to my brilliant critique partners, S.E Gilchrist and Sue Bellamy. My Editor Deadra Krieger, cover artist, Fiona Jayde Media, and my formatting team at Author E.M.S.

CHAPTER ONE

Nick Flanagan closed the car door and breathed in the familiar scent of tamarind trees. Their huge canopies cast a welcome shade and offered respite from Broome's blistering afternoon heat. He rolled his shoulders to ease the building tension. Anxiety or anticipation? It was a toss-up, but there was no turning back now.

The hangar had been a place he'd haunted as a teenager and then again while on breaks from the Army Aviation Corp, and later the SAS Regiment. Nothing had changed, although it seemed unusually quiet. He let his gaze drift over the other vehicles—Barry's dusty Nissan and a top of the range, black jeep. He'd expected the parking area to be full this time of year. Pushing the thought aside, he headed for the hangar's staff entrance.

Nick paused as his mentor's raised voice reached him.

"I'm not bloody interested. Now get the hell off my property before I call the cops."

Edging around the office, Nick focused on a heavy-set bald guy standing right up in Barry's personal space.

"You're making a huge mistake, Sanders. How long can you operate a charter business without pilots? I suggest you take the offer. Retire while you can."

Barry's cheeks flamed and his forehead glistened with sweat as he faced the larger man. "You tell your boss to take his money and shove it up his arse. I'm not selling and that's final. And you can tell him I'm installing security cameras and an alarm, so next time you sabotage one of my choppers, I'll take you and your boss to the cleaners."

"You're a fool, old man. How ya gunna fly with a broken arm?" The stranger gripped one of Barry's arms and twisted it behind his back.

Barry yelped and Nick leapt forward, punching the stranger in his kidney. As Barry fell sideways, Nick bent the stranger's arms up his back and kicked his feet from under him, dropping him to the concrete floor.

The man grunted and tried to twist away.

Nick rammed his knee into the middle of the guy's back and wrenched his arm higher. "I don't know who the fuck you are, but you ever touch Barry again, I'll break every fucking bone in your body. You got that?"

"I got it." The man sucked in his breath.

Nick stepped back and snatched a long handled spanner from the bench. "Not so nice on the receiving end, is it? Now get off these premises before you really piss me off."

The man clambered to his feet. "You don't know who you're messing with, hero."

"Neither do you, arsehole, but I'll give you a word of warning. You so much as sneeze near Barry and I'll come looking for you. Now fuck off."

The man glowered before barging out of the hangar.

Nick turned to find his old friend leaning against the bench. "You all right, Barry?"

"Yeah," he rasped, breathing heavily. "Thanks."

"What's going on? Who was that guy?"

Barry rubbed his chest. "He works for a rich bastard by the name of Damon Pearce. They want to buy me out. I refused to sell so they poached Dave and Max. I need those two chopper pilots to keep this place running. I even had to rent my house out and move in with my sister just to stay above board."

Nick frowned. "What's this about sabotage?"

"Water's been added to my fuel, the phone-lines cut, and last week someone smashed a chopper console. I can't prove it's them, but I got to tell you, mate, it's bad for business. I've taken to sleeping here just to keep an eye on things, and I hate to admit it, but I'm scared shitless." He rubbed his arm. "I know you've got a job in Sydney, but you couldn't help me out, could you?"

Nick placed the spanner on the bench. "I've taken a couple of weeks off to sort out some personal stuff, but I'll do what I can while I'm here." He looked round the hangar. "First off, we need to get your surveillance cameras up and the alarm system installed."

"It's all here. I just haven't had the time to do it."

Nick glanced at his watch. He'd been flying or in transit for ten hours, so crawling around the roof of a hangar in this scorching heat didn't appeal. He also needed to track down his quarry and he couldn't wait any longer. "Are you okay physically?"

"Yeah, the old ticker is not what it used to be. My doctor wants me to slow down or retire, but flying's my life. I can't go fishing every day."

"You can if you want to." Nick grinned. "There's something I need to do, but I'll be back this evening to install the cameras and alarm. It'll be a lot cooler and you can tell me about Pearce."

"You're a good man, Nick."

"Only because of you. I hate to think what would've happened to me if you hadn't taken me under your wing."

Barry laughed. "You certainly were an angry young man. It's a pity things didn't work out with..." He flushed. "Sorry, I know you don't like to talk about her."

"Actually, that's why I'm in town. I've discovered Ava left England four months ago and moved to Broome."

"Here?"

"Yep. And she never married."

"But that would mean her father..." Barry's mouth dropped open.

"Lied to me." Nick shook his head in disgust. "I knew he despised me, but being a minister of the church, I didn't question his word. And he was so bloody convincing."

Barry frowned. "Why Broome?"

"The pearl industry. Ava once said the best pearls in the world came from Broome. One of her dreams was to use them in her designs."

"It's a wonder she hasn't been out to see me."

"She's probably avoiding you." Nick exhaled. "I'd better go. I need a shower before I delve into the past. I'll give you a call later." He saluted Barry and strode out of the hangar. There was no sign of the black jeep.

Ava Mitchell replaced the magazine on the small table in the solicitor's waiting area then glanced at her watch. She needed to sign several documents and then she would legally own half a Jewelry shop. Helen Davis was in her fifties, and a divorcee with one son in Queensland. She'd been looking for a partner and it presented an opportunity Ava couldn't resist. Her own online business was thriving, but to have a prime location in Broome where she could display and sell her creations was a Godsend. Helen fast became a friend and confidant.

Ava chewed her nail. She wasn't an impatient person, but sitting here thirty minutes past her appointment time was beginning to grate. If they didn't hurry up, she'd miss the courier and have to wait to send her consignment until Monday. She also needed to deliver some new designs to Helen and pick up the love of her life. An arrow of pain shot through her heart. *The second love of my life.*

She looked at the wilting lilies on the counter and then at the receptionist, a frosty-faced woman who wore her graying hair in a severe bun. The only touch of softness a pair of pearl earrings set in an intricate filigree swirl—a popular design that Ava was particularly proud of creating.

The receptionist glared at Ava's foot, which she hadn't realized she was taping against the leg of the low table. "My husband is extremely busy, Miss Mitchell. He may have slotted you in, but if his next client arrives on time, you'll have to wait."

Ava raised an eyebrow. It was obvious who wore the pants in their relationship. "I'm also a busy person, Mrs. Bell, and I would have been happy to come on Monday, only Mr. Bell insisted." Ava smiled sweetly, trying to soften up the frosty battle-axe.

"Be that as it may, I will not disrupt our regular clients who made their appointments well in advance. You will have to wait."

Ava dug her fingernails into her palms, resisting the urge to take the lilies and hurl them at the frustrating woman. Her heart sank as the outer door opened and an older couple walked in. By their clothing and the woman's jewelry, Ava guessed they weren't short of a dollar.

A huge smile transformed Mrs. Bell's face. "Mr. and Mrs. Henderson, it's so nice to see you. Frank won't be long. How was your trip to Spain?"

Ava watched in astonishment as the woman fawned over and

flattered the couple. It was a wonder she didn't curtsy as she ushered them through a door, offering to make them tea or coffee. Shaking her head, Ava crossed her arms and waited. If Mr. Bell hadn't insisted she sign today, she'd get up and walk out. *I'm too obliging.* That's what Maggie had been telling Ava for the last four years. She needed to grow some balls, be assertive, stop letting people walk all over her. Ava glanced at her watch. It looked like today was the day.

The receptionist strutted back into office looking well pleased, even smug. That did it. Ava stood. "Please ask Mr. Bell to have the documents delivered to me at the shop. You can also inform him I shall be taking my business elsewhere. Oh, and those earrings your wearing—I designed and made them." Ava picked up her purse and hat then stalked out, delighted to see the woman's mouth hanging open.

She felt a little mean, but who the hell cared. *I will not allow anyone to take me for granted ever again.* Pain lanced Ava's heart, swift and sharp, causing her to stumble. It often came on like that, no warning. One thought of the past and bam. *Will I ever move on?* She stepped onto the footpath where the oppressive humidity almost smothered her. "And will I ever get used to this damn heat?" She jammed her wide-brimmed sun hat on then glanced at her watch. "Argh, where has the day gone?"

Nick dropped his duffle bag on the bed, wiped the sweat off his forehead and hit the air con. His shirt and pants stuck to him like a second skin. He needed a shower and a shave before confronting the woman he should have married four years ago.

She might not even speak to me. If I'm honest, it's what I deserve.

He stared out over the resort's pool to the deep blue of the ocean beyond and the fluffy cloud mass gathering overhead. Wet season in the tropic of Capricorn was an experience he'd always found fascinating. Most days were hot and humid with random, short-lived downpours. Occasionally there'd be violent storms, impressive lightning displays and monsoonal winds. A sight to behold, which brought Nick back to the reason he'd come to Broome. It was time he laid his ghosts to rest, confronted the woman he couldn't forget, and learned the truth. Then, maybe he could move forward.

Pulling out his wallet, Nick withdrew the photo he'd carried for seven years. He stared at the fiery redhead with exquisite emerald eyes She'd captured his attention the second he laid eyes on her. She'd called him the love of her life and he'd almost believed her.

Nick slipped the photo back in his wallet and withdrew the address Simon gave him. A jeweler's shop here in Broome, where the designs of Fantasy Pearl Creations were sold. *At least one of Ava's dreams came true.*

As he stepped into the bathroom his satellite phone vibrated against his hip. It wasn't a number he recognized. "Nick Flanagan speaking."

"Hey, mate. It's me, Ryan. I've just arrived on the island."

"G'day, mate, how's Sam and Talos?"

"As happy as pigs in mud, now that they're back with Kallie and Jane. Simon's here with me and we're wondering how you're making out in Broome?"

"It's bloody hot." Nick kicked off his shoes. "I'm glad I don't live on this side of Australia anymore."

"You're soft, mate. The SAS guys handle that heat carrying a thirty kilo pack."

"Yeah, that's why you and me joined Six Av." Nick chuckled. "We wanted to fly Black Hawks, not tramp about in the hot sun all day with heavy packs."

"So, have you caught up with Ava yet?" Ryan's voice held a note of wariness.

"No. I'll ask for her number at the jewelers."

"You reckon they'll give it to you?"

Nick flicked the shower nozzle on. "They will when I tell them I want her to make a piece of jewelry for a member of the royal family."

"Which royal family?"

"I haven't decided yet."

Ryan laughed. "Good luck, mate, but if things don't work out, you can still make it to Fiji for the nuptials."

"Yeah, I know. Thing is, Valentine's Day had a special meaning for Ava and me. That's why I decided to hang off until now. If there's a chance at winning her back, Valentine's Day might be it. What's the latest on Vietnam?"

"The boss reckons it's sorted. We're in the clear and the police over there have shut down the ring's trafficking operations. Another successful mission and another fat payment. I'm not complaining."

Nick dragged his damp T-shirt over his head and dropped it on the floor. "What about Ming? Did the Vietnamese authorities agree to our proposal?"

"Yep. The kid's set for life and a far sight better off than if we hadn't come along."

"Great. That's been playing on my mind."

"I've got to go, mate. I've spied a tasty morsel."

"As in a female?"

"Oh yeah. She's a dark eyed beauty with attitude, and by the way Gibbs warned me off, she's either his sister, a close relative, or his intended."

"Then you've got no hope in hell. See ya, mate." Nick ended the call and stripped off the rest of his clothes. He stepped under the showerhead, relishing the jet of cold water over his heated body. Once he'd spoken to Ava, he would install the cameras and alarm system for Barry.

৯৵

Nick parked the car in the only bit of shade he could find and climbed out into the humid heat. Glancing around, he wasn't surprised to see most cars carried several layers of red dust. The shrubs along the street island looked in need of water, and although there were plenty of vehicles about, there were only two men having a conversation further up the street. It made sense that most people would be in the air-conditioned shopping center.

Nick closed the car door and stared at the jewelers. Four years was a long time apart. He'd changed dramatically from the young chopper pilot who'd let the love of his life walk away. His job had toughened him both physically and mentally. It had also made him realize just how much he'd lost, which then led him down a path of casual encounters with women he immediately forgot.

A green CRV parked several cars away and a woman in sunglasses and a wide-brimmed hat exited the driver's seat. She hurried round the vehicle then leaned into the passenger side. Nick's gaze slid over the navy skirt, and down toned legs to her dangerously high red sandals with small bows, just like Ava once wore.

Could it be?

Nick's gaze shot back to the woman's face as she straightened. *Ava.* Gone were the fiery, luscious long curls he'd loved running his fingers through. She looked sophisticated, stylish, and sexy. But then Ava had looked sexy in a pair of worn jeans and an oversized jumper, or his Guns and Roses T-shirt.

Hands fisted, Nick stepped onto the footpath. His chest tightening with a fear he'd only ever experienced in hostile combat situations. Ava nudged a shoebox under one arm, stacked her purse and a folder on top, and raised a phone to her ear. Fumbling with the box, she closed the door with her backside then laughed. The familiar sound drifted over Nick like a silken scarf, so vibrant he could hardly breathe.

"Okay, it's a date. I'll see you at seven. Now I really must run. Bye." She laughed again before ending the call then entered the shop he'd been heading for.

Damn, she's seeing someone. Gutted, Nick turned to retrace his steps then abruptly stopped and raised his sunglasses. *I can't walk away without speaking to her.*

His stomach in knots, Nick strode along the footpath and glanced in the shop's window. Delicate pearl necklaces, bracelets, and rings were displayed on black velvet stands. He pushed the door open.

Ava had her back to him as she spoke to a fair-haired woman at the rear. The floppy hat sat on a glass counter between them. A surge of delight shot through Nick. She hadn't chopped off her beautiful hair. It was caught up in a thick braid. He closed the door softly and stepped forward as Ava opened the shoebox.

"These are a little different, Helen, but I wanted to appeal to younger women."

The other woman's attention remained riveted on the contents of the box. "They're stunning, my dear. You have a remarkable talent."

"Thanks. I was hoping you'd like them."

"Oh, I do." The woman looked up and noticed Nick. "I won't be a moment, sir."

Decision made, Nick drew in a deep breath. His body was as tight as a coiled spring, but he wasn't walking away. Not this time. "It's Ava I'm after."

Ava's whole body stiffened and her phone dropped from her hand as she twisted round. The anguish on her now pale face stunned him. "Nick." It came out strangled, hardly more than a whisper. Confusion and shock battled in her green eyes. She raised a shaking hand toward him, as if he were a specter.

Nick caught her as she fainted. Not exactly the response he'd been expecting. Scooping her into his arms, he looked around for somewhere to put her.

"Oh my goodness." The woman bustled from behind the counter. "Who are you?"

"Nick Flanagan—I used to be engaged to Ava."

The woman looked thunderstruck. "Well, that's sure to put a dent in the kingpin's plans." She picked up Ava's purse and the shoebox then pointed to a doorway. "Bring her through to the back. I'll wet a cloth to cool her down."

Nick registered a large room with a kitchenette on one side and office on the other, but his brain had frozen. Having Ava back in his arms was akin to waking from a deep coma. Was it any wonder no other woman could hold his attention? He needed to focus.

"Who is the kingpin?"

"Damon Pearce. He's been chasing Ava since she arrived in Broome. Now I understand why he hasn't been successful." The woman's gaze flitted over Nick. "I understand perfectly."

Nick stilled. *The man harassing Barry.* "It sounds like you don't think much of this Damon Pearce."

"I don't." She handed Nick the damp cloth then pulled out a chair for him. He lowered himself carefully. A powerful surge of possession settled over him as he cradled Ava in his arms. This was where she belonged, where she'd always belonged.

"I'm Helen Davis." The woman sat on the only other chair, her gaze on Ava. "Since Damon Pearce came to Broome, he's been buying businesses, running them on a shoestring, and forcing the rest of us to either sell or close. If it hadn't been for Ava agreeing to a partnership, I'd have lost everything."

The shop door opened and Helen stood. "Excuse me, I'll see who that is." She bustled out.

Ava's eyelids fluttered open and she stared at him with her luminous green eyes. "It's really you?"

Nick placed the cloth across her forehead. "It's really me, Angel."

Her breath hitched. "Nobody's called me that since..." She pushed the cloth away and struggled to sit up, her fingers clutching his shirt. "I was told you died in a training accident."

Nick frowned. "By who?"

"An officer from the Army came to my parents' house with the news, then they rang me in England." Ava bit her lip. "I tried to ring you and then your friend Ryan, but couldn't get through."

"I don't know who would tell your parents I'd been killed, but I swear, I'll find out." He stroked the side of her face. "I've missed you, Angel."

Her eyes widened, then she scrambled off his lap, and glared at him. "Nicholas Flanagan, you can't just waltz back into my life after four years of silence and tell me you missed me. Not after all the pain you've put me through. I thought you were dead."

"I'm sorry, Ava. I should have talked to you about the SAS, and I should have taken your feelings into account. I was a selfish prick with a dream that took precedence over all else. I thought if I gave you a little time, you'd come back to me. I didn't expect you to take off to England with some other guy."

"What!" Ava's mouth dropped open. She sounded as incredulous as he'd been. "That's ridiculous. I was in love with *you*. Why would I run off with someone else?"

Nick's heart swelled. "I wanted to find you, steal you away, but your father told me you were happy. He refused to give me your address."

"My father?" She held her hands out wide, clearly bewildered.

"Yes. He told me you'd married someone else. I only recently discovered that wasn't true, but then your parents never thought I was good enough."

She backed away from him, shaking her head. "That doesn't excuse you deserting me." Two fat tears tracked down her cheeks.

"Ava." Nick stood and reached for her.

"No." She held up her hand, halting him. "I can't think at the moment."

"Angel, we need to talk. To sort this out."

She swiped the tears away. "I gave up so much for you, then you chose the SAS over me. When I needed you most, you weren't there."

The pain in her eyes had Nick's stomach twisting. "I'm sorry, Angel."

"I went home, desperately hoping you'd come after me and transfer back to the Army's Aviation Corp. That was a big mistake. My...parents didn't want me. They suggested I go live with my aunt Maggie in England. If it hadn't been for Maggie, I'd have had no one."

"I know your parents hated me, but that's no reason to reject you."

"They're narrow minded people, Nick. In their eyes, I'm a fallen woman."

"Because we lived together?" He frowned. *I'm missing something here.*

Ava stared at him stonily then picked up her purse. "It's taken me a long time to get over you, and for you to turn up now is... I need to think." She turned and ran through the shop, then out the front door.

"Ava, wait." Nick strode into the shop only to collide with Helen. "Sorry, are you all right?" He craned his neck to see Ava climb into the green CRV then drive off.

Helen barred his way. "Now what have you done?"

"It's a long story, but I intend to fix it. Can you give me Ava's address?"

"Not on your life."

A vibrant musical beat resonated from under the display counter. Nick leaned down and retrieved Ava's phone. "Hello."

"Oh, hi. This is Fiona Jennings. Is Ava there?"

"No, sorry, she's not. I'm Nick Flanagan, can I pass on a message?"
Silence.

"Hello?" He frowned at Helen, who was watching him carefully.

The woman on the phone stuttered. "S...sorry, I thought... I was told... Did you say your name is Nick Flanagan?"

"Yes, that's right."

"Mr. Flanagan, you're not on our emergency pick-up list, but we run a daycare center for children between six weeks and five years. Liam's taken a fall and hurt his arm. Do you know where we can reach Ava?"

"Liam?" Perspiration gathered on Nick's lip and forehead.
Christ, she's got a kid.

No wonder her parents rejected her. Hector and Shirley Mitchell were martinets who dictated the virtues of clean living and strong morals. Nick had been a thorn in their backsides. He scowled as a suspicion began to form in his mind.

I bet there was no Army officer. Hector Mitchell lied to keep us apart. Bloody hell, Ava must have hooked up with some guy on the rebound and fallen pregnant. And that's why her parents rejected her.

"Mr. Flanagan, are you still there?"

Shit. He had no idea what the woman had been saying and Helen continued to watch him like a hawk. "I've only just arrived in Broome. Can you give me the address?"

Helen passed him a notepad and pen.

"Thanks." He held the phone to his ear again. "Ava's left her phone behind, so I can't reach her at the moment, but I can take the little fella to the hospital and get his mum to meet us there."

"I'm sorry, I can't release Liam to you without someone confirming your identity."

"Just a sec." Nick glanced at Helen. "It's the daycare center. Liam's been in an accident. Are you able to verify who I am?"

"Of course." Helen took the phone and quickly confirmed his identity then ended the call and handed the phone back to Nick.

Still in shock, he slipped it into his shirt pocket. The thought of Ava having a child was akin to being hit by a fully loaded concrete truck.

"From your face, I take it you didn't know about Liam?" Helen held the shop door open for him.

"No, I didn't. Thanks, Helen, it was nice meeting you."

"You too, Nick." She smiled. "I hope Liam's all right. He's a lovely little boy."

Nick strode from the jewelers and jogged along the path to the car he'd hired at the airport. He tried to put himself in Ava's position. Telling him she had a child was probably the last thing on her mind at the moment.

Nick mulled over the baby bombshell as he drove. He wasn't thrilled, but more astounding was the fact that the father had walked out on Ava.

The vibrant beat of Ava's phone blasted from his shirt pocket.

Steering the car to the side of the road, he swiped the screen. "Hello, Angel, forget something?"

"Who is this?" a clipped, male voice demanded.

"Nick Flanagan. Who are you?"

"That's my business. What are you doing with Ava Mitchell's phone?"

Nick stiffened at the man's tone. "Now, why would I tell you that when you haven't had the courtesy to introduce yourself?" He ended the call and turned the phone off. *That guy needs to work on his people skills.*

Nick parked outside the childcare center and strode across the crunchy grass to the front entrance. His thoughts were in a jumble as he entered the small foyer. If things had been different this child could have been his. Was the father on the scene? Did Ava have feelings for him? Maybe they were in a de-facto relationship. Maybe Damon Pearce was the father. *Fuck.*

A young, dark skinned woman smiled at him from behind the desk. "Hi, I'm Fiona. You must be Mr. Flanagan? I just need to see your driver's license."

Nick pulled out his wallet and handed over the license. "How's Liam?"

"Much brighter since we informed him you were on your way."

"Oh?"

She handed back the license. "Liam is always telling the other children that the angels are looking after his dad. We assumed you'd died. I'm sorry."

Nick's throat tightened. Fiona thought he was Liam's father. *I wish.*

"Where is Liam?"

"This way." She opened the door and led him along a hall decorated in colorful drawings, paintings, and craftwork. Fiona smiled. "Without being on the emergency pickup list, we wouldn't normally let you take Liam, but we're short staffed and Helen Davis did vouch for you." Fiona stopped at a blue door with a giraffe on it. "This is our three year-old's room."

Three year-old? So it was a rebound thing.

Several children slept, while others played quietly on the floor. He skimmed them quickly, coming to rest on a child with chestnut hair clutching a toy helicopter.

Fiona knelt beside the boy. "Look who is here to take you to the hospital, Liam."

Hazel eyes locked on Nick, then the little boy's face broke into a sweet smile.

Nick's heart leapt riotously. His lungs squeezed so tight, he could barely breathe. They'd broken up because Ava was terrified he'd be killed in the SAS, leaving her to raise any children they might have. She'd never keep him from his own son. Yet Liam not only had hair and eyes the same color, he'd also inherited a dimple in his right cheek. There was no doubt in Nick's mind.

Liam was *his* son.

The boy clambered to his feet, favoring one arm, but Nick doubted it was broken.

"I knew you'd find a way to get through the clouds, Daddy."

Fighting for control, Nick dropped to his haunches as confusion and anger threatened to overwhelm him. *How could Ava do this to me?*

He held out his arms and Liam shyly stepped into them. "I love you, Daddy."

Chapter Two

Ava had never suffered from jittery nerves until now. Her heart pounded so hard it was in danger of bursting from her chest. Nick wasn't dead. He was alive, and in Broome. Her emotions seesawed between anger and bemusement. Worse still, her precious baby had been hurt and she hadn't known. Her hands were shaking so badly she drove into the gutter in her haste to park outside the hospital's emergency department. "Shit." She reversed a little, then turned off the engine, and ran. *My poor baby, he must be so frightened.*

Entering the emergency waiting room, Ava quickly scanned the people. She couldn't see any of the daycare staff so she approached the triage nurse at the counter.

"Hi, I was told you have my son here. He fell off play equipment at his daycare center."

The woman looked at her computer screen. "Your son's surname?"

"Flanagan."

"I don't have him on the register. Are you sure he was brought here?"

"Yes. I got home to find a message on my answering machine. It cut out before the message finished, but the director said Liam had been brought here. I assumed by one of the staff. Maybe it was in an ambulance."

"We do have a Liam Mitchell though."

"I'm Ava Mitchell. Liam has his father's name."

The woman looked over her spectacles. "It was his father who brought him in."

"His father?" Ava's heart began pounding fiercely and for the second time in her life, she felt light headed. "Nick's here with Liam?"

"Is that a problem?" The woman frowned at her.

"No...I left my phone behind. Nick must have picked it up. Of course, and when the daycare center rang, he would have answered." Ava clenched her fingers. *Shit.*

"Can I please see my son now? Is he all right?"

"Yes and yes, but I'll need his Medicare card and date of birth. His father didn't know."

Ava gave the nurse Liam's details and passed over her card.

The nurse typed the information into her computer then handed the card back and pointed to a door. "Please wait and I'll let them know you're here."

"Thank you." Taking a deep breath, Ava paced over to the door. She'd wanted to break the news to Liam gently. Not like this. What must he have thought when Nick turned up alive? Her temper rose. *Why did the daycare staff release Liam to a man they don't know?*

She chewed on a fingernail as she waited. *Nick is alive.*

Alive and with Liam. Shit.

The door opened and Nick stood there staring at her with eyes as hard as flint. She could understand his fury, but it wasn't her fault. "How's Liam? Where is he?

When Nick spoke, his voice held a chill she'd never heard before. "I may have been a selfish bastard four years ago, but what you've done to me is far worse than anything I ever did to you. I had a right to know you were pregnant with my child."

Ava shivered at the coldness in his eyes. She was reminded of an arctic wind cutting across a glacier. "Don't you dare judge me, Nicholas Flanagan. I didn't know I was pregnant when I left you, and by the time I realized, my parents had told me you were dead. Why didn't you come after me? You knew I loved you. Why would I run off with someone else?"

His body seemed to pulse with fury.

Ava took a step back. "Where's Liam?"

"They've taken an x-ray, but the doctor doesn't think the arm is broken." He almost spat the words out.

"Nick, I told you the truth." Why was she defending herself? Nick was the one who canceled their wedding. He hadn't even thought her important enough to discuss his decision to join the SAS. Bottom line—he hadn't loved her.

"Come through," muttered Nick. "This is not the place to discuss it."

"Discuss what? You chose the SAS over me. End of story."

"I said, we'll discuss it later." He strode across the hall and ducked behind a curtain, leaving her standing in the doorway.

Who are you? He was bigger in the chest and shoulders and certainly more assured than he'd been four years ago. Raw sexuality rolled off him in waves, but then he'd always been a handsome devil. The coldness was new and scary.

Her temper simmering, Ava pushed the curtain aside to see Liam sitting up in a bed with the side rails raised. He held his wooden helicopter and wore a huge grin on his face. She leaned down and gently cradled him to her chest, then kissed his forehead. Seeing him whole, safe, and happy brought tears to her eyes. "Are you okay, munchkin?

"Yes, Mummy." He dropped the helicopter to grip her fingers. "I told you the nice angels would bring Daddy back."

Nick narrowed his eyes at her. "One angel brought me back, but I'm not so sure she's a nice angel."

Liam laughed as if it was the best joke he'd ever heard. "Can you take me for a ride in a helicopter, Daddy?"

"You bet." Nick brushed a wayward curl off Liam's face. His voice had gentled considerably. "There's no rush, I'm not going anywhere." He sat on a chair against the cubicle wall and met Ava's gaze. "Without my son, that is."

Ava's temper clicked into second gear. She handed Liam his helicopter then sat on the chair beside Nick and lowered her voice. "How dare you breeze back into my life and then treat me like a cold hearted bitch."

Nick flicked a quick glance at Liam zooming his helicopter around and imitating the whooping of rotor blades. "I'm not the one who left, Ava."

She stared at him, her temper well alight as she clenched her fingers tight. "You callous jerk. You didn't want me. My parents didn't want me." A sob caught in her throat. "By the time I realized I was pregnant I thought you were dead. I tried ringing your phone and I left messages with Barry. He never called back."

Nick met her gaze. "The first three weeks after you left, I was on a training mission. We didn't have phone access and I had no idea where to find you."

Uncertainty prickled Ava's spine. "What about Barry's land line? I left messages."

Nick's chest expanded as he leaned back in the chair, his eyes never leaving her face. "Christ. That would have been when Barry's wife died. He went to stay with his daughter in New Zealand for a few weeks. Your messages were probably wiped by the other pilots."

Ava clasped both hands to her heart as the slither of uncertainty crept into her bones. "Thinking you were dead, I called my parents. They said I wasn't to come home unless I gave the baby up for adoption. They couldn't abide their good name being sullied by my promiscuous ways."

He hunched forward, his fingers interlocked as he stared at the floor. "They conspired to keep us apart."

She leaned closer to hear his softly spoken words.

Nick shook his head. "I thought I'd give you a little time to come around. Those first weeks of training were full on, but then I went to see your parents. They refused to tell me where you were. I tried again a couple of months later and your father told me you'd married someone in England." Nick glanced up at her, his eyes duller than she'd ever seen them. "You knew me better than that, Ava. I would never abandon you or my child?"

"I thought you were dead." She sagged. "I adored you. How could you believe I married someone else?"

"Fuck."

"Shush." Ava shot a glance at Liam. He was sound asleep with the helicopter sitting on his chest. Wiping a stray tear away, she stood, needing to pace, but not having the room. "I've been to hell and back since leaving you."

"Your parents must have known it was my child. Why would they keep us apart?"

"Who knows? I haven't spoken to them since they insisted I have the baby adopted."

"I'm sorry, Ava." He came to his feet and stepped closer. "If I'd known you were pregnant, I..."

"So you could let me go, but not your child?"

"That's not what I meant. After the childhood I had, I never would have left you to raise Liam on your own, whether *you* wanted me in your life or not."

"Are you still in the SAS?"

"Only as a reservist. Ryan Dutch and I left six months ago along with four others in our unit."

Ava frowned. "Ryan?" He'd been Nick's best friend in the Army's Aviation Corp.

"Yes. Both of us were selected to join a special ops unit within the SAS. We now work for a security firm that's owned and operated by our ex-colonel."

"Do you regret joining the SAS?"

"No, but I do regret not talking to you about it and I regret losing you because of it."

The curtain swished back and a dark-haired woman smiled at Ava. "Hi, I'm Doctor Kate Chandler. I've got the x-ray report and there's no break. It looks like Liam dislocated his shoulder and it popped back in on its own. I'll put a sling on, but I recommend Liam take it easy over the weekend. You can give him a little Tylenol if required."

"Thank you, Doctor," said Ava.

Once the sling was on, Nick handed Ava her phone then gently lifted Liam into his arms. "You should let the daycare center know everything's okay. And in case you're wondering, Helen vouched for me. They know I'm Liam's father."

"Right. I couldn't understand why they'd let a stranger take Liam, but Helen is my emergency contact so that explains it. It's not hard to see the resemblance."

Ava rang the daycare center and quickly brought Fiona up to date, then she turned to Nick. "Shall we go?"

"After you."

She picked up her purse and the helicopter. "I need to get Liam home. It's past his dinner time and I'm starving. I haven't eaten since break... Oh no." She clamped her hand over her mouth. "What's the time?"

"About six, why?"

"I was going out tonight with...a friend, but with you turning up and Liam getting hurt, I completely forgot." She held the door open for Nick.

Nick's eyebrow rose. "A date?"

"Yes. Damon has been giving me business advice for several months. He's going to be disappointed if I stand him up."

Nick's smile didn't quite reach his eyes. "I'm sure he'll understand."

"Yes, but he was planning something special." She turned her phone on then selected Damon's number.

"Ava! I've been trying to reach you.

"Hi, Damon. Nick turned up in Broome this afternoon."

"The guy that had your phone? Who is he?"

She hesitated. "Liam's father."

A hiss erupted from the phone. "I thought you said he died in an Army accident."

Her gaze collided with Nick's. "That's what I was led to believe."

"I see. I hope this isn't going to interfere with our dinner plans?"

"Damon, I can't leave Liam." Her gaze dropped to her precious son who stirred in Nick's arms.

"Mummy?"

"Get Helen to babysit for you," said Damon.

She took a couple of steps away from Nick in an attempt to gain a little privacy. "Liam was hurt today. He needs me."

"Ava, they would keep him in the hospital if he wasn't okay. Let me spoil you for once. I've hired a chef to prepare a special dinner for you on my boat. I thought we'd spend tonight enjoying each other's company. Get to know each other."

"I know." Talk about timing. She finally met a man she liked enough to replace the one who broke her heart. She'd even bought a pack of condoms. Ava glanced at Nick to see him pointing at Liam. She lowered the phone. "What's wrong?"

"Liam doesn't feel well."

"Okay." She raised the phone again. "I'm sorry, Damon, but Liam's my priority. I'll talk to you soon." She ended the call then opened the car door. "Strap him in his seat and I'll take him home."

"Daddy come too."

Nick buckled the safety harness. "I'll follow you in my car, buddy."

Ava clasped her hands, concerned she should maybe take Liam back into emergency. "Do you feel sick, munchkin?"

"No, Mummy."

"But you told Daddy you don't feel well?"

"No, I said, I need to wee."

Ava closed the door and narrowed her eyes at Nick. "You said…"

He shrugged. "Sorry, I must have misheard."

"Hmm." She opened her door and slid into the seat. "Where did you park your car?"

"Along the end of this row. I'll follow you home." He closed the door.

Ava buckled her belt then started the engine as locked away recollections bombarded her. Nick's laughing eyes and sense of humor. Their limbs entwined as they lay exhausted from their love making. Weekends spent exploring coastal hamlets on his motorbike, not a care in the world. Then came the memory of devastating pain, rejection and loss.

Ava drew in a shaky breath. *Nick is going to want Liam in his life, but where does that leave me?* She gave herself a mental shake. Nick had put the SAS before her. If he'd been told she'd married someone else, why hadn't he come after her to find out for sure? He must have known how much she'd loved him?"

"Mummy, I need to do a wee?"

"Sorry, munchkin. We'll be home in two minutes."

On reaching her rented house, Ava rushed Liam out of his seat and inside, leaving the front door open for Nick. When she heard his knock, she called out, "We're in the bathroom. Won't be long."

"How about I find us some take away for dinner?" he called back.

"Thanks, that would be great." Ava helped Liam wash his hands then they came out of the bathroom to find Nick leaning casually against the wall.

"From now on, I'll take care of you." He grinned. "And your needs, just like old times."

"What's that supposed to mean?"

"As I recall, I never left you unsatisfied." He grinned then strode down the hall.

"Nicholas Flanagan!"

"Mummy, what does unsatisfied mean?"

Nick's deep chuckle echoed in the narrow space. "It means your mummy always sleep well."

The front door closed, leaving Ava glaring at the frosted panel.

"Mummy, I like Daddy."

"That's good, honey. Let's get you in your pajamas."

"What about my bath?"

"Not tonight, munchkin. I don't want you splashing about and hurting your arm."

Liam's bottom lip pushed out. "But I like my bath."

"How about I give you a sponge bath. Daddy loves them."

"Really?"

Ava swallowed. The memories that surfaced had her body heating. "Yes." She filled the basin with warm, soapy water then undressed Liam.

Ava had Liam in his pj's and the sling back in place when the doorbell rang.

"Daddy's back." Liam raced off down the hall. "Hurry, Mummy."

"Okay." Ava unlocked the door. "You've only been back in my life a couple of hours and I'm running after you... Oh, Damon!"

Damon's cool blue eyes met hers as he handed her an enormous box wrapped in red paper. "It's a train set. I thought it might make Liam feel better."

"That's so thoughtful. Thank you." Her eyes flitted over his perfectly cut fair hair, black silk shirt, and pressed trousers. She wasn't surprised he was listed as one of Australia's most eligible bachelors.

Liam scowled at Damon. "Where's my daddy?"

"Right here, buddy." Nick bounded up the steps then carefully scooped Liam up in one arm. "I'm Nick, you must be Damon Pearce."

Ava cringed as both Nick and Liam looked at Damon with the same mildly interested expression. She stepped back against the wall. "Come in, Damon. We were about to have takeaway. You're welcome to join us."

"I'll come in, but I won't eat. I've lost my appetite along with my dinner date."

"I'm sorry." She led the way along the hall and into the kitchen. "You didn't have to buy a present, but it was very nice of you." She frowned at Liam. "Don't you have something to say to Mr. Pearce, sweetie?"

"I don't like trains. I like helicopters."

"Liam!"

"Thank you for the present." Liam wrapped his good arm around

Nick's neck and plastered a sloppy kiss on his father's cheek. "Thank you for bringing dinner, Daddy."

Oh my God. They're like peas in a pod. I'm going to kill the two of them. Ava glared at them before turning to Damon. "Can I get you a glass of homemade lemonade?"

"Thanks." Damon pulled out the chair opposite Nick and sat. "What have you been doing for the last four years while Ava's been raising Liam on her own?"

Ava's breath hitched. The old Nick would tell Damon to get stuffed. The new Nick smiled lazily. "I was in the Army until six months ago."

"And now you're unemployed and what? Drifting until you find yourself?"

"I work for a security firm in Sydney."

Ava took the lemonade from the fridge. "I can't believe you left the Army."

"I'd had enough." He sat Liam on the chair beside him and lifted the lids off the takeaway containers. Instantly the kitchen filled with the aroma of garlic and ginger. He'd bought Pad Thai, Chili and Basil Lamb, and Black Pepper Soft Shell Crab. Her favorites. Nick's gaze settled on her. "I've recently been in Vietnam and the food there was amazing. Will you pass over some plates, Angel?"

So that hasn't changed. If Nick doesn't want to talk about something, he changes the subject. She set the table then poured four glasses of lemonade. "Here you are, gentlemen. Sorry, I don't have any beer or wine."

Damon took a sip then stared at Nick. "Security. What does that involve? Night watchman, department stores, or are you a nightclub bouncer?"

"Something like that. What do you do, Damon?"

"My holdings are extremely diversified. I own a diamond mine and pearl farm several hours from here. I also own a resort and an assortment of small businesses in Broome and Melbourne. If you're looking for work, I could possibly find a use for you in one of my establishments."

"Nah, I'm good." Nick served Liam then pushed the containers across to Ava. "Eat up, Angel. You'll need your energy for tomorrow."

"Tomorrow?" Ava frowned at him.

"Yes. As it's Saturday, I would like to take you and Liam up to Cape Leveque for a picnic, if you're agreeable?"

Damon raised an eyebrow. "You obviously don't comprehend how big the Kimberley region is. Cape Leveque is hours away over corrugated dirt roads."

Ava bit her lip as Nick slowly laid down his fork.

"I've lived in the Kimberley region most of my life. I know where Cape Leveque is. We'll be going by helicopter." His voice had a steely quality to it.

"Helicopter?." Liam's little face broke into a wondrous smile. "Mummy!"

Ava looked at Nick. "As you can see, Liam's inherited your love of helicopters."

Damon pursed his lips. "You won't get a charter this late. The local companies are booked out weeks ahead. I know because I own one."

"I'm not interested in a charter flight. I'll borrow a friend's chopper and fly Ava and Liam up there myself."

"You're a pilot?"

"It's what I did in the Army." Nick picked up his lemonade and drained the glass.

Ava's gaze ran along his muscled arm and stopped at his raised bicep. *And it wasn't just the Army. It was a specialized unit within the SAS.* She lifted her gaze to meet his and swallowed. The Nick she once knew lived life to the fullest and had a wicked sense of humor. The SAS couldn't have been easy and although he'd always looked great, the change in his physical stature along with his nonchalant attitude appealed to her. *Don't go there.*

Ava looked at Liam who stared at his father adoringly. Whatever the future held, those two would not be parted. That was one thing she knew for certain, which could be a problem if she and Nick were living on different sides of Australia.

Damon cleared his throat. "How long do you plan on staying in Broome, Nick?"

"I've no idea. That depends on Ava."

She picked at her dinner, still reeling at the turn of events. It would take time to come to terms with Nick's return, and what she had learned today. She wanted to hate him, but ten minutes in his company and her treacherous body was betraying her. She needed to protect her heart, as it wouldn't survive another round of punishment. And, what was in Liam's best interests?

Ava smiled at Damon. "Are you sure you wouldn't like something to eat?"

"No, thank you." He narrowed his eyes at Nick. "Why would it depend on Ava? She has an established clientele here, which is due to my help. You can't expect her to give up her dream to live on a security guard's wage?"

Shocked, Ava glared at Damon. "I appreciate your advice, but I've worked jolly hard to get where I am and Nick knows better than anyone about my dream to become a designer. He would never ask me to give it up."

"Are you sure? What if he isn't prepared to live in Broome, or he puts his career above yours—again?"

Ava cringed. She wished she'd never told Damon about Nick and their breakup.

Nick pushed his chair back and stood. "It's been a tough day, so I think I'll head back to the resort. If you've got something to say, Damon, let's take it outside."

"Very well." Damon reached across and covered Ava's hand. "Don't be annoyed with me. I'm concerned for you and Liam's wellbeing. I don't want to see you hurt."

"Thank you, Damon, but I'm not going to let that happen."

"Mummy, I want Daddy to stay here with us." Liam's bottom lip trembled.

She scooted round the table. "Daddy is staying at a resort."

"Why can't he stay with us? I don't want him to get stuck behind the clouds again."

Nick placed his hands on Ava's waist, sending a riot of quivers shooting along her nerve endings as he eased her aside and squatted beside Liam's chair.

"Buddy, I wasn't stuck behind the clouds. I haven't been around because I didn't know about you. Naughty people told your mummy and me lies that kept us apart."

"But why can't you sleep here? Mummy's got a big bed."

Damon coughed. "I'll wait outside." He strode down the hall, the screen door slamming behind him.

Ava's cheeks warmed as Nick's gaze rose to meet hers. He had a wicked glint in his eyes as he spoke. "I'd like to share Mummy's bed, but I haven't got my pajamas with me."

"Oh." Liam wriggled off his chair and stood between Nick's thighs. "You go get your pajamas and come back. Then we can all sleep in Mummy's bed."

This is getting out of hand. Ava rubbed Liam's back. "Give Daddy a hug, munchkin, and we'll see him tomorrow."

"No! I want Daddy to sleep here." Liam wrapped his good arm around Nick's neck. "Don't go, Daddy." He began to sob.

Nick raised an eyebrow at Ava. "Hey, buddy, if it's all right with Mummy, I'll come back and sleep on the couch, but first I have to help an old friend install an alarm."

Liam's tears dried instantly. "Can I come with you?"

Ava sighed. "Liam, it's getting late." She looked at Nick. "What friend?"

"Barry Sanders. He's been the target of some serious vandalism by a man who works for Damon Pearce. I'm going to install an alarm and security cameras."

Ava's skin prickled as she stared at Nick. "You're kidding me, right?"

"No. Since arriving in Broome this afternoon, two people have told me Pearce is not a nice guy. He may be rich, but he doesn't care who he puts out of business."

"Now you're insulting my friend? I think you'd better leave, Nick."

"I've never lied to you, Ava, but by all means come with me and talk to Barry. He'd be delighted to see you, and tell you what's going on."

"You may not have lied to me, but you definitely withheld the fact you'd applied to join the SAS. And it took you four years to find me."

"Angel, I didn't tell you about the SAS because it's extremely hard to get into. The recruiting process is savage and lots of recruits don't make the cut. In my case, the Army had spent a lot of time and money training me as a Black Hawk pilot. The only reason I tried out for the SAS was because they needed two chopper pilots for an experimental sub-unit within the group. I bypassed some of the more severe stuff."

"You told me you were going on an intensive training camp."

"It *was* intensive. The chances of making the cut are very slim.

There was no point telling you if I didn't qualify."

"I beg to differ. You should have told me." She straightened and crossed her arms.

A horn blasted from out the front of the house.

"I never meant to hurt you, Ava. You're the only woman who has ever meant anything to me." He stroked a finger across her cheek then ruffled Liam's hair before striding from the kitchen.

And you're the only man I've ever given my heart, body, and soul to. She kissed Liam's forehead, more confused and angry than ever.

"Mummy, after dinner, can we go see Daddy's friend?"

Ava stared into Liam's solemn eyes. She needed answers. "Yes, sweetheart."

Chapter Three

Nick squared his shoulders and paced down Ava's front path to a silver BMW. "All right, Pearce. Let's get this over with."

"Very well. What will it take for you to leave Broome and never come back?"

"You're shitting me? I've just discovered I've got a son. I'm not going anywhere."

"Would fifty thousand change your mind?"

Nick held back, aware Ava had opened the front door and watched them. "I don't want your money, Pearce. I just want what's mine."

"One hundred thousand and I'll see you get the kid during school vacations. That's more than generous for a guy who has nothing."

By sheer will, Nick kept his stance relaxed and his back to Ava. "Financially I am well placed to provide for Ava and my son. That aside, I know the sort of man you are, so back off from Barry Sanders and stay away from Ava."

Pearce blinked. "That was you who threatened my man today?"

"You better believe it. Barry Sanders has worked hard to build that charter business and I won't allow you or anyone else to drive him out."

"You're making a big mistake. I have the money and power to do whatever the fuck I like, and no *security guard* is going to prevent me getting what I want." He glanced toward the house and gave a friendly wave to Ava. "Or who I want."

Nick faked an air of indifference when all he wanted to do was smash the smugness off the other man's face. "A word of warning, Pearce. You mess with my family or my friend and I'll annihilate you."

Pearce hesitated. "You're a big talker for a man with nothing." He got into his car then gunned the engine and drove off, his wheels spraying Nick with sharp bits of gravel.

Fuckwit.

In serious danger of punching something, Nick climbed into his vehicle then drove down the street. Pearce might follow through on his threat. He was just the sort of arrogant bastard to do whatever it took to get what he wanted. The sooner Barry got the security cameras up the better. Maybe it would be worth asking Simon to check into Pearce's background or at least notifying Jarred in case things went belly up.

Nick's thoughts drifted to his teammates. All ex-commandos who were highly trained in advanced weapons, close quarter fighting, anti-counter surveillance, personal protection, and reconnaissance. Their elite squad had been formed within the SAS as a secret task force that could be deployed swiftly to any situation, worldwide, hence the need for two Black Hawk pilots and a communications specialist. It had been the initiative of the Defense Minister, and operated efficiently for three and a half years until a new Defense Minister disbanded the elite squad. Biggest mistake the minister ever made. Now the government paid a fortune for their unique services.

Would Ava consider moving to the east coast so Nick didn't have to give up his job? He strongly doubted it, but the thought of leaving the team—his mates—didn't sit well. Pushing the thought away, Nick drove through the open gates and parked beside the hangar's staff entrance. A sensor light immediately illuminated him and the empty car lot.

"I thought you were going to ring me?" Barry stood in the doorway holding a rifle.

"Sorry, I got sidetracked. You got a license for that thing?"

"No, I don't, but I need something to keep the vermin out."

"Find something else. If the cops hear you've got a rifle, they'll have you behind bars before you can blink."

"It's not right. A man should be able to defend himself."

"Guns are illegal, mate. Like it or lump it, that's the way it is. Let's get this security system in and you can tell me everything you know about Pearce."

They'd been working an hour when Nick heard a car approaching.

He climbed down the ladder, grabbed a towel, and wiped the sweat off his face and chest. "I'll see who it is. You stay near the phone."

"Righto." Barry wiped his hands down his shirt and hurried into the office.

Picking up a crow bar, Nick opened the side door as a small, green CRV came to a stop beside his vehicle. *Ava.*

She climbed out of the car, shut the door, then stared at his chest. "You've certainly..." She cleared her throat. "I want to talk to Barry...about Damon."

Nick's gaze skimmed the soft blue T-shirt clinging to her shapely breasts then dropped to her tight fitting jeans. This was the Ava he remembered. "Where's Liam?"

"With me of course." She opened the rear door and leaned in, presenting him with her very nice arse. "Out you come, squirt."

Nick's cock twitched. Four years and she remained the only woman who could bring his body to instant attention. He leaned the crowbar against the corrugated iron wall and held out his arms. "Hello, mate. Isn't it past your bedtime?"

"I came to help you, Daddy."

Ava's intoxicating green eyes were on Nick's chest and his hand brushed against the side of her breast as she passed Liam over. She jerked back, her breath hitching. The fact she still reacted to his touch thrilled Nick.

"Barry will be delighted to see you. It's been a while." Nick held the door open for her, then picked up the crowbar and followed her through, locking the door behind him.

Liam began squirming, his eyes wide. "Mummy, look, helicopters."

Nick carried Liam to the nearest chopper, a Bell 204—a compact but powerful workhorse. He opened the door and sat his son in the cockpit. "Look, but no touching, okay."

"Okay, Daddy." Liam sat transfixed, staring at all the dials on the control panel.

Ava folded her arms. "Seriously, Nick. You can't expect him to be that close to his biggest obsession and not touch."

She gave him such a blasé look that Nick wanted to pull her into his arms and kiss her. It was what he would have done four years ago. "You're right. It's not fair at all."

Her eyes widened as he stepped closer. "Nick!"

"Well, ain't you a sight for sore eyes." Barry ambled over, his gaze riveted on Ava before he noticed Liam in the chopper. He looked from Liam to Nick. "Good Lord, how come you never told me you had a kid? He's the spitting image of you."

"I only found out myself today. His name is Liam." Nick put his arm around Ava's shoulders, pretending not to notice her fluttering hand against his stomach. "Ava's father told her I'd died in a training accident."

"You don't say?" Barry held out his arms. "Hello, Ava. It's been a long time."

"Hello, Barry." Ava stepped away from Nick and hugged Barry. "I'm sorry to hear Kerrie died. Your wife was a lovely person."

"Yeah, it knocked me for six." He grimaced. "I have to tell you, honey, when you left Nick, it knocked him around too. He acts the tough guy, but he was angry and hurting for a long time."

Ava's gaze lifted to Nick's. "It seems we both were."

Nick gave a tight smile. "Barry had to put up with my ranting and raving when I thought you'd married someone else. I came up here whenever I wasn't on deployment to help Barry with his charter flights. The rest of the time my team-mates kept me busy."

"Mummy, look, I'm a helicopter pilot." Liam now sat in the pilot's seat with his hand on the cyclic control. "You want me to take you up in the sky?"

"Soon, munchkin." Ava pursed her lips. "Barry, I'm a friend of Damon Pearce, and I find it hard to believe he would be behind any scheme to put you out of business."

Barry shot a look of disbelief at Nick. "She's involved with Pearce?"

"He's been giving Ava *business advice*. Tell her what's been happening while I finish wiring the alarm."

"Yeah, okay. Let's jump in the back of the chopper. The young fella can take us for a spin while I talk to you."

Nick appreciated Barry's gesture to appease Ava and Liam. He left them to it and climbed up the ladder to finish running wires along the steel beams. As he worked, he listened to Barry tell Ava how he'd been harassed over the past several months. How Pearce had bribed his two pilots into leaving with the promise of more money. How the bald guy who worked for Pearce had physically intimidated him on several occasions and all but admitted to vandalizing the office and chopper.

Every now and then, Nick would climb down to move the ladder and wink at Liam as he played at flying the chopper. The little guy's sound effects were brilliant.

Eventually Liam curled up in the pilot's seat and fell asleep. Ava had gone very quiet as she listened to Barry describing other tourist operators whose businesses were suffering because of Pearce.

With the last of the wiring done, Nick descended the ladder to test the cameras. In the office, a large monitor with six screens lit up and, even though it was dark outside, the high-resolution images of the parking area, helipad, and approach to the hangar clearly showed via the infrared filter. He checked the alarm next, hitting the kill switch at the first piercing scream. The steel shutters over the office window were sturdy and a new addition since he'd been here eight months ago.

Nick leaned over the workshop basin, drenching his head and chest in cool water, when Ava wandered over.

Her gaze dropped to his chest for several heartbeats before she met his eyes. "You said you met two people today who have been bullied or trampled by Damon. Who is the other?"

"Your partner, Helen. If you hadn't bailed her out, she would have lost everything. She told me Pearce is determined to acquire what and whom he wants. Pearce told me the same thing, before offering me one hundred grand to walk away from you."

Ava's mouth dropped open. "I don't believe you."

"No? Well he also promised me I could have Liam every school vacation as long as I agreed to leave Broome tonight. It was all I could do not to hit the bastard."

"Why didn't you?"

"I was trying to make a good impression on Liam."

"Once upon a time, you'd have hit a man for much less."

"That was before I knew better, Ava. In the last four years I've learned control, patience, and planning. And while we're speaking truths, I now work for Steele Intelligence and security services with Ryan and four ex-SAS soldiers. Some of our work is highly classified and there is an element of danger."

She blinked several times. "So you could still be killed. Is that what you're saying?"

"I could be killed crossing the road. We take precautions and watch each other's back. Most of our work is security for politicians and celebrities, but occasionally we contract to the government, running undercover operations, which is when I get to fly the Black Hawk."

"Like what? I need to know what you do."

He expelled a breath. "Recently we went after an underworld figure and rescued two women he would have killed. That mission led us to Vietnam where we disbanded a ring of human traffickers and freed several young girls from a brothel."

Her eyes widened. "I see." She chewed a fingernail, looking lost in thought as he scrubbed his hands. Then she frowned at him. "How did you find out I wasn't married?"

Nick grabbed a towel and dried his face and chest. "One of the women we saved had green eyes and unbeknown to me, she'd been given a red wig as part of her disguise. I came into a room and for a split second I thought it was you. I reacted badly. She convinced our communication expert to do an intensive search on you. Simon discovered you'd never married and were living in Broome, running Fantasy Pearl Creations. The name alone told me it had to be you."

She smiled. "Fantasy Pearl Creations was always my dream."

"I'm happy you achieved it, Angel."

She pursed her lips. "If I were to let you back into my life, and I'm not saying I will, but if I did, would you give up working for Steele Intelligence and move here?"

Nick's lungs constricted. He loved flying the Black Hawk, even though it was rare these days, and working with Jared and the boys was so varied and interesting that any other job paled in comparison. His mates were the only people other than Ava and Barry who'd ever cared about him.

"Is that what you want, Angel. To live here in Broome for the rest of your life?" He knew he was dodging the question, but he couldn't help it. He needed time to think.

"Probably not, but I want to know I come first in your life. Not second or third."

Nick hesitated. "And where would I come? You have Liam and your business now."

"You still don't get it." She had to stop from grinding her teeth or she wouldn't have any left. "Children are a precious gift for us to love and raise, then they go their own way. My business is important, but I loved you more than anything or any person in the world. You were my life." *And you crushed my heart.*

He raised a hand and stroked her cheek. "You still love me, Angel."

She reared back as if he'd struck her. "I don't know how I feel. We have to take this slowly. I need to know I can trust you and that you… trust me."

Tires screeched outside the hangar. Nick ran to the office to find Barry watching the monitor. "This ain't good, mate."

Looking over Barry's shoulder, Nick saw two battered sedans doing doughnuts in front of the hangar, leaving rubber burn marks all over the tarmac. "I'll secure the staff door; you ring the cops. Those guys are wearing balaclavas so they've come here to do more than bloody burnouts."

Nick sprinted to the side door and fixed two steel bars across the width. He turned to see Ava behind him, her hands on her hips as she stared at him.

"I don't believe Damon is behind this. He's not violent."

"He wouldn't expect Barry to have the cameras up this fast or that we'd be here." Nick glanced across the hangar. "I need you to get Liam into the back of the chopper. We may need to make a quick get-away."

Barry yelled out from the office, "Nick, they've got rifles."

"Fuck." Nick rubbed his jaw. "Let the cops know."

"I have and they'll be here as soon as they can, but someone slashed their tires."

Ava gasped. "What are we going to do?"

"I'll go out there and try to talk them round."

"No!" She clutched his arm. "You can't take on a bunch of thugs by yourself."

"I won't endanger you and Liam."

"Please, don't go out there. Liam needs you in his life."

"All right, Angel." He looked around the hangar, his gaze falling on the giant doors. "There's another way." He snatched her hand and ran to the chopper. "Move Liam into the back and buckle up."

He sprinted back to the office. "Barry, bring the security camera hard drive and get in the chopper. Where's the rifle?"

Barry's hand shook as he pointed to the corner. "What are you planning, Nick?"

"We may need to fly out."

"Christ." Barry unplugged the hard drive then ran to the chopper.

Nick shrugged his shirt on then picked up the rifle and locked the office. He was climbing the ladder when something heavy smashed against the side door.

Clenching his jaw, Nick opened a window high in the corrugated iron wall. One car continued doing burnouts. Several masked men stood below watching as another rammed a steel bar into the door. Nick fired a couple of warning shots into the sky, hoping it would scare them off.

It didn't. They returned his fire using semi-automatic rifles. Bullets sprayed into the corrugated iron wall, peppering it with holes. The noise was deafening.

"Fuck." Nick descended as fast as he could, picked up the remotes to the alarm and hangar doors, then ran to the chopper. Ava had flung herself over Liam in the back, protecting him with her body. After checking their belts and headsets, Nick hit the alarm then handed the rifle to Barry and put his own headset on. It was the fastest start up he'd ever attempted. "Let's do this."

Nick disengaged the rotor brake, then flipped the battery master switch on and checked his gauges. All looked normal, so he cracked open the throttle as he held in the starter button. The engine spun up and as the rotor blades began to revolve, he glanced over his shoulder. Liam looked about excitedly.

Nick meet Ava's anxious eyes. "I know what I'm doing, Angel."

"I hope so." Her voice shook through Nick's headset.

Fury raced through Nick as he switched on the generator, and checked the hydraulics and governor. *How dare Pearce put Ava and Liam in danger.* He pressed the other remote and the doors began to slide apart. "Hopefully those idiots won't hear us with the alarm blaring."

"Bloody hell." Barry stared at him. "I've always used the wheels or the dolly platform to move the choppers out of the hangar. This is crazy."

"What's a dolly platform, Daddy?" Liam's little voice jolted Nick.

"It's a low platform on wheels, mate. The chopper sits on the platform making it easier to tow in and out of the hangar, but I'm going to fly us out this time."

"Christ," mumbled Barry. "If it was anyone else, I'd shit myself."

"You still might. Let's hope those pricks stay at the rear of the hangar." Nick knew that as soon as he lifted the collective enough to lift off, the helicopter's downwash would blow all sorts of debris around the interior of the hangar, possibly endangering the rotor blades. "I need to minimize the hover, so I'm going to nose it over and fly straight forward off the dolly. The tarmac is going to look awfully close!"

An old beat up Ford careened out onto the helipad tarmac. It slammed to a stop and two masked men jumped out. They both raised their rifles then seemed to think better of it. Nick breathed a sigh of relief. "They've realized you've got company."

The two men ran off round the side of the hangar, presumably to warn the others. Nick did a final quick scan around the instrument panel, making sure his gauges were indicating in green. "Here we go. As soon as we're clear, shut the doors."

"Okay," croaked Barry.

Nick raised the chopper just enough to give him room to push the nose down and accelerate around the parked Ford and then around the hangar.

Several men came running toward them carrying rifles. Nick flew straight at them, sending them diving for cover. "Hopefully the doors will be closed before they get to them." Nick redlined the turbine engine and quickly accelerated and climbed away to the right before the men could get to their feet and start firing. "Pearce just picked a fight with the wrong guy."

"I can't believe men were shooting at us, or that Damon is involved," Ava said.

Her voice wobbled so badly Nick thought she might be about to burst into tears. That he couldn't handle right now. "Pearce wouldn't know you and Liam were here tonight."

"Daddy, this is fun."

Nick shot a glance over his shoulder. Liam had a huge grin on his face. Ava raised a fine eyebrow. "He doesn't realize."

"Thank God." Nick returned his attention to the front. "We'll report this to the police, but I doubt we can prove Pearce is behind it."

"What about the security video?" Barry patted the hard drive. "We can at least identify their vehicles."

"They're probably stolen. I'm going to land on the oval. It's not far from the police station. Ava, while you're filling out the statement, Barry and I will fly a couple of cops out to the hangar. We might get lucky and catch the bastards."

"Will you come back to my place later, so I know you're all right?"

"It's going to be very late."

"I won't be able to sleep and Liam wants you there."

"Okay." Nick silently cheered, his anger dissolving to be replaced with anticipation. *Pearce might just be his own worst enemy.* "Angel, I'd appreciate it if you didn't mention Barry's rifle to the police."

She huffed. "I wasn't going to."

CHAPTER FOUR

Ava rubbed her weary eyes, but she couldn't sleep. One minute she wanted to hit Nick with a very big bat for all the hurt he'd given her, the next she wanted to have his arms around her, kissing her like he used to. Every car that passed the house had to be checked in case it contained those men with guns. Her head felt fit to explode. She'd never, ever had a day filled with so much tension or emotion and fear. Good Lord, Nick arising from the dead with the intention of taking up where they left off was bad enough. She didn't even know if that was possible. Then Liam's accident had scared the living daylights out of her. Not being there when he needed her was unforgiveable.

She shivered at the thought of those men with guns. They could have killed Liam. How could a nice man like Damon be behind such hooligans? She'd been a mass of nervous tension on the flight back into Broome, terrified they might be shot out of the sky. She was angry, shaken, and jumping at every little noise. This wasn't her safe, ordinary life. It hadn't seemed to bother Nick that much, but she supposed he was used to people dying in combat or pointing guns at his helicopter, trying to shoot him down. That thought made her nauseous. "This isn't helping. I'm just making myself sick."

Confusion engulfed Ava as good and bad memories bombarded her. Their carefree life together before Nick went on that training camp. The grief when she'd been told he died. Nick's reappearance would change the life she'd mapped out for her and Liam. Was that a good or bad thing? Were they safe here?

Tiredness dragged at her eyelids, but she couldn't fall sleep, not until she knew Nick was safe. Apparently she still cared a little. She threaded another exquisite pearl onto the silk thread, listening for the sound of his footsteps on the veranda.

"Mummy, is Daddy here yet?" Liam sat his wooden chopper on her worktable.

"Oh, honey, what are you doing out of bed?" She pulled off her cotton gloves and covered her latest creation. "Would you like to sleep in my bed?"

Headlights lit up the blinds. "It's Daddy." Liam ran into the hall.

"Liam, wait." She dashed after him, thankful he couldn't reach the lock. "Let me check. I don't want you opening the door to a stranger."

Liam hopped from foot to foot as Ava unlocked the door and spied Nick striding across the lawn.

"It *is* Daddy."

"So it is." Ava's pulse skipped as she observed the cheeky grin on Nick's face. He wore a fresh white T-shirt that defined his broad shoulders and chest. A sensual thrill shot straight to her core, leaving her with a deep longing she hadn't experienced in a very long time. "Nick." It came out as a croak.

"Hello, Angel." He opened the screen door and scooped Liam up. "What are you still doing up, mate?"

"We were waiting for you, Daddy. Now we can all sleep in Mummy's bed."

Nick's gaze locked on Ava. "What a good idea."

She swallowed and stood aside. "I don't think we'll all fit, Liam."

"Yes we will." The little rascal wrapped his good arm around Nick's neck.

The big rascal winked at her. "Just until Liam nods off, and while we're waiting, I can bring you up to date on those thugs." His gaze dropped to her nightshirt and his dimple appeared, making her body heat all over again. He chuckled. "That's my Guns and Roses T-shirt."

Ava crossed her arms over her breasts in an attempt to hide her hardening nipples. "No, it's my Guns and Roses T-shirt. You never liked it."

He laughed out loud, the sound curling round her heart like wisps of forgotten pleasure. "Actually it wasn't that I didn't like the T-shirt." He leaned in close to her ear. "I just preferred you out of it."

"I..." She stared into Nick's intense hazel eyes as erotic thoughts raced through her mind. Desire filled her veins, infusing every cell in her body. Her heart thundered in her ears and her breasts ached. If not for Liam's presence, she'd be in serious danger of falling into Nick's arms without a thought for the consequences. *Shit, that's exactly how I got pregnant.*

"Can we go to bed now?" Liam yawned and laid his head on Nick's shoulder.

"Of course, munchkin." Ava turned her back on Nick and closed the front door. She needed to be strong. She needed time to work out what the hell she was feeling. "You show Daddy the way. I need a couple of minutes to pack up my tools."

Ava escaped to the kitchen and drank a glass of iced water. The thought of sharing a bed with Nick had her body throbbing. Not that they'd be on top of each other. Liam would be a safety shield between them. The glass shook in her fingers. *Have there been other women in Nick's life?* "Stupid question. Of course there have." She rolled the cool glass across her forehead. The thought irritated her.

"Are you all right?"

Ava spun round and stared at Nick, lounging against the doorframe. "I was thirsty." She placed the glass on the sink and rubbed her arms. "Today has been one shock after another and I'm...I'm very confused and angry, Nick."

He straightened and sauntered across the kitchen, taking her hands in his. "That's not surprising, Angel. What do you want to know?"

"After we parted, did you... Have there been other women?"

"I'm not a monk, Ava, and I thought you'd married someone else. But you're still the only woman I've ever wanted a permanent relationship with."

"I see. Well, apparently you were harder to forget than I was. Every time a guy got close, I'd be consumed with memories of you and run for the hills, until Damon. If you'd turned up in another week, I probably would have been in a serious relationship with him." *Okay, maybe not a week.* Ava drew in a deep breath and was instantly assailed by Nick's masculine scent—a mixture of citrus and spice. A profound yearning for what they'd once had invaded her soul. "I missed you dreadfully. If it hadn't been for Liam, I don't think I'd have survived."

He drew her closer and kissed the top of her head. "You're a beautiful and strong woman, Angel. Failure and negativity are not in your vocabulary."

Ava pulled back before she did something embarrassing like kiss him, or slap herself for being such a fool. "I need to put my latest creation away."

"I'd love to see it."

"Okay." Ava led him into her workroom and uncovered the pearl choker she'd almost completed. "I still have a few pearls to add and then the French wire and clasp."

"It's magnificent." Nick reached out to touch the choker.

"No, not without gloves." Ava caught his hand and stilled as his fingers curled around hers. "That choker is worth twenty thousand dollars."

"You're kidding."

Ava dropped his hand, afraid he might pick up on her quickening pulse, and padded over to the meter-high safe. "Wait until you see what I have in here." Kneeling in front of the safe, she keyed in the eight-digit code then turned the handle and pulled the heavy door open. "Damon suggested I get this to store my gems. It's secured to the floor." She withdrew the velvet-lined box she kept her stock of pearls, diamonds, and precious stones in.

Nick stood aside as Ava placed the box on the table and lifted the lid. He gaped at the collection of pearls, and sparkling gems. "Wow."

"I know." Ava smiled. "I've been given a commission by a media mogul. He wants me to make his wife a matching set of earrings, necklace and bracelet, using these pearls and gems."

Nick shook his head. "What are they worth?"

"Somewhere in the range of five hundred thousand I believe."

"Holy cow, Ava. Who else knows you have these here?"

"Only Helen and Damon." Ava grinned. "Wait, there's more." She went back to the safe and lifted out three small boxes. "I designed and made these in England. They're personal favorites that I can't part with." Opening the lids, she showed him a filigree ring with an emerald in its center, a necklace of twisted miniature pearls and a wide wristlet of pearls to match the necklace. "You like?"

He shook his head. "I'm lost for words, Ava. They're exquisite."

"Thank you." Ava preened as she closed the lids then returned everything to the safe. "We should go to bed."

Nick's dimple appeared. "I thought you'd never ask."

"I meant—" Ava hesitated. She didn't know what she meant.

"It's all right, Angel. I'm messing with you. I can sleep anywhere."

"You might *have* to sleep in my bed. The couch and Liam's bed are too short for you." She led the way to her room, stopping in the doorway to gaze at her little treasure spread out like a starfish. "He likes to take up the whole bed, just like you."

"Hmm, that's not going to work with three of us in the bed. I should go back to the resort." Nick leaned over the bed and dropped a light kiss on Liam's forehead.

"You can't go." Ava crossed her arms to stop from reaching for him. "You haven't told me what happened after I left the police station. I worried with those men on the loose, and Liam is going to be disappointed if he wakes and you're not here." She shivered.

He slowly straightened to his full six feet, his gaze never leaving her face. "Do *you* want me to stay?"

So much for hating him until the end of time. Swallowing her pride, she nodded. "Yes."

"Then I'll stay." He bent over the bed again and rearranged Liam into the middle. "I take it you still like the left side?"

A giggle escaped. "I never liked the left side and you jolly well know it."

"I distinctly remember waking up with you on my left every morning."

Ava strolled round the bed. "Yet, I distinctly remember climbing into the right side every night. Amazing."

"You're safe tonight." His deep chuckle sent a quiver of excitement down her spine. She'd missed his teasing and wonderfully wicked laugh.

Her smiled died and she cast her gaze on Liam, sound asleep. "I was so hurt when you chose the SAS over me, but that was nothing compared to the pain of discovering you were dead."

"When I catch up with your parents, I'm going to wring their spiteful necks." He paced around the bed, put a finger under her chin, and lifted until she was forced to meet his eyes. "I was crazy about you and they knew it."

Ava nodded. "Yes." *But being crazy about someone isn't the same as loving them.*

Nick drew her into his arms. "I'm so sorry you went through it alone."

Her eyes watered. "I gave you an ultimatum and it backfired. I thought you'd choose me over the SAS."

"And I thought you'd forgive me and come home." He released her and pulled back the covers. "You're tired. Hop into bed and get some sleep."

"After you tell me what happened tonight." She scooted under the covers and watched him walk around the bed. "Were those men still at the hangar?"

"No." He stripped off his T-shirt and sat on the bed to remove his shoes. "The police have the security footage and we took them out to the hangar to have a look around. They're going to have a word with Pearce and his off-sider, but so far there's nothing to connect them to the thugs."

Ava's gaze roamed his broad shoulders and the angel on his upper right arm. The tattoo was another thing her father had hated about Nick. Her gaze continued across his muscled back and came to rest on a raised welt below his left shoulder blade. "How did you get that scar?"

He pulled his jeans off. "I was guarding an underworld guy when his accomplice arrived with a female hostage. He threatened to shoot her unless I laid down my gun. I had no choice. The bastard shot my mate's dog and then me. It wasn't a good day."

Nick turned to face her, touching a small scar above his chest. "Luckily the bullet went straight through without doing any major damage."

Three inches lower and it would have ploughed into his heart. An icy finger of fear slid down her spine at how close he'd come to dying. It served as a reminder of the life he'd chosen over her. She dreaded the thought of her precious son finding his father only to lose him again. Liam had always hero-worshipped Nick; now they would be inseparable.

Her gaze skimmed Nick's chest, flat stomach, muscled thighs and the substantial bulge in his black jocks. Butterflies skittered across her stomach and her mouth dried as heat infused her face. "Did you get him?" Ava dragged her gaze back to Nick's face.

"In the end the bastard got his just reward, and we rescued the hostage—" Nick smiled. "She is the lady who pestered me into finding you."

Ava rolled onto her side, adjusted the covers over Liam, and stared at Nick. "Tell me the whole story."

He settled back against the pillows and raised both hands behind his head. "I guess I can. It's going public in a few days anyway." He drew in a breath. "My boss, Jarred Steele, was our colonel in the SAS. When our special ops unit was deactivated, he decided he'd start his own special ops security service."

"Which is how you came to be watching a bad guy?"

Nick nodded. "As I said, we normally provide security for politicians, celebrities, royalty and millionaires. Sometimes we do covert work for private organizations and the Australian Government."

"So what happened?"

"We were sent to a small town in northern New South Wales to find a mobster who disappeared fifteen years ago. He was rumored to be living there under an assumed identity and about to steal a rare diamond. We found five men matching his general description. So we went in undercover, and that led to a chain of events, which in turn took us to Vietnam in search of a ring of human traffickers."

Nick rolled on his side to face her. "While we were in Vietnam a journalist by the name of Madeline Shaw got caught up in our investigations. Jarred didn't want any leaks, so he promised Madeline the story if she'd keep a lid on it." Nick chuckled. "But to be sure, Jarred left her and the two women we were protecting on a private island off Fiji, without any social media and under twenty-four hour guard."

"I've met Madeline Shaw." Ava moistened her lips. "She's an incredibly talented journalist and beautiful."

Nick reached over Liam and feathered his fingers down her cheek. "You are the most talented and beautiful woman I know." He withdrew his hand. "How do you know, Madeline?"

How to explain? Until Ava was sure about Nick's intentions she needed to protect those closest to her. "Madeline was in London doing an article on a politician hosting a charity gala. I attended as a guest and I'd donated a couple of my designs for auction." Ava yawned. "After seeing my designs, Madeline commissioned me to make her an Opera necklace."

"What's an Opera necklace?"

"It's a long string of pearls." She yawned again.

Nick rolled onto his back, reached out, and turned the bedside lamp off. "Go to sleep, Angel. You're tired."

"But I want to know the whole story. Did you...were you involved with either of the woman you were protecting or Madeline Shaw?"

"No, I wasn't. I'll tell you the whole story tomorrow. Goodnight, Angel."

Ava snuggled into her pillow, breathing a sigh of relief. "Goodnight, my dar... Nick."

She heard his soft chuckle and drew the sound deep, letting its warm tendrils wrap around her heart, infusing her with a serenity she hadn't felt in a long time. *I'm a fool.*

Ava woke slowly, coming out of her lethargic trance bit by bit. She stretched and lolled as she pondered the reason behind her unusual contentment. Opening one eye, she spied Liam playing on the floor beside her. He had his helicopter balanced on the trailer of his truck, pushing it back and forth. He wore the old aviation jacket Maggie had given him before leaving England. The sling had disappeared. Ava's thoughts jumped to the events of yesterday.

Nick!

She twisted round, her eyes searching the empty space beside her. There was no sign of him. She sat upright, listening intently, but other than Liam's mimicking of rotor blades, there was no other sound.

No, I can't have imagined him. I can't. "Nick!" She scrambled out of bed, clasping her hand over her mouth to hold in the sobs as she ran down the hall. "Nick!"

"Mummy?" Liam's frightened voice followed her.

"Nick!"

He stepped out of Liam's room, catching her in his arms. "What's wrong?"

"Nick." Ava clung to him, her tears running freely as she sobbed into his T-shirt. "I woke up and you weren't there."

"Oh, babe." He hugged her close, running his hands up and down her back in long soothing strokes. "I'm not going anywhere."

"You don't understand. I used to dream everything was fine, we were happy and together, then I'd wake up and...you were gone. I was alone and my heart would break all over again." She hiccupped, gulping in air as she tried to compose herself.

"Christ. I wish I'd been there for you."

Ava turned away and noticed Liam staring at her with huge eyes. "I'm sorry, munchkin. Mummy had a nightmare." She lifted her gaze to Nick's. "Where were you?"

He turned so they were facing Liam's room. Two albums lay open on the bed. One crammed with images of her and Nick over their four years together. The other had photos of her pregnant, Liam as a baby, and then the two of them over the last three years. On the bookcase stood a framed photo of Nick in his Army fatigues, smiling as he leaned against a Black Hawk.

Nick rubbed her arm. "Even though you thought I'd deserted you and then that I was dead, you still made me a part of Liam's life. Thank you."

"He deserved to know who his father was... Is."

"I would have loved to watch you grow big with my child, and to help you through his birth. I wish I'd been there to see his first smile and first steps."

"So do I."

He inhaled. "The album helped."

She may have been mad at him to begin with, but his death had almost destroyed her. What would have happened if she hadn't left? Would he have married her? Would she have ended up a doormat? Would she have her design business? Maybe it had been fate and now they had a second chance to do things right.

Ava hesitated. "Do you know what tomorrow is?"

"The same day I walked into a florist in Adelaide and fell under your spell. And then two years later, it was the day I asked you to marry me. Valentine's Day."

She smiled and eased away. "I'll bring the camera today and take photos of us all."

"Thank you." He lifted Liam, then walked into the kitchen. "Breakfast is almost ready."

Ava gasped. The table was laid with a crinkled cloth and a bunch of beautiful wild flowers, roots still intact in a jug of water. Bacon, eggs, and tomatoes crackled in the pan. "You cooked breakfast?"

"Just like old times." He sat Liam on a chair and dropped a couple of pieces of sourdough into the toaster. "I hope your neighbors are understanding. I pinched the flowers from their garden."

"I thought you might have. They're lovely, thank you."

"After breakfast, I thought we could pack a hamper then head out to Barry's for our flight up to Cape Leveque. It's really quiet up there and we can talk."

"That would be lovely, but I need to finish the string of pearls. If you'd like to spend a couple of hours with Liam, I can pick up everything we need and meet you at the hangar."

"Sounds good. I've set up the train set, but I'd like to take Liam to the beach if that's okay with you?"

Ava glanced at Liam who beamed from ear to ear. "Would you like to spend the morning with Daddy?"

"Yes, but then can we go in the helicopter?"

"Sure." She kissed his dimple. "I love you, munchkin."

"I love you, Mummy, and we love Daddy too, don't we?"

Her heart thumping wildly, Ava met Nick's steady gaze. She'd once loved him desperately, but it hadn't been enough. He'd loved her with his body, lavished her with attention, but never admitted the words. *Why?*

She smiled at Liam. "Go and put your board-shorts on and don't forget your hat."

Liam ran off and Nick raised an eyebrow. "You didn't answer his question."

"I'm not going to build up his hopes, and I'm not rushing into anything." How could she? Especially when Nick's job terrified her. He hadn't said he would give it up. Troubled, Ava turned away. Last night she'd been cowering in a helicopter, fired upon by masked men. No matter how much she still desired Nick, what she needed was time to think and decide what was best for Liam.

Chapter Five

After tidying the kitchen, Nick went to Ava's workroom where he found Liam on the floor surrounded by the train track Damon had given him. A fine thread with an S-hook on the end hung from Liam's wooden chopper as he hovered it over an upturned engine.

"Daddy, watch this." Liam hooked the engine with the S-hook then raised the chopper. "The Black Hawk is lifting the train back on the track."

Nick chuckled. "He's got it bad, hasn't he?"

Ava looked up from the necklace she was threading with pearls. "You have no idea. Once Liam left his chopper at daycare. I had to climb onto a garbage bin, get over the fence, and hunt in the dark. It might be wise to leave the helicopter here today."

"That okay with you, buddy?"

"Yes, Daddy."

"Nick, before you go, can you get me my thread box out of the safe?" Ava held up her gloved hands. "The combination is—"

"Don't tell me." Nick stepped over Liam and keyed in the code then turned the handle and opened the door. He handed her the box.

"You saw the numbers last night," she accused, narrowing her eyes.

He laughed. "Guilty as charged, but in my defense, you didn't try to hide it."

"Okay, smarty. You better get moving if you want to have that swim. Take my car, it's got Liam's safety seat in it."

Unable to resist, Nick kissed her glorious auburn head. "See you soon, Angel."

She nodded, her lovely eyes warily meeting his. "Liam tends to get boisterous, so watch he doesn't hurt his arm."

"I'll put the sling back on for now." Nick lifted Liam into his arms and strolled out of her workroom. "Okay, buddy, let's hit the beach."

"Yay."

After refitting the sling for Liam, Nick grabbed Ava's keys then opened the front door where he found an enormous bunch of red roses blocking his way. A woman's head appeared around the arrangement.

"Hi, I have a delivery for Ava Mitchell."

Ava came running along the hall. "For me?" She looked at Nick.

A sour taste filled his mouth. "I didn't send them."

She accepted the roses from the woman. "Thank you."

"It's a pleasure." The woman bustled down the steps and over to a small van.

Ava opened the card. "They're from Damon. He'd like to have dinner with me tonight."

A hard knot twisted in Nick's stomach. This would ruin his surprise unless he used dirty tactics, which he was quite prepared to do. "Are you going to accept, because that will mean cutting short our time at Cape Leveque."

She considered him. "I'll ring Damon to thank him for the flowers and explain why I can't have dinner with him tonight. No matter what you think he's done, he's been good to me. That said, I am looking forward to our trip to Cape Leveque."

Nick's heart swelled as he leaned down and dropped a kiss on her lips, lingering over the contact. "Me too."

A soft blush rose in her cheeks. "I need to finish this necklace." She pushed him out the door. "I'll see you in a couple of hours."

⤷∘⤶

Nick idly ran his fingertips along the counter as he waited for the resort's receptionist to finish her phone call. He looked down at the tiny plump fingers he held in his own large hand, still reeling that this beautiful child was his. The enormity of what Ava had gone through threatened to bring Nick to his knees. The decision not to go after her had been one of the hardest things he'd ever done, but her father had said she was marrying a good man. He'd said she was too refined for a tattooed ruffian who didn't even know his father's identity, and whose mother had been a loose-living addict.

Ava's father had convinced Nick that if he cared about her at all, he would let her go. So he had. *The worst fucking decision I've ever made in my life.* From the moment he'd met Ava, her innocence, beauty and kindness had called to him. In his heart he'd known she loved him, known she'd believed in him, known she wouldn't run off with some other guy.

Then why the fuck didn't I go after her?

Because he'd wanted to be someone people respected and looked up to. He'd needed to prove he was someone worthy of her. Ironically, he now realized he'd never had to prove anything to Ava. He didn't regret the last four years only that he'd lost her. Yet could he live a quieter, less dangerous life? What other job would give him such satisfaction? He'd told Ava he wasn't going anywhere, but giving up a job he loved and the friendship of men who were closer than brothers was not something he could do lightly. A mundane job would send him stir crazy, but having Ava and Liam in his life was as vital as oxygen.

Nick tapped his fingers on the counter, searching for an alternative. He wasn't taking anything for granted. He would keep his room at the resort for now and make the most of the gym and pool facilities. Before going to Ava's last night, he'd loaded the chopper for the trip he was planning then returned to the resort for a shower and clean clothes. The receptionist had informed him that two men had been in earlier asking for his room number. She hadn't given it to them, but Nick knew they'd be back to make a point. They would have to wait.

The receptionist finished the call and smiled. "How can I help you?"

"Hi, I am expecting a couple of visitors but I may have missed them this morning."

"Yes, you did. I rang your room but there was no answer."

"Thanks. I'm sure I'll catch up with them somewhere."

She smiled down at Liam. "What happened to your arm?"

"I crashed my helicopter and Mummy had to give me a sponge bath." Liam giggled. "Mummy used to give Daddy sponge baths when he was hurt and he liked them a lot."

Nick had to grin at Ava's ingenuity and pretend he hadn't noticed the receptionist's deep blush. All being well, a sponge bath would definitely be on his future agenda. He smiled. "If my visitors come back, can you ask them to leave their details and I'll call them tomorrow afternoon?"

"Certainly."

"Thanks." Nick detoured around the luxurious pool so that they approached his room from the other direction. No one lingered nearby so he unlocked the door and entered, casting a swift glance around the interior before stepping inside. "I need to change clothes, buddy, then we might build a castle on the beach and have a swim here in the resort's pool."

"Can I take this sling off?"

"Sure." Nick rubbed Liam's head. "But you have to take it easy, okay?"

The next two hours were amongst the happiest Nick had ever experienced. They built castles, dug holes, searched for shells, and splashed in the shallow seawater. Liam was an inquisitive and amusing little boy with Ava's good-natured disposition. Nick couldn't fathom how Ava had come from two such dour parents. It ripped his heart to shreds that he'd missed out on the first three years of Liam's life. If he ever crossed paths with Hector and Shirley Mitchell, all hell would break loose.

"Okay, buddy, it's time to go meet Mummy."

"And Barry and the helicopter."

"Yep." Nick took Liam's hand and they made their way back to the car park via the resort's gardens. Nick drove to Ava's house, parked in her driveway, then took Liam inside with him to grab everything they'd need for a night away. He stuffed it all in a large plastic bag, collected Liam, then locked the front door behind them.

It was another humid day in Broome and Nick was looking forward to a swim in the ocean. He'd found the secluded cove two years ago while on a charter flight. A honeymoon couple had asked him to drop them on a deserted beach for several hours. Nick had obliged then flown another ten minutes up the coast to a tiny cove where he explored and swam in the crystal clear water. *Now I can share my little paradise with Ava and Liam.*

After parking Ava's car outside the hangar, Nick unbuckled Liam and assisted him out. He straightened to see Ava strolling toward them. She wore a short, flowery dress, flat sandals, and a wide brimmed hat. Nick's gaze lingered on her long tanned legs and his pulse quickened. He felt like a horny teenager.

"Hello, Angel. Did you miss us?"

"As a matter of fact I did." She bent down and kissed Liam's cheek, hesitated, then blushing prettily, lightly kissed Nick's cheek. "I've got our picnic, towels, and my camera in the helicopter. Helen has offered to take Liam tonight, if we'd like time to talk."

"That's nice, but I've got something planned." He stepped close, meeting her gaze. "You look gorgeous."

"Thank you." Her hand fluttered to his chest and held him from coming any closer. "Did you have a nice time with Liam?"

"Yes. I don't think we'll win any awards for our sandcastle, but we had fun." Nick turned away, grabbed the plastic bag, and shut the door. "Let's go." He picked Liam up and they walked round to the front of the hangar where two Bell Jet Rangers sat on dolly trolleys. The third chopper sat inside the hangar waiting on repairs.

Barry stood talking to a man in sunglasses and a cap beside one of the choppers. They looked across then Barry came striding over. "Hiya, Nick. Your chopper's fueled and ready to go, and I've packed those extra supplies you wanted."

"I appreciate that, Baz."

"Take your time; you're paying for the fuel and I've only got one charter tomorrow." Barry appeared to hesitate then met Nick's gaze. "Could you spare five minutes? That guy behind me is one of the pilots Pearce coerced into leaving me to work for him. Dave's got some disturbing news and I don't know what to do about it."

"I remember Dave." Nick passed Liam to Ava and stowed his pack in the side hold of the chopper, then opened the front door. "Give me a sec to strap in my co-pilot."

Liam glowed, his face a canvas of sheer delight.

"I guess that means I'm in the back." Ava sighed dramatically. "I suppose it's only right that the two pilots sit in the front."

Nick fought to stop grinning. "That's right." He took Liam from her and secured him in the seat belt, adjusting it to fit his small frame, then held the rear door open for Ava. A picnic basket sat on the far seat with a blanket over the top. As Ava slid onto the seat her dress rode up her thighs and without a second thought, he ran his hand across her bare leg as he reached for the seatbelt. "You really are gorgeous."

Her breath caught. "You keep telling me that and my head will be too big to get out of this chopper."

"Never. I'll be back shortly." He closed their doors then jogged across the tarmac to where Barry stood with Dave beside the other chopper. "I'm surprised you've got the guts to come back after leaving Barry in the lurch."

A dull red flush covered Dave's face. "The deal Mr. Pearce offered Max and I was too good to knock back, but I'm definitely regretting it now."

"Oh?"

"Look, I know you used to be with Special Forces and Barry tells me you're freelancing with some of your old crew."

Nick sent Barry an annoyed grimace before returning his attention to Dave. "I'd prefer you kept that information confidential. Barry said you have disturbing news?"

"Yeah. Mr. Pearce only has one chopper but he wanted the two of us on his payroll." Dave drew a deep breath. "When we're not flying Mr. Pearce between Broome and his other businesses, we're at the beck and call of a guy called Lex Walsh."

Nick crossed his arms, impatient to be gone. "What's your point?"

Dave glanced around as if expecting to catch someone spying on them. "Max and I suspect Pearce and Walsh are up to something illegal. Each week we take them out to a diamond mine and then onto a pearl farm. Then after dropping Pearce back in Broome, we take Lex to either Roebuck Bay where Pearce has a luxury yacht with an armed crew, or to a heavily guarded place in the King Leopald Ranges. I wouldn't be telling you this except the last time I spoke to Max he intended to do a little snooping. Now he's disappeared."

Nick narrowed his eyes. "Disappeared?"

"Completely and without a word." Dave stared at the ground. "Max sent me a text yesterday saying he needed to talk to me urgently, but he never showed."

"Could he have gone off on a bender?"

"Max doesn't drink."

Nick rubbed his chin. "Does Pearce or Walsh know of your suspicions?"

"I don't think so. Pearce asked me yesterday if I'd spoken to Max lately, as he couldn't reach him. I told him I hadn't."

"I suggest you report Max as missing and tell the police what you've told me."

"I have. They think I have an over-active imagination and Pearce's crew are licensed to carry guns at sea, in case they're attacked by pirates." Dave shuffled his feet. "I've asked Barry to fly me down to Cape Villaret where I plan to lay low."

Nick nodded. "I don't like Pearce, but that doesn't mean he's responsible for Max's disappearance or that he's up to anything illegal. If Max hasn't turned up by tomorrow, I'll ask my boss to pull a few strings and widen the search."

"Thanks." Dave shook Nick's hand. "I appreciate it."

Nick inclined his head then strode back to the other chopper. He pushed all thoughts of Max out of his mind. The man would more than likely turn up.

As Nick climbed into the chopper, Ava met his gaze. "Is everything all right?"

"Barry's worried about a friend who's gone AWOL. If he hasn't turned up by tomorrow, I'll see what I can do." Nick adjusted Liam's headset. "Ready, partner?"

Liam nodded, his gaze following Nick's every move.

"First, we make sure our collective and cyclic levers, and the tail rotor pedals are moving freely and everything is centered." Nick finished the safety check then disengaged the rotor brake and turned the battery master switch on. "You should be able to hear me through the headset now. Okay?"

Liam nodded.

"Now we check outside to make sure no one is standing close then we feed it a little fuel with the throttle, hold the button, and let the starter turn the engine. You'll hear the engine noise change as the starter disengages and the engine lights up and spins under its own steam."

The blades began to turn.

"I have to contact Broome Tower to get clearance. We don't want to bump into anyone up there."

Nick listened to the recorded weather information automatically transmitted by the tower, and adjusted his altimeter. He then radioed the control tower.

"And now we look to see that all those red and amber lights have turned green." Nick checked that the rotor disk was spinning at 100% rpm, and beeped the governor slightly to make sure it was exactly right. "You see this?" He pointed at a pea-sized ball in a curved tube on the instrument panel. "This is the skid ball. It looks like a little beetle sitting on a dotted line. We have to keep him exactly in the middle of the gauge when we're turning."

"How do you do that, Daddy?" Liam stared at the gauge.

Nick smiled. "I use the pedals. They change the pitch on the tail rotor. When you're a big boy, I'll teach you to fly, but in the meantime it's very important you don't touch any of the switches or levers, okay?"

"Okay." Liam nodded, his hazel eyes shining. "Daddy, is a Seahawk the same as a Black Hawk?"

"The Seahawk is a Navy chopper named after a sea bird, so it's one word. It's very similar to the Black Hawk, which is two words and named after a famous American Indian."

"Everything okay in the back, Angel?"

"Super. Do I get a lesson too?"

"I always meant to teach you. How about I give you a lesson on the way back?"

"It's okay, I don't need to know how to fly a helicopter."

"It won't hurt to have a little knowledge under your belt."

Liam squirmed in his seat. "Daddy, can you take me in a Black Hawk too?"

"We'll see, buddy." Nick turned his attention to the controls. Besides Ava, his other passion in life was flying Black Hawks and the adrenalin rush of being on a mission. The thought of giving it up was numbing.

"Here we go." Nick raised the collective lever and the helicopter lifted smoothly off the dolly platform. Once they were hovering in front of the hangar, Nick did a final check that all indications were good, then eased the cyclic lever forward and to the right taking them sweeping out to the pristine coastline. He smiled as Liam forgot about the gauges and exclaimed excitedly over a line of camels carrying tourists and plodding along the sand.

Liam spotted a pod of dolphins. "Mummy, look."

"I'm looking, I'm looking. Isn't the water a beautiful color, and so clear?"

Nick glanced over his shoulder. "Wait until you see the little cove I'm taking you to. There is no road access and boats can't cross the reef. The only way in is by foot or helicopter, so we should have the place to ourselves."

"I can't wait." Ava's eyes met his and she smiled.

Nick turned back to his windshield. Elation didn't come close to what he was feeling. Up until several weeks ago he'd been emotionally dead, drifting from one shallow hookup to the next, never interested in anything more than casual sex. Today he felt alive and on top of the world. He now had Ava and this amazing little boy in his life. If all went according to plan, that's where they'd stay.

Nick kept to the coast, taking the chopper down lower whenever Liam or Ava spotted something they wanted a better look at. The flight took them an hour and as they approached the little cove he'd marked as his own, Nick was relieved to see nothing had changed. It lay protected on three sides by hilly outcrops. The reef lay clearly visible beneath the calm clear water, providing an impassable border and ensuring no sea-going vessels or sharks could slip into the cove. The white sand served as a stark buffer between the ocean and the dense foliage. They would have complete privacy.

"We're here. What do you think?" Nick took the chopper in a wide arc, allowing Ava and Liam a bird's eye view of the tiny cove.

Ava had her nose pressed to the glass. "I can see why you liked to escape here."

"I see fishes, Mummy."

Nick smiled at the excitement in Liam's voice. "I've packed a fishing rod so we can catch some for our dinner tonight."

"Dinner?" Ava turned to him. "How long are we staying?"

He turned back to concentrate on a small open area on the bank above the sand. "I want to show you the spectacular sunset and then when it's dark, the stars, which can only truly be appreciated away from town lights. So, if you're agreeable, I'd like to stay the night."

"Where will we sleep, Daddy?" Liam turned questioning eyes to him.

"I've brought a tent with us, buddy. Just in case."

"A tent! I've never slept in a tent." Liam bounced with excitement.

"I'm not sure I like being manipulated like this," said Ava. "What about crocodiles. Aren't they a danger?

"I've never seen crocs here. They're usually in estuaries and fresh water rivers, although I believe a few have been sighted further up the coast. This cove is protected on three sides by the steep ridges around us. That's not to say a croc couldn't come in from the ocean at high tide though." He winked at Liam. "If Mummy says we can stay, I'll pitch the tent on this bank and our camp fire will scare off any unwelcome visitors."

Liam grinned. "I'm not afraid."

"That's good, but you should always keep your eyes open for anything dangerous."

Nick brought the chopper down on a grassy verge overlooking the brilliant white sand. He wound the throttle to idle, gave the engine a few seconds to stabilize, and then shut off the fuel. There wasn't a footprint or track to be seen. It was as if no human or animal had ever ventured onto this beach since the beginning of creation.

Ava sighed. "It's beautiful."

"Just like you. A beautiful angel I didn't deserve." Nick shut off the fuel and master switch. "That's the only thing your father and I ever agreed on."

Chapter Six

After climbing out of the chopper, Ava stood motionless, absorbing the gentle breeze as she took in the pure white sand, powder blue sky, and aquamarine water so clear she could see all the way to the reef. As each wave hit the larger rocks, a spray of foam surged into the air then cascaded across the reef and into the bay with barely a ripple. After the traumatic events of yesterday, this was exactly what she needed. Time to unwind and evaluate where Nick fitted into her and Liam's lives. No rushing. They would take things slowly and see if they had a future.

Nick strolled around the chopper carrying Liam in his arms. "What are you thinking, Angel?"

They looked so natural together. Ava sighed inwardly, accepting it wasn't going to be easy to keep this man at bay. He may have left the SAS, but from what he'd told her, his current career was just as dangerous. Did she want that type of stress in her life? In Liam's life? She'd asked Nick whether he'd give up his current job for them. The fact he sidestepped her question hadn't escaped her.

He looked at her with a raised eyebrow. "Penny for your thoughts."

She managed a smile. "I'm thinking I'm hot and I need to cool off."

He met her gaze. "A swim won't make you any less hot in my eyes."

"Nicholas Flanagan, behave. Our son has a way of repeating things at the worst possible moment."

"I've noticed. The hotel receptionist now knows you like to give me sponge baths when I'm hurting."

"Oh my God." Heat flooded Ava's face. "I said that because of

Liam's arm. He wanted a...a...bath." She spluttered. "You see what I mean?"

His eyes held a wicked glint. "But I *did* like your sponge baths. I just can't recall hurting, unless of course you meant a particular part of my anatomy that often got stiff?"

"Nick!" She glared at him, aware Liam was trying to follow their conversation. "Let's see who can be first into the water."

"Me, me." Liam wriggled until Nick placed him on the ground. Within seconds he had his sling off and was scrambling down the bank.

"Good thing his arm was only dislocated." Nick leapt off the bank, throwing off his T-shirt, runners, cap, and sunglasses as he chased Liam across the sand.

Ava smiled when Nick scooped their son up in his arms and plowed into the ocean, Liam's high-pitched laughter shrill with excited glee. Nick's deep, masculine laugh warmed her soul. "This is how it's supposed to be."

Ava slipped off her sandals and jumped down onto the heated sand. Nick's words tore at her heart. Had he always felt he didn't deserve her? She'd been eighteen when he'd walked into the florist where she'd worked part-time. It had been her escape from a strict home life and endless studying during her first year of uni. The flowers had always soothed her and the majority of customers came in with romance in mind—such a contrast to the stilted relationship of her parents. Nick pursued her for months. He turned up at the florist every Saturday to walk her home, unless he was on an Army maneuver. He'd wait for her shift to end then take her to a cafe for hot chocolate. She'd never let him walk her the whole way home, as her parents would have freaked. He'd been her fantasy lover, until the day he stole a kiss and turned her world upside down.

"Hurry up, Mummy. Come and see the fishes."

Ava waved at Liam then picked up Nick's discarded bits and pieces. Her toes sank into the warm sand as she walked toward the only two people in the world who had the power to destroy her. One almost had. The other had saved her.

This could be a second chance for all three of us, as long as Nick doesn't take us for granted. As long as he gives up his dangerous job. As long as he loves me.

"Mummy, come on!"

Ava waved. "Hold your horses." She spread out a towel and dropped Nick's things in the middle then removed her own hat and dress. Nick's intense gaze raked over her as she waded toward him. The carnal lust in his eyes heated her all over, which only made the cool bite of the water starker against her hot skin.

Ava stared at Nick's naked chest and shoulders where rivulets of water trickled down his deeply tanned skin. Her gaze moved to the angel tattoo, which he'd had done after making love to her for the first time. After she'd confessed her love for him.

"Only delinquents and gang members have tattoos and that man will be the ruination of you. He's a heathen with a black soul." Her father's words had been bitter, his face twisted in fury.

Ava gasped at the memory. She'd been so angry that she'd run to the one person who made everything right, who lavished her in compliments and delicious kisses. When it came to souls, Nick's was much purer than her father's. Nick made her feel wanted and cherished. He'd brought so much laughter into her life. She'd never told him why she suddenly agreed to move in with him. He'd been too happy.

He was laughing at her now. "Come on, Angel, the water's not that cold, but I can warm you up if needed."

A scorching flood of desire leapt through her veins. "I'm coming."

"Oh you'll come, Angel. That's a certainty."

Her body went from hot to molten. "Nick!"

"Sorry." He skimmed Liam through the water like a dolphin surfing the tiny waves. "But witnessing you...come for me...is something I've never forgotten."

"Nicholas Flanagan!" Ava tried glaring at him as lust roared through her. She was in danger of internally combusting. There was only one solution. She dived under the water, breast-stroking for several meters before bursting to the surface to inhale a lungful of air. Her clip had come out and her hair streamed down her back. She searched for it and found Nick and Liam watching her.

"Mummy looks like a mermaid, doesn't she, Daddy?"

Nick's eyes danced wickedly, his lips curved. "Exactly what I was thinking, buddy."

Ava huffed. "I bet." She waded closer. "I think your daddy wants to hook me on his fishing line and then eat me."

Nick raised an eyebrow. "What a good idea. Tasting you is very appealing."

Liam giggled. "You can't eat Mummy. Who will look after me?"

Ava threw her hands up in mock disgust. "Liam, I expect you to save me because you love me, not because I look after you."

"But, that's what mummies do."

A shadow passed over Nick's face. "Not all mummies look after their children, Liam. You're a lucky boy to have a mummy who loves you so much."

Ava stared at Nick. He'd told her so little about his childhood. She knew his existence was due to a short-lived affair. That his mother had become an addict and he'd spent considerable time in foster care. And, if not for Barry, Nick would have ended up in a juvenile detention center.

Ava had told her father this to show him how much Nick had overcome, but it made Hector Mitchell more determined to keep them apart. A shiver ran down Ava's spine. If Nick hadn't come into her life, she never would have discovered she'd been adopted. Hector and Shirley had raised her as their own child and she'd loved them or at least tried to. They'd always been distant, even with each other. She'd never realized how distant, until Nick showed her a warmth and closeness she'd never known. Yet he hadn't said he loved her. Was he afraid of that emotion? *Possibly. Probably.*

She turned her face up to the sun. "I'm a lucky lady to have two handsome pilots who can set up the tent and catch fish for my dinner."

Nick laughed. "Come on, buddy, I really am hungry, and if you don't want me to gobble your mummy up, we'd better get stuck into that picnic lunch."

Liam roared with laughter and hugged Nick tightly round the neck with both arms, obviously no longer in any pain.

Ava followed, relieved to see Nick's good humor restored. She wondered how he hadn't turned to a life of crime with such an unstable childhood. And then a terrible thought hit her. *Until I came along, did anyone love Nick? He didn't think he was good enough for me. Oh, God, is that why he didn't come after me? If I give him a second chance, will he break my heart again?*

"Come on, Mummy, or Daddy and I will gobble you up."

Quickening her pace, Ava decided she would get the truth out of Nick later. "Okay, hold your horses, I'm com...my legs aren't as long as Daddy's."

Nick's gaze dropped to her legs and she could almost see all the wicked responses he wanted to say, but he refrained and instead, slowly raised his eyes.

"We should eat before my appetite brings out the Neanderthal in me." He lowered Liam to the sand and jogged up to the chopper.

"Mummy, what's a Neanderal?"

"Neanderthals were alive thousands of years ago and they're like a close relative to people. They're different but similar, like orangutans and gorillas. They used to hunt for their food and"—*Damn you, Nick*—"if they were hungry or...lonely they might fight other Neanderthals for their food or their mate."

"Like lions?"

"Yes." Ava drew in a giant breath and relaxed. "Exactly."

Liam giggled. "I won't let Daddy gobble you up. I'll protect you, Mummy."

"Thanks, munchkin." Ava dropped to her knees and hugged him. "I know you will."

"And Daddy will protect you from the Neanderals."

"Luckily, Neanderthals don't exist anymore."

Liam's expression turned solemn. "But if they did, Daddy would protect you because he's very strong."

Nick chuckled from behind Ava. "That goes without saying." He ruffled Liam's hair, then placed the basket on the sand and tossed Ava the blanket. "After our lunch settles we should take a hike up to the top of the ridge. It's an easy walk and quite impressive."

"Sounds good." Ava spread out the blanket then opened the basket. "We've got fresh rolls, ham, chicken, coleslaw, grapes and..." She pulled out a cooler. "Water."

"Yay." Liam scampered over the blanket, accepted the bottle, and then helped her take out the food.

"Yay," Nick mimicked weakly as he lowered his body to the blanket. "You wouldn't have something stronger?"

She reached into the cooler and passed him a beer. "I'd hate to disappoint you."

He grinned. "You wouldn't know how, Angel."

"But I did, didn't I." She chewed her bottom lip. "Just like your mother. I'm sorry, Nick. I really thought you'd come after me."

His hand stilled in the act of raising the can to his mouth. "Ava, you are nothing like my mother. You care about people. If you want the truth, I didn't come after you because I thought you were better off without me. I was still trying to prove I could be someone worthwhile."

"You never needed to prove anything to me. And I'm ashamed to say, I would have used my pregnancy to blackmail you."

He frowned at her. "Blackmail me?"

"A soldier in the SAS is such a dangerous occupation. You know I couldn't stand the thought of you being killed. I would have used my pregnancy to make you leave."

He laughed. "I do believe you would have."

"What does blackmail mean?" Liam looked from Ava to Nick.

"Damn." She put her head in her hands. "Your turn. I dealt with Neanderthals."

Nick took a couple of swigs from the can. "Blackmail is when a person makes you do something you don't want to, because they know something about you that's a secret, or they have something you want."

"What did Mummy want you to do?" Liam's questioning eyes went between them.

Nick cleared his throat. "I had a dangerous job and your mummy didn't want me to get hurt, so she would have insisted I leave that job to look after you. Unfortunately, another person told Mummy I...was stuck in the clouds, so she stayed in England."

"With me and Grandma."

"Sorry?" Nick frowned at Ava. "Grandma?"

Ava bit her lip. "I lived in England with my aunt Maggie who is considered the black sheep of the family. When I realized I was pregnant I rang my parents. My father went crazy and began ranting. He said, like mother like daughter and that he rued the day he decided to adopt me. That's when I discovered they weren't my real parents."

He covered her hand and gently squeezed. "I'm sorry, Ava. I always wondered how you could come from such sour parents. It makes sense, you're nothing like them."

"No, but I was still rocked. My aunt went berserk. She swore so crudely that I was shocked into a stunned silence. She slammed cupboards, threw a plate at the wall, and then rang her brother. The things she screamed at him would have shocked even you. No one has ever spoken to him like that, but she was relentless. Then she hugged me tight, so tight I could barely breath, and kept saying she was sorry. That's when the truth hit me. Maggie is my mother."

Nick enveloped her in his arms and lifted her across his thighs. "Bloody hell."

Liam gasped. "Daddy! You said a naughty word."

"Shit."

"Nick!" Ava spluttered then clung to him, laughing, until she was gasping for air. He laughed too, his chest quaking under her hands.

Liam gave a high-pitched squeal and launched himself into Ava's lap, causing the three of them to fall backward in a tangled heap, delirious with laughter.

"Stay there." Ava sat up, searched out her camera, and took a couple of shots of Nick and Liam laughing up at her. Then she fell back into Nick's arms and held the camera above them. "Smile."

"My arm is longer." Nick took the camera and held it above them as he tickled her. She squealed, which set them off into another fit of laughter.

"All this noise is going to scare the wildlife away." Nick murmured the words against her earlobe, his breath tickling her sensitive skin. Then his fingers feathered across her tummy sending a blast of desire shooting through her body.

"We can't have that." She scrambled up, hiding her heated face as she sorted through the containers. "I'll bring my camera on our walk and take lots of photos."

"Ava."

"And after our walk we can have another swim. We'll probably need it by then."

"Ava, look at me."

She swallowed and raised her eyes. Liam stood beside the basket, playing with her camera. Nick sat very still, his hazel eyes dark and intense.

"I didn't comprehend what you meant to me until you were gone. No one has ever cared about me the way you did or made me so happy. I never told you what you truly meant to me because I couldn't put it into words. You were my world."

Ava wasn't sure who moved first, but suddenly she was in Nick's arms, held so tightly she could barely breath. They stayed like that for several minutes, clinging to each other as if their lives depended on it. Then he released her, eased back, and framed her face with his hands. He lowered his head and kissed her, at first gently then when she responded, he parted her lips and claimed her greedily. She welcomed him with energetic enthusiasm.

Liam giggled.

Ava gasped, shocked to find she desperately wanted more. Much more. She had no words.

Liam beamed at her. "I took a photo of you and Daddy kissing."

"What a clever boy." Nick raised an eyebrow at her as he reached for a bread roll. "Lucky he interrupted us when he did."

"Let me see." Ava held her hand out for the camera. "Thank you, Liam."

The image was nothing short of spectacular. It showed them plastered to each other in a kiss of frenzied passion. But passion wasn't enough. Her hand shook as she passed the camera to Nick.

He stared at the photo for a minute then winked at Liam. "Great photo, buddy."

Liam preened then sank to his knees and waited patiently as Nick filled the roll with chicken and coleslaw for him. "Thank you, Daddy."

Ava passed another roll to Nick and filled her own as her mind raced back and forth. It was no longer a case of if they made love, but when. She was still in love with Nick and had no idea what she intended to do about it.

Nick decided against hiking to the top of the ridge as Ava and Liam only wore sandals. Instead, they spent a couple of hours fossicking along the beach, building sandcastles for Liam to jump on and taking photos of each other. Then Nick unpacked the chopper and pitched the tent while Ava and Liam played in the shallow water. He'd just finished erecting the tent when Barry rang.

"Nick, I've got bad news."

"Oh."

"The police found Max's body. They say he was washed off rocks while fishing."

"I'm sorry to hear that, Barry."

"Yeah. I've been thinking seriously about taking Pearce's offer."

"What?"

"He rang me this afternoon to see if I knew where Dave was. I told him I had no idea. Then Pearce apologized for his man's heavy handedness, and said he didn't have anything to do with the thugs last night. He also doubled his original offer."

"But the choppers are your life. What's really going on, Barry?"

"I don't won't to end up dead, like Max."

"I thought you said he was washed off the rocks?" Nick didn't like where this was going.

Barry sighed. "Max hates fishing. He doesn't even own a rod."

"Then we need to find out why he was there and where that rod came from."

"It's probably Dave's," Barry said. "His wife can't stand the fishy smell, so he keeps his rods and gear in Max's garage. There's no way in hell Max would go fishing though."

"Christ." Nick's gaze settled on Ava chasing Liam up the sand, the deep green of her bikini showcasing her fair skin and fiery red hair. His eyes lingered on her long legs before moving up to her delectable breasts. He cleared his throat. "Tell Dave to stay out of Broome and not to answer any calls but yours. I'll ring my boss when I get back. In the meantime, don't tell anybody about your suspicions and don't take Pearce's offer."

"Righto. Thanks, Nick."

"No worries. See you tomorrow." Nick gritted his teeth. He would have to speak to Jarred. If Pearce was behind Max's death, then he was a deadly adversary to have and Ava could get caught in the crossfire. Nick tossed his phone in the tent, jumped off the bank, and crouched to catch Liam. He'd deal with it tomorrow, for now his family was safe. "Come on, buddy. I'll protect you from that gorgeous mermaid."

CHAPTER SEVEN

Ava leaned against Nick's solid chest, cocooned within his arms as they gazed at the descending moon and its golden light casting a path across the ocean. His warm breath tickled her ear as he spoke. "Between March and October it's even more spectacular. They call it stairway to the moon."

She sighed. "I've never seen anything like it."

"When the moon disappears, the stars become brilliant. I always wanted to bring you to Broome so you could experience it, too."

Ava tilted her head and met his gaze. "I wish you'd come after me."

"I almost did, so many times. It would have been easy for Simon to find you."

"Simon?"

"He's our communications wizard. There are very few computer systems Simon can't hack into. He could have traced your whereabouts through your credit card, driver's license, or tax file number. And, even though the thought of you married to some other man gutted me, I figured you would have children and I couldn't bring myself to wreck your life, so I'd physically exhaust myself with exercise, get drunk, or get laid."

The thought of Nick with other women nettled. "You're the only man I've ever been with. The only man I ever *wanted* to be with."

His arms tightened. "And *you're* the only woman I wanted as my wife. That's why no one else could hold my attention. They weren't you."

Ava touched his cheek. "So you think you're good enough for me now?"

"I was always good enough for you, babe. It just took me a while to realize it." He turned his mouth into her hand and placed a soft kiss on her palm. "My childhood was shitty. I never knew whether I'd come home to an empty house, or to find some creep banging my mother." He grimaced. "I spent a lot of time in foster care, which I preferred, but eventually my mother would turn up and convince Child Services to give me back."

"Oh, Nick." Ava lowered her hand. "Why couldn't your mother leave you in foster care?"

"If she didn't have a boyfriend to live off, she needed the child support money."

Ava wriggled round to face him then sat back on her heels. "You only ever gave me snippets of your childhood. How did you end up with Barry?"

Nick grimaced. "When I was fifteen, my mother's boyfriend beat me up. I was questioned at school and decided to out the bastard. The school counselor and a cop went to visit my mother and found her as high as a kite. She was so out of it that they called an ambulance."

Ava gasped. Her own childhood may have been rigidly strict, but she'd always been cared for and never beaten. She gripped Nick's arms. "Then what happened?"

Nick's lips twitched. "Barry caught me spraying graffiti on his hangar. He hauled me down to the police station and discovered it was my second offense. I'd recently been caught stealing a car in an attempt to get away from my mother."

"Oh no." Ava's shoulders sagged. "That wouldn't have helped."

"No, but before I went to court, the school counselor spoke to the magistrate and Barry. The next thing I know I'm working my butt off every afternoon and weekend at the hangar. It was that or a juvenile detention center. I would lock up at night, just so I didn't have to go home. Barry never said anything but he knew I slept there. He kept the fridge stocked with leftovers, which I helped myself to. A few weeks later my mother was admitted to a rehab center in Perth. I moved in with Barry and never heard from her again."

"You didn't find out who your father was?"

"She hinted once that he might have been in the Army, but who would know? She got around."

"Hmm." Ava looked down, worrying her bottom lip. This was the most Nick had ever divulged. Earlier he'd told her about some of his missions with Steele Intelligence. What else could she learn? She glanced up to find him watching her with amusement.

"Ask whatever you want, Angel."

He could always read her so easily. She hesitated. "I know Barry taught you to fly, but why join the Army?"

"Barry figured I needed structure. He said the Army would make a man of me and if I worked hard, I might get to fly Black Hawks. He was right."

"Barry is very proud of you." She smiled. "Thank you for telling me about the missions to Willaroi Downs and Vietnam. I don't know how Kallie and Jane can sleep knowing Sam and Talos might be injured or killed." Her smile faded. "I know I'd be sick with worry." *Do I want to live like that?*

"They seem to take it in their stride."

She frowned. *I need to meet them. Ask how they cope with knowing the next phone call could carry the worst possible news.* "It's a pity you're missing their weddings tomorrow."

"Weddings aren't my thing and finding you was more important." He looked toward the sinking moon. "I'll leave my job, if that's what it will take to keep you and Liam in my life, but I don't know what else I can do."

"You could go into partnership with Barry and fly charter flights around the Kimberley."

"That's one possibility." His lips twitched. "Is Liam a heavy sleeper?"

Ava glanced at the tent. They'd zipped the flap closed in case of mosquitoes. "Yes, why?"

"I wouldn't want him to catch us making out." He brushed a kiss against her ear.

Delicious shivers ran down her spine, chasing her misgivings about a future together from her mind. "There's no chance of that."

He frowned. "No chance he'll wake, or no chance of us making out?"

A thrill of elation surged through Ava. What harm could there be in taking a little pleasure. "Liam didn't get much sleep last night and you wore him out today. The poor little fella could barely keep his eyes open to eat the fish you caught." She danced her fingertips across Nick's broad shoulders then down his T-shirt, stopping to circle a hard nipple. "I doubt my screaming would wake him."

"Is that so?" Nick drew her closer. "I'd like to test that theory." He lowered his head and brushed his lips across hers. "God, I've missed you, babe."

Ava tensed. "The last time you said that was the day you got back from what I thought was a three-week training camp, when in fact it was an SAS selection course."

"Hmm, I barely made it through the front door when you had your way with me."

Ava drew back. "That must have been when I fell pregnant. We were so frantic we didn't use protection, then a couple of days later you announced we should postpone the wedding because you'd been accepted into the SAS."

He cupped her bottom and lifted her closer. "Let's put that behind us and concentrate on the future. I want us to be together, Ava, like we were meant to be." He drew her against his hard chest, holding her tight in his arms, then lowered his head and kissed her gently, almost reverently, like he had for their very first kiss.

She could feel his locked muscles under her fingers, his rigid length against her belly. Sense the supreme effort it took to keep his demons under control. She ignored the warning bells as a tremor of wicked delight danced over her belly. He kept the kiss light, trying to draw her in slowly, but she wasn't having any of that. She parted her lips, touched her tongue to his, and deepened their kiss, jubilant when he groaned and spread his hands across her bottom, dragging her hard against his erection.

Ava pushed, knocking him backward in an attempt to keep the upper hand, but Nick rolled, his heavy body pinning her to the blanket. She wrapped her legs around him, desperate to be closer. The kiss was voracious, the bristly whickers on his chin scratching her skin. She didn't care. His control hung by a thread and she intended to break it.

Nick's hand closed over her breast and she moaned, pressing into his palm as she wrestled to get his T-shirt up. She needed skin against skin.

He reared back and yanked his T-shirt off then pulled her sundress off, hurling it toward the bank, along with his control.

Thrilled, she wrestled with his shorts, his erection making it impossible to get the zipper down. "I want you."

"Hold that thought." He leapt to his feet.

"What?" She blinked in confusion. "Where are you going?"

"Condom." He bounded up the bank and jogged to the helicopter.

Ava leaned up on one elbow and watched with amusement as he wrenched the pilot's door open, dug through his wallet, then tossed it over his shoulder, uncaring where it landed as he ran back. He dragged his shorts off, then fell on her, and straight back into their incendiary kiss.

She traced her hands over his shoulders and biceps, enthralled by the hard muscles under her fingertips. His erection pressed against her almost painfully as he pulled aside her bikini-top then ran his hands over her tingling breasts. Desire swamped her. The heat between her thighs threatened to burn her alive, but it still wasn't enough. She pulled the strings of her bikini-pants and yanked them off, then locked her legs around him and pressed closer.

"Now, Nick."

"God, Ava, wait." He tore the packet open with his teeth, sheathed himself, then touched her. "You're so wet, I've got to taste you."

Ava moaned. "Next time. I want you inside me now."

He ignored her and slid down her body, leaving a fiery trail of kisses over her breasts and stomach. She could smell her own desire as he pushed her legs wide then kissed the inside of her thighs. She tried to pull him up, aware he was deliberately slowing things down. He didn't budge. "Please, Nick."

A deep chuckle sounded then he slid his hands under her backside and lifted her to meet his lips. She bucked and cried out as his mouth closed over her sensitive skin. He circled her nub and thrust his tongue deep, tormenting her into a quivering mass of hyper-awareness. Then he sucked hard and her body exploded like fireworks on New Year's Eve. She screamed, shaking violently then stiffened, clamping her thighs around his neck as her body soared higher than the glorious moon.

Nick unlocked her legs, then wiped his mouth and moved over her. "I love how you come for me, Angel."

She closed her eyes, boneless and unable to lift a finger. "I can't move."

"You will." He kissed her mouth then eased his thick erection inside her.

It felt wonderful, like coming home. She groaned and lifted her lids to see him watching her.

His dimple appeared. "I can see I've got your attention."

"Yes, but can you keep it?"

"I'll do my best." He withdrew and slowly pressed in, all the way, then did it again a little faster.

Life infused her limbs as she absorbed his scent—a mixture of spice, sweat and lust. She moaned and lifted her hips to meet him. "Harder."

He thrust deep, quickening his speed as his own need built. Ava clung to his shoulders, tilting her head to allow him access to her neck and collarbone. His warm breath caressed her skin. With each powerful thrust, his chest hair chafed her nipples until they were so sensitive she could barely breathe.

He rocked into her hard and fast, building to a frenzied crescendo, then took one nipple in his mouth and sucked at the same time he brushed his thumb over her clit. She shattered, crying out his name as she soared over the edge and into oblivion again.

Nick thrust once more and roared his own climax, before collapsing on top of her. He lay breathing heavily, still buried deep inside her, his weight a soothing balm to her scattered wits.

After a minute he rolled to the side, keeping her locked in his arms. Neither said a word; it was too special a moment and they both seemed to need to savor it.

Ava was still high in a euphoric daze when a cool breeze skipped over her skin. She shivered and cuddled closer.

Nick pulled away and wrapped the blanket around her. "I'll be back in a minute."

Too sated to move, she closed her eyes and breathed a sigh of contentment. Her world had been ripped apart four years ago, could this be a second chance at a happy ever after?

Eventually, Nick came back and knelt beside her. "Wake up, Angel. We can't sleep out here."

"Why not?"

"Dingoes, spiders, snakes. Take your pick."

"What?" Ava shot to her knees, the blanket forgotten.

Nick laughed and held out her Guns and Roses T-shirt. "Here, put this on. I've also got your toothbrush if you want to clean your teeth."

Ava struggled into the T-shirt and glanced nervously around the dark beach and nearby scrub. "You're joking about the wildlife, right?"

"No, I'm not. We're better off up on the bank in our tent than down here on the sand. It is possible for a croc to come up the beach, and without the fire other animals might get curious."

"Okay." She had another look around before climbing the bank.

While Nick smothered the fire with sand, Ava made quick work of cleaning her teeth then followed him into the tent.

As predicted, Liam was still sound asleep. She zipped the tent flap closed and turned to find Nick holding the edge of a sleeping bag open for her to climb in beside him. He'd also laid one open beneath them, making a double sleeping bag.

"I thought you might need my body heat to keep you warm," he whispered.

"That's very noble of you." She wriggled in beside him and turned straight into his arms. "That resort you're staying at must be expensive. Maybe you could stay with Liam and me, while you decide what you want to do?"

"I'd like that," murmured Nick.

Okay, I'm officially a lost cause. I want Nick to make love to me again, and it makes sense for him to stay at my house so he can be with Liam. Who am I trying to fool?

"Nick, if you decide to go into partnership with Barry, what will you tell your boss and the rest of your team?"

He sighed. "The truth. They'll be disappointed but I think they'll understand."

"You're very close to them all, aren't you?"

"We've been through a lot together and the boys are like brothers. I'd trust each of them with my life, and yours if it came to it."

Ava traced her fingers aimlessly across his broad chest. "Will you be content living in Broome with me and Liam?"

"I'll be happy anywhere as long as the three of us are together. Finding a job as exciting as what I do now isn't going to happen, but as long as I'm flying, that will help."

"But is that enough? What if Barry isn't interested in a partnership?"

He hesitated a moment too long and Ava experienced a pang of guilt. What right did she have to expect him to give up the friends and profession that made him the man he now was? A profession that had earned him respect and admiration.

Nick kissed the tip of her nose. "As long as I don't have to work for Pearce, I'll be fine." He caressed her arm in long, soothing strokes.

Well after Nick had fallen asleep, Ava lay staring at the roof of the tent. She wanted Nick with her and Liam more than anything in the world, but all he knew was flying helicopters and being a soldier. How would he cope? *If this is going to work, I need to know I can trust Nick with my love. I need to know he will choose me over his work, that he'll always put Liam and me first. But is it fair to expect him to give up a profession he loves?*

A sudden weight landed on Nick's shoulder. His eyes flew open to find a tousled-haired little boy grinning down at him. "You want to go fishing, Daddy?"

"Fishing? What time is it?"

Ava stirred beside him. "Too early, Liam." She yawned and stretched, her bottom pressing against Nick's morning erection. She made a purring sound.

Nick groaned. With Ava's enticing body so close, there was only one rod he wanted to cast, and it had nothing to do with fishing.

"The sun is awake." Liam tapped Nick's cheek. "Come on, Daddy."

"Okay." Nick rolled away from Ava and caught Liam before the little fella's knees did some serious damage to his disappointed rod. "How about we catch our breakfast, then after we've eaten, we'll pack up and have a swim before flying home?"

"I want to stay here with you and Mummy." Liam pouted.

"We can come back another time. Besides your helicopter is at home."

Liam brightened. "I forgot." He crawled to the tent flap.

Ava mumbled from her cocoon, "Wake me when breakfast is cooked."

Nick leaned back and dropped a kiss on her warm neck and whispered, "If it wasn't for Liam, I would have woken you in a completely different way and you would be on this side of the mattress."

Her skin quivered under his lips. "There's always tonight."

Nick chuckled. "Count on it. And this time we take the slow road. Happy Valentine's Day, Angel."

Chapter Eight

After agreeing to meet back at Ava's house, Nick drove to the resort to collect his gear and checkout. He gave up trying to keep the grin off his face and paced toward his ground floor unit, scanning the immediate area for unwelcome surprises. On the flight back he'd convinced Ava to sit up front and given her a flying lesson. She hadn't been keen, in fact she'd been downright terrified, but with a little coaxing she'd learned to relax her feverish grip on the cyclic stick between her legs, making only tiny movements of the cyclic and pedals to keep the skid ball centered on the little horizon inside its tube.

Nick had been impressed by her understanding and questions as he explained each of the controls and what to do if a bird crashed through the windshield incapacitating him. Once she'd had enough, Nick resumed control then told her about Max and the fact he didn't fish or own a fishing rod. If Max had been murdered, then Ava needed to be wary, especially if Pearce was involved.

His room was exactly as he'd left it, yet the hairs on the back of his neck bristled. He checked the bathroom and wardrobe then stood in the center of his room. He could just detect the smell of stale cigarettes and body odor. *Someone's definitely been here, but who and why?*

Latching the door, he paced to the bathroom, stripped off, then stepped into the shower. The cooling spray took the heat out of his body yet the sense of unease wouldn't abate. He'd left the do-not-disturb sign on the door and the cleaners hadn't been through, yet someone had been in his room.

He flicked the spigot off, grabbed a towel, and briskly dried himself then shaved. He was pulling on a T-shirt when his phone rang. "Hey, Angel. I won't be long."

"Nick, I've had a break in." Ava's voice shook badly.

He tensed, a knot of unease twisting inside his gut. "Is anything missing?"

"They opened the safe. It's all gone. The diamonds, the pearls, everything, and they smashed Liam's chopper." She choked on a sob.

"Shit." Nick ran a hand through his damp hair. "I'll be there as fast as I can."

"No." She snuffled. "Apparently Damon dropped by to see me, saw the broken glass, and called the police. They were here when I got home and asked to see the safe's master key, which was still where I'd hidden it. Damon told them about you and that he doesn't trust you. The police are very keen to speak with you."

"I don't have a problem with that."

"There's more. A neighbor gave the police your description. She saw you coming out my front door with a black plastic bag. She didn't know if you had a car because she got a phone call and my driveway is blocked from her view by shrubs."

"I stopped by your place to pick up clothes for you. Shit, I used your keys and had Liam with me. Ava, you can't possibly think I'd do that to you?"

"Of course not, but Damon does, and my neighbor obviously didn't see Liam." She sniffed. "Nick, the police know about your juvenile record."

"That was years ago. You didn't mention Barry's rifle did you?"

"No, but your fingerprints are going to be on my safe. What are we going to do?

He rubbed his forehead. "You do have insurance, don't you?"

"Yes, but it's not easy making a claim like that. The insurance company will launch their own investigation and most of those gems were purchased specially by the media mogul. My reputation is everything and bad publicity will destroy me."

"Try not to worry. I'll ring my boss and get his take on this. It could be a couple of hours before you hear from me. I need to think this through."

"Okay."

Nick dropped the phone on the bed and stared at the ceiling. *Pearce has got to be behind the robbery. It seems he'll do anything to keep me away from Ava.*

Voices drew Nick's attention to the window. He strode across the room and with one finger slightly moved the blind. Two uniformed policemen were talking to the manager further along the path. One cop kept touching his Taser gun.

"Fuck." Nick's gaze raked the room, the uneasiness growing. He dropped to the floor and checked under the bed. *Nothing.* He opened the bedside drawers then lifted the mattress. *Where would I hide something?* His gaze fell on the mini fridge. Dashing across the room, he opened the fridge and searched the contents, then the small cupboard beside it.

A loud knock sounded at the door.

Nick stilled, barely breathing as his heart pounded. Another two knocks sounded as he edged into the bathroom. The vanity had a shelf underneath with a spare towel, toilet rolls and a hairdryer. He checked behind the toilet and in the cistern. *Nothing.*

Hearing one set of footsteps receding, Nick padded over to the window, parted the blind a fraction and peered through. One policeman stood with his back to the window. The other marched toward reception. *He's going for the key.*

Nick stepped away, his gaze coming to rest on his duffle bag. *Fuck.* He almost pounced on the bag, dragging all his neatly packed clothes onto the bed, along with one small velvet box and a drawstring pouch. *That bastard. How the hell am I going to explain this to Ava?*

He opened the drawstring bag and stared at the collection of sparkling gems and pearls. About a third of what Ava had shown him. The small box held the emerald ring she'd created. *I'm in deep shit. I need to get out of here and hide this stuff fast.*

Ramming his clothes back in the duffle bag, Nick grabbed his hooded jacket then stuffed the box and pouch into his pockets. He risked another peek out the window to see the other policeman leaving reception with the manager.

Silently unlatching the door, Nick ran to the bathroom and slid the window open. He lifted the tabs, eased the screen out and let it drop to the grass below. It was a tight squeeze but he levered himself out then put the screen back before sprinting through the garden toward the car park.

He'd almost reached his vehicle when two men of average height and wearing balaclavas and wielding baseball bats stepped across his path.

Fuck. Taking a defensive stance, Nick raised his fists and found his balance as the first guy swung high, looking to connect with Nick's head.

Nick ducked then sprang forward as the man's rotation continued, leaving him open and unbalanced. It took one savage kick to the kidneys to put the guy down on his knees, gasping for air.

Nick snatched up the bat and swiveled in time to block the other man's incoming blow. The bats collided with a resounding boom, the vibration ricocheting up Nick's arm. He regained his balance and stepped forward to meet the next blow, then launched his own attack, going straight for the guy's kneecap. The sharp crack was followed by the man's agonized scream as he collapsed to the ground, spewing a mouthful of Chinese curses.

Adrenaline pumping, Nick spun as the first man, now on his feet, roared and charged. Deeming his bat useless, Nick hurled it aside and sidestepped. Avoiding most of the impact, he let the man's momentum throw him off balance then delivered a hammer punch to the guy's solar plexus.

The man gagged and crashed to the ground then a woman yelled from across the car park. Deciding it was time to get out of there, Nick dispensed a kick to the man's thigh then leaped over him and sprinted for the beach. He'd been trained to think on his feet and that's what he needed to do.

If Pearce is this determined to get me out of the way then I need help to protect Ava, and if Max was murdered then I wouldn't put it past Pearce to dispose of me too.

He eventually reached a fenced compound containing boats in drydock. It seemed as good a place as any to lay low. The yard appeared deserted, so he squeezed through the bent gate and broke into a yacht that looked as though it had been sitting there for months.

First he rang Barry to give him the heads up and get some food and water dropped nearby, then he rang Jarred's phone. It was switched off, so he tried the next in command. Sam Locke had been a Lieutenant Colonel in their SAS unit and today was his wedding day, but it couldn't be helped. Ava was vulnerable. Some of the tension left him when he heard Sam's voice.

"G'day, Nick. I hear you're in Broome."

"Sam, there's something big going on over here that involves a rich guy who wants me out of the way. Is the boss with you?"

"Yeah, hang on a minute." Nick listened as Sam called out to Jarred, their ex-Colonel in the SAS and founder of Steele Intelligence & Personal Protection Services.

"Jarred here."

Nick gave his boss the run down on Damon Pearce, his intimidation tactics, the break-in, Max's death, and his own ambush. "Aside from that, Pearce is fixated on Ava and wants me out of the way. Will you help me?"

"Of course. Hang on, Simon's here."

Nick listened as Jarred asked Simon to do a search on Pearce. Then he heard Madeline Shaw's voice.

"Damon Pearce is a self-centered playboy from Melbourne. He's full of his own importance, and it's common knowledge he usually gets what he's after."

Jarred's voice came on again. "Did you hear that, Nick?"

"Yeah, that's him. Ava thought he was a nice guy because he's been giving her business advice and acting the charmer, but he definitely wants me out of the way and I think he'll do anything to achieve that. I'm scared Ava will get hurt in crossfire."

"Give me an hour. I'll be in touch."

Exactly an hour later, Jarred rang. "I've had a meeting with the boys, Inspector Gibbs, and Madeline Shaw. Except for Gibbs, the rest of us are coming to Broome."

"Thanks, but why are you bringing Madeline Shaw?"

"Because she's a bloody journalist and if I don't, she'll poke her nose in anyway." He sighed. "I don't want any leaks and she might actually be of help to us."

"Fair enough. What's the plan?"

"Simon will pose as Ava's cousin, enabling him to keep a close eye on her. Initially, I planned to contract the Black Hawk then have Ryan and Sam fly it over, but with all the refueling stops that would take maybe three or four days. So Gibbs has arranged for an extra Hawk to be loaded onto a C-17A Globemaster that's leaving Richmond Air base for Perth tomorrow. Sam and Ryan will also be on board with Ajax; he may come in handy."

"That's a huge order, boss. Do we really need the Black Hawk?"

"Forget the expense. Gibbs believes there's a substantial smuggling ring operating between Asia and the Kimberley region. He's heard rumors of diamonds going out and someone is bringing illegals in. Defense is prepared to help us out, and the government will fund our costs, but they expect results."

"Okay. How can we protect Barry?"

"Sam and Ryan will go undercover as his new chopper pilots. Madeline Shaw is arriving in Broome under the pretense of seeking an interview with Damon Pearce. Talos will act as her bodyguard, which won't seem odd after her recent death threats. I will be my usual pain in the arse and demand a thorough investigation."

"Christ, they won't know what hit them." Nick exhaled, the tight band around his chest easing with the knowledge he had the team's support.

"Inspector Gibbs wants to be kept in the loop and will add his assistance if required. In the meantime, stay out of sight and don't talk to anyone."

"Ava needs to know, otherwise she'll panic if I just disappear."

"Very well. I'll be in touch."

"Does Simon want Ava's address?"

"He has it."

Nick laughed. "Of course he does. Thanks, Jarred." He ended the call and fell back on the bunk. *What would I do without those guys? They always have my back. Working for Jarred is nowhere near as dangerous as the SAS. Maybe I can talk Ava into coming over to the east coast.* He pushed those thoughts to the back of his mind.

Staring at the ceiling, Nick went over his conversation with Pearce, then everything Dave and Barry had told him. If Pearce were involved in Max's death and the robbery, he'd soon discover he'd made a grave mistake.

Nick began to pace the yacht's living area as he considered every alternative, every possibility. If he'd missed just one gemstone, the police would issue a warrant for his arrest and that would complicate things.

The way he saw it, the team would have to plant cameras and listening devices on Pearce's yacht and in his house, tap his phones and place Ava under surveillance.

"Fuck." Nick ran his hands through his hair. The last thing he wanted was to put Ava in danger. He sighed, pulled out his phone, and selected her number.

After the fifth ring, she answered, breathlessly. "Nick, where are you?"

"Why are you puffing? What's happened?"

"I ran down the garden so the police and Damon wouldn't hear me talking to you. Where are you?"

"Keeping a low profile until I know who set me up." Nick inhaled. "Ava, when you called earlier, I was suspicious someone had been in my room, so I searched and found a small amount of gems and your emerald ring."

He heard her gasp. "I don't understand."

"I swear I didn't take them. They were hidden amongst my clothes in the duffle bag I left in my room, but the rest of the gems, your necklace, and bracelet weren't there. Whoever is trying to set me up has the rest of your stuff. You have to believe me, Ava, I wouldn't do this to you."

There was a long pause before she spoke. "What do you want me to do?"

It bothered Nick that she didn't say she believed him, but who could blame her? "Nothing at the moment. I've spoken to my boss, and he's offered to help. I'll come to your house late tonight and we'll talk."

"That's not a good idea, the police are watching my house. I have to go, Damon's coming."

"Don't trust him, Ava."

"I'll talk to you later." She hung up.

Nick prowled back and forth like a caged tiger, his fists clenched, his body tense. "Pearce has no idea who I am or what I'm capable of doing. He wants to play dirty then so be it. I will not lose Ava a second time."

A soft click had Ava fully alert. Darkness shrouded her bedroom, which made it impossible to see, yet she sensed company. A rustle sounded at the end of the bed.

"Nick?"

"Yes. Sorry it's so late, but I couldn't risk coming any earlier."

"It's not safe. The police are still outside." She pushed the tangled sheet away then switched on the bedside lamp. Her gaze fixed on his naked chest. He stood there like a statue of Apollo, staring at her, then a slow, sexy smile appeared.

"You're more temptress than angel, sitting there with your tousled hair about your shoulders, blinking those lovely green eyes at me. Do you have any idea how beautiful you are?"

"The police?"

"I wanted to let you know what's happening. My boss has a contact in the Federal police who promised to keep an eye on things. If it looks like the local police are going to arrest me, he'll step in. My team is going to help us find the person who broke into your safe. Everything's going to be okay, Angel."

"Are you sure? I don't want you arrested."

"Yeah." He placed his wallet on the bedside table, then dragged his shorts and boxers off, and tumbled onto the bed.

Ava's heart began to race. "You could have told me that over the phone. Why did you risk coming here?"

"It's still Valentine's Day and I need to hold you in my arms." He reached for her, pulling her against him, the contact sending a tremor cascading through her body.

"And, this time we're taking the slow road." He leaned into her, pressing her back amongst the pillows as he claimed her lips.

She responded to Nick's kiss with gusto, wrapping her arms around his neck and pressing against him flagrantly. Then she lifted her thigh over his, rubbing against his erection, taunting him.

"No, Angel, I won't be rushed, not tonight." He caught the edges of her T-shirt and stripped it up over her head then raised his hands to frame her face. "Tonight I want to show you all you mean to me, all that we are together."

He kissed her greedily, deepening the kiss until she grew restless, shifted against him, and tried reaching for him. He caught her wrists, anchoring them on either side of her head. "Behave," he ordered.

Ava had no intention of behaving. "Make me." She arched, pressing her breasts against the crinkly hair on his chest, which only made her more desperate. "We have the rest of our lives to go slow, Nick."

He lifted his head, smiled lazily, then covered her lips again, drawing her into a voracious kiss that scattered her wits. Heat bloomed between her thighs as she rubbed against his erection. He groaned, so she rubbed again.

He pulled away, shaking his head. "Slow road."

"Argh." She pulled her hands free and pouted. "I'm desperate."

He chuckled against her collarbone. "Not as desperate as you will be." He lowered his lips to one breast, leisurely licking and kissing her sensitive skin, momentarily soothing the growing ache. Then he closed his hand over her other breast, kneading gently, weighing, then rolling the nipple between his finger and thumb. He moved lower, closing his lips over her furled nipple. He sucked and she cried out as pleasure lanced through her body. He clasped her hip preventing her from wriggling as he feasted like a hungry wolf, driving her to the brink of insanity. She clutched at his hair, frantic to have him inside her. All her senses were reeling as she urged him to take her, but he stubbornly refused to be distracted.

The hand holding her hip drifted inwards, his fingers tracing across her belly then moving lower, brushing over her curls. A delicious shudder ran down her spine. "Yes."

He chuckled. "Not yet." Releasing her, he sat back on his ankles and smiled knowingly. His gaze locked on her face then slowly raked over her swollen breasts still throbbing from his ministrations, then skated over her belly.

"Open your legs." A husky growl laced his request.

Quickly she complied, glorying at the width of his shoulders, the open desire in his eyes, and his magnificent erection. She reached for him, but he gently brushed her hands aside and leaned over to claim her mouth again until she gasped and trembled. Finally, he touched her where she ached, stroked her swollen flesh, then slid two fingers inside her and thrust deeply back and forth compelling her to rock against his fingers, panting and writhing, her body tightening.

He lifted his head and withdrew his fingers. "Not yet."

"Please." She tried grasping his hips to pull him back.

He captured her wrists again, trapped them on either side of her body, then shifted lower. "Soon. I haven't finished tasting your breasts yet." He licked, laved, and suckled until she cried out in frustration.

"Slow road." With a wicked smile, he released her hands, slid further down her body, and pushed her thighs wide. He lowered his head and devoured her, slowly, deliberately, totally. He continued to circle her nub and thrust his tongue deep, eliciting a cry of pleasure from her. "Fly for me, Angel." He suckled hard.

Ava came up off the bed, crying out in ecstasy as she soared out of this world.

Nick leaned back on his ankles and watched as his angel floated back to earth, a serene, well-satisfied smile on her face, naked and spread before him like a gift from the gods. "I'm not finished with you yet, babe." He reached for his wallet and a condom.

Her eyelids fluttered open, the devotion in her gaze humbling him. He couldn't fathom it, but this woman called his very soul. No one else would ever do.

She held out her arms and beckoned. "Take me, my darling, I'm yours."

Thank God. Nick silently cheered. She'd finally said it; called him her darling and meant it. Never again would he take those words for granted. Slowly he lowered himself on top of her, settled between her thighs, and kissed her deeply until she was writhing and rubbing against him impatiently. Only then did he seek her entrance and drive home.

She arched underneath him, moaned, and clung to his shoulders. Nick let his desire and passion run free. Let go of his tightly held control and showed her how much he craved her. He drew her legs around his hips and thrust deeper, harder, closing his eyes as her body tightened gloriously around him.

"Yes." She gasped and dug her fingernails into his back, meeting each thrust, urging him to ride her faster. She'd always been liquid fire in his arms, but tonight he was determined to give her a thorough loving.

He reveled at the sensation of her breasts against his chest and her delighted gasps as he filled her. Sensing the ripples of her release, he ploughed into her and roared as she climaxed, taking him with her over the edge. Together they flew, then Nick collapsed on top of her, spent, breathing hard and deeply sated.

Eventually he rolled to the right, pulling her into his arms and simply held her, elated to see the familiar dreamy smile on her lips. He'd have to leave before dawn, but for now he was content to hold her and savor his good fortune while she drifted off to sleep. Once the boys arrived she would be well guarded and he would be free to deal with Pearce.

Chapter Nine

Cozy as a fire on a winter's night, Ava barely registered Nick slipping out of her room at dawn. Several hours later she woke wondering if she'd dreamt his midnight loving, but jettisoned that thought when she discovered stubble rash on her breasts and a stiffness between her thighs as if she'd been riding a bronco horse. "Pretty close." She rolled out of bed, grinning and determined to keep a positive attitude all day. Having a police presence out the front might make it harder for Nick to come and go, but it gave Ava some peace of mind.

After breakfast and after the locksmith had replaced her front door and changed all the locks, Ava drove Liam to daycare then called in at the shop to catch up on orders and put a call into the insurance company.

The shop and clients kept her busy until a representative from the insurance company rang late in the afternoon. He told her they were launching their own investigation and made it clear if they found she'd been negligent they wouldn't cover the loss. If that happened, how on earth would she pay back the money?

Ava had just collected Liam when Sergeant Evans rang, asking her to drop by the station. When she got there, he had more questions regarding her relationship with Nick. Then, he produced two perfect diamonds his officers had found in Nick's duffle bag. She couldn't help feeling the police thought she was in cahoots with Nick regarding the theft and insurance money.

Exasperated and anxious for Nick and herself, Ava left the station deciding to engage a lawyer for any future interviews and wondering if Damon was indeed behind the robbery. If he was, what would he do next and how was this going to impact on Liam? She and

Liam reached her car to find Damon waiting. *Great, that's all I need.*

"Hello, Ava. I was driving past and saw your car."

"I'm tired, Damon. What do you want?"

"How much do you really know about Nick Flanagan? He turns up out of the blue after four years and then five hundred thousand in gems disappears from your safe. I hear he's done a runner, so you can't blame me for suspecting the worst."

"You and Helen know I have master keys. Either of you could have stolen the gems."

Damon's eyes widened. "You can't possibly think either of us would break into your house?"

Ava rubbed her forehead in an attempt to ease the growing tightness. It was after seven and she was tired and hungry. "Damon, Nick didn't steal those gems and he hasn't done a runner." She unlocked the car and helped Liam into his seat then turned back to Damon. "I'm sorry, but I need to get Liam home."

"Ava." Damon sighed. "You're too soft hearted and Nick's playing on that, whereas I genuinely care for you. I'm worried about you. Please come and stay at my house?"

"No!" Liam screamed, his little face screwed up in fury. "Get away from my Mummy. She belongs to Daddy and me."

"Liam, sweetheart, it's okay, I'm not going anywhere." Ava glared at Damon. "Please go, you're just making things worse."

"I'm sorry, I didn't mean to upset the boy. Call me if you need anything." He waited for an assurance she didn't give then strode toward his BMW.

Expelling a deep sigh, Ava buckled Liam into his seat, then climbed in the front and drove home. As she pulled up in the driveway she noticed a police car pull into the curb on the other side of the road. *So now they're following me too.*

She climbed out, opened the rear door, and unbuckled Liam. "Come on, sleepyhead, we're home."

"Is Daddy here?"

"He doesn't have keys, honey." She lifted him out, closed the door, then ran across the lawn. After unlocking the new front door, Ava stepped into darkness and total silence. Liam pushed past and ran to his bedroom.

"Daddy?

"He's not here, honey." She switched on lights and closed the door, her heart heavy with worry for Nick, their future and her career.

"He could be hiding." Liam dashed past her again as she dropped her keys and bag on the hall table. In the kitchen, Ava opened the fridge and stared halfheartedly at the contents. *I guess I could barbeque some chicken thighs and make a salad.* She put the chicken on the bench and flicked the porch light switch. Nothing happened.

"Damn, that's a new bulb. Well there goes that idea." She closed the blind, sank onto a chair, and put her face in her hands. *Where are you, Nick?*

Liam's little feet pounded down the hall. "Neanderal."

"It's Neander*thal*, honey." She saw panic in his eyes. "What?"

"He's in your workroom."

"Who?" Her chair crashed to the floor behind her as she jumped up.

"The *Neanderal.*"

Ava froze as a huge, muscle-bound, dark-eyed man stepped into the kitchen.

"Don't be alarmed. I'm not here to hurt you." His deep voice sounded non-threatening, but he watched her as if he might pounce at any second.

She ran forward, snatched Liam up in her arms, and backed away. Was he responsible for the break-in? Had he come back looking for more gems? Or was he after Nick. Ava's heart pounded in her ears.

Her gaze fell on the knife block. She lowered Liam to the floor, eased him behind her, then lurched for the carving knife and pointed it at the man. "Come any closer and I'll stab you."

"Not if you hold the knife like that." A deep, amused voice sounded to her left.

Ava whirled to find another tall, dark-eyed man standing just inside her back door. She pulled Liam against her thigh and backed toward the living room. "The police are out the front." She waved the knife back and forth between the two men. "Get out of my house or I'll scream and they'll be straight in."

The floor creaked behind her. Before she could react a man's arm imprisoned her against his rock-hard body. His other hand clapped over Ava's mouth cutting off her scream. The big man in front lunged, caught her wrist and held it, preventing her from stabbing anyone.

The man behind her spoke. "Miss Mitchell, my colleague told you the truth, we are not here to harm you. However, I advise you to release the knife before you hurt yourself." His deadly calm voice held a mountain of warning.

The big man in front extracted the knife from her fingers.

"Get away from my mummy." Liam slammed his little fists into the big man's legs.

The man placed the knife on the bench, then leaned down and swung Liam up into his arms. "We won't, I promise." He narrowed his eyes. "This kid looks like..."

"Let him go." Ava struggled, but the man's hold was unbreakable.

Liam glared at his captor. "My daddy is a Black Hawk pilot and he's going to be really mad."

Ava drew a shaky breath. "Please, I don't know where Nick is." She heard a sudden intake of breath behind her.

"Miss Mitchell, am I right in assuming this child is Nick Flanagan's son?"

Oh God. She squirmed. "I'm not telling you anything!"

The man swung her to face him and captured both her wrists, leaving Ava staring up into cold gray eyes and a face that could have been carved from granite. She shivered.

"My name is Jarred Steele." He nodded at the big man holding Liam. "This is James Talarico, we call him Talos. The man on your right is Sam Locke. We're here to find out who framed Nick and why. I apologize for not introducing ourselves earlier and for breaking into your home, but we had to make sure you were alone. Until I know who framed Nick, I don't trust anyone and I would prefer no one else knows about our team."

Ava drew a shaky breath. "I want to see some identification."

He released her wrists to pull out his wallet then he showed her his license. "Satisfied?"

She sagged, the relief making her light headed. "You're Nick's ex-Colonel?"

"Yes."

"Mummy, are they Neanderals?"

"No, honey. They're daddy's...friends."

The kitchen seemed tiny with three big, intense men surrounding her. The mystery of her blown porch-light now made sense. Ava waved them to the table. "Please sit down, you're crowding me."

"Thank you." Jarred picked up the fallen chair and sat. The man called Sam took a chair at the end of the table opposite Jarred. The big man, Talos, passed Liam to Ava. "Can I make us all a coffee? It's been a long day."

Ava nodded then sat on the nearest chair and hugged Liam. "I thought you were in Fiji."

Sam gave her a genuine smile. "We were. Talos and I got married yesterday." He laughed. "Not to each other. We left our brides to come and help Nick."

"What about your honeymoons?"

Talos leaned back against the kitchen bench and crossed his massive arms. "Nick is our friend, Miss Mitchell. There isn't anything we wouldn't do for him, and he wouldn't have asked for our help if it wasn't serious."

Ava rubbed Liam's back, relieved to see he was sneaking curious peeks at the men, but that didn't excuse their behavior. They could have traumatized Liam for life. "My name is Ava." She glared at Jarred. "You have no right to break into my house and frighten us like that."

"I'm sorry. With the police sitting out the front and doing random checks around your house, we couldn't risk staying in the garden. There was also a man in a silver BMW who stopped by several times."

"That's Damon Pearce." Ava sighed. "He doesn't trust Nick and they don't like each other. Damon discovered the robbery and rang the police. And the police have incriminating evidence and a witness who saw Nick at my front door."

Jarred's eyes narrowed. "What witness and what evidence?"

"One of my neighbors saw Nick leaving my house on the day of the robbery. I told the police Nick had a key and called in to pick up some clothes for me, so he didn't need to break in, and Liam was with him."

"What is the incriminating evidence they've found?"

Ava blinked. Jarred was the most intimidating man she'd ever met. Slightly taller than Nick and a little broader in the shoulders, but it was the barely-veiled lethal power emanating from him that set him apart. It wasn't hard to imagine him as an SAS Colonel.

"The police found two diamonds in Nick's duffel bag and they brought up his juvenile record. I explained he only stole a car when he was fifteen to get away from a drug-addict mother and her abusive boyfriend."

Sam turned to Jarred. "The diamonds are going to be a problem."

"I'll get Gibbs to intervene there."

Talos groaned. "Great."

Ava glanced between them. "Who is Gibbs?"

Sam chuckled. "A Federal Police Inspector who Talos accused of being corrupt."

Talos huffed. "He shot the only person who could have confirmed that fact."

Sam smiled at Ava. "By shooting that person, Gibbs saved the woman Talos is now married to, which makes the big fella beholden to the Inspector."

A look of disgust swept over Talos' face. "And Gibbs loves it. How do you like your coffee, Ava?"

"White with one sugar. Thank you." She glanced at Jarred Steele to find him watching Liam. His gaze rose to her face.

"As we didn't know Nick had a son, I must assume he didn't either?"

"No. My parents told me Nick had been killed in a training accident before I discovered I was pregnant. It seems they did it to keep us apart."

"Jeez." Sam shook his head. "How did Nick take that?"

"He was furious."

The kettle whistled and they silently watched as Talos made four mugs of instant coffee then brought them to the table. He looked at Ava. "Has Nick contacted you this evening?"

"Not yet. He said he'd see me tonight. I know he didn't break into my safe."

"What makes you so sure?" Jarred stared at her as he tapped a finger against the coffee mug. "Perhaps the temptation was too much."

Ava stiffened. "Nick wouldn't do that to me and he certainly wouldn't smash Liam's helicopter. What are we going to do?"

Jarred's lips curved upwards, but the smile didn't reach his eyes. "You don't need to do anything. My team will do whatever is necessary. We have already swept your house for listening devices. Two of my men will pose as chopper pilots, thus keeping Barry Sanders and his helicopters safe. Simon will stay with you, posing as your cousin."

Things were moving way too fast for Ava. She tried to stare down the intimidating leader of this special ops team and failed. "I'd like a say in who stays in my house, and I don't have any cousins."

"You do now."

Jarred Steele's dismissive manner annoyed Ava, but having someone in the house to protect Liam was a plus. "Okay. What will you and Talos be doing?"

"I will be myself, here as Nick's boss to find out what's going on. Talos will act as a bodyguard for Madeline Shaw, a journalist who is assisting us."

Ava blinked. "I know Madeline Shaw. We met in London."

"I see." He rubbed his chin thoughtfully. "We'll use that connection. Madeline can do a story on your rise to fame. That will give you a reason to meet regularly without drawing undue attention."

Talos frowned. "It's not the type of story Madeline normally does."

"Neither is an interview with Pearce," said Jarred. He looked at Ava. "If Damon Pearce is behind the robbery you could be in danger."

"I find it hard to believe Damon would do something like that."

Jarred raised an eyebrow. "Let me make one thing clear, Miss Mitchell. My team would not be here if we thought Pearce had nothing to hide." He took a gulp of coffee. "I hope it's not inconvenient, but Simon will have a dog with him."

"A doggy." Liam sat up, a big smile on his face.

Ava frowned. "How did you get a dog here?"

"He came in the big Air Force Bird, along with the Black Hawk and two of my men."

Liam slid off Ava's knee and ran out of the kitchen.

She sipped her coffee and glanced around the table. These men were very much like Nick. They were strong, silent types, large, inherently powerful, and a touch arrogant. All appeared calm and controlled on the surface, but they were warriors at heart and she sensed they were all capable of manipulation, deadly if crossed, and ruthless in pursuit of an enemy, especially Jarred Steele.

Ava rubbed her temples in an attempt to relieve the tightening across her forehead. So much for her fear of Nick's high-risk job. It was her association with Damon that had brought danger into her home.

CHAPTER TEN

Liam raced back into the kitchen and placed the broken bits of his helicopter on the table between Talos and Sam. "The Neanderal broke *my* Black Hawk."

"Is that so?" Talos examined the bits of wood and body of the chopper. "Your daddy and I can replace the blades and skids so this chopper looks just like a real Black Hawk. Would that be all right with you?"

Liam nodded solemnly.

A light tap sounded then the back door opened and Ryan Dutch stepped into the kitchen. Ava hadn't seen Nick's best friend in four years, but there was no mistaking his deep-ocean-blue eyes or sun-bleached, sandy-colored hair.

His gaze fell on her. "Hello, Ava. It's been a long time."

"Hello, Ryan."

He ambled over and kissed her cheek. "Who's the little guy?"

"This is Liam, my son."

Liam gave Ryan a dimpled smile. "My daddy flies a Black Hawk."

Ryan stared at Liam for a couple of seconds then looked at Ava aghast. "I hope you have a good reason for keeping him from Nick?"

Jarred pushed out a chair with his foot. "She does. Her parents led her to believe Nick had been killed in a training accident."

"You're joking?"

"No. What's happening outside?"

Ryan took the offered chair. "Two cops are still watching the house, and a bald guy in a black jeep is parked three doors down."

"Run the plates." Jarred's phone beeped. "It's a text from Simon.

He'll be here in five minutes, which will undoubtedly bring the police in to investigate."

The back door creaked and Ava looked up to see another man entering in a hooded jacket. He closed the door and flipped the hood down.

"Nick!" She jumped up and ran into his arms. "I've been so worried."

"Daddy." Liam crashed into their legs.

Nick lifted Liam in one arm and wrapped his other around Ava's shoulders. "Sorry, Angel, I couldn't risk coming near you until the boys arrived." He grinned at the other men. "Hi, fellas. I see you've met Ava and my son."

"About time you showed up." Jarred stood, drained his coffee, then crossed to the sink and rinsed the cup. "We need to get moving. Our vehicle is on the next street." He clapped Nick on the shoulder. "Simon will be here shortly with Ajax." Jarred hesitated. "They will keep your family safe."

Nick gave a nod. "Thanks, Colonel."

The other three men rinsed their cups then followed Jarred out the door, leaving her, Nick, and Liam in a tight embrace. Ava didn't want to let go. "Please be careful."

"I will. Simon's a good guy and Liam's going to love Ajax."

He eased her away and kissed Liam. "Buddy, I need you to look after a dog for me. He's not used to kids, so don't rush at him."

"Okay."

"Good boy."

Nick lowered Liam to the floor and hugged Ava again. "I have to go, Angel." He kissed her then flipped up his hood and strode out the door.

Ava ran after him. "Nick, wait."

He turned in time to catch her in his arms. This time their kiss was deep and fervent, full of urgent need and desperate longing.

The doorbell chimed, tearing them apart, both breathing heavily.

"That'll be Simon." Nick kissed her again. "Warm the bed, I'll be back later. Oh, and I'll give your ring and gems to Jarred. I can't afford to be caught with them and at this stage only the real culprit knows I have them so don't tell anyone. Not even Helen." He jogged down the garden and disappeared over the back fence.

"Mummy, there's someone at the front door. It could be the doggy."

"Yes, it will be." Ava dragged in a breath, blinked away her unshed tears, and climbed the steps. "Let's go and welcome my cousin Simon and his dog."

Liam raced ahead of her to the door, squealing when they heard whining and scratching on the other side. "The doggy wants to play."

"Remember what Daddy said. Don't scare the dog." She opened the door and stepped back in alarm. A huge black and tan German Shepherd stood on his hind legs against the screen door looking her in the face. "Oh my God."

Liam wrapped his arms around her leg, his eyes wide. "Mummy!"

The dog dropped to its hindquarters, tilted his head from side to side, then barked.

Ava and Liam both jumped.

The handsome man standing beside the dog laughed. "I don't think Ajax has ever seen a child before. Hi, you must be Ava. I'm Simon Hawke, your cousin, I believe."

She looked into friendly green eyes filled with flecks of hazel. Simon Hawke had short, chestnut-colored hair, a build similar to Nick, and an easy-going smile.

"Hi, Simon. I wasn't expecting such a big dog. He won't bite, will he?"

"Not unless you attack me. Ajax is ex-military, but a big softy. May we come in?"

Ava picked Liam up before pushing the screen door wide. "Of course."

The dog squeezed between Simon and the door, then trotted down the hall and into the kitchen.

Ava gasped. "The chicken." She ran, breathing a sigh of relief when she found the dog sniffing at the back door and whining.

Simon grinned. "He's picked up a familiar scent, probably Sam's. Come here, boy."

Ajax trotted over and sat beside Simon, where he again tilted his head from side to side as if trying to figure out Liam.

"Mummy, I want to get down."

"All right, but no sudden moves." She kept her eyes on Ajax as she lowered Liam to the floor, but the dog didn't move. "He has a beautiful coat." She reached out and let Ajax smell her fingers before rubbing him under the chin. "Good dog."

Ajax gave a massive yawn, exposing a mouth full of sharp fangs. Liam fell to his knees, screeching with laughter. Ajax instantly bristled and backed away.

Ava grabbed Liam. "No sudden movements. If you frighten him, he might bite."

"But I want to play with him."

"Let me introduce you." Simon dropped to his haunches and took hold of Ajax's collar then held out a hand for Liam. "Come to Ajax slowly and keep your hands down."

Liam pulled away from Ava and did as Simon asked, taking baby steps. Ava watched with her heart in her mouth, ready to lunge forward if needed.

Ajax craned forward and sniffed Liam tentatively, then licked his fingers. Liam giggled.

"Now I'll show you how to pat him," offered Simon, taking Liam's hand and stroking the dog. Ajax wagged his tail and nudged Liam's chest.

Ava relaxed. "I'm going to make a chicken salad if you're hungry."

"Yeah, thanks. Where can I dump my kit?"

Ava bit her lip. "Maybe in the living room. I only have two bedrooms and Liam's bed is too short for you."

"I have a bedroll or I can take the couch."

"The couch is too short for a man your height."

The doorbell peeled and Ava glanced at Simon. "That will be the police."

"You open the door. Ajax and I will stay here."

She hurried down the hall and opened the door to a young policeman. "Hello, officer, what can I do for you?"

His hand rested on a Taser gun. "Miss Mitchell, I'm Constable Milligan, may I come in?"

"Of course. Do you have news?" She led the way down the hall.

"Mr. Pearce thinks you might be in danger, so we've been watching the house. Who is the man you just let in?"

Not comfortable with lying, Ava bit her lip. "My cousin, Simon. Come through to the kitchen and I'll introduce you." She entered the kitchen to find Sergeant Evans leaning against the back door. The sly fox must have thought to cut off Nick's escape via the back door. Only it wasn't Nick.

Simon hadn't moved from the bench and was slicing chicken. Ajax sat perfectly still, his steady gaze riveted on the sergeant, completely ignoring Liam's bear hugs and giggles.

Ava eased Liam away from the dog. "Hello, Sergeant, I see you've met Simon. What's going on?"

Sergeant Evans straightened. "I apologize for the intrusion, Miss Mitchell, we mistook your cousin for Nicholas Flanagan. I take it you still haven't heard from him?"

Ava crossed her arms. "I appreciated you leaving officers here for our protection, but shouldn't you be looking into the death of Max Williams? Did you know he hated fishing and didn't even own a rod? Or, you could be investigating the vandalism and threats Barry Sanders has had to put up with. Nick is innocent, and someone is trying to set him up."

"That remains to be seen. The other night when Mr. Flanagan reported the conflict at Barry Sander's hangar, he didn't mention he'd been in the Army."

"Why would that be relevant?" asked Simon, giving the sergeant a sidelong glance. "Ava said Damon Pearce offered Nick money to leave town."

Ava nearly choked. She'd never told Simon any such thing, but obviously Nick informed his friends of the outrageous statement.

Sergeant Evans raised an eyebrow. "We only have Mr. Flanagan's word for that. Miss Mitchell wasn't privy to the conversation."

"All right. What about the fact Damon Pearce and Ava's business partner knew she kept master keys to the safe here and at the shop?"

Ava blinked. She didn't want to involve Helen in this.

The sergeant inclined his head. "They have been interviewed and both have reliable witnesses who can verify where they were yesterday and this morning. The fact remains, however, that a neighbor saw a man matching Mr. Flanagan's description leaving this house while Miss Mitchell was out yesterday morning. And we found a couple of loose diamonds amongst his belongings."

Ava huffed. "I gave Nick my keys, which he used to collect some personal items for me. He had no need to smash the glass. You track down the specialty pieces I made and you will have your thief."

Sergeant Evans held up his hands. "This can all be sorted if Mr. Flanagan comes into the station." His cell phone chimed. "Excuse me."

Ava paced to the fridge. Obviously the police had made up their minds and who could blame them. The diamonds in Nick's bag were damning.

Sergeant Evans ended the call. "There's an SAS Colonel at the station waiting to see me." He frowned at Ava. "It seems Mr. Flanagan received a military medal for bravery while serving in the SAS, and now does specialized work for the government." His eyes narrowed as he considered Simon. "Is Mr. Flanagan here on an undercover mission?"

"I can't comment on that. I'm just here to make sure Ava comes to no harm."

"Hmm." Sergeant Evans nodded at Constable Milligan. "Let's get back to the station."

Ava showed them out and returned to the kitchen to find Ajax sprawled near the back door allowing Liam to pat his head. Simon was busy frying the chicken in a pan. She set about making the salad.

"I don't think the sergeant believes you're my cousin."

"Neither do I, but he will now look into things far more carefully." He chuckled. "Sergeant Evans doesn't know what's in store for him. Jarred didn't make SAS Colonel by being polite."

"He is intimidating."

Simon raised an eyebrow. "You have no idea. Jarred will do whatever is needed to exonerate Nick and so will the rest of us."

"Nick told me you all watch each other's backs and that he'd trust you guys with his life and mine. And, he told me about your last two missions."

Simon tilted his head. "If it hadn't been for Nick's chopper skills in extremely bad conditions, two women and two young children would be dead."

Ava stilled, recalling what Nick had told her about his mission in Vietnam. Again she wondered if she had the right to ask him to walk away from his team—men who saved lives. She frowned. "Nick said it was Talos and Jarred who rescued them."

"Yes, but the ladies and kids were trapped on the ledge, in a storm, with a person who meant to kill them. It was Nick who battled to keep the chopper close enough and steady enough for Talos to wound their attacker. It was Nick who flew them to safety."

Ava stared at Simon, her heart racing at the danger Nick had faced. He'd played down his own involvement. Typical. Could she be any prouder of him? "Nick made it sound like Talos and Jarred did the whole rescue. He didn't mention his part."

"I bet he didn't tell you he's one of the bravest Black Hawk pilots in the business either, or that he received that medal for a rescue mission in Afghanistan?"

"No, he didn't." Again she experienced a glowing pride for the man Nick had become and who she was trying to change. A heavy guilt descended over her.

"Well, now you know." Simon smiled. "I think all of us at some time or other, owe our life to Nick's skills as a pilot. He's never shown any fear, but I guess that's because he thought he'd lost you."

Ava frowned. "Why do you say that?"

"We've only ever heard Nick talk about you when he was drunk. I got the impression that without you he didn't have anything to lose. I hope you two work things out. Nick's a good guy and he deserves to be happy."

"Yes." *But will Nick be happy without his friends? Can he settle for life with Liam and me, here in Broome? Am I asking too much?* She tossed the chicken in the salad and placed it on the table.

Simon chuckled. "I think we can safely say Liam and Ajax have become friends."

Ava turned and smiled. Ajax's head rested on his paws, eyes half closed as he watched her. Liam lay sprawled across the dog's back sound asleep. "It's been a big day. I guess Liam's too tired to eat now."

Simon picked Liam up. "I'll be working most of the night. If he wakes I'll feed him."

"But you need a bed."

Simon shook his head. "Honestly, my bedroll is fine for tonight. Tomorrow I'll pick up an inflatable mattress." He carried Liam to his bed and left Ava to tuck him in.

What a nice guy. She kissed Liam and turned to find Ajax settling himself in Liam's beanbag under the window. "I guess it's okay for you to stay in here."

Tired, hungry, and concerned for their future, Ava wandered back to the kitchen. A lone tear slid down her cheek. She'd imagined ending the day in Nick's arms. Instead, he was on the run from police and it was her fault. *There must be something I can do to clear his name.*

CHAPTER ELEVEN

Staying close to the heavily shadowed fence-line, Nick warily crept across Ava's back garden. The wind had risen and an occasional strike of lightning lit the black sky. The heavens were about to open and he had no intention of being caught in the downpour. The storm could rage for all he cared as long as Ava lay in his arms.

Nick stepped onto the back porch then sidled to the edge of the kitchen window where a slither of light peeped through the blind. He could see Simon at the table, frowning heavily at his computer. Nick lightly tapped the window. "Simon, it's Nick."

Seconds later, Simon opened the back door. "I figured you'd be back."

Nick shrugged. "It's not that I don't trust you to protect Ava, but now that I've found her, I want to keep her close."

"I don't blame you, she's one hot lady." Simon closed and locked the door. "Liam's asleep in his bed with Ajax on guard and Ava's in her room."

"Great." Nick dropped his jacket over a chair and kicked off his shoes. "You look worried. Is there a problem?"

"I think my emails are being hacked." Simon shook his head. "With all the safety nets I've set up that shouldn't be possible."

"Unless the hacker is as good as you."

Simon's lips thinned. "That's what worries me. I'm initializing a tracking program, so there'll be a footprint for me to follow the next time I'm hacked."

The pitter-patter of rain sounded on the roof along with a low rumble in the distance, reminding Nick of the approaching storm. "Happy hunting, I'll let myself out before dawn."

"No worries." Simon returned to the table and his computer.

Nick stepped across the hall to the small bedroom where a night-light cast a faint glow. He found his son sprawled across Ajax on a beanbag. Nick's lips twitched at the affronted look in Ajax's brown eyes. "Sorry, fella, but I think you've made a friend for life."

Nick crouched down, rubbed Ajax's head, then scooped the little boy up and carried him to the bed. "Sleep tight, little buddy." He dropped a light kiss on Liam's head then headed for Ava's room.

The door opened soundlessly, then he stood for a minute savoring the scene. The bedside lamp threw a soft, muted light over the room. The left side of the bed was turned down invitingly, while she was curled up on the right, facing the middle and sound asleep. Nick smiled, closed the door, and discarded his clothes. Their battle for the right side of the bed had always been a prelude to their lovemaking and it only ever ended one way. She might start on the right, but she would always wake on the left and they both knew it.

He crawled onto the bed, slid under the covers and lowered his head to place a gentle kiss on her lips. She stirred, smiled and lifted her face. "More."

Pulling the covers from between them, Nick reached for her, lust flaring when he found her naked and warm. "I'm going to ravish you and you're going to enjoy every single second."

"Hmm." She licked her lips. "Am I allowed to ravish you back?"

"No, tonight I'm in charge." He pressed her into the mattress, lowered his head, and claimed her lips, hungrily, ferociously, giving her no chance to turn the tables. He wasn't gentle. He ran his hand down her right thigh then pushed both thighs wide and settled between, the head of his cock nudging her heat.

She arched, rubbing her breasts against his chest then locked her ankles over his arse and rocked into him, seizing his senses, urging him to take her quickly.

Not tonight. Breaking the hold but not the kiss, he shifted to the side and closed one hand over her ripe breast. She shuddered and pressed into his palm, raked her fingers through his hair, gripping his skull as she battled to get closer.

He released her breast and sent his hand skimming over her ribs, waist, hip and the firm globe of her bottom where he squeezed then caressed her heated flesh before lifting her against the hard ridge of his erection. Hunger and want pounded through his veins, but he needed to draw their interlude out.

She broke their kiss, drew her fingers down his neck, over his shoulders and across his chest, her nails lightly scoring and leaving a fiery blaze on his skin. Then she reached for him, her hand closing firmly around his cock.

Nick groaned. "I should have tied you up."

"Maybe you should have. I'm beyond desperate, so you're dreaming if you think we're going slow tonight." Ava ran her fingers down his hard length.

Nick fell back on the bed, letting her have her way with him. She came up on her knees and stroked him slowly back and forth then straddled him. She was a vision spread out before him. Her smooth skin glowing with health, her curvaceous breasts begging for attention, the delicate column of her neck and collarbone, her lovely face, so familiar he ached to kiss every inch. His gaze drifted lower to her flat stomach and the thatch of auburn hair between her thighs. "So beautiful."

She smiled. "I'm in awe. You've been working out."

Nick raised both hands to her breasts and kneaded the swollen mounds, brushing his thumbs over her tight nipples. She quivered under his fingers and pressed her breasts harder into his palms. He tried to think of disassembling a rotor blade but then she lowered her head, let her hair brush his hip, and laved him with her tongue and lips before taking him in her mouth. His body tensed but he couldn't sum up the will to stop her. She traipsed a hand across his stomach then down one thigh and up the other. She cupped his balls and squeezed lightly.

"God, Ava, that's so good." His voice dropped to a low growl. He allowed Ava to lavish attention on him for another minute then took hold of the reins again. He wanted to fill her and possess her but not until she was panting and begging, writhing beneath him. Framing her face, he eased her away, tumbled her backward, then set his lips to her breasts, licking, suckling, worshipping her as she moaned and dug her fingers into his shoulders. He slid lower, spread her thighs wide then swept his tongue through her slick folds. She cried out. He circled her tight nub then thrust inside her hot, wet haven, lapping up her precious nectar.

"Harder." She pushed against his mouth. "Make me come."

Rudderless and reeling, Nick drew her swollen flesh into his mouth once more then pushed two fingers into her tight sheath and worked them deep, elated at her quivering gasps. She was a tempest under his hands, her tantalizing scent rising to commandeer his senses.

Another roll of thunder rumbled, closer this time and with it came heavier rain, loud enough to mask her soft cries and moans, but it wouldn't mask her scream.

"Nick, please."

Chuckling, he leaned over the edge of the bed, riffled through his shorts, then ripped the tiny packet open. "The next time I make you pregnant, it's going to be planned." He sheathed himself then lifted over her, braced himself on both hands, and fitted his hips between her thighs. "Ready to tango with me, Angel?"

"Always, my darling." She clutched his shoulders and arched into him.

Nick flexed his hips and entered her in one powerful thrust then slowly withdrew and thrust again and again, plundering her body relentlessly.

She sank her fingernails into his arms and matched his vigorous rhythm as he drove into her with unbridled lust. His gaze held hers as every nerve tightened and he spiraled toward paradise. He lifted one hand, framed her jaw and claimed her mouth, muffling her scream as a wave of pure ecstasy blazed through his body, rose up and crashed over him. She clenched around his length as ripples of aftershock pulsed through his veins. Nothing had changed. She was the only woman who could bring him to his knees.

Wow. Nick floated on a cloud of euphoria, happy to lie over Ava as her heart thudded against his chest. Her fingertips tracing up and down his back.

Eventually he stirred, kissed her then rolled to the right. "I'll be back in a minute. Just need to dispose of this condom." He planned to hold her all night, secure in his arms, just like he always had and if fate were kind, always would.

Ava woke several hours later, warm and cozy, cocooned within

Nick's arm, her hand over his heart as the heavy rain drummed into the roof. Surprised to see the lamp still on, she raised her gaze to find Nick staring at the ceiling. "What's wrong?"

He glanced down and smiled. "Nothing. I was just reminiscing."

"About?"

He stroked her arm. "I never told you this, but the day I walked into the florist where you worked, it was to buy flowers for a woman who'd been stringing me along. I stood there watching you serve all those men. Your smile never wavered as you helped each guy pick flowers for the woman in his life and then you helped them all write a unique message. I kept hanging back, encouraging more customers to go before me."

"I noticed. Why did you do that?"

"Because you were forbidden fruit. An exquisite angel with a fiery red halo and sparkling emerald eyes. Everything about you was pure and good, and once you served me, I'd have to leave, so I kept putting it off."

"Oh, my darling." She reached up and stroked his face. "I noticed you the second you walked in and I couldn't stop peeking. I thought you were a biker or at the very least a rebel. You hadn't shaved and wore a leather jacket that screamed bad boy. I was a bit intimidated—until you smiled. Your hazel eyes were warm and that dimple was so cute. You instantly became my ultimate fantasy."

He chuckled. "Then that gay guy walked in."

Ava cringed. "He wanted flowers to match his partner's eyes, which were powder blue so I made up an arrangement of nigella, scabious, irises, and lily grass. It was gorgeous and then he asked me to write an ode to his partner, *Keith*. I must have gone every shade of beetroot."

Nick laughed. "You did blush but the ode was perfect and he left walking on air, then you served me and I knew I couldn't stay away from you."

She squeezed him tight. "I'm glad you didn't. We had so much fun and you opened my eyes to so many things. Without you I wouldn't have Liam or found out I was adopted." She bit her lip. "I never stopped loving you, and even though you never said you loved me, I knew you cared for me."

Nick came up on one elbow and leaned over her. "More than you'll ever know, but I couldn't fathom what you saw in me. No woman has ever shown me the warmth you lavished on me. No person understood me like you, but I didn't have words strong enough to express what you meant to me." He stroked her cheek with the back of his hand. "I've spent the last four years regretting that. So here goes."

He leaned down and placed a gentle kiss on her lips. "You are the fire within my soul. Your smile is like the brightest star in the galaxy. Your heart is as pure as a newborn baby, and your laugh is like warm silk on my skin. I desire you, I adore you, and I want us to be together for the rest of our lives. You, me, Liam, and any other children we are blessed with. I love you, Angel."

Her eyes filled. "That's the loveliest thing you've ever said to me." She hugged him tight. "I love you too, my darling. So much my heart is bursting with it."

Nick eased her away, a serious expression on his face. "I'm prepared to leave the team if that's what it will take to have you and Liam in my life. I love you." He captured her lips and kissed her with such gentleness that her heart quivered. This man of so many layers had finally opened his soul to her, given his heart into her care, and gifted her with his trust. *Alleluia.*

She urged him onto his back then straddled his thighs. "I think we should celebrate, don't you?"

He placed his hands round her waist. "I'd like nothing better, Angel, but I don't have any more condoms and tasting you wouldn't be enough for me."

"It's okay. I bought a packet of condoms last week in case my relationship with Damon got serious." She circled the head of Nick's impressive erection and wriggled closer. "It's a good thing you turned up when you did."

"A very good thing, Angel." He shuddered then caught her in his arms and drew her against his chest, imprisoning his erection between them. "It would have gutted me to find you, only to lose you again." He tangled his fingers amongst her long curls as he gazed into her eyes. "I've always loved your hair." He trailed kisses down her neck and across her collarbone, then claimed her lips like a marauding pirate, stealing her breath then giving it back as his hands cruised down the curve of her spine, over the globes of her backside and along her thighs.

Ava wrapped her arms around his neck then rubbed against him, sending hot flashes of desire throughout her body.

"Two can play at this game." He gripped her hips, edged her back slightly and ran his fingers up the indent of her waist, then closed his palms over her breasts to leisurely knead, and torment her as he continued to plunder her mouth.

Eagerly, she met each stroke of his tongue, her hands caressing his shoulders and chest wantonly, as wild as him. "I want your mouth on me."

"So impatient." Nick closed his lips over her nipple, circling the bud with his tongue, as he caressed her other breast with his fingers.

"Nick, I can't wait any longer." She rose on her knees then pulled open the bedside drawer and grabbed a condom. Once she had him sheathed, she shamelessly rubbed her slick folds over his engorged head. "Now."

With a savage growl, Nick gripped her hips and impaled her in one powerful thrust, then held her there for a second before lifting her and thrusting again, and again.

Ava tried to mask her cries of pleasure as she gripped his shoulders and matched his pace, but he felt like a flaming torch inside her, driving her rapidly toward release. Delirious with desire, she arched back as he lowered his mouth and recaptured her nipple, sucking hard as he drove into her faster. She jolted, clenched around his cock, then cried out. He roared his own climax and pumped into her.

They fell amongst the pillows, boneless and replete. Ava lay in an unbelievable state of bliss as her heart rate slowed and Nick soothingly stroked her backside.

He eventually roused himself and kissed her shoulder. "You have no idea how much I've missed this. You and me, how we are together."

"I do," she murmured drowsily against his chest, unable to raise the energy to shift the veil of hair covering her face. "We're two halves of a whole, my love."

"I couldn't have said it better." He kissed her lips then eased her alongside him, brushed her hair away and kissed her eyelids. "I love you, babe."

"I love you too, my darling." Ava closed her eyes as Nick pulled the covers over her. He continued to caress her as she rested her hand on his chest and listened to the storm raging outside. "I missed you so much."

"I know. Go to sleep then I'll sneak out."

"Kay."

Chapter Twelve

Still floating from Nick's heartfelt words and their love making, Ava hummed as she redressed the shop window. Everything would work out—how could it not? Nick's friends would investigate the missing gems and exonerate him. His impassioned declaration had her walking on air all morning. She would cherish his words forever.

Smiling, she positioned a choker over the velvet bust, careful not to let the pearls touch the sand or shells in her display. "I think we need a couple of starfish and crabs, then it will look more like the ocean floor."

Helen looked up from the glass cabinet she was cleaning. "You could try the Bargain Basement. I know they have a small treasure chest that's quite realistic."

"Fantastic. I can stuff some white satin in it then drape several strings of black Tahitian pearls over the top. What do you think?"

Helen strolled over and examined the display. "You certainly have a flair for this." She pursed her lips. "Sergeant Evans came by this morning to check if the master key to your home safe was still here. He also asked about Nick Flanagan."

Ava's breath caught. "What did you tell the sergeant?"

"That you fainted when Nick walked in and that he didn't know about Liam. I hope that's all right. I don't want to make trouble for you."

"You're only being truthful, Helen. I'm sorry you've been dragged into this."

"Don't apologize, dear. The police wouldn't be doing their job if they didn't speak to me and Taylor."

Taylor! "Who is Taylor?"

"A teenager doing work experience. She was here on Friday and Saturday. Sergeant Evans wanted to know if anyone could verify my whereabouts. He even asked about Friday evening."

"The key I have hidden at home hasn't been touched." Ava began cleaning up her mess. "I think the thief was a professional safe-cracker."

Helen grimaced. "Are you sure it wasn't Nick who broke in? After all, he had the time and opportunity with you here at the shop."

"It wasn't Nick." Ava lifted her chin. "He wouldn't do that to me."

"Then perhaps it's Damon Pearce. What if he paid someone to break into your safe then set Nick up to take the fall? Damon wants you in his life, Ava. The last thing he needs is for your ex-fiancé to turn up and steal you away."

"I don't know what to think." Ava swept up some sand then leaned across her new window display to rearrange a conch shell. A tap sounded on the glass and she looked up to see Madeline Shaw waving. Behind her stood the big guy, Talos.

"Come in," mouthed Ava, and beckoned them with her hand.

Slim, graceful, perfectly groomed, and wearing killer stilettoes, the journalist breezed through the open doorway, leaving Talos out on the sidewalk.

"Ava, it's so nice to see you again." Madeline's dazzling sapphire eyes glowed with warmth. She hugged Ava, cloaking her in an exotically delicate fragrance.

Bemused, Ava noted the peach-colored designer dress, which worked beautifully with Madeline's eyes and butterscotch-blonde hair.

"Hello, Madeline. I couldn't believe it when I heard you were here."

"It was too good an opportunity to miss. When did you leave England?"

"Four months ago. A pearl broker I buy from introduced me to Damon Pearce in London. He suggested I set up business here and then I met Helen who was looking for a partner to run this shop."

"So that's how you know Damon?"

"Yes. He gives me business advice whenever I need it."

"I bet he does," Madeline murmured sarcastically.

Ava raised an eyebrow. "You know Damon?"

"We met at a charity function in Melbourne last year. Let's just say he found it hard to take no for an answer. Anyway, Jarred Steele suggested I do a story on Damon and while I'm in Broome I'd like to interview you as well."

"Wow. You normally do articles on high profile people or the repression of women, and human trafficking, etc. Why me?"

"I have a vested interest in helping your career. I love your designs and Nick helped save my life in Vietnam."

"I heard you've trodden on some dangerous toes lately and it's resulted in death threats and a few close shaves."

Madeline shrugged. "That's in the past. No one will get near me with Talos and the boys around." She glanced at Helen hovering toward the back of the shop then lowered her voice. "I convinced Jarred Steele to let me interview Damon so I could tag along. I know there's something bigger here. I have a sixth sense about these things."

"I see." Ava watched Talos enter the shop. His gaze rested on her for a couple of seconds before drifting to Helen.

Madeline also looked at Helen then leaned closer. "We can't talk here."

Ava was about to say it was fine when Talos spoke. "We don't want any locals knowing what we're up to, not even your business partner."

"Fine, but it would be rude not to introduce you." Ava caught Helen's eye and raised her voice. "Helen, this is Madeline Shaw. We met in London last year when Madeline was doing a story on a prominent British politician I know."

Helen bustled forward and shook Madeline's hand. "Welcome to Broome. Are you on holidays or is this a business trip?"

"A bit of both. I'm here to interview Damon Pearce, but now that I know Ava's here, I want to interview her as well."

Ava laughed. "I'm not that interesting."

"Oh, yes you are," enthused Madeline. "Not only are your designs stunning, but the British people would delight in your parents' story. How they fell in love while studying at Cambridge University."

Ava gasped. "How did you know they were my parents?"

Madeline smiled. "Your father told me during our interview." She grinned at Talos. "He's the prominent British politician."

Stunned, Ava stared at Madeline. "I can't believe he opened up to you."

"I told you I have a sixth sense when it comes to secrets, and I know just how to make people relax enough to talk to me. Well, most people." She smiled. "You have your father's eyes. After I saw you together I speculated, then he told me the truth."

"I don't want it to get out. My father's reputation could be damaged.

"Actually, it will gain him empathy, especially as he didn't know about you."

"I would need to speak to him before you printed any of those details." *And Nick deserves to know before the rest of the world.*

Helen raised an eyebrow at Talos. "And who is this fine looking man?"

Madeline laughed. "This is James, my body guard. I've had several death threats in recent months so my editor insists I'm protected at all times." She smiled at Talos. "Not that I'm complaining."

Helen's lips quirked. "I wouldn't complain either." She turned to Ava. "Why don't you take Madeline and James to that café you like. I can look after things here."

"Thanks, Helen, I will."

They left Helen and strolled to the café. Over coffee and then lunch, Madeline and Talos revealed more details behind the team's last two missions. It was an eye-opener for Ava as the full impact of Nick's job hit her.

Madeline squeezed her hand. "Why don't you and Liam come to our condo at Cable Beach? I love to cook and the team is planning to go over our tactics for tomorrow. I think you should be there."

"Thank you, Madeline, but what's happening tomorrow?"

"I've managed to convince Damon to let me interview him on board his yacht."

"Why the yacht?"

"We want to get a look at the crew and install cameras so we can see who or what is being brought onto that yacht."

Talos raised an eyebrow. *"We?"*

She ignored him and focused on Ava. "I presume you've met Jarred Steele?"

"Yes, last night. He's rather intimidating."

Madeline scoffed. "The man's a law unto himself. He's stubborn, bossy, demanding, and a pain in the arse."

Talos chuckled. "Funny, that's exactly how Jarred describes you. You started it."

Madeline crossed her arms then scowled at Talos. "I was simply dropping off papers for my husband when Jarred exploded onto the terrace and crash-tackled me into a pool. He ruined my phone, my purse, and my favorite pair of shoes."

Talos' lips twitched. "He also saved your life on two separate occasions."

"And I'm grateful, but that doesn't mean he can tell me what to do or imprison me on an island for a month." She pushed back her chair. "I need to make a call. I'll be back in a minute."

Ava picked up her purse. "I would love to hear that story, but I need to pick up some props for my window display before I collect Liam from daycare."

"Wait." Talos put his large hand over hers. "Simon's busy with Nick and Jarred at the moment so how about you let me escort you to the shops then pick up Liam and drop you home."

"I'll be fine, Talos. It's not as if anything is going to happen to *me*."

"It takes less than twenty seconds for a reasonably fit man to drag a light-weight woman into a vehicle. Nick would never forgive me if you disappeared."

"All right. Can we stop by the Bargain Basement?"

"No worries." Talos picked up their bill then shook his head as Ava opened her purse. "My shout. I'm hoping you'll take a commission to make earrings for my wife."

"Do you have a recent picture so I can judge what style would suit her?"

"Sure." He pulled out his phone and after a couple of seconds passed it over. "Scroll through the photos. They were taken at our wedding and around the island. Her name is Jane and the baby is Eloise, but we call her Ella. The Vietnamese child is Ming, who we found in Vietnam and have since adopted."

Ava studied the happy family and the radiant bride with big green eyes, very similar to her own. "She's lovely, Talos. It looks like you all had a wonderful day. Hopefully I'll get to meet Jane and Sam's wife in the not too distant future."

Madeline spoke from behind Ava's right shoulder. "It could be very soon from what Nick was telling Jarred this morning." She shook her head. "I don't understand why some parents can't accept their children's choices. It's like they're still living in the dark ages and anyone who's different or doesn't conform to their set of rules is unacceptable. Then they wonder why their children rarely visit or live secretive lives. It makes me so angry."

Nonplussed, Ava gaped. She'd never seen Madeline anything but charming and composed. As a journalist she had a reputation for being levelheaded and painstakingly thorough. Ava suspected Madeline was ranting about something much more personal than what had happened to her and Nick.

Blushing softly, Madeline glanced around, obviously embarrassed at her outburst. "Sorry, I just needed to vent. It's been a tough couple of months. I'm glad you and Nick have found each other again, but it's a shame he's leaving the team."

Ava blinked in surprise. She hadn't expected Nick to speak to Jarred so soon, or for Madeline to know about it. "We are taking it slowly." *Well that's a big fat lie for a start.* She lifted her chin. "Nick said he's prepared to leave the team for me, and Barry might be open to a partnership." Even as she said it, she felt a weight of guilt on her shoulders.

"Leave the team?" Talos frowned at Ava. "Do you realize it's our team that kept Nick sane these last four years? We don't only work together, we hang out, and we're there for each other. No job here would pay so well or allow Nick so much time off. He'll go nuts in a place like this."

Ava clutched her hands in her lap. She didn't doubt what Talos said, but the fear of losing Nick tragically far outweighed money or holidays. Nick could easily work as a chopper pilot and still meet up with his friends. "He wants to be with me and Liam. Is that too much to ask?"

"No, it's not." Madeline raised an elegant eyebrow. "But be warned, once Kallie and Jane find out, they'll be on the first plane to Broome. I spent a month with them on a Fijian island and they plan to see each of these guys enticed into a loving relationship. So if they think they can help your romance along, they will."

Talos groaned. "Bloody hell, you're right. We'll just have to make sure they're not told anything until we've cleared Nick and looked into Max's death."

❧

Out in Roebuck Bay, Nick surfaced by the small boat Jarred had hired and pulled out his regulator. "All done."

"No problems?" Jarred leaned over and took the weight belt from him.

"Nope. I've attached the GPS tracker to the yacht's hull."

"Good. If they leave this bay, we'll have a heads up."

Nick threw his goggles and flippers over the side. "Did you see any crew?"

"Yes. A couple of Asian men and a solid looking bald guy."

"That'll be Lex Walsh." Nick shrugged off his oxygen-tank and passed it up. "Do you think it's wise to let Madeline Shaw interview Pearce tomorrow?"

"She'll be fine. Talos will be there and it's the only way we can get on board to plant the bugs and surveillance cameras."

Nick hauled himself out of the water and into the boat. "Are you sure the fishing boat we're hiring is up to chasing them if we have to?"

"Of course. By the way, I think one of the men who ambushed you is on board. I noticed an Asian man with his leg in plaster. You must have broken his kneecap."

"It's a pity I didn't break his head." Nick glanced across the bay. "None of the crew saw you watching, did they? We don't want Pearce getting suspicious."

"No. I was extremely careful. If anyone looked this way, all they saw was a fisherman in a large hat. Just remember, those guys might have ambushed you, but that doesn't mean Pearce sent them."

"No, but it figures," murmured Nick.

"Simon did a background check on Pearce and nothing remotely felonious came up. Lex Walsh, however, has a rap sheet as long as my arm. He's done time for break and enter, armed robbery, and assault."

"So Pearce hired him to do a little strong arming and possibly run a smuggling operation out of the Kimberley. It fits with what Dave, the chopper pilot told me, and the rumors Gibbs has heard."

Jarred looked toward the yacht. "Until we have irrefutable proof, we don't want to scatter our pigeons or jump to conclusions. Once we get back to the condo, I'll contact Gibbs and let him know. In the meantime, you need to keep a low profile. I want Pearce and Walsh to think you've taken off."

"What about the police?" Nick dragged his wetsuit off his shoulders.

"Gibbs has informed Sergeant Evans that you have the backing of the Federal police and you're part of an investigation into a rumored smuggling ring. Sergeant Evans has agreed to keep that information classified and provide us with backup if and when required. However, he's reserving judgment on whether you're guilty or not."

Nick grunted. "In that case, can you collect some clothes and toiletries for me? I can't keep borrowing stuff from the boys."

"No worries. What's keeping Simon?"

"He's planting the detonator in case we have to disable the propeller. Here he comes now."

Simon surfaced on the far side of the boat and, after handing over his tank and flippers, he slid over the side, pulled off his mask, and grinned.

"If we have to set that little demon off, they won't know what hit them."

"Excellent." Jarred handed him a towel. "I'll drop you both at the beach then go shopping. Madeline Shaw just rang with a list of bloody groceries she wants me to pick up. Apparently she's managed to organize our meeting in her condo tonight, where she's cooking dinner."

Nick started the engine. "You've got to give her full points for ingenuity. By the way, she's a great cook, which you'd know if you'd stayed on the island longer."

"If I'd stayed on the island any longer I would have strangled the damn woman."

Simon looked up. "Why, what happened?"

"I told her due to safety concerns she couldn't leave for a month. Nor could she have Internet or social media access as I didn't trust her not to leak the story."

"Uh-oh." Nick grimaced. "That wouldn't have gone down well. What did she say?"

Jarred's lips twitched. "She called me Chief Steel Feather and informed me she wasn't my squaw to order about. So, I said, if she was my squaw I'd drag her to my teepee and service her with my steel feather for insubordination."

"You didn't?" Nick gaped at their boss, barely able to contain his astonishment.

"Yes, unfortunately I did. Then she threw a bowl of muesli and yogurt over me, told me I could stick my steel feather where the sun doesn't shine, and sailed out of the kitchen. I have no idea how her husband copes with her."

Nick and Simon both doubled up with laughter.

Simon shook his head. "I can't believe we've found a woman capable of ruffling your feather." He broke into another fit of laughter at his joke.

Jarred raised one eyebrow. "I don't find it that amusing, Major Hawke."

"Oh, it is, Colonel. It really is."

Nick and Simon chuckled all the way to shore.

CHAPTER THIRTEEN

Ava watched with amusement as Fiona and the other child-care staff ogled Talos. She couldn't blame them; he was an impressive man with his huge shoulders, towering height, and soft brown eyes. What she found surprising was his ability to interact with Liam, a shy little boy who generally shunned strangers. At the moment he had Talos by the hand, proudly showing him the sandpit and climbing equipment.

"He's a nice guy, isn't he?" Madeline murmured beside her.

"Yes. So is Simon, and I've always liked Ryan. I haven't got to know Sam or Jarred yet, but Nick thinks a lot of them."

"As a team, they all work incredibly well together."

Ava glanced at Madeline. "But you don't like Jarred."

"Jarred?" Madeline's eyes widened then she blushed softly. "It's not that I don't like him. He's a very effective leader. We just got off to the wrong foot and we rub each other up the wrong way."

"Why?"

"I have no idea. Sometimes I think he sets out to antagonize me, just so I'll bite. My husband, Elliott, thinks it's hilarious that Jarred and I clash so fiercely."

"Your husband doesn't mind you traveling all over the world to do stories that put you in danger?"

"Not until recently. He's based in Vietnam and I'm based in Melbourne so he doesn't always know what I'm working on until it's done. My latest death threats scared him and that's why he let Jarred detain me on an island for a month."

"Couldn't you catch one of those island hopping ferries to the mainland?"

Madeline huffed. "It was a private island with its own security detail and although Jarred only stayed a couple of days, he made sure at least two of his men were there to watch over us women. No way off. Believe me, I tried."

"So, if you and your husband are living on different continents, when do you get to spend time together?"

She lightly shrugged her shoulders. "Family celebrations and the odd week here and there. I know it sounds like a strange marriage, but it works for us."

Very strange and by your sad smile, it's not working that well. Ava touched Madeline's arm. "If you're not happy with your life, it's up to you to change it."

Madeline blinked several times, seemingly lost for words before clearing her throat. "I'm fine, Ava, and Elliott is a wonderful man. He's not the least bit controlling."

"Mummy." Liam wrapped his arms around Ava's legs. "Quick, we have to hurry, Talos said Daddy is almost finished fixing my helicopter and Ajax is missing me."

"Oh, is that so? And what about me? I didn't get a proper hug or kiss." She leaned down, opened her arms, and presented her cheek.

He giggled, gave her a big hug and kiss, then leaned back. "I see you all the time, Mummy." He glanced at Madeline and smiled shyly.

"Liam, this is Mrs. Shaw. She is a journalist who is going to write stories about me and Mr. Pearce for people to read."

He screwed up his face. "I don't like Mr. Pearce. Why don't you write a story about Black Hawk helicopters or catching fish? That would be good."

Madeline laughed. "I don't know anything about helicopters or fish, Liam, but I'd like it if you called me Maddy?"

He thought for a few seconds then grinned. "My daddy knows about helicopters and fish. Let's go ask him." He gripped Talos' hand again.

"Let's." Talos swung Liam up in his arms and strode to the car. Ava and Madeline followed, both chuckling.

They stopped by Ava's house so she could change into jeans, a blouse, and flat shoes, then Talos drove them to Cable Beach. The condos Jarred had hired were side by side, sharing a common wall and located amongst a tropical garden of coconut and banana palms, cycads, bromeliads, and masses of golden-cane palms.

Ava looked about with interest. "Staying next door to Nick's team is sure to make Damon suspicious."

"I don't plan on inviting him over for dinner so he won't know." Madeline frowned at Talos. "Unless, he's got someone following Ava.

"No, we would have noticed," said Talos. "And, for now we don't want anyone to know Nick is holed up here with Jarred and the boys."

Ava frowned at him. "Where are you staying?"

"I have a room in Madeline's condo. I'm her body guard, remember?" He grinned. "There's a connecting door, so we can move between both places without drawing attention."

"Wouldn't Jarred love that," murmured Madeline, climbing out of the car.

Ava followed her into a stylish dwelling of polished floorboards, cream walls, and soft lighting. Passing a bedroom, she noticed a queen sized bed with a thick white coverlet, three vibrant, decorative cushions, and a red shawl draped across the foot of the bed. *I bet it's not cheap to stay here.*

Madeline led her through the condo and out onto a private terrace where Nick and the rest of the team were relaxing around a table, each with a beer. They called out cheerful welcomes.

"Daddy." Liam's high-pitched voice startled a Willie Wagtail from the overhanging tree. "Maddy needs to know about fishing and helicopters."

"Does she?" Nick stood, kissed Ava then picked Liam up. "What would Maddy like to know?"

"Everything. It's more better than talking to Mr. Pearce."

Ava and Madeline grinned as confused faces turned toward them. Madeline reached out and smoothed Liam's unruly hair. "I have to agree with you, sweetie, but I still have to interview Mr. Pearce for Chief Steele Feather here."

Jarred choked, sending a mouthful of beer across the table. After several coughs he narrowed cool gray eyes on Madeline. "Do not call me that unless you wish to deal with the consequences."

She smiled. "I suppose I could just call you chief."

His lips twitched. "That I can live with, but can you?"

She gave a light shrug. "Yes, but it doesn't make you my lord and master."

Nick chuckled. "Just keep that Steele feather under control, Chief."

The whole table erupted in raucous laughter, leaving Jarred rolling his eyes and Ava frowning at Nick.

"I'll explain later, Angel."

Jarred shook his head. "So much for loyalty. I should have known you boys wouldn't keep that to yourselves."

Simon shrugged. "It's rare we get something this titillating on you."

The men burst out laughing again, Sam and Ryan wiping their eyes.

Madeline took Ava's hand. "Come into the kitchen. I'll tell you about it while I get you a drink."

"Okay." Ava followed Madeline. "Can I give you a hand with dinner?"

"Definitely. Would you like beer, wine, or something else?

"Wine, please."

Madeline picked up two bottles of wine and read the labels. "We have Cabernet Sauvignon and a Shiraz." She put them on the counter and opened the fridge. "If you prefer white, there's Pinot Grigio or Sauvignon Blanc."

"Shiraz, please." Ava took two wine glasses from an open shelf. "Can I get Liam a glass of milk or orange juice if you have it?"

"Of course, help yourself. Would you pour me a Cabernet Sauvignon while I change into sandals and something more comfy?"

"Sure." Ava opened the wine so it could breathe then poured a glass of milk and took it out to Liam who played with Ajax. The men were still ribbing Jarred about his steel feather, which, by the smirks on their faces, she assumed referred to a certain part of his anatomy. Ava met Nick's gaze, smiled, then returned to the kitchen. It would do him good to spend time with his mates, but how would he feel once they went back to Sydney without him? If the weight of her guilt got any heavier, she'd flatten like a pancake.

Ava was pouring the wine when he came into the kitchen behind her, wrapped his arms around her, and nuzzled her neck. "How was your day, Angel?"

"Interesting. I redid the shop window, then had lunch with Madeline and Talos, where I learnt a lot about you and the other guys. How was your day?"

"Besides thinking about you all day, I went diving then repaired the top of Liam's helicopter so the blades now spin freely."

"They never spun freely, they were fixed."

He smiled. "Not anymore. Talos stopped by the hardware store for some bits and pieces so we could fashion new blades and skids then we attached them to the body of the helicopter. All I need do now is paint the chopper to resemble a Black Hawk."

"Oh, Nick, Liam's going to love that." She turned in his arms and hugged him. "So why did you go diving? Talos gave me the impression you were up to something with Jarred and Simon."

"Yeah. Jarred hired some scuba gear and a small boat. We motored over to Roebuck Bay where Simon and I attached a GPS tracking device to the hull of Damon Pearce's yacht."

"Are you expecting him to disappear?"

"It's possible, and with Madeline interviewing him tomorrow, it's better to be safe."

Ava frowned. "What if Damon or one of his crew saw you?"

"They didn't." Nick nuzzled her neck. "I need to stay out of sight a while longer so Pearce and his off-sider think I've done a runner. That doesn't mean I'll stay away from you. Do you want me to come over tonight?"

Ava bit her lip. "I do but..."

"You think we're rushing things?"

"Yes— No— Maybe. It's just that you've got a strong bond with your mates and I don't want you to rush into a decision that you might regret for the rest of your life. I want us to be together more than anything, but I want you to be happy."

His arms tightened. "You and Liam are my life now. I will never regret any decision that keeps us together. I love you, Angel."

"I love you too, my darling." She leaned back and smiled into his warm, hazel eyes. "Can you spend the whole day with us tomorrow? Liam won't be at daycare and the three of us could go to the beach."

Nick sighed. "Not the whole day. Madeline and Talos are meeting with Pearce at four. The rest of us will be observing and listening from a fishing boat nearby."

"Then we can spend the morning together. Being a parent is one of life's biggest pleasures." She locked her hands behind his neck and kissed him deeply.

"Okay, you two, move it or lose it." Madeline clicked into the kitchen wearing silver sandals and a tropical flowered caftan. She'd redone her hair in a thick topknot and added vibrant blue earrings. Glamorous and perfectly groomed as always, but Ava caught a glimpse of immense sadness in Madeline's eyes before she turned away.

Was it the kiss, or the idea of being a parent? Maybe Madeline can't have children.

Jarred strolled into the kitchen as Madeline retrieved a plastic tray stacked with meat from the fridge. She held it out to him. "Perfect timing, chief. You can take these scotch fillets and sausages outside and fire up the barbeque. Ava and I will have the salads ready in twenty minutes or so."

"I live solely to serve you," said Jarred dryly as he accepted the tray.

Ava noticed a smile return to Madeline's lips and a hint of mischief light her eyes before she answered him. "Hmm, I like that."

"You would." Jarred glanced across the kitchen. "Nick, can you bring more beers? My hands are rather full."

"Sure."

"Wait." Madeline ripped open a large packet of Honey-Soy chips and emptied them into a plastic bowl. "Take these with you too, in case they're hungry."

"Thanks." Nick took the bowl and a six-pack of beers, winked at Ava, and followed Jarred onto the terrace.

"Right. If you don't mind doing the pear and rocket salad, I'll boil these baby potatoes and make up a parsley, mayonnaise, sour cream, and lemon dressing."

"Yum, that's sounds delicious. I'd love to be able to come up with dishes like that."

"Stick with me, kid, and before you know it, you'll be turning out warm duck salad with beetroot and pomegranate, and apple dumplings in caramel sauce. I love to cook. It's my way of winding down."

Madeline opened the fridge and began piling the bench with so many items, Ava wondered if they were feeding one Army or two. "So tell me about Chief Steele Feather."

Madeline did just that with an enthusiasm that had them laughing so hard, tears ran down their cheeks. By the time they finished making the fruit salad accompanied by a passion fruit laced cream, Ava recognized a real camaraderie growing between her and Madeline. One she would love to continue.

After a very satisfying meal, Ava rubbed her full belly then leaned back on her chair. "Thank you, Madeline. That was delicious."

"More fruit salad?" Madeline pushed the bowl across the dining table.

"No, thanks. I couldn't eat another bite." Ava's gaze drifted to the kitchen where Liam and Ajax sat on the floor at Nick's feet as he conversed with the other men. They were busy washing up or packing the dishwasher. She glanced back at Madeline. "It's been a very enjoyable evening, hasn't it?"

"Yes, it has." Madeline put the lid on the fruit salad bowl and held it out to Jarred. "Would you please put this in the fridge, chief?"

"Certainly, Pocahontas."

As soon as the kitchen was tidy, the men joined them at the table then Jarred outlined the following day's plan. "Any questions?" He looked around the table. "Good, after that delicious meal, I suggest we adjourn to the terrace for coffee."

Jarred returned to the kitchen to make the coffee while the rest of them drifted onto the terrace to either sit at the outdoor setting or stand about talking.

Ava joined Madeline at the railing and looked out over the ocean at the round moon glowing brightly in the darkness. "It's beautiful, isn't it?"

"Amazing. I've never seen that effect on the ocean before."

"It's called Stairway to the Moon. A couple of days ago Nick took me to a little beach way up the coast, where we sat on the sand late at night and gazed at the moon. It gave me a sense of well-being and filled me with optimism for the future."

"I could definitely do with some of that."

"Some of what?" Jarred's deep voice sounded behind them.

Madeline stiffened beside Ava. "You wouldn't understand." She turned away but Jarred reached for her arm.

"Try me."

"It's nothing."

Ava frowned at Madeline's departing back. "That's the third time today that I've got the feeling something's very wrong in Madeline's life."

Jarred's gaze settled on Ava's face. "See if you can find out what it is then let me know. God knows why, but her husband has left Madeline in my care."

"I'll try." Ava left his intimidating presence, wandered over to the terrace steps, and sat beside Nick. He watched Liam throw a tennis ball for Ajax, who kept bringing it back, to Liam's delight.

Nick put his arm around Ava's waist. "Besides a real family, I always wanted a dog. Maybe we can get one for Liam before he gets much older."

"He'd love that." She leaned her head against Nick's shoulder and slid her hand into his. "You will be careful tomorrow, won't you? I don't like the sound of Lex Walsh or the armed crew."

"Talos is the only one who will be on the yacht with Madeline. The rest of us will be on the fishing boat across the bay. I'll be fine, Angel, I promise."

Tiring of their game, Ajax wandered inside the condo and Liam followed. Ten minutes later Ryan gave a friendly wave and left for his night shift at Barry's hangar. Then Sam called out goodnight and strolled through the side gate with his phone to his ear. Ava noticed Jarred and Simon were deep in conversation by the barbeque. Talos had moved further down the garden and also held his phone to his ear.

Nick smiled. "Calling their wives to say goodnight."

Ava yawned. "That's sweet. We should probably go too. It's past Liam's bedtime."

Nick stood and pulled her to her feet. "Simon, you ready to leave?"

"Yeah, no worries. I'll just get my computer."

Jarred joined Ava and Nick as they followed Simon into the living room. Liam and Madeline were curled up on the couch together, sound asleep while Ajax sprawled on the thick rug, his eyes half closed.

"I'll get Liam." Nick eased Liam out of Madeline's arms and scooped him up.

Ava glanced at Jarred. "We can't leave Madeline there; she'll end up with a stiff neck. Would you carry her to her room?"

"I prefer to stay well away from married women and journalists, especially that one. She bites."

"Oh come on. She can't bite you in her sleep."

Jarred sighed heavily. "Very well." He gently lifted Madeline into his arms, juggled her against his chest then, muttering under his breath, carried her to her bedroom.

Ava darted around them and pulled the thick white cover back so Jarred could lay Madeline down, then waited as he slipped her sandals off and drew the covers up.

He raised an eyebrow at Ava. "Happy?"

"Yes. Thank you, Jarred."

He grimaced. "First it was Kallie McNeil enticing Sam out of bachelorhood, then her friend Jane sideswiped Talos. Now you turn up and Nick is jumping ship. This is turning into a damn conspiracy."

"Shush, you'll wake Madeline."

He threw his hands up and lowered his voice to a growl. "She's the worst of the lot. What the hell did I do to be plagued by so many bloody-minded women?"

He stalked off leaving Ava grinning at Nick who leaned against the doorjamb. "I think your Chief Steele Feather is on the warpath."

"You might be right, Angel. Let's go home before he starts emitting smoke signals."

She stretched up and brushed her lips across his, lingering over the sensual contact. "Stay with me for the whole night? I miss waking up in your arms."

"So do I. There is no place I'd rather be than with you."

Ava lowered her voice to a whisper. "And tonight, I'm taking care of you." She poked him in the arm. "No arguments."

He chuckled. "I wouldn't dare."

CHAPTER FOURTEEN

After spending the morning with Liam and Ava on a deserted beach well away from Broome, Nick arrived back at the condo ready for action. As Simon attached the miniature camera and microphone to the outside of Madeline's navy handbag, Nick watched Jarred pace back and forth across the terrace, unusually tense for such a minor operation.

Talos seemed to agree. "What's eating you, boss?"

"Under no circumstances is she to take any risks or push Pearce too far."

Sam looked up from Simon's computer screen. "Colonel, if you think Madeline's in danger then call off the interview. We can get Pearce some other way."

Jarred halted. "Lieutenant Colonel, the woman is safe as long as she does exactly what I've told her and doesn't take unnecessary risks."

They all stared at Jarred. Although Sam had indeed been a Lieutenant Colonel, since leaving the SAS they rarely referred to his full rank.

Talos straightened from where he'd been leaning against the wall. "I'll be there to protect Madeline if Pearce tries anything."

"Damon will be putty in my hands." Madeline swept onto the terrace looking to Nick like she'd just stepped off a Parisian catwalk. Her hair was caught up in an intricate roll, her make up accentuated her iridescent sapphire eyes, and she wore a figure hugging, cream dress with navy edging.

Nick's gaze traveled down her long tanned legs to the navy high heels. Everything about her appearance was designed to draw a man's eyes and would leave most men floundering. He almost felt sorry for Damon Pearce.

"Wow." Simon shook his head and handed Madeline her handbag. "If you were interviewing me, I'd tell you anything you wanted to know."

She blew him a kiss. "I'll keep that in mind, Simon, for when I want inside information on Steele Security Services. I'm sure Jarred has lots of juicy secrets."

Nick glanced at Jarred and watched, fascinated as his knuckles whitened. "If Pearce suggests going below deck, don't. If he suggests meeting somewhere private, don't. If you feel at all uncomfortable, signal Talos and leave."

She rolled her eyes. "Jarred, I'm not a novice at this sort of thing."

"Perhaps not, but the fact his crew carry weapons while anchored in a safe bay is cause for alarm. Sergeant Evans and I have spoken to the Harbor Master and Water Police. Between us all, we are keeping Pearce's yacht under twenty-four-hour surveillance. Nobody gets on or off that boat without us knowing about it, but I do not want you putting yourself or my men at risk."

Nick frowned. "They won't move the yacht further up the coast because they don't have a pilot to fly them back and forth."

Sam grunted. "Lex Walsh stopped me today as I was leaving Barry's compound. He offered me a job flying his boss's chopper. The salary is beyond tempting—it's fantastic. I told him I might be available as long as it doesn't clash with my work for Barry. It'll be interesting if Walsh approaches Ryan as well."

Jarred nodded. "I'd rather it was you flying Pearce's chopper. I need Ryan and Nick free in case we have to use the Black Hawk."

Madeline looked up from examining the fake clasp. "Damon will never guess this is a camera, but I'll keep moving my bag so you can see and hear him at all times."

"No need." Jarred took her handbag and sat it on the lid of the barbeque. "This camera has a wide angle lens. You need to place the bag where we can see the whole room." He gestured at Simon's computer. "Take a look and you'll see what I mean."

Madeline peered at the screen, where Nick could also see the clear picture of them all on the terrace.

"What's the range of the microphone?" asked Madeline.

"As long as you stay in the same room as your bag, we'll hear everything."

"Not a problem. I have no intention of going below deck with that man." Madeline collected her bag. "We should go, Talos. Damon's driver will be here soon."

"Lead the way." Talos saluted them and followed Madeline out of the condo.

Jarred exhaled. "That woman is going to drive me demented."

"I don't understand why you agreed to bring her," said Sam. "She's everything you avoid rolled into one woman. A journalist, married, and far too impulsive or naive."

"Hardly naïve, Lieutenant. She's been married for six years and a hard hitting journalist for almost as long."

Simon scoffed. "Colonel, she goes after incredibly dangerous people without much thought for her own safety, and brushes aside death threats as nonsensical. If someone doesn't stop her, she's going to get herself killed and I'd hate that to happen."

Jarred narrowed his eyes at Simon. "Major, is there something between you and Madeline Shaw?"

Simon gave Jarred an incredulous look. "Of course not. As you said, she's married." He picked up his computer and strode inside. They heard the front door slam.

Jarred rubbed the back of his neck. "I'll talk to Simon later and see what the hell is eating him."

Simon was waiting by the hire car as Nick and Jarred left the condo. "Sorry, boss. I'm concerned that having Madeline here might have a negative impact on our mission."

Jarred grimaced. "All right. After she's done this interview, I'll send her home.

Nick met Jarred's gaze. "I think that's a good idea."

They drove to Roebuck Bay, parked, and strode down to the water's edge where a Port Authority employee had a tender waiting to take them out to the fishing boat.

Ryan lowered his binoculars as they entered the fishing boat's cabin. "About time you fellas showed up. I need to get back to Barry's." He passed the binoculars to Nick. "Pearce arrived by speed boat about ten minutes ago with the bald guy. I've spotted another two men on board, both Asian. I didn't see the guy in plaster."

Nick nodded. "The bald guy is Lex Walsh, a real piece of work." He took Ryan's position on the lounge and focused the binoculars on Pearce's multi-million dollar yacht. "I can see Pearce talking to Walsh on the back deck. An Asian guy is mopping the forward deck and another is up on the bridge cleaning the inside of the glass windshield. No guns visible."

Nick scanned the impressive yacht. "Walsh is climbing into the speed boat. He must be going in to pick up Madeline and Talos."

Simon set up his computer on the table. "I'll have sound and visual in a few minutes."

Nick kept the binoculars trained on Pearce who casually strolled to the railing and stood watching as Walsh sped toward shore. Several minutes later he returned with Talos and Madeline. Nick moved the binoculars to watch Damon help Madeline on board then stand aside as Talos boarded.

The audio clicked on and they could hear Madeline's voice. "This is James, my bodyguard. I'm not allowed to go anywhere without him."

Pearce's voice sounded surprised. "Why do you need a bodyguard?"

"I've had death threats. I'm not happy about it, but that's how it has to be."

"We have a visual," murmured Simon, turning the computer slightly.

Nick lowered the binoculars and joined Jarred to watch the screen over Simon's shoulder. The picture bounced around as Madeline strolled across the deck. "It's rather warm out here, can we go inside?"

"Certainly," replied Pearce. "Would you or your body guard like refreshments? Tea, coffee, a glass of wine?"

"Not for me." Although out of view, Talos' voice came through loud and clear.

"I'd like a cup of tea, please." Madeline placed her handbag on a counter and moved it slightly, giving Nick and the boys a view of the luxurious surroundings. Deep blue carpet covered the floor's surface. Three white leather lounges formed a large U-shape around a polished coffee table. Large tinted windows covered the walls, framed by white curtains with red swirls.

Nick watched Madeline settle herself on one of the couches. Pearce sat opposite, resting his right ankle on his left knee. Talos had taken up a stance near the door, where he was purposely out of earshot.

Pearce smiled. "You look well, Madeline. I'm surprised you want to interview me after our conversation in Melbourne. I believe you said I was the last man on Earth you'd consider spending any time with."

"I must apologize for my bluntness, but you were very persistent and I am a married woman."

"Why the change of heart? This isn't your normal style of interview and it's a long way to come just to talk to me."

"You're right." Madeline relaxed into the lounge and leisurely crossed one long leg over the other.

Nick noticed he and Pearce weren't the only men who followed the movement. Jarred scowled. "Bloody woman is flaunting her assets."

Madeline smiled at Damon. "You have been voted as one of Australia's most eligible bachelors, both in looks and fortune. My boss wants the inside story. He also wants me to interview Ava Mitchell, an up and coming jewelry designer, who I met in London last year. In return for doing these two interviews, my boss has agreed to send me to India, so I can research the repression of women there."

He laughed. "That sounds more like you."

Madeline pulled out her notepad then asked Pearce a couple of innocuous background questions, which he answered easily.

An Asian man entered the saloon carrying a tray, which he set down on the low table then left. Pearce leaned forward. "How badly do you want this story, Madeline?"

"I beg your pardon?"

"I'll answer your questions but there's something I want in return."

"Bastard." Jarred narrowed his eyes. "Get her out of there."

"Wait." Nick held up a hand. "She won't fall for that."

Madeline looked directly at the camera and gave a tiny shake of her head then glanced back at Damon. "I would hate to jump to the wrong conclusion, Damon. What exactly do you want?"

"Have dinner with me tonight at my house, and leave your

bodyguard behind. There's something I'd like to discuss with you that could lead to a mutually satisfying outcome."

"Fucking bastard." Disgust swept Jarred's face. "I'm going to beat the crap out him."

"Get in line." Nick clenched his fists. "Who the hell does he think he is?"

They watched Madeline calmly pour a cup of tea then add milk. "I don't think so." She wrinkled her nose as if Pearce had requested she squash a frog with one of her dangerously thin heels. After taking a couple of sips, she placed her cup on the low table. "If you're not interested in doing the interview, then I'll move on to Ava Mitchell."

"What if I expose your clandestine life? It's going to be a big shock to your family, once they know you're living a lie. And how's it going to affect your husband?"

"I don't know what you're taking about, Damon." Her voice shook slightly.

Nick raised an eyebrow at Jarred. "What clandestine life?"

Pearce laughed. "You know exactly what I'm talking about, Madeline. You've been living a half-life for years, and I know why. I'm offering to help you. Think about it."

Nick exhaled. "Drugs?"

"No way, we would have seen evidence in Fiji." Simon turned up the volume.

Madeline glanced at her bag and then Pearce. "Let's go outside, I need some air?"

"Certainly." Pearce stood and followed her onto the deck.

"What about the bag?" Sam called. "Take the bag."

"She's left it behind on purpose." Jarred pulled out his phone and selected Talos' number. "Follow them. Don't let her out of your sight."

Nick swiped up the binoculars and trained them on Madeline and Pearce. "They're arguing. She looks like she wants to hit him. Here comes Talos with the bag."

"I'll expect you at six, Madeline." Pearce's voice sounded smug.

"Go to hell."

He followed her across the deck. "I'm not a bad guy, Madeline. I want to help you."

Nick kept the binoculars on Madeline. "She's climbing into the speedboat. Talos is right behind her and he just gave Pearce a diabolical look." Nick lowered the binoculars to find Jarred staring out the window.

"Simon, I want to know everything there is to know about Madeline Shaw. Dig deeper."

"Yes, boss."

They waited until Lex Walsh returned to the yacht, collected Pearce, and then departed for the shore again. Once they'd left the beach, Nick and the others climbed aboard their tender and were taken to shore.

They arrived back at the condo to find Talos pacing. He nodded toward Madeline's bedroom door. "She wants to be alone. Pearce said something to upset her."

"He's blackmailing her." Nick knocked. "Madeline, we need to talk to you." He leaned against the door and listened. "I can't hear anything."

Jarred exhaled. "Open the door."

Nick pulled out his penknife, fitted the blade into the groove on the handle, and twisted. "We're coming in, Madeline." He pushed the door wide to reveal an empty room. Madeline's navy high heels lay discarded on the floor and her cream dress had been tossed carelessly on the bed. Several drawers hung open as if she'd grabbed clothes in a hurry and the glass sliding door was wide open. "Shit, she's done a runner."

Sam checked the wardrobe. "Her suitcase and clothes are still here."

Jarred looked about the room. "She hasn't taken her bag. Talos, go for a run on the beach, she may just be letting off steam. Sam, you take a look around the nearby streets. Simon, stay here and find me Pearce's address then ring it through and get started on Madeline's background check. Nick and I will see if she's gone to Ava's house. Ring me if she shows up."

Nick doubted Madeline was involved in anything illegal. Even so, none of the team would tolerate her being blackmailed. It just remained to be seen which of them would pay Pearce a visit to explain that fact.

Having just changed out of her bikini and sarong for a cool, cotton dress, Ava padded out of her bedroom as the doorbell peeled. She opened it to a fuming Madeline, dressed in gym gear and runners, and looking as if she wanted to punch something.

"Madeline, what's wrong?"

"Damon Pearce is a low life, slime ball and he's trying to blackmail me."

"Arh, you'd better come inside." Ava unlocked the screen door. "Liam's playing with Ajax in the back garden. We can talk out there."

"Thanks."

Ava had a quick look up and down the street, but there was no sign of the police or the black Jeep. She locked the door and led Madeline into the kitchen. "I need to put these potatoes in the oven then we can talk." She quickly opened the oven door and placed the pan of potatoes on the shelf under the lamb roast.

"Done. Let's go out the back." Ava pushed the screen door open and held it for Madeline then they strolled toward the park bench. Ajax had a tennis ball in his mouth and was pouncing at Liam then leaping away, all to Liam's delight.

After brushing leaves off the garden seat, Ava patted the wood beside her. "Why don't you start at the beginning?"

Madeline sank onto the park bench. "Talos and I went to Damon's yacht where I started the interview then he propositioned me. I knocked him back and he threatened to expose something I'd rather keep private. The team would have heard most of it and Jarred will want all the facts, which I'm not prepared to go into." Madeline massaged her temple then focused on Liam and Ajax. "Elliott and I have been married six years, but I've loved him since I was twelve."

"That's so sweet."

Madeline's gaze stayed on Liam. "As a teenager I dreamed of marrying Elliott, then traveling all over the world with him and eventually having our own family." She bit her lip. "We grew up in Sydney and our parents are good friends." She cleared her throat.

"Elliott wanted to go to Melbourne University to get away from his family. Not that they're horrible or anything, just very parochial in their beliefs. He needed space, so I followed him four years later. We got married when I was twenty and then shared a house with Elliott's friend, Trang."

She sighed. "I finished university and got a great job with a leading newspaper then Elliott and Trang quit their Corporate Law jobs to start a software company in Vietnam. My career was just taking off and I didn't want to leave Melbourne. Elliott was cool with my decision but our parents weren't happy. Even though our mothers both have careers, they think a woman's place is with her husband."

Ava frowned. "Couldn't Elliott and Trang have started their company here?"

"Trang's father is very wealthy and offered major financial support if they set the company up in Vietnam. It proved to be a sound investment. They are continually expanding." Madeline's gaze stayed riveted on Liam. "It works for us, but Damon is going to ruin everything."

"Jarred could speak to Damon and warn him off."

Madeline put her head in her hands. "No, that will only make things worse. I need my privacy and I need to get Damon to back off without involving Jarred."

Ava rubbed Madeline's back. "What can Damon do to hurt you?"

"Leak the truth about things I don't want aired publicly. Our parents have no idea Elliott and I spend so much time apart. They're always on about a grandchild, which isn't going to happen."

"You don't want children anymore or you can't have children?"

"I would love children, but it isn't possible."

Ava leaned back against the backrest of the park bench. "We need to get something on Damon and then switch the tables on him."

Madeline raised an eyebrow. "I've searched. He's either very careful or clean."

"I know his housekeeper, Renata, and I'm sure she'd let us in to the house to wait for him. While I keep her busy, you could search for something incriminating. If that fails, we could set him up. I'll hide while you get him to repeat his offer, which I'll record. Blackmail is a criminal offence after all."

"What about Liam and the dog?"

"I'll ring Helen and see if we can leave Liam with her and I'll lock Ajax in the house. We should go now before anyone comes looking for you."

"Jarred is going to be a problem."

Ava chewed her fingernail. "Not if we convince him that it's a trivial matter and a confrontation with Damon would compromise the investigation."

Madeline nodded. "Thank you for helping me, Ava. I don't have anyone else I can turn to."

"That's what friends are for. Let's do this."

Chapter Fifteen

Helen was more than happy to look after Liam, assuming Ava and Madeline were having dinner to discuss their upcoming interview. Ava didn't correct her supposition, just thanked her then drove Madeline out to Roebuck Bay.

As they passed Damon's lavish two-story home, Ava spotted his BMW in the driveway. She parked further down the street and tapped the steering wheel with her finger. "What if I ring and ask him to meet me at his office in town? I'll say it's important. Then as soon as he leaves we go in and search the house."

"Will he go for it?"

"Yes, and when I don't turn up, he'll eventually come back home."

"Do it."

Ava felt a sliver of guilt at the concern in Damon's voice but dismissed it. He wasn't the upstanding man she thought him. He was a blackmailing two-timer. Even though they hadn't officially gone out yet, he was supposed to be keen on her.

Two minutes later they observed him reverse out of his driveway and speed away in the opposite direction.

"Let's go," murmured Madeline.

Renata, Damon's plump but efficient Malaysian housekeeper, opened one of the double doors to them. "Oh, Miss Ava, Mr. Damon, he just go into town."

"That's okay, Renata, he's expecting us, so we'll wait for him, if that's all right? This is Madeline."

"Hello, Miss Madeline. You very beautiful lady."

"Thank you, Renata."

"Come in, please. I'm cooking dinner for Mr. Damon. You wait in living room?"

Ava hesitated. "Actually, I'd like to show Madeline through the house. I'm sure Damon wouldn't mind."

"Oh sure. It very lovely home." Renata closed the door and toddled across the wide foyer and through the rear door to the family room and kitchen beyond.

"Let's start in his study." Ava opened a solid door on the right of the foyer. "If he's got something to hide, it's probably in here."

"Or his bedroom." Madeline closed the door, paced to the desk, and tried a drawer. "Locked." She pulled out two flat metal rods. One had a hook on the end, the other looked like an L-shaped Allan key.

Ava gaped. "Are they lock-picks?"

"Yes, but Bobby pins will work too." Madeline inserted the L-shaped pick into the bottom of the top drawer's keyhole. "This is called the tension wrench. I need to apply a little pressure then insert the other pick into the upper edge and feel for the pins."

Ava watched in fascination as Madeline inserted the hook pick and concentrated.

"Now, I push the pins up until they lock into position, while maintaining torque on the cylinder. It prevents the pins falling back down." She closed her eyes and concentrated. "It takes patience, but once all the pins are locked into position, you turn the tension wrench and *Voila*." She grinned at Ava and pulled the drawer open.

"Wow. Who taught you to do that?"

Madeline inserted her picks into the next drawer. "A seventeen-year-old reformed thief from my pole-dancing class. I locked my keys in my apartment and she offered to pick the lock. I invested in a lock-pick set after that."

"You do pole-dancing?" Ava knew her mouth was gaping but couldn't help it. Madeline was one surprise after another.

"It's fun and keeps me fit. I also do a martial groove class." She opened the drawer. "You start searching while I get the rest of these drawers open."

Ava mentally shook herself. They had a job to do and time was moving on. She skimmed through an accounts ledger and several folders of future investment proposals. "My goodness, Damon's got his fingers in a lot of pies."

Madeline began sorting through the bottom drawer. "Among those in the know, his business skills and talent for investment opportunity are considered brilliant. Why he has to be such an arrogant, self-centered, blackmailing jerk, I don't know."

Ava turned her attention to the bookshelf. "He's always been nice to me and he's never once stepped over the line or put the hard word on me."

Madeline began relocking the desk drawers. "Maybe you brought out the chivalrous side of him, or he was wooing you into a false sense of security."

"Maybe." Ava turned to the filing cabinet. "These drawers are locked too."

"Let me see." Madeline went to work on the lock while Ava looked through Damon's diary. "Appointments, meetings, and lunches. Nothing devious or criminal." She saw her own name circled with the word dinner on the day Nick had arrived.

Madeline pulled the top drawer of the filing cabinet open and skimmed through files. "These are all businesses he owns or has shares in." She closed the drawer and opened the bottom drawer. "Tax, bank accounts, warranties, insurances. Let's check upstairs." She closed the drawer and relocked the cabinet. "He'll have a safe somewhere, but I have no hope of breaking into that."

Ten minutes later, after ignoring five calls from Damon, Ava descended the stairs with Madeline, having found nothing more interesting than a walk-in-robe full of designer suits, shirts, shoes, and ties.

"Now what?" Madeline slowly revolved in the middle of the vast foyer. "Perhaps he keeps sensitive stuff on board the yacht."

"With an armed crew. We have no chance of searching the yacht."

Ava's phone blared. "It's Nick."

"Don't tell him where we are."

"I'm not going to lie to him." Ava hit answer. "Hi, Nick."

"Angel, I'm at your place. Where are you?"

"I'm with Madeline. There's a leg of lamb and potatoes roasting in the oven, would you turn the heat down a little and make me some gravy?"

"Sure. Is Madeline all right?"

"Yes, she's fine. We won't be long. I have to pick Liam up though. He's at Helen's apartment which is over the shop."

"Did Madeline say anything about Damon Pearce blackmailing her?"

"Yes, but everything's fine. We have a plan and we don't want you or Jarred confronting Damon or you could ruin everything."

"What plan? Ava, where are you?"

The soft purr of an engine sounded beyond Damon's front door. "I have to go, Nick. Please stay there. I'll see you soon." She ended the call and silenced her phone.

"You have to hide." Madeline grabbed her wrist and dragged her into the living room opposite Damon's study. They both looked through the drapes to see Damon closing his car door. "Quick, hide behind the sofa," whispered Madeline.

Ava slid behind the chocolate colored leather sofa and put her phone on recorder mode ready to go. "Sit down and try to relax."

"Shush, he's coming." Leather rustled as Madeline slid onto the couch.

The front door opened and heavy footsteps crossed the foyer. Ava pressed record just as Madeline spoke. "Hello, Damon."

"Madeline? What are you doing here?" He sounded stunned to Ava.

"I thought that's what you wanted?"

"Yes, but after our discussion today, I didn't expect you would come."

"Damon, I'm not here because I'm agreeing to submit to your outrageous proposition. I'm here to talk you out of blackmailing me."

"Madeline, I had no intention of following through with my threat. I wanted to get you alone so I could convince you that this is no way to live your life. I tried talking to you in Melbourne, but you refused to have anything to do with me."

"My private life is none of your business."

Ava's mind raced. Damon sounded sincere but why did he think he had the right to interfere in Madeline's life?

Softer footsteps alerted Ava to Renata's imminent arrival.

"Arh, Mr. Damon. You home. I have tea and cake for Miss Ava and her friend."

"Ava?" Damon's voice rose an octave.

Damn. Ava rose from behind the sofa. "Thank you, Renata, but we won't be staying." She met Damon's incredulous eyes as she slid the phone into her pocket.

He stiffened as his gaze dropped to her pocket. "Surely you can stay for one cup of tea, Ava. At least give me a chance to explain." His eyes implored her.

Renata placed a silver tray on the low table in front of Madeline. "You stay and talk to Mr. Damon. I get another cup." She trotted off seemingly not the least curious as to why Ava would be behind the couch.

Edging out, Ava shot a look at Madeline. She was frowning at Damon. "How did you find out about Elliott and me?"

Ava glanced at Damon to find his eyes not on Madeline but on her. His jaw rigid, he slowly turned to Madeline. "I had an opportunity to do business with your husband last year. It was a high-risk venture and as such I had my people investigate him, his business-partner, his family, and you—thoroughly."

"I see." She drew in a deep breath. "I think I need that cup of tea after all." She reached for the china teapot and began pouring as Renata bustled back into the room with a cup for Damon. "You tell me if you need anything else, Mr. Damon?"

"Thank you, Renata. That will be all."

Ava sank onto the couch beside Madeline, mystified. *There had to be more. What did Damon know about Madeline?*

He sat on the couch opposite and contemplated them. "I am not the immoral and devious person you both think I am. I did not break into your safe, Ava, and I knew Madeline wouldn't speak to me unless I didn't give her any choice." He shook his head. "You are both intelligent women. Why can't you see I'm trying to help the two of you?"

Ava shifted uneasily. "I don't know what to think, Damon. When Madeline told me you were blackmailing her, I was shocked. That's why we decided to confront you."

He loosened his tie. "So why get me to drive into town?" He stiffened then leaned back. "You wanted me out of the way, why?"

Ava swallowed then wiped her palms down her jeans. "We thought we might find something we could use to bargain you out of blackmailing Madeline."

He raised one eyebrow. "You searched my house?"

Madeline straightened. "It was that or report you to the police."

Squealing tires turning into the drive heralded another arrival. Ava shot to her feet. "Oh God, that'll be Nick."

"Good. It's about time somebody taught that swine a lesson." Damon shrugged off his suit jacket and threw it as he strode from the living room. The jacket hit a porcelain figurine, knocking it to the tiles, where it smashed into tiny pieces.

Panicked, Ava ran after him. The last thing they needed was Damon confronting Nick. "Stop, please," she yelled, grabbing Damon's arm.

"Shit." Madeline clutched his other arm as the double doors flew open, slamming against the walls behind them.

Nick and Jarred stepped through resembling two avenging warriors. Their faces were set like stone, their eyes promising retribution. Then to Ava's horror Nick plowed his fist in Damon's face, snapping his head back and splitting his lip.

Blood splattered Damon's shirt as he pulled his arms free of Ava and Madeline.

"No," yelled Ava. She tried to step in front of Damon, but Nick hauled her into his arms, then Jarred delivered two fast, heavy punches into Damon's stomach, dropping him to his knees like a sack of potatoes. He gasped for air as blood dripped on the apricot tiles.

"Let me go." Ava fought to get free but Nick held her locked in his arms.

"What are you doing?" Madeline leapt in front of Jarred. "I was handling it."

Jarred lifted Madeline to the side. "I'll deal with you after I've taught this piece of shit a lesson." He snatched Damon's tie and hauled him to his feet. "I'll show you what happens to men who prey on defenseless women." He raised his fist.

Ava gasped as Madeline flung herself against Jarred's chest and clung, preventing him from dispersing any more punches.

"Jarred, please. Damon wasn't serious about the blackmail. We've sorted it out and I am not defenseless."

For a minute Ava didn't know what Jarred would do. His cold gray eyes glowered at Damon as if nothing but grinding him into the dust would suffice. The muscles in Jarred's left arm bulged as he held

Damon upright. His right arm held Madeline protectively against his chest, as if he didn't want to let her go either. *Interesting.*

Ava exhaled as Jarred released Damon, who dropped to the tiles clutching his stomach. "Will someone tell me what the fuck is going on before I have you all arrested?"

Ava could feel Nick's heart pounding against her breast as he stared down at Damon. "We know about the blackmail."

Still holding Madeline, Jarred snarled. "If anyone is going to be arrested, it's you."

A sharp crack drew Ava's attention to the back of the foyer, where Renata stood pointing a rifle at them. "Mr. Damon, you want me to shoot these men?"

Before Ava could do more than gasp, Nick thrust her behind him. She noticed Jarred attempting to do the same thing to Madeline.

She fought to stay in front. "No. I will not be responsible for your death."

"Damn it, Maddy. For once in your life, do as you're told." He lifted her off her feet and propelled her through the front door then turned his back on her.

Damon staggered to his feet. "Put the gun down, Renata."

"But, Mr. Damon, these men hurt you and try to take the ladies?"

"It's a misunderstanding, Renata." Damon scowled at Ava. "I hope you know what you're doing?" His eyes moved to Nick and turned icy. "If you hurt her in any way, I'll see you crucified. Now get out of my house. All of you."

Nick stood his ground. "I'll never hurt Ava and I didn't break into her house or safe, but I'm damn well going to find out who did." He caught Ava's hand then strode to his car, towing her in his wake.

"Nick, slow up. My legs aren't as long as yours."

He halted and spun round, causing her to run into his chest. "Do you have any idea how worried I was, Ava? You and Madeline could have been in serious danger."

"I'm sorry, but maybe someone else is behind the robbery. Damon said he just wants to help Madeline and he's worried about me."

"Like I'd believe anything Pearce says." He marched her to his car and was about to open the front door when Madeline shrieked.

Ava looked back to see Jarred carrying Madeline over one

shoulder. She was thumping his back. "There is nothing to find out, you blasted maniac."

Jarred opened the rear door. "Tell me what he knows, or I'll go back and beat it out of Pearce."

"I told you, he doesn't know anything. He just wanted to talk."

"It looked like he was dragging the two of you off somewhere against your will."

"*We* were holding him back. You hit a defenseless man."

Jarred tossed her onto the rear seat. "He deserved it."

She scrambled up and glared at him. "You're not responsible for me, Jarred."

"Thank God for that. I'd be a mental case if I was."

"Argh. You make me so mad." She flung herself back in the seat and glared at him.

Jarred turned to Nick. "Take her to Ava's. Talos can meet you there and drive her back to the condo to pack. I'll drop Ava's car off and take Ajax for a long run. He's probably as frustrated as me. Why you three guys want a woman messing with your life is beyond me. They're just trouble."

Ava raised an eyebrow. "We're not messing with their lives, we're complementing them." She handed him her car keys. "A man and woman who have communication, chemistry, and compatibility in their lives are far better off than those who don't, believe me, and if they're in love, then they have it all."

Jarred shut Madeline's door then turned to Ava and lowered his voice. "Pearce is not a man to be taken lightly. If he has something on Madeline, you need to tell me."

Ava's cheeks warmed. "I won't betray her confidence."

"What if it gets her killed?" Jarred shook his head then strode down the drive.

"You need to trust us, Angel." Nick opened her door. "To protect Madeline, we need to know what we're up against."

Chapter Sixteen

Nick parked in front of the shop and waited with Madeline while Ava ran in to collect Liam, then he drove them all to Ava's house. Talos was sitting on the front step with Ajax.

Ava glanced at Nick. "How did Ajax get out? I locked him in the house."

"Locks won't keep us out, Angel." Nick turned into the driveway then stopped in front of the garage. "If I'd wanted to break into your house, I could have done it without smashing the glass in your front door."

Madeline opened her door. "Thanks for the lift, Nick."

"You might want to thank Jarred. He promised your husband he'd look after you and Jarred never breaks a promise."

Without replying, she slid out of the car and wandered over to Talos and Ajax.

Releasing his own seatbelt, Liam scrambled after her. "Wait for me, Maddy."

Nick reached for Ava's hand. "Whether Pearce is behind the robbery or not, you need to be extra careful. The police will take me in for questioning if they see me, which is why I need to keep a low profile. I can't protect you if I'm in custody." He rubbed his forehead. "Ava, promise me you won't do anything reckless like today." He raised her hand to his lips then kissed the inside of her wrist. "It would tear me apart if something happened to you."

"It won't." She leaned over the kissed him. "I have you to protect me."

"Ava."

"I need to check on my roast dinner."

"I'll be in after I have a quick word with Talos." He grinned. "I'm happy to see you learned to cook."

She squeezed his hand and climbed out of the car. "Maggie managed to teach me a few skills." Her eyes suddenly flared. "Oh, cripes, I meant to tell you about my father."

"What?" Apprehension slithered down Nick's spine.

"I didn't just find my mother in England. I found my father too. He's a lovely man and a respected politician. When this is all sorted out, I'd like the two of you to meet."

The tension in Nick's shoulders eased. "How come he and Maggie didn't raise you?"

"My father didn't know I existed because his parents convinced Maggie she wasn't good enough for him. Sound familiar?"

"So how did they get back together?"

"Maggie was my father's one true love, and he suspected his parents might have chased her off. He remained a bachelor until Maggie contacted him four years ago. Now they're back together and very happy."

"Why did Maggie give you up to Hector and Shirley?"

"She wasn't able to look after me, go to work, and attend university. Hector and Shirley couldn't have children. So in his righteous way, Hector convinced Maggie she was unfit to be a mother and that I'd be better off with him and Shirley. It's strange to refer to them by their names, but I will never call them by anything else now."

"Hector manipulated your mother's circumstances."

"Yes, but that's in the past. Why don't you ask Jarred to dinner? I think Madeline could do with some alone time."

"Sure." Nick watched Ava run across the lawn, sweep Liam up in a bear hug, kiss him, then put him down again and jog up the steps. He smiled. She was right in what she'd told Jarred. Communication, chemistry, and compatibility were far better than a life of casual encounters. She wouldn't convince Jarred though. His father's affairs had scarred Jarred's teenage years and turned him off marriage.

Nick climbed out and leaned against the car, hidden from the neighbors by the shrubs. He observed Madeline sitting on the grass, idly patting Ajax as Liam told her about the big fish he'd caught. Her attention shifted to Jarred as he parked Ava's car on the road then strode up the path.

Jarred paused and then continued across the lawn to speak to Talos, yet his gaze kept dropping to Madeline as she chatted to Liam.

Nick grimaced. Madeline was a stunningly attractive, intelligent, and engaging woman. She was also married to Elliott, a decent guy who'd helped them out in Vietnam. None of the boys would cross the line, but Madeline embodied a distraction Jarred didn't need.

She suddenly stood up, dusted bits of grass off her backside, and scowled at Jarred. Something he said had her hackles bristling *again.*

Pulling his cap lower, Nick strolled across the lawn and met Talos' concerned gaze. "What's up?"

"Jarred wants Madeline to fly home first thing in the morning so we can concentrate on Pearce without the risk of her getting caught in the middle."

"I'm not about to let an egotistical brute rule my life," said Madeline stubbornly. "I came to Broome to help you get close to Damon. We did that today and you now have his crew under twenty-four-hour surveillance. I'm not leaving until I interview Ava and give her the publicity she deserves."

"Madeline." Jarred's voice deepened in warning. "I will not allow you to hinder our investigation. We were lucky today that my team's cover wasn't blown."

"I didn't ask you to come after me. And in future I'd appreciate it if you'd all mind your own business. I am perfectly capable of looking after myself."

Nick shifted impatiently. "How long will it take to interview Ava?"

"No more than a couple of days. I need some photos for the spread and then I'll get out of your hair." Her phone rang. "Hi, Elliott... I'm fine." She narrowed her eyes at Jarred. "No, I haven't been doing anything out of the ordinary. How's things with you?" Her eyes widened. "What are you doing in Sydney?"

Nick glanced at Jarred who also followed the one sided conversation.

Madeline turned her back slightly. "Elliot, I need to talk to you, face to face, and I've decided to sell the apartment and move back to Sydney. Can you hang around for a few days?"

Suddenly the color drained out of Madeline's face. "When— Was anything stolen? Did they do any damage?"

Nick raised an eyebrow at Jarred then lowered his voice. "You think it's something to do with her death threats?"

"Possibly."

Madeline sighed. "Okay, ring me at exactly ten-thirty tomorrow night. I'll be at the apartment by then. I will, bye." She drew in a deep breath. "Looks like you get your wish. Somebody broke into my Melbourne apartment last night. My neighbor couldn't reach me, so he rang Elliot. I need to go home."

Jarred frowned. "Perhaps you should go to your parents in Sydney until we make sure the break-in is not connected with your death threats. I'll speak with Elliott."

Madeline crossed her arms under her breasts and glared at Jarred. "You dealt with those people in Vietnam, and since when are you and my husband such good buddies?"

Jarred held up his hands. "Madeline, Elliott contacted me. He's concerned there may be another crime syndicate after you. Why don't you stay with your parents?"

"No." She turned her back on them. "I'll say goodbye to Ava then I'm jogging back to the resort *by myself*."

Nick watched her stalk into the house. "How does Elliott stay sane?"

Talos shrugged. "I believe Elliott and Madeline hardly spend any time together. It doesn't say a lot for their marriage."

Nick turned to Jared. "Will you inform Elliott about the blackmail?"

"Not yet. Simon's doing a deeper background check on the Shaws and their families. If Pearce discovered something worthy of blackmail, then I want to know what it is." He looked at Talos. "Tail Madeline. Ajax had better stay here."

Hearing his name, Ajax trotted over to head-butt Jarred's thigh.

"Hey, mate. "Jarred gave him a brisk rub. "I know you'd like a run, but we can't blow your cover."

Ajax barked as if in total agreement.

Liam scampered across the grass and threw himself at Nick. "Daddy, you want to go fishing? We can show Maddy where Ajax chased the seagulls today."

Nick picked Liam up. "It's too dark, buddy, and Mummy has our dinner cooking. How about we go to the beach tomorrow with Sam and Ajax?"

"'Kay."

Nick met Jarred's gaze. "I meant to ask if Simon's discovered who hacked into his email account?"

"Not yet. I've contacted Fergie and he reckons no one has been in my house other than the cleaner, and she has been with my family for years. If someone did gain entry to my house, they'd still need to breach our operation's room."

"So they have to be hacking Simon externally, but why?"

"That's what we need to discover. I'll phone my cleaner later tonight. In the meantime, Simon's set a trace for when our hacker logs in again. So far he's staying one step ahead of us."

"That's interesting. I've never known anyone to get the better of Simon."

Talos nodded. "Which is why he's agitated. Simon knows all the computer scientists within Australia's universities and intelligence agencies. This is someone with a unique footprint, similar to the professor who mentored Simon."

"Which means what?" Nick asked, lifting Liam up to sit on his shoulders.

Jarred slowly rubbed his hands together. "It means the hacker more than likely studied under the same person as Simon."

"So let's speak to this professor. He might click to who it could be."

"We can't. He fell or jumped to his death in Nepal four years ago after being accused of cyber fraud. Millions of dollars were embezzled from global financial institutions via a complex virus that harvested online transactions. The money was wired to untraceable accounts. It's known as botnet—a robotic network, which is a network of computers covertly operated by talented hackers. It was Simon who found the footprint leading back to his old professor."

"Did they find his body?" asked Talos.

"No, the mountain was covered in treacherous ice and snow. By the time a recovery team got up there, no one could identify the right crevice."

"Could the professor have faked his own death?"

"Simon thinks it's unlikely. An experienced Sherpa was with him when he disappeared and the professor's family meant the world to him. Initially they were monitored in case he tried to contact them. He didn't."

"Well, if anyone can track our hacker, it's Simon."

"Yes. In the meantime, don't post anything sensitive or confidential in your emails. We'll use our sat phones."

The screen door opened and Madeline stepped onto the veranda. She waved to Liam then skipped down the steps. "I'll see you round. Good luck with the investigation."

They watched her jog to the end of the street then Talos gave a salute and set off after her. Nick rubbed the bristles on his chin. "I think you should inform Elliott Shaw about the blackmail. He has a right to know what Peace is up to."

"What if Madeline doesn't want her husband to know?"

Nick frowned. "You think she's hiding an affair?"

"I don't know, but she's hiding something."

"Ava has cooked a roast dinner, you want to eat with us?"

"Sure, it smells great."

Nick chuckled. "And you've got Buckley's chance of Madeline inviting you to dinner. Maybe you could relax a little and show Ava you're not so imitating."

Jarred snorted. "By the way she stood up to us the other night and then ordered me to carry Madeline to bed, she's not intimidated in the least. I must be losing my touch."

After a quick scan of the street, Nick called Ajax and they trooped into the house.

Ava was covering the roast as they converged on the small kitchen. "I'm just resting the meat. There's beer in the fridge or wine if you'd prefer."

"Beer." Nick opened the fridge and handed Jarred a Crown lager. "I see Simon's stocked the fridge with the essentials."

Ava laughed. "Yes, there's more beer in there than food. Where is Simon?"

Jarred lounged against the back door watching Ava whisk the gravy. "He'll be here shortly. I have him working on something."

Nick drew out a couple of chairs then lifted Liam over his head and sat him on the one with a booster seat.

Ajax immediately rested his head on the edge of Liam's chair, his soulful eyes glued to the little boy's face. "Friends for life." Nick grinned at Ava. "What would you like to drink, Angel?"

"A glass of Shiraz, please."

Jarred pulled out a chair and sat. "Nick told me what happened to keep you two apart, and I've since made my own enquiries. No official from the Army or any other defense branch informed Hector Mitchell that Nick had been killed."

"So we figured."

"At least you know the truth now and who your real parents are."

Ava's gaze shot to Nick. He held up his hands. "I didn't say a word."

Jarred's lips twitched. "We occasionally take special assignments from several government agencies, which is why we have approval to use a Black Hawk on occasion. In return I am given certain favors. When Talos informed me your real father is a prominent member of the British Government, I had it verified. What interesting parents you both have."

Nick snorted. "Ava yes, but not me. My mother was a waste of space and God only knows who my father is."

Jarred raised an eyebrow. "Still in denial?"

Ava met Nick's gaze. "What is Jarred talking about?"

"Nothing of substance." Nick scowled at his boss. "Just rumors and hearsay spread by bureaucrats within the defense force who have nothing better to do."

"Hmm." Jarred turned to Ava. "When I was selecting my special ops team in the SAS, I did a background check on all the applicants. I only wanted the best of the best. I needed two Black Hawk pilots and although Nick was on top of my list, he had a reputation for being a little too daring, which can be good and bad. I was considering my options when two highly ranked officers came to see me. They had a personal interest in seeing Nick on my team."

"Why?"

Nick shifted uncomfortably. He'd worked damned hard to get where he was and hated people assuming he'd been fast tracked because of who his father *might* be. "Forget it, Ava. It's not important."

She looked at Jarred. "Tell me?"

Jarred inclined his head. "I don't like being manipulated, so I gave the men a choice to tell me what their interest was, or I would dig for the truth. They knew I had the resources and meant every word. They confided off the record that one of them might be Nick's father."

"His father?" Her gaze locked with Nick's.

Jarred's lips thinned. "The two officers did their SAS training together, and unknowingly each indulged in a brief liaison with Nick's mother at the same time. She approached each of them for money to terminate an unwanted pregnancy, which they agreed to. They wouldn't have known Nick existed except for the fact his mother went after them for more money years later."

Ava gasped.

Nick shrugged. "My mother probably played that card on lots of guys."

"Possibly." Jarred lightly tapped his fingertips on the table. "However, they went to Broome to confront her and discovered Nick had recently been beaten up by his mother's boyfriend, and was in serious trouble for theft and property damage. It drew some ugly attention, which could have reflected on these men, who by now were well on their way up the military chain of command."

"What did the officers do?" Ava's knuckles whitened as she clenched her fists.

Jarred's smile didn't reach his eyes. "They paid a visit to Nick's mother and her boyfriend. The boyfriend got what he deserved then the officers threatened to have them both locked up if they ever touched the boy again or tried to extort money. The officers met with the school principal, councilor, local magistrate, and Barry Sanders. For a kid who'd been left to fend for himself most of his life, Nick had a quick mind and extremely good grades. The two officers and Barry decided to take an interest in his future."

Ava's eyes widened at Nick. "That's the reason Barry urged you into the Army."

"Or because I developed a love of helicopters." Nick stood. "How about I carve the roast."

Ava ignored him and turned back to Jarred. "In your opinion, is one of these men Nick's father?"

"Yes." Jarred's gaze flicked to Nick then back to her. "I've interacted with both men over the years and each has kept a keen interest in Nick's career." He hesitated. "I don't know which of them is his father, but neither was happy when he opted out of the SAS. They pressured me to persuade him to stay in the Army."

Nick laughed. "Like you, Jarred, I don't like being manipulated."

"So why leave our team? It's what you've fought for all your life—respect, recognition, admiration, and the camaraderie of men who are closer than brothers. We are alive many times over because of your damn skill and calmness under duress."

A cool breeze flowed through the kitchen window, rattling the blind before wafting around Nick's neck. A shiver ran down his spine as his gaze moved to Ava. He felt like he was being ripped in two. She hadn't said a word, but stared at him with anxious eyes. Nick cleared his throat. "My decision stands. I want to be with Ava and Liam."

Jarred spread his arms. "Then relocate them to Sydney. I've looked into Ava's business model and it can be run from anywhere in the world."

Nick clenched his jaw. "Ava and Liam are my priority. They want to stay here, so this is where I need to be."

Liam looked up from patting Ajax. "Daddy, I don't like it here. It's too hot. We can come live with you then I can play with Ajax, and fly Black Hawks, and teach Maddy how to fish. That's a good idea isn't it?"

Nick's gaze shot to Ava fidgeting with her napkin.

Her troubled eyes lifted to Jarred. "What makes you so sure one of the officers is Nick's father?"

"They're identical twins, and he's the spitting image of them."

"Oh, Nick." Ava's heart melted for him.

CHAPTER SEVENTEEN

Ava had so many thoughts crashing round in her brain she couldn't concentrate on her designs or accounts. She'd even snapped at Liam over breakfast, which was a first and had them both in tears. So chirpy and excited, he'd barely been able to sit still, positive they were about to pack up and follow Nick anywhere in the world. Once upon time she would have. Now she didn't have a clue what to do. Liam would be devastated if his daddy left. And there lay Ava's biggest fear. If Nick stayed, would he lose his zest for life, and resent her for taking him away from the job and people who inspired his sense of worth? Did she have the right to demand he give that up? Jarred was right, she could run her business from anywhere, but what if Nick's job killed him? "God, I don't know what to do."

He'd made love to her so tenderly last night, as if he knew how fragile she was feeling. Neither slept as they clung to each other. Had he been as terrified as she was that they wouldn't get their happy ever after? Was it better to love him with every fiber of her being, knowing that one day he might not come home, or slowly watch his thirst for life shrivel up doing a job that bored him to death?

"Hello, anyone home?" Madeline called from the front door.

"Screen door's unlocked. I'm in the kitchen." Ava wiped down the bench then threw the dishcloth in the sink. "Want a cuppa?"

"Love one." Madeline swept into the kitchen looking gorgeous in an electric blue blouse, white jeans, and red-heeled sandals. "You ready to do that interview? I've got a couple of hours before I have to be at the airport." Her butterscotch-blonde hair swung loosely about her shoulders, longer than Ava had imagined, her make-up so well applied it emphasized her vibrant blue eyes.

"Wow, you looked fantastic, Madeline."

"Thank you. I love your earrings. Are they one of your creations?

Ava touched a teardrop pearl. "Yes, these are from last year's collection. Sorry I'm not organized. I had a restless night and Nick didn't wake me when he left this morning."

"No rush. My flight doesn't leave until eleven."

"Do you need a lift to the airport?"

"No." Madeline rolled her eyes. "Talos dropped me here and Jarred is picking me up in two hours to personally deliver me to the airport. Chief Steele Feather is determined to see me out of his hair." She opened her handbag and took out a notepad and camera. "I have this nagging feeling I shouldn't leave."

Ava filled the kettle. "You've already been a great help and you need to check on your apartment."

"I know, but when I get these feelings, they're usually right." She sighed. "Still, I need to put my apartment up for sale, and I've arranged for Elliott to ring me at ten-thirty, so I really can't stay."

"How do you want to do the interview?" Ava checked her white blouse and black skirt for any of Liam's jam fingerprints.

Madeline considered her for a moment. "Do you have something softer or even vibrant, that shows your creative energy?"

"Erm, sure. You want to look through my wardrobe?"

"I'd love to, and then we'll work on your hair and make-up."

"I tend to like the natural look or very light makeup."

"I'm thinking just a hint of color to highlight your eyes and what you're wearing."

"Okay."

In the end Madeline chose a dramatic jungle print caftan and a vibrant purple blouse. Yet Ava couldn't help unzipping the protective cover to a delicate full-length chiffon gown in the softest shade of cream. It had a sweetheart neckline and hundreds of miniature pearls embroidered into the bodice. She brushed her fingertips over the delicate fabric, swallowing the lump of emotion welling in her throat. She'd only tried the gown on once, in a boutique in Perth, and it had been love at first sight. She'd imagined herself a princess from a fairytale, awaiting her dragon slayer knight. This would have been her wedding dress.

It could still be.

Ava chewed her bottom lip. "Let's go with the purple blouse."

"Sure." Madeline pulled her white jeans off and handed them to Ava. "Wear these with the blouse. Black is too harsh. I'll wrap a towel around me, in case you have any visitors."

Ava dressed then they went into the bathroom and Madeline scooped Ava's red mass of curls up in a soft style, leaving several long coils draped around her shoulders. Then she applied a light make up, showing Ava how to accentuate her eyes and cheekbones.

Other than moisturizer, block out, and a little lip-gloss, Ava rarely used makeup unless she attended a special function, but she'd never looked like this. The woman in the mirror looked like a glamorous cover girl.

"Now we need to take a photo of you at your work desk and another out in the garden with Liam and Ajax. They're very quiet, where are they?"

Ava smiled. "Simon took them to the beach to meet Nick."

"We'll get them to come back in an hour. We should be finished with the interview by then. I can't get rid of this feeling I should stay. I'm not superstitious, but...never mind."

"Can someone else check out your apartment?"

"No. Show me your work room."

Ava picked up her jewel box and led Madeline down the hall, then sat at her table and pretended to work on a pearl choker. The thief hadn't stolen any jewelry from Ava's bedroom, which seemed mighty unusual.

Madeline took several shots then morphed into the professional journalist, asking Ava a stream of questions, her pen flying as she wrote everything down in shorthand.

They were sitting on the bench in the back garden having a cup of tea when Simon strolled out of the kitchen with Liam and Ajax on his heels. "Ladies, you might want to lock the front door in future. Anyone could walk in."

Ava bit her lip. "Sorry, we got sidetracked. Where's Nick?"

"He's staying out of sight until a senior inspector in the AFP gives us the all clear. The last thing we need is a cop attempting to arrest Nick. It wouldn't end well for the cop. I'll be inside if you need me."

"Okay, thanks, Simon." Ava smiled at Liam. "How was the beach, munchkin?"

"So fun." His eyes were shining as he clambered onto Ava's knee and wrapped his arms around her neck. "You look beautiful, Mummy."

Madeline encourage Ajax to lay at Ava's feet then stood back and shot what seemed like a hundred photos. Liam, oblivious to the camera, prattled out every minute detail of his morning adventure.

Ava ached with love for this precious child and Nick who owned her heart and always would. They were meant to be together, but what did the future hold for the three of them? She squashed down the panic threatening to overwhelm her and hugged Liam tightly. "I'm sorry I snapped at you this morning, sweetheart. I didn't sleep well and that made me a big cranky puss."

"That's okay, Mummy. I get cranky when I'm tired too."

Jarred strolled round the side of the house looking his usual, suave self in a pair of jeans and white T-shirt, but for all his good looks there lurked a lethal quality just under his skin that scared the life out of Ava. She could easily imagine him the leader of an elite, SAS anti-terrorist group. A shiver ran down her spine. Was he still the leader of a *privately* run anti-terrorist group? Was there a lot more to his security firm than met the eye?

His gaze fixed on Madeline. "All done?"

"Yes." She dropped the camera into her bag and turned to Ava. "I'll type up my notes on the flight to Perth then email it and the photos to my editor before my connecting flight to Melbourne."

Ava hid her grin as Jarred's gaze dropped to the bath-sheet around Madeline's waist. "You want to ditch the towel so we can get going?"

"If you insist." Madeline whipped it off and tossed is loosely over one shoulder before sashaying past Jarred. The sheer blouse just covered her butt, highlighting her long tanned legs. As Madeline climbed the back steps, Ava caught a glimpse of the white thong she wore under the blouse.

Madeline opened the back door then sent Jarred a sultry smile. "Give me five minutes, Chief." She blew him a kiss. "Then I'm all yours."

Ava almost choked at Madeline's audacity. The woman had to have a death wish to take on someone like Jarred. What if he took her bravado the wrong way?

Surprisingly his lips twitched. "One day that sassy mouth is going to get you into deep shit, sweetheart. Elliott must be very sure of you, or he's got his head buried so deep in the sand he's brain dead. If you were mine, I wouldn't let you out of my God damn sight."

Ava caught her breath as Madeline laughed vivaciously, her stunning eyes shining with devilment. "Honey, if I was yours, you'd be the luckiest *God damn* man alive."

As the door closed behind Madeline, Jarred turned his attention to Ava. "Inspector Gibbs has spoken to your insurance company and the owner of the missing gems. They've agreed to wait for our findings before they take further action. Inspector Gibbs has set up a conference call at the police station at four-thirty and would like you there."

"Okay." Ava lowered Liam to the ground and took his hand. "I'd better return Madeline's jeans." God this man rattled her. Taking a deep breath, she started toward the house then stopped. "Madeline has a funny feeling she shouldn't leave."

"She's a journalist, Ava, and she'll say anything to stay in the loop."

"I don't think so. She said these feelings are rarely wrong."

"And you believe her?"

"Yes, I do." Ava climbed the steps. She needed to finish her accounts and order the pearls for Talos' wife's earrings. The media mogul would have to wait. No way could she afford to replace those gems. Hopefully, Helen would watch Liam while she attended the tele-conference. The rest she would figure out later.

Nick sat between Ava and Jarred at a large table in an interview room of the police station. The humidity was building, as was a storm by Nick's reckoning. Two police officers stood either side of the door, looking like they wanted to cuff him then toss his ass into a cell and throw away the key. On the opposite side of the table sat Senior Sergeant Evans and a woman from Ava's insurance company. At the end of the table sat a lawyer representing the media mogul, who had agreed to play along as a favor to Madeline Shaw. Nick slid his sweaty palms along his cargo shorts. If not for Madeline, Gibbs, and Jarred, he'd be incarcerated in a cell awaiting trial for a crime he didn't commit.

Nick appreciated their efforts, but why the fuck couldn't people look at his exemplary Army record, or his bravery award for saving a bunch of civilians and elite soldiers while under hostile fire in the middle of a war zone? Shit, any of the fucking missions he'd risked his life for. Why did his past always come back to haunt him? As a kid, he only stole food when he was desperate. The car had been an attempt to escape the horrors of his home-life. The graffiti a cry for help. Fucking hell, he'd been beaten up, starving, and terrified.

Thankfully, he had some powerful people in his corner, but it still pissed him off to have an act of desperation held against him. He was fricking over it.

The phone rang and Sergeant Evans hit a button. "Inspector Gibbs, you're on speaker." He introduced everyone at the table.

Gibb's voice resonated round the room. "How you doing, Nick?"

"Other than being pissed off, I'm fine. What's this all about?"

"We've notified all the major gem wholesalers to keep an eye out for the stolen goods and we're got people watching the black market trade. My gut feeling is the gems are still in Broome."

"So give me carte blanche. I'll get the thief to talk and find the gems."

"No, we want you to do nothing for the moment."

"You can't be serious." Nick stood, sending his chair crashing to the floor. The two policemen by the door reached for their Tasers.

Jarred slowly came to his feet beside Nick, his eyes deadly cold as he stared at the two officers. "Put those toys away. This man could kill you with his bare hands before either of you got those prongs anywhere near his body."

Ava and the woman from the insurance company gasped.

Shit. Nick closed his eyes. "Too much information, Boss."

Jarred raised an eyebrow. "You are an elite soldier who has put your life on the line fighting terrorist organizations all over the world. These people can fucking give you the respect you deserve." He looked at Ava and the other woman. "Excuse my language, ladies, but I will not have one of my men treated like a criminal."

"Calm down." Gibbs's order had everyone looking at the phone. "For those present, Jarred Steele and his team are officially investigating another matter with the full backing of the AFP, which means everything said in this room comes under the Secrecy Act. If any of you repeat anything you hear, you will be arrested and dealt with severely."

The two policemen holstered their Tasers.

Nick glanced at Ava's pale face. *Shit.*

Gibbs continued. "Nick, you are to keep your head low. I want your word you won't let your personal dislike for Damon Pearce influence your actions."

"Yeah, you got it."

"Good. In the meantime, keep working on unearthing that smuggling ring. They could be tied in with Ava's thief. Sergeant Evans will assist if needed."

Nick placed his hands on the table. "Personal dislikes aside, Pearce is involved."

"You have no evidence. Keep tabs on his house and boat. I don't want him to scratch himself without us knowing. I should be in Broome tomorrow morning. If anything urgent comes up, you can reach me on my cell."

"Not if you're on a commercial flight," said Nick.

"I'll be traveling by private jet."

Nick raised an eyebrow at Jarred. An enigmatic Arab owned the jet that Inspector Zac Gibbs had used to get the team out of Vietnam. The Arab also owned the Fijian Island they'd retreated to while things cooled down. Add the fact Gibbs lived in a penthouse overlooking Sydney Harbour, drove a luxury car that a person on his salary couldn't afford, and—according to Simon's checks—didn't have a birth certificate, was it any wonder they viewed him with suspicion? Gibbs may have assisted them in Vietnam and helped saved Madeline and Jane's lives, but by shooting the trafficking Kingpin, he also buried any possibility of the team discovering if the AFP had another mole.

"What about my client's missing gems, Inspector Gibbs?" asked the lawyer, a balding, round-faced man in a black suit and white shirt that strained across his fat gut.

"When Jarred's team uncover the smugglers and the true thief, Miss Mitchell will get the gems back and finish his order. Please pass on our thanks to your client for his patience. I will be in touch as soon as we have any new information."

A musical ringtone broke the silence. "Sorry." Ava glanced at her phone. "I need to take this." She turned to the window and put the phone to her ear. "Helen, I won't be much longer. Is everything okay?"

Gibbs continued to speak, but Nick tuned out to concentrate on Ava. She'd gone unnaturally still. Her gaze lifted to his. He read shock, then terror before she dropped the phone and slid down the wall to the floor, her haunted eyes locked on him.

"Fuck." He dropped to the floor and pulled her into his arms, then scooped up the phone. "Helen, this is Nick Flanagan. What's wrong?"

"T...two men in balaclavas barged into the shop. They...punched me in the f...face and then t...tied me up. They've taken Liam and they s...said if you or Ava call the police he dies. I'm so sorry, I tried to stop them."

Ice filled Nick's veins. *I'll fucking kill them.* "We're on our way." He stood and helped Ava up then met Jarred's hooded gaze. "Two masked men snatched Liam from the shop. One of them punched Ava's partner before tying her up."

Everyone in the room stood, the shock evident on their faces. Nick shook his head. "You know nothing. The kidnappers said they will kill Liam if we go to the police." He gritted his teeth. Rarely was there a good outcome from a kidnapping.

Jarred nodded and pinned Sergeant Evans with his steely-eyed gaze. "We are better equipped to handle this than you. I'd appreciate your word you will stay out of it."

"Look here, Colonel..."

Jarred strode round the table and opened the door for Nick and Ava, then turned to face the other occupants. "Not a word to anyone or that little boy's life could be in danger."

Sergeant Evans exhaled. "We have people who can handle this sort of thing."

Jarred's deadly eyes flicked from Nick to the sergeant. "Not as fast or as effective as my people. Gibbs, tell them to stay out of it and get here as fast as you can." He closed the door and strode ahead of Nick as he pulled out his phone. "Sam, get the team together and meet me at the hangar. Liam's been kidnapped."

In a daze of shocked disbelief, Ava couldn't stop shaking and sobbing.

How could this happen? Nick screeched to a stop outside her shop and Ava bolted for the door. Finding it locked, she searched her handbag for the key then dropped it twice. Nick took the keys and unlocked the door then held her back as he pulled a gun from under the back of his jacket and silently crept toward the back office.

"She's here." Nick knelt beside Helen tied to an upturned chair on the floor. The back door stood wide open.

Ava's gaze dropped to Helen and she gasped at the blood congealed on Helen's lip and a large bruise forming under her left eye.

Helen had one arm free and the phone in her hand. "I'm so sorry. It happened so fast, they took me by surprise."

"Stay with her, Ava. I'll check out back." Nick ran out into the lane.

Ava shook so violently; she struggled to untie the knots as tears poured down her face. "Are you hurt anywhere else?"

"No."

She helped Helen to another chair then grabbed some ice from the fridge and wrapped it in a hand towel. "Here, put this against your face."

Nick strode through the back door. "Describe the men."

"I can't, they wore balaclavas." Helen wiped her running nose.

"Accents. Did they sound Australian, Asian, what?"

"The one who hit me sounded Australian. I thought they wanted to rob the shop, but he dragged me out here then tied me up. The other one picked up Liam who started kicking and screaming. I begged them not to hurt him but then one of the men hit me again. He said to tell you not to call the police or Liam would die. He said they'd be in touch with you."

"Me personally, or Ava?"

"His exact words were, 'tell his parents we'll be in touch.'"

Nick remained so calm, Ava wanted to shake him. This was their baby, an innocent little boy who wouldn't hurt a fly. "How do they know my number or Nick's? This is bullshit, we need to get the police involved."

"No." Nick stared at Helen. "Describe them, height, build, hands, what were they wearing, anything?"

Helen drew in a shaky breath, ringing her hands as she looked from Ava to Nick. "They wore dark clothes and sunglasses, not skinny, not fat." She swallowed. "Average builds and height. I don't know them."

"I take it they came in through the front of the shop? I need to look at your surveillance footage."

"There isn't any. The camera hasn't worked in a long while, and I didn't have the money to get it repaired."

"Geez. All right, tell me exactly what happed."

"Liam wanted to draw so we were out here. He'd been telling me you were all going to live together on the other side of Australia with someone called Ajax." She touched her swollen lip. "The bell on the shop door tinkled so I went to see who it was. What are you going to do?"

"Nothing at the moment. I'll ring a taxi to take you to the hospital, but please promise me you won't contact the police?"

"I don't need the hospital, and I won't say a word. I don't want anything to happen to Liam."

"Thank you." He glanced at Ava. "Sweetheart, we need to go to your place and wait for their call."

"How can you be so calm?" Ava wanted to throw up, rant and rave, punch something. "I need Liam back. You've got that team of elite soldiers three minutes away. Go get your team and find our baby."

"I will, Angel."

"What could grown men want with an innocent little boy?" *Maybe they're perverts.* "Oh my God." Agony ripped through her heart. She didn't care that her screams sounded like a wild animal. She was being ripped to shreds. "He must be terrified."

Nick pulled her into his arms. "Whatever it takes, I promise I'll get him back. I need you to believe in me, Angel. To trust me."

He'd said those exact words to her after he'd announced he was joining the SAS and canceling their wedding. She stared into his hazel eyes, the deeper hue mirroring his emotions. It was like looking into his soul. The sincerity rocked her.

"I do believe in you. I do trust you. I always have. I always will."

Chapter Eighteen

Almost two am and no word. Nick paced back and forth across the small kitchen. He had his gun holstered, his knife in its sheath strapped to his right leg, and the sniper rifle lay with his bullet proof vest on the kitchen bench. He'd never prayed or sworn so hard in his life.

He looked over Simon's shoulder at the two state of the art computers set up on the table. One ready to run a trace the second the kidnappers called, the other ready to map out their route. These computers were cutting edge, their technology years ahead of anything the average person could get their hands on, but would they be enough?

It didn't ease Nick's frustration one iota. He looked across to Sam set up at the coffee table in the lounge, manning the bugs on Pearce's boat. If the kidnappers hadn't called by morning, the team would swoop, searching Pearce's boat, house, office, and any other business he owned. He and every one of his employees would be interrogated.

Nick gnashed his teeth. History showed most kidnappers killed their victims and got rid of the bodies before the ransom was paid, or soon after. It was rare for victims to survive. Nick had been involved in several kidnappings, which only ended well because the team had ignored protocol and gone in fast and hard.

It was a battle to stay positive. He drew in a deep breath and glanced out the window. The storm had been raging for a couple of hours. Jarred stood on the veranda, phone to his ear idly scratching Ajax's head. How Jarred could remain level headed and cool was beyond Nick. In SAS circles the colonel was known as the man of ice and steel. Madeline's analogy of Chief Steele Feather was right on target. It was only since assembling his special ops team that Jarred had lightened up a little and shown them his sharp sense of humor, although he remained a competitive son of a bitch. They all were. Nick could only be thankful Jarred had come to his aid. He might have been a tough commander, but he always backed his men and did what needed doing.

Nick adjusted the cuff of his black body suit. Slash resistant, lightweight, flexible and worth every cent. Jarred and Talos had gone out to the Black Hawk earlier to retrieve their weapons, suits, and night vision goggles from the purpose-built storage safe behind the back seats. The team was now dressed, locked, loaded, and ready to move the second they had a location.

Ryan had stayed at the hangar and carefully pre-flighted the Black Hawke, ensuring it was ready for startup. He had the auxiliary power unit running so that they would have the best possible chance of being ready for takeoff the minute they got to the hangar.

Gibbs had eyes at the bus terminal and airport. He kept in constant communication with Sergeant Evans and Jarred. They had confiscated CCT footage from local businesses. It hadn't helped.

Nick slipped into the hall to check on Ava. Her bedroom was empty, so he strode to the bathroom and leaned against the door. He relaxed at the sound of running water. Ava's distress had played on them all. It shredded Nick to see her like this, and God help him, he didn't know how she'd recover if things turned out badly. Whoever did this was going to die a very painful death. Nick returned to the kitchen and pulled out a chair. Doing nothing was sending him demented. "Where's Pearce?"

Simon glanced up. "Still at his house according to Sergeant Evans."

"What about Walsh? Has anyone seen him?"

"No. He hasn't been near the house this evening and neither has anyone carrying something big enough to conceal a small boy. Gibbs is organizing warrants so the police can search every property and business owned by Pearce the minute they come through."

"Shit, I feel so powerless. Why haven't the bastards called?"

Simon shrugged. "They're making us sweat. Helen's called a couple of times. I introduced myself as Ava's cousin and told her we haven't heard anything yet."

The back door opened and Jarred strode in. "We've got troops arriving at dawn to begin a foot search. You heard anything?"

"No." Nick rubbed his bristly jaw. "They set me up, but what could they gain by taking Liam? These bastards don't know who they're tangling with, but they will once I get my hands on them."

"Did they ring?" Ava stood in the doorway wearing jeans and a T-shirt, her eyes puffy and red-rimmed.

Nick stood then wrapped his arms around her. "Not yet, babe."

Jarred's phone rang. He whipped it out. "Talk to me."

Nick held his breath as Jarred sank onto a chair, closed his eyes, and clenched his fist so hard the knuckles turned stark white against his tanned skin. Nick broke into a sweat as the color drained from Jarred's face, leaving a grey tinge.

Fuck, what the hell?

"What is it?" whispered Ava, her nails digging into Nick's waist.

Jarred opened his eyes then shook his head at them. "Don't fuck with me, Gibbs. Was she there or not?" He stood and turned his back to them. "Christ, I watched her board the fucking plane. Yeah, keep me informed." He placed the phone on the bench then dropped his head into his hands. "Fuck."

"What?" Nick flicked a glance at the others. In all the hostile and deadly situations they'd found themselves, never had the colonel been anything but controlled.

Jarred scrubbed his face with his fingers then drew in a deep breath and turned around. "A small bomb detonated in Madeline's apartment. The neighbors on one side and below suffered extensive damage." He swallowed. "Gibbs said three people have been hospitalized. Madeline isn't among them."

"When did this happen?" Simon almost croaked it out.

"Ten-thirty eastern standard time. Half an hour ago. Exactly when she arranged for her husband to call."

"No." Ava deflated in Nick's arms, babbling. "She can't be dead. She can't be."

Shocked to his soul, Nick held Ava against his chest as she bawled. He met Jarred's dead gaze. "Maybe she's not there. Simon can ping her phone location."

"It's been done. Gibbs said they couldn't get a reading. It's either off or...."

"Pearce was pissed at Madeline, and he wouldn't know she's gone home, but would he resort to something like this to settle a score?"

"It could be the person who sent her the death threats," murmured Sam.

Simon cleared his throat. "We need to pay Pearce a visit. If he's behind the robbery, then he's behind Liam's kidnapping and possibly the bombing."

Ava lifted a tear stained face. "What if Liam recognizes his kidnappers?"

Nick didn't want to think about that. The odds of getting Liam back were slim to none unless they got a break soon.

Jarred raked his fingers through his collar-length hair. "Stay here, I'll take Talos with me and talk to Pearce. Keep monitoring the boat and house. If he moves, I want to know."

Jarred's phone rang. He swiped it up. "Gibbs?"

The room was silent as everyone waited on tenterhooks. Nick held his breath, hoping for good news.

"Thanks. Let me know when you land." Jarred laid his phone on the table then linked his fingers and stared at his hands. "Madeline's neighbor noticed a light on in her apartment as he arrived home from work. Twenty minutes later he was climbing into bed when he heard her phone ring. He knew it was Madeline's because her lounge room is right next to his bedroom wall and the phone bugs the hell out of him when he's on night shift. He thinks it rang about five times before being answered. Next thing there was a deafening roar and he was thrown out of bed and across the room. He thought it was an earthquake until he got outside and saw a big hole where Madeline's lounge room used to be."

Jarred scrubbed his face again. "I need some air." He yanked the door open and ploughed into someone in the doorway. "Jesus Christ."

Nick stared unbelievingly at the disheveled woman Jarred had grabbed by the shoulders. She raised her grubby chin mutinously. "Don't you dare yell at me, Jarred. I've got blisters, I'm soaked to the skin, and my neck is killing me. It's a good thing I came back because..."

Jarred yanked her off her feet and into his arms. "Be quiet for one minute."

Madeline shrieked. "I will not. I demand to be released right this instant."

"Of course you do." Jarred kept his arms around her.

She struggled. "What in God's name is wrong with you?" She pummeled his chest. "Let me go."

He laughed. "Believe it or not, I'm delighted to see you."

"Madeline!" Ava ran across the kitchen and hugged Madeline as Jarred released her. "We thought you'd been killed in the explosion."

"What explosion?"

"Someone blew up your apartment. We thought you were in it."

Madeline blinked then spread her hands wide. "Someone blew up my apartment? That's just great. Now I don't even have a home." She frowned at Jarred, "That's why you hugged me. You *really* are happy to see me?"

He huffed. "I should have known a mere bomb wouldn't stop you meddling in our operation."

Nick's gaze ran over Madeline's matted, wet hair, scratched arms and filthy gym clothes. "We're happy you're safe, Maddy, but what the hell happened to you?"

"It's a long story." She stalked to the sink, filled a glass with water, then gulped it down. "Bring me up to date on what's happened here first."

Ava's lips trembled. "Liam's been kidnapped."

"I know, hence my appearance. They're holding him in a heavily guarded private property about three hours from here, so what are we going to do about it?"

"How the blazes do you know that? Wait." Jarred picked up his phone and scrolled through it. "I'll let Gibbs know you're alive so he can notify your husband and family."

"Thanks." Madeline filled her glass again and drank while Jarred spoke to Gibbs. He hung up. "Okay, let's have it?"

Madeline rubbed the back of her neck. "On the flight to Perth I kept getting this premonition I shouldn't leave. I'm not psychic, but I get these feelings occasionally and they're never wrong." She shrugged. "Lucky I didn't go home. Anyway, when the plane landed, I caught the next flight back to Broome."

She looked at Jarred pointedly. "I hired a car, as I figured you wouldn't pick me up, then as I parked near Ava's shop I saw an Asian man shoving Liam into a black jeep, and that bald guy from Damon's boat jumped in a car behind them. I couldn't ring you as my phone battery is dead, and I couldn't risk losing them, so I sunk down in the seat until they drove past. I didn't see where the bald guy went because I followed the jeep.

"My hire car is black and once we left the main road, I stayed well back and turned my lights off. But I hadn't figured on them driving to the middle of nowhere."

"Where did they take Liam?" Nick tried to dredge up what Dave had said about the places he'd flown Pearce and Walsh. He noticed Simon had brought up a map of the Kimberley region.

Madeline rolled her shoulders. "Up on a plateau. I don't know where it is exactly, but I'd recognize it from the air."

"When did you last eat?" Jarred lifted a piece of pizza and handed it to her.

"Breakfast—thanks." She took a bite, chewed then swallowed. "Once I saw their brakes lights come on and stay on, I pulled off to the side of the road and waited while they drove through big gates. I changed into dark clothes, put my hair under a cap, and used the trees to hide. Luckily I saw the armed guard at the gates before he saw me. So I hightailed it along an electric fence until I found a mound that I could take a run off and clear the fence."

Simon laughed. "Geez, Maddy, you're my hero."

"It wasn't a good landing." She held up a grazed elbow. "I jerked my neck too. I think I've pinched something."

"That was damned foolish," snapped Jarred. He moved behind her and began massaging her neck. "You shouldn't have entered the property at all."

Nick could see a pulse beating in Jarred's throat. The boss was rattled.

Madeline shivered. "I didn't have a choice." She took another bite of the pizza. "I eventually got to the house and saw a helicopter in the courtyard, and several men with rifles, so I climbed up to a second story balcony."

Sam raised an eyebrow. "May I enquire how?"

"When I'm bored I do a bit of rock climbing. I saw Liam through a window. He looked like he'd been crying and was glaring at the door, but he didn't appear harmed in any way. I couldn't risk a rescue on my own because there was no way to get him out unseen."

She finished the pizza and wiped her hands down her muddy gym pants. "I saw the bald guy from Damon's boat pacing under the balcony. He was on his phone and I heard him say, 'Nicholas Flanagan and his macho soldier friends won't do anything while the kid is being held', and something about a surprise waiting for you. When he went inside I got out of there."

"How do they know about us?" Talos beat a rapid tattoo on his thigh. "Other than the people in the meeting today, no one knows who or what we are."

"Helen knows." Ava met Nick's gaze. "When we untied her I yelled at you to get your soldier friends to find Liam. Maybe she went to the police."

"Maybe."

Ava drew in a shaky breath. "I'm going to get Madeline some dry clothes, then we can leave."

Nick crossed the kitchen in two strides. "Angel, you said you trust me. Please stay here with Madeline and wait for Gibbs. I'll bring Liam back to you."

"I do trust you, but I'm not waiting here." She turned to Madeline. "Make yourself a hot drink and have a shower. You'll feel much better."

"Thanks. I ran out of petrol so set out on foot through mud and this torrential downpour. Luckily a guy on a Harley gave me a lift."

"Jesus, Madeline, what if he'd attacked you?" Jarred shook his head as he continued to work on the back of her neck.

"He was a good guy, chief. I would have kicked his ass if he tried anything."

Nick exhaled. No way would he want the worry of a woman like Madeline. She thought nothing of going after kidnappers, jumping electric fences, and hitching rides with bikers. A bomb that should have killed her barely gained any reaction, other than irritation. Madeline was obviously an adrenaline junky. *Poor Elliott.*

Ava squeezed his fingers. "I know you'll do whatever it takes to get Liam back safely, but let me wait at the hangar, please."

"Babe, I need to know you're safe."

"I will be. Nobody can get into the hangar. I'll watch the surveillance cameras and if I see someone, I'll ring the police."

"Okay, folks." Simon waved them over. "I've enlarged a map of the Kimberley. Which road did you take out of Broome? I'll calculate your speed and time traveled to come up with the area we need. Then I'll bring up an aerial shot."

Madeline smiled at Jarred. "Thanks, my neck feels much better." She toed off her muddy runners and threw them out the back door. "It's a huge house on top of a plateau." She pointed a torn fingernail. "This is the road. They drove through Derby then after about thirty minutes the surface became gravel."

"There," said Nick, indicating a dirt road on the map.

Madeline touched a dot labeled *Kupingarri*. "I saw a sign post with that name on it, and remember thinking it would take two hours to get there, but the jeep made a right hand turn about an hour later."

Nick nodded. "The King Leopold Ranges. There's a military training area northwest of there. We know it well."

"Hm." Talos lay a paper map on the table. "Nick, if you can land the Black Hawk close enough, we'll hike in. Bring up an aerial view of that region, Simon."

"Ahead of you."

Nick stood behind Simon and studied the landscape. "Zoom in a little."

"There." Madeline indicated a group of buildings nestled against a ridge.

Simon shifted to the other computer, his fingers flying over the keys. "It used to be an eco-lodge, catering to rock climbers and backpackers. It's now privately owned."

"No way we'll be able to hike in." Jarred pulled on his bulletproof vest. "Simon, did Pearce make or receive any calls between seven and nine?"

"Give me a sec." Simon's fingers sped over his keys. "Yes. He received one call then made two. Give me a minute and I'll have names for you. The caller could have informed Pearce about us then he warned Walsh."

"Perhaps." Jarred glanced at Nick. "Alert Ryan to warm up the Hawk. Madeline, go have a hot shower before you freeze to death."

Ava squeezed Nick's fingers again. "I want Liam back, but please don't do anything crazy. I love you, and I want you back too." She took Madeline's hand and towed her out of the kitchen.

Jarred met Nick's gaze. "You okay, Lieutenant?"

"Just peachy, Colonel." Nick pulled on his vest then rang Ryan.

"Mate, our cover's been blown. Get the Hawk ready to fly; we'll be there in twenty. Have you heard from Barry? I can't reach him."

"Yeah, he left a note saying he's taken a charter up the coast and won't be back until tomorrow."

"Probably a good thing. This way Ava can't talk him into following us."

"Yeah, but it's strange he didn't mention the charter earlier, and there's nothing in the book. It must have been a walk-in."

CHAPTER NINETEEN

Nick kept the chopper at 8,000 feet. There was no air traffic to worry about as the control tower had been advised to clear the area. And with the heavy cloud cover, rain, and rumbling thunder, their approach would be masked until the last minute.

Nick checked the two compasses and the GPS then adjusted the heading a little to the right. "Target five minutes away, Colonel. You sure you don't want to hike in?"

"Positive. We have the element of surprise on our side." Jarred's voice came through the headset so clearly Nick might have been sitting beside him in the back of the chopper rather than up front in the cockpit. "Stay to the north-west until the last minute then we'll drop in right on top of them. You know the drill."

"Copy that." Nick checked that his seatbelt was locked and tight then lowered the collective lever. "Expect some turbulence on the way down." He dropped through the heavy cloud then followed the river winding its way into the gorges of King Leopold Range. Thanks to the occasional lightning, Nick could make out clumped trees, tussocks, and boulders.

"Two minutes, Colonel." He lowered the collective further, increasing the rate of descent. Flying charters for Barry wouldn't be anywhere near as exhilarating. "I'm going to miss our missions."

Ryan glanced across the cockpit. "You'll be bored silly without us and the Hawk. This is your life."

"Ava and Liam are my life now."

"Why can't you have both?" asked Simon.

"Exactly," interjected Sam. "Ava seems like a reasonable woman. Talk to her, mate. Tell her how you feel."

Nick grimaced. "I appreciate your concern, fellas, but I lost Ava once and I won't lose her again." He pointed southeast. "That plateau is our target. Let's hope they don't have a sentry posted."

"Unlikely," said Simon. "The overheads show a steep rise behind the main residence and sheer cliffs on three sides. Only way in is via the front gate or scaling those rock faces. Except for us and the gatekeeper, nobody will be out in this weather."

As if to validate his words, they hit a stomach-rolling pocket of turbulence and the heavens opened, pounding the Hawk with rain and strong gusts. Sweat drenched Nick as he battled to stay on course against Mother Nature at her wildest. Visibility instantly reduced, forcing him to fly by the instruments, hoping to Hell they weren't catapulted against the rock face. A bolt of lightning lit up the landscape ahead. Nick breathed easier. They were okay. "Thirty seconds to run, decelerating now. You're okay to open the back doors."

"Doors are back and locked," called Talos.

"Weapons to action. Go on my signal," shouted Jarred.

Nick's heart hammered inside his ribs. They'd only get one shot at this. He needed to keep his wits about him and trust the guys to do their part once he got them in safely. He swiped the perspiration off his forehead.

"I see external lights on the largest structure," called Ryan.

As suddenly as it hit, the rain eased to a steady drizzle, taking with it a little of Nick's anxiety. He divided his attention between his instrument panel and the largest of the three buildings. Talos and Sam would rappel onto the roof then drop to the balcony. While Talos ran interference, Sam would locate Liam then get him the hell out of there. Jarred and Simon would hit the ground running, find shelter, then lay down heavy fire. Anyone stupid enough to engage would be annihilated. Ryan's job was to keep unfriendly fire away from the chopper while Nick kept it high enough to prevent unwanted passengers hitching a ride.

As plans went, it was swift and effective. He prayed it would work. "Target three, two, one."

"Go," yelled Jarred.

Nick held the chopper steady as Talos and Sam dropped to the flat roof, disengaged their harnesses from the lines, and vanished over the side. "Clear." Nick jettisoned their lines as he swept over the large courtyard.

Jarred and Simon leapt out with several feet to go, then sprinted for cover, their AK47's unloading a hammering barrage of bullets as they disappeared into the shadows between the smaller buildings. Ajax bounded out after them.

Gunfire sounded from the main house as Nick lifted the chopper clear of danger above the action. He hit the floodlight, illuminating the house and courtyard like the Eiffel Tower on New Year's Eve.

Ryan slid his window open. "Keep her steady, Nick. One tango with weapon approaching fast on foot from the gatehouse." Ryan raised his rifle and sent down a volley of shots, blasting the ground in front of the man, who dropped his rifle and dived for cover among shrubs.

"If you've got any sense, you'll stay there," muttered Ryan.

Perspiration covered Nick's top lip. He couldn't see the chopper Madeline had referred to. Barely a minute had passed yet it felt like ten. Did Sam have Liam? He glanced at the balcony as another shot blasted from the house. "Come on, boys, where are you?"

"Stay cool, mate," came Sam's voice through Nick's earpiece. "We've got Liam, and the house is secure. Come on in and we'll see what these bastards are up to."

Nick drew a calming breath and cleared his throat. "Thanks, boys, I owe you."

"Nah," said Talos. "You've saved our butts enough over the last few years."

Nick flicked off the floodlight and set the chopper down on the gravel.

An Asian man stepped out of the shrubs with his hands above his head. Jarred followed, his rifle aimed at the center of the man's back. "Any casualties?" He picked up the discarded rifle.

"One dead, two injured," came Talos' voice. "Bring the medi kit."

Nick grinned at Ryan. Talos was not only their weapons expert; his whole body was a lethal weapon. Add his size and strength, and anyone on the receiving end would need more than a medi kit.

Ryan frowned. "Where's Simon?"

"Double checking the perimeter," replied Jarred. "Ryan, you stay with the chopper."

"Copy that."

Nick grabbed his rifle and the medical kit, then ducked low and made a dash for the house. As he reached the portico, the brickwork exploded beside him.

"Fuck." Nick dived behind a huge clay pot. "We have a shooter out here." He checked that Ryan was safe inside the chopper then flipped down his night vision goggles. Another shot rang out, the bullet hitting the tango in front of Jarred and leaving a gaping hole in his chest.

"Christ." Nick raised his rifle and lay down cover as Jarred zigzagged around the Hawk toward him.

"I see him," came Simon's voice. "Right hand corner of the house."

Nick's gaze searched. "Can you get a shot off, Sime?"

"Negative. We need to cut off his back door."

"I'm on it." Nick pelted off round the left side of the house. "Someone hit the external lights so he can't see me."

Within seconds the lights went out. Thanks to his goggles, Nick could see everything as clear as daylight only in green. Keeping to the edge of the building he crept forward, ducking under windows as he scanned the surrounding area. At the far corner he edged behind a shrub and poked his head around.

There you are. Nick crouched as a heavy set white guy backed toward him, his head whipping from side to side as he searched the darkness. It wasn't Walsh.

I'm right behind you, dickhead.

Nick lay his rifle down then his goggles and charged, hitting the man hard in the midsection. The rifle went flying as they crashed to the ground with a rib-cracking thud.

"I need lights," yelled Nick.

The man bellowed and kicked out, twisting to dislodge his attacker.

Nick smashed his gloved fist into the guy's nose. It made a resounding pop and blood gushed. Nick got a quick jab in then rolled away as the lights came on. The guy roared and charged. He was built like a Sherman tank on steroids.

Nick sprang to his feet, dodged a swinging arm, then came in fast with an upper cut to the guy's hard jaw. The man's head snapped back then he gurgled and dropped to the ground.

Nick's hand hurt like hell, but it felt good to work out some of his rage. Pulling out two zip-lock ties, he rolled the dazed man on his side then secured his hands and feet. "Tango incapacitated."

As Nick entered the open front door, Sam stepped out of a room on the right, his rifle held loosely in his hands. "About time you joined us. Talos has Liam in the room at the end of the foyer.

"Thanks." Nick glanced at two men hunched side-by-side on the sofa. One held his bloodied arm cradled across his chest and wore a plaster cast on his right leg. The other sported a swollen face, split lip, and broken nose. They were the injuries Nick could see. He'd be surprised if they didn't have a few broken ribs as well. As the medic on the team, Ryan could assess them later.

Nick ran across reddish tiles and opened the door Sam had indicated.

"Daddy!" Liam shot off Talos' knee and threw himself at Nick.

Ajax gave a woof and trotted from behind the desk.

"Liam." Nick's lungs seized. He didn't have the capacity to draw breath as he dropped to his knees, caught and clutched his son in his arms. His throat clogged. Emotion threatened to overwhelm as he kissed Liam's head, felt tiny fingers clinging, his heartbeat thudding. His little mate was alive.

The anguish still gnawed at Nick as he thanked God, the universe, and every deity he could think of for protecting his son. Eventually he calmed enough to open his eyes and ease Liam away.

"Can we go in the Black Hawk now, Daddy?"

"Soon, buddy." Surprised to see Liam's eyes shining with excitement, Nick raised an eyebrow at Talos, who sat behind the desk with one foot resting on his knee. "Did they hurt him in any way?"

Talos shook his head. "No. The little guy locked the door and climbed onto a chest of drawers to look out the window. We spotted him as soon as we hit the balcony. Amazingly he recognized me straight away, even in all this gear. He hasn't stopped smiling since."

Liam put his little hands on either side of Nick's face and stared him straight in the eyes. "Daddy, I was very scared when the Neanderals took me, but I tried to be brave and I didn't cry a lot." He grinned. "I knew it was Talos, cause he's the biggest man I ever saw, and he jumped out of your Black Hawk."

"I see." Nick ruffled Liam's hair. "You are a very brave boy."

"I'm hungry, Daddy."

Nick's heartbeat slowed with the relief. Liam appeared unharmed in any way. It went a long way to easing his panic. "I'll see what I can find in the kitchen." He looked at Talos. "Best Liam doesn't see the results of your handy work."

"Too late. Sam was carrying the little fella as we were working our way downstairs. Two tangoes tried to stop us, so I dealt with them. Sam managed to shield Liam from most of it, but he saw the end result. I've explained to him that men who hit ladies and steal children make men like us very angry. They got what they deserve."

"Any sign of Walsh?"

"No, but I had a chat with one of our captives. This property belongs to Pearce, and his crew maintains it when not manning the yacht. Pearce plans to turn this place into a five-star retreat for the rich and famous."

"Using armed guards?

"Apparently."

"What did Pearce think he'd gain by kidnapping Liam?"

"Who knows? Feed the little guy and we'll ask our captives."

Nick kissed Liam's head again then followed Talos out of the study, but headed for the kitchen, a workspace that would have any chef green with envy. He'd noticed a dining room with a table that would easily sit twelve. This place would have made Pearce a stack of money as a get-away for the wealthy.

"We'd better ring Mummy so she knows you're safe."

"Okay, Daddy. Come on, Ajax."

Unable to get through to Ava's cell phone, Nick tried the hangar's landline only to be put through to message bank. Unsettled, he poured Liam a glass of milk, then dropped some bread into the toaster. He spread the toast with butter and honey then took Liam back to the study.

"You stay here with Ajax while I see what's happening."

"When can we go fly the Black Hawk, Daddy?"

"Soon." Nick left the door ajar and strode across the hall to an expensively furnished sitting room. One wall housed a fully stocked bookcase. The tango Nick had knocked out sat on the floor against an armchair, his face and shirt covered in blood, his eyes unfocussed.

Simon lounged by the bookcase concentrating on his phone. A dead Asian guy covered in mud and blood lay at his feet. The two on the couch had their terrified eyes locked on Jarred, standing over them menacingly. Talos leaned by the archway, his deadpan face and casual stance in no way masking his hostility.

Jarred drew his handgun. "I'm not a patient man, so I'll only ask this once. If I don't like the answer, I will shoot you in the foot, then work my way up. You will die slowly and painfully. Who hit the woman and took the boy?"

The man on the left swallowed. "I follow boss's orders. I carried boy to car. I not hurt him and I not hit the woman. Boss must have hit her after I leave."

"I need your boss's name."

"Lex. Lex Walsh."

"Isn't Daman Pearce your boss?"

"We paid by Mr. Pearce, but Lex give us our orders."

Nick pulled his handgun, stepped forward, and pressed the barrel against the head of a man who had his right leg in plaster. "We've met before, haven't we?"

"I just follow orders. Lex said you come to Broome and make Mr. Pearce unhappy. It bad for business. So he set you up for robbery, hoping lady kick you out and Mr. Pearce happy again."

"Are you saying Pearce didn't know about the robbery?"

The man was sweating profusely as he looked nervously at his buddy. "Maybe, maybe not."

Pulling the gun away, Nick narrowed his eyes. "Why would my coming here be bad for business?"

The man on the left shifted restlessly. "We not know."

"You've lost a lot of blood," Jarred said coldly. "If you want medical attention, you need to start talking."

"We take orders from Lex, not Mr. Pearce."

Jarred aimed the butt of his rifle at the man's crotch. "Who broke into Ava Mitchell's house and stole the gems?"

"Lex."

"How did he get into the safe?

"He know where to find key."

"Who planted the stuff in the hotel room?"

"I see Lex do it."

"Where are the rest of the stolen gems?" asked Nick.

"Lex say he give them to his partner."

"Damon Pearce?"

"Maybe."

Nick stared at the two men. "I still want to know why is my being in Broome bad for business?"

The man with the plastered leg began wringing his hands. "Mr. Pearce unhappy you take his lady. If you leave, Mr. Pearce happy, and business good."

"What fucking business?" Talos whipped out his deadly blade, then paced behind the sofa, and dragged the guy's head back. "Spill your guts or I'll slit your throat."

"Lex collects pearls and diamonds each week then every few months we take them out to sea to meet ship. They take gems to Asia and we bring back workers for the mine."

"I think we just found the smuggling ring Gibbs is after." Nick looked at Jarred. "Pearce is bringing in cheap, illegal labor then pilfering his own gems and selling them on the black market. By avoiding paying tax he'd be making a fortune."

"Never assume anything. Pearce may not know what's going on right under his nose," Jarred said.

Nick stared at the man in plaster. "Where is Walsh now?"

"He left in helicopter before you arrive."

"Who is piloting the chopper?"

Both men averted their eyes and shifted uneasily.

Jarred waved his rifle at them. "I'm losing patience."

"We not know. Lex keep him tied up then use gun to make him fly chopper."

Nick's heart began to race. He had a very bad feeling. "The pilot, Max Robson, was found floating in the ocean. How did he get there?"

Both men looked at the big guy Nick had taken down.

He snarled back at them. "I'm gunna freaking kill you bastards."

Simon drew his knife and pressed it against the man's ear. "Answer the question."

"I didn't knock the pilot out. That was Lex. I just helped dump him in the ocean and scatter some fishing gear over the rocks."

Nick gritted his teeth and stepped closer. He wanted to smash the guy. "What were you planning to do with my son?"

"Lex didn't say. We just had to keep him here."

"Describe the pilot with Walsh."

"He's a grey haired bloke that Lex had a gripe against. I don't know his name."

Barry! Nick's skin crawled. "You are going to prison for a long time." He punched his fist into the guy's broken nose, knocking him out again, then turned to Jarred. "We need to get back. Ava isn't answering the phone."

Jarred nodded then turned away. "Boys, load our passengers and the bodies. We'll hand them to the cops when we get back to the airport."

Nick selected Barry's cell number. Hopefully he was wrong and his old friend was asleep and would go off like a firecracker at being woken this early in the morning. The call went to message bank.

He could have turned his phone off. Nick stopped at the study door and selected Ava's number. She wouldn't let anyone she didn't trust into the hangar. *What if Pearce had a cop on the payroll? What if that's how Walsh found out about us?* "Come on, Angel, answer the damn phone." It was possible her battery died.

Shit, I hope that's all it is.

He skimmed his contacts then rang the hangar's landline. It went to message bank again then dropped out. *Why the hell doesn't Barry clear his messages?*

Could Pearce have Ava? Nick pushed that thought away. There was a chance she was in the bathroom. It was a flimsy hope and the chill infusing his body kept spreading.

He pushed the study door wide. Liam lay asleep, curled up beside Ajax on a thick, expensive looking rug. The empty plate sat under Ajax's nose. He lifted his head from his paws and gave Nick a sheepish look.

"Gave you his dinner, did he?" Nick picked his precious son up and cradled him against his chest. "Let's get you home to Mummy, sweetheart."

A roar from Talos, then pounding feet on the stairs had Nick stiffening and Ajax growling. Holding Liam against his shoulder, Nick drew his gun then edged into the wide hall as Sam landed in the foyer.

"The building is rigged with enough explosives to blow the top off the damn plateau. It's a tricky detonator and Talos says he's not sticking round to defuse it. We gotta get out of here now."

"They knew we were coming or planned to cover their tracks." Nick holstered his gun, then adjusted Liam and sprinted for the Hawk, bending low to avoid the long rotor blades. Liam woke and clung to Nick's neck, reminding him the deafening noise of the Black Hawk's twin engines were much louder than the small chopper they'd taken up the coast.

Ajax leapt in the rear of the Hawk ahead of Sam, who then held out his arms. "I'll take Liam."

Nick hesitated. He would have preferred to keep Liam with him, well away from their captives, but taking him into the cockpit wasn't an option. Talos waited with a headset that he quickly fixed over Liam's head then hauled the door closed.

Nick swung into his seat. "Let's get the hell out of here before she blows."

Chapter Twenty

With barely fifty feet below them, and the throttle fully open, Nick pushed the cyclic stick forward and swept off the top of the plateau. If the blast didn't knock them out of the sky, then the debris would be catapulted into the finely balanced rotor blades. His priority was to get Liam and the Hawk as far away as possible before the explosives detonated.

Nick radioed Broome Tower and requested they contact Inspector Zachary Gibbs to meet them at the airport along with an ambulance and prisoner transport.

Just as he finished speaking, a ball of blazing flames lit up the sky to the southeast of them. Nick fought for control as shock waves hit the chopper, throwing them about in their seats for several seconds.

"Jesus." Ryan shook his head. "That was close."

"Daddy, the sky is on fire." Liam's speculation rammed home how close they'd come to dying. The knot of unease in Nick's stomach tightened.

Through the background static in his headset, Nick heard Broome tower calling. Assuming the tower needed more information, he responded.

"Broome Tower, this is Delta Romeo Whisky, what can I do for you?"

"Delta Romeo Whisky, this is Inspector Zachary Gibbs. I take it you have rescued the child?"

To say he was stunned to hear Gibbs was an understatement. "That's affirmative." Nick adjusted the intercom settings so the whole team could hear. "What are you doing in the tower, Inspector?"

"It's easier to speak to you all over this channel than by

phone. The AFP has a situation that we need your assistance with."

"Another one," drawled Jarred. "What is it this time?"

"Perth Radar reported a code 7500 squawk several hours ago."

"The global hijacking code?" said Talos.

"Yes. As it wasn't a commercial flight and neither Perth nor Broome could radio the pilot, they thought he might have intended to log a 7600, the code for loss of communication, but hit the five instead of the six. The AFP's Counter Terrorism Branch was notified as is mandatory and instantly issued a tracking order. The aircraft made three landings! The first two locations were southwest of Broome, then in the King Leopald Ranges. Not exactly the typical behavior of a hijacker. The pilot activated another 7500 forty minutes ago, just before he disappeared off radar, which is when it was brought to my attention."

Every muscle in Nick's body locked. "The pilot could be Barry Sanders and the hijacker is a man by the name of Lex Walsh. Have the police check on Ava at the hanger and Madeline, who is at Ava's house?"

"No worries. I'll get back to you with any news."

Ryan met Nick's gaze. "You think they've got Ava?"

"That's my biggest fear. Try ringing the hangar again."

For the next fifteen minutes Nick stewed over several possibilities. None good. Then the radio crackled.

"Delta Romeo Whisky, this is Broome Control Tower. I have Inspector Gibbs for you."

"Broome Control Tower, this is Delta Romeo Whiskey. Go ahead, Inspector Gibbs. What can you tell us?"

"No sign of anyone at the hangar, but there's fuel on the ground as if someone did a sloppy job of refueling. The police also found a smashed cell phone and the surveillance cameras shot out."

"Christ. What about the hard drive?" asked Nick.

"Gone, but Madeline is still at the house. Sergeant Evans has left an officer with her. Oh, and Pearce isn't at home. He must have got away on foot."

"Someone should have stayed with Ava." Nick set his jaw as Jarred began peppering Gibbs with questions.

"Hold up," called Gibbs. "Something's happening. I'll get back to you."

Nick glanced at his white knuckles then forced his attention back to flying the Hawk. The tension riding him far exceeded anything he'd faced in the Army, SAS, or since. The thought of Walsh hurting Ava made his stomach churn. His heart raced. Perspiration soaked his shirt and forehead. His mind reeled with possible locations they could search. Pearce's house—diamond mine—pearl farm—office. *No, they won't take her anywhere obvious.*

Where are you, Angel? I can't find you if I don't know where to look.

Strapped in the front passenger seat of the training chopper, Ava sneaked a peek at Barry's battered face. One eye had completely closed up, a huge bruise covered his left cheek.

Her fault.

When she'd seen the chopper land then Barry get out, she hadn't stopped to think before opening the hangar door. Not for a second had she imagined anything other than he was returning from a chartered flight. Then she'd seen Lex Walsh and the gun he had leveled on Barry. Her mind had gone absolutely blank until Barry noticed her and began yelling for her to get back inside and lock the door.

Ava stood on the cusp of fright, then flight. She'd been about to obey him when Lex Walsh smashed his gun into Barry's face, knocking him to the ground. In obvious pain, the older man had crawled to his knees only to have Lex kick him hard in the stomach, leaving him curled in a ball, gasping for air.

Disgust and fury erupted from Ava, and before she'd considered the consequences, she'd screamed then run to Barry's aid. He'd tried to wheeze out a warning, but Lex kicked him again, and then turned the gun on Ava. Her stupid, stupid actions had given Lex another hostage and bargaining power. Barry had no choice but to refuel the chopper or watch Lex shoot her.

I should have stayed in the hangar. Nick will go out of his mind when he finds me missing.

She glanced at Barry. He hadn't said a word for several minutes as he battled to get the chopper up in the air. A near impossible task with his wrists tied together. Ava licked her lips and glanced down to where her hand grasped the collective lever between their seats. Barry had control of the cyclic stick and pedals, but he was relying on her to follow his instructions to the letter.

They hit an air pocket and her stomach dropped. "For goodness sake, please untie Barry. He isn't going to try anything while we're in the air."

"Shut your mouth, or I'll shut it permanently."

Ava shuddered and glanced back at the bald man aiming a gun at her.

Barry suddenly cried out then let go of the cyclic stick and clutched his chest.

"What's wrong?" Ava grabbed his shoulder. "Barry?"

"Pain." He gasped for breath, then his eyes rolled backwards, and he went limp like a wet rag.

"Barry?" Oh, God. Her hands were shaking as she grasped the cyclic stick in front of her, a dual control to the one Barry had been using.

Nick's voice reached through her shock. *"If anything ever happens to incapacitate me or some other pilot, you need to know what to do. Being familiar with the controls will help. Unfortunately, most choppers won't have a second set of controls like this, so you're doomed. But if it does and your pilot is unable to fly, get him off the controls and take his headset so you can radio for help."*

"Shikes." She leaned over and knocked Barry's feet off the Pedals. "He's unconscious. We need to radio for help."

"Do you know how to fly a chopper?" Lex gripped Barry's shoulders and pulled him back against the seat.

"I've had one lesson." She pulled off her headset and grabbed Barry's, forcing down the bile in her throat as she tried to concentrate, tried to remember Nick's instructions.

"The main control stick that sits between your legs is called the cyclic. Push forward, nose goes down. Pull back, nose goes up. Push left, chopper banks left. Push right, it banks right. The radio Com switch is on the cyclic."

Or was it the button on the cyclic. She glanced down quickly and pressed the button. Immediately she heard Lex Walsh swearing under his breath. *Okay, not the button.* She flicked the switch and prayed someone would hear her, but what could she say that wouldn't alert the man holding a gun on her.

"I'm in control of a chopper that I don't know how to fly." Her voice shook so violently it was coming out in near sobs. "Jarred Steele and his team of special operatives will come after you for kidnapping me, Mr. Walsh."

"Just fly the fucking chopper."

"Don't swear at me. I'm trying to remember what to do with the pedals."

The memory of Nick's calm tones overrode her panic. *"Pedals control the tail rotor. Push the left pedal to turn the nose left, push right to turn the nose right. Keep the skid ball on the center mark to stay in a straight line. Ninety percent of flying is looking out the windshield and remember, nothing sudden. Use small, gentle movements."*

She glanced ahead at the moon barely visible through the haze of cloud. They were heading out to sea. "I need to turn back." She applied a little pressure to the cyclic and the right pedal. The chopper began to tilt to the right.

Not a sound from the back seat.

Ava shot a glance at Barry's grey face, unable to tell whether he was breathing. Her heart hammered in her chest. This kind man was a father figure to Nick, his mentor, his rock. "I think Barry's had a heart attack." Perspiration ran down the valley between her breasts. "I'm supposed to do something with this lever between the seats. I think it controls the rotor blades and the throttle is on the end of the lever?"

"The throttle controls the engine speed. It's set at 100%; don't mess with it."

Nick's words had her snatching her fingers away. "Nick said the collective lever makes the rotor blades blow more or less air. When you pull up, all the rotor blades tilt slightly, so each blade takes a bigger chunk and more airflow is pulled through the rotor system."

"We're climbing," said Lex.

"Get the aircraft flying straight and level. That's critical. Don't let the nose stay above the horizon. This will cause your airspeed to decrease and you will come to a stop."

"Shikes, I can't see the horizon ahead." Ava eased the stick between her legs forward, very gently. It worked. They leveled out. She eased it right and pressed firmer on the right pedal. Three seconds later they were banking toward the coast.

Ava wiped the sweat off her face. She could probably do this all night, but eventually they would run out of fuel and then they would crash. *Not if I can help it.*

She flicked a gaze at Barry then gripped the cyclic stick. Every muscle rigid, her eyes shooting from gauge to gauge to gauge. She was in a real live nightmare.

"Once the chopper is under control, you need to think about landing. A big airport is best as they have all the safety equipment. Avoid power lines and try to land like a plane. If you attempt to hover you will crash."

"Nick said helicopters can land like planes, but we need a big area."

"We're going to land on a beach."

Tears ran down Ava's face. If Barry was alive he was in a very bad way and needed medical attention urgently. That's if she could get them down safely. *I can't lose my marbles now.* "At this height we'll fly straight over it."

Her tormentor tapped Ava's shoulder with his gun. "Fly further up the coast. I'll tell you when to land."

"Are you crazy? We need to go back toward Broome. I don't know how to land."

"If you want to help Barry, you'll do exactly as I tell you."

Ava swallowed the lump in her throat. She trusted that Nick and his team had rescued Liam. They were the best of the best. She had to remain positive and hope someone out there could hear her. "Okay, I'm turning left up the coast."

They were still very high. She eased the cyclic to the left as Nick's calm voice flittered through her mind. *"Once you're lined up with the runway, gently lower the collective lever to start a slow descent. Keep the nose slightly down then sight the place you intend to land on your windshield."*

Nick had shown her other things but she had been side tracked by the tenor of his deep voice, sexy eyes, and smile. His instructions had brushed over her as memories of their lovemaking, of their connection, of their future drowned him out.

He'd mentioned another communication button on the floor but she was too scared to take her eyes off the dark coastline ahead. She could only pray that someone in the control tower was listening, someone who could alert the authorities. And if they were listening, she prayed they'd be able to help her.

Drawing a shaky breath, she glanced back. "Mr. Walsh, I don't appreciate you holding a gun to my head while I'm trying to figure out how to land. We should be flying in the opposite direction, toward Broome airport where we have a chance of being talked down safely. If you shoot me, we all die."

Lex prodded her ribs. "There's a long beach further up the coast. That's where we are going to land."

"I can't," she all but wailed.

"You will, or I'll shoot you."

Ava bit her lip. *I have to get a grip and land this thing. Liam needs me. Nick needs me.* "Then you die too. Do you realize by kidnapping Liam and now me, you have taken on a team of special ops soldiers? They are not going to let you get away with this. They are more than likely already on your trail, and they know you took Liam to that lodge in the King Leopold Ranges. When they discover me missing, they are going to hunt you and your boss down. You have no idea who you're tangling with."

"Your heroes don't rattle me, sunshine."

Ava licked her dry lips. "I haven't seen lights for a long time. What's going to happen when we land?"

"Once I've dealt with two more loose ends, we're taking an ocean cruise."

"On Damon's yacht?"

"Yeah. We may as well be comfortable."

It didn't sound like he meant to kill her yet, but there were worse fates than dying quickly from a bullet. He could throw her in the ocean with the great white sharks that inhabited this coastline, or keep her onboard for his crew's entertainment. She shuddered. *Positive thoughts. If someone is listening, they need every bit of information I can give them.*

"You haven't thought this out," snapped Ava. "If you hurt me in any way, Nick and his friends will hunt you down, and when they find you, they will tear you apart."

He sneered. "Maybe once upon a time, but not now. We planned on taking the kid to keep your boyfriend off our backs, but then thanks to you, we discovered who he really is. That made things a little more challenging."

Ava frowned. "Thanks to me, I don't understand?"

"You told Nicholas Flanagan that he and his team of elite soldiers, who were only three minutes away, should be out looking for your son. Isn't that right?"

Yes, but the only other person who could have heard that was— *Oh no.* "What have you done to Helen?"

"You mean besides hitting her when we snatched the kid?" He laughed cruelly. "You'd be surprised what one can learn by being in the right place, at the right time."

Ava's stomach churned. She tried to push down the sickening fear wrapping its barbed tentacles around her heart. Had they got to Helen too? "Why are you so sure Nick won't come after us?"

"Did you think my men wouldn't notice they were being followed?"

She gasped. "Madeline was sure they didn't see her."

"The journalist? If I'd known it was her, I would have had her brought in. Still, she served a purpose. The only way she could have entered the property was through the main gate, which didn't happen. My men reported the car had left so we continued with our plan."

"Madeline did enter the property by vaulting the fence. She saw where you had Liam then she went for help. The AFP know your identity, so you and your boss are going to jail for a long, long time." Ava bit her lip. She shouldn't antagonize him.

Lex sneered. "Your bravado is admirable but wasted. When I discovered who Nicholas Flanagan and his friends were, I paid Barry Saunders a visit at the hangar. With a little persuasion, he flew me up to King Leopold Ranges. I figured once your heroes knew where the kid was, they'd come get him, so I left a man watching your house. He reported six men and a woman left the house at two-thirty this morning and drove to the hangar."

Ava swallowed. "By now they've rescued Liam and are on their way back. You are in big trouble."

His laugh turned ugly. "I allowed them time to fly up there and attempt a rescue. By now they've been blown sky high from the explosive reception I left them."

Ava looked over her shoulder and a chill ran down her spine at the pure evil she saw in his eyes.

His chuckle sounded malicious. "Your hero and kid are dead."

"No!" Ava's heart cleaved in two as pain tore through her body. She refused to believe she'd never again hear their voices, or laughter, see their precious faces. Never again hold her baby in her arms, his life cut short before it had begun. She couldn't bear the thought of losing the two people she loved most in the world, their bodies blown to smithereens. "No, I won't believe it."

He has to be lying. Nick and his friends are ex-SAS. They would have gone in and got out fast. Lex wouldn't know they had a Black Hawk helicopter that is bigger, faster, and stronger than most other choppers. She couldn't give up hope or she'd be doomed. She couldn't let this wanker beat her. Ava's thoughts jumped about like a grasshopper on speed. *I need to get help to them. Maybe it's not too late.*

Lex tapped her shoulder. "You're landing on the beach round the next headland.

"Nick, where are you?"

Lex sneered. "He ain't helping you."

Her headset crackled. "Angel, stay calm. I'm here."

Ava jumped as Nick's deep familiar voice sounded through her headset. One swift glance back at Lex told her he hadn't heard. Or was her imagination doing overtime?

"Nick?" It came out barely a whisper.

"I'm here, sweetheart. Liam's safe, and Walsh can't hear me on this channel, but he can hear you. Now, without alerting him, I want you to look at the altimeter and tell me your height?"

Ava's heart soared. Her boys were alive. "We're at two thousand feet."

"How many knots are you doing?"

"Sixty knots."

"All right, Angel," soothed Nick. "Point your nose slightly below the horizon. Do you remember me telling you to keep the place you want to land on a spot on your windshield?"

"Ah ha." She glanced out the windshield at the long beach ahead. "I can see the beach I'm going to land on."

"Good, girl. Press the cyclic lever forward slightly. Slowly lower your collective and keep watching your spot. You'll gradually lose height. Just keep your target in the same spot on the windshield."

She did. "We're coming down."

"I don't need a running commentary," Lex snarled, shakily.

"Just shut up, Lex," yelled Ava. "Talking helps me stay calm."

"Ignore him, babe," came Nick's voice. "How's Barry?"

She glanced sideways. It was hard to answer without alerting Lex. "I think Barry's had a heart attack. He's unconscious and lost all color."

Lex grunted. "Forget about Barry and watch where you're going."

Ava heard Nick exhale. "You're going to land like a plane. In the last few seconds before touchdown, don't pull up on the collective or cyclic levers. Use the pedals to keep the nose straight. The toes of the skids are curved upward and will act like a sled, cutting through the snow."

"Sand is like snow, right?"

"Right. Is your seat belt locked and tight?"

"Ah ha."

"Okay, Angel. How much beach have you got and what's your height?"

"It's a long beach. We are at one thousand feet."

"Good. Ease down on the collective slightly to continue your descent. Think of a piece of string connecting you to the mid-way point on the beach. Now fly along the string line. Keep the nose marginally down so your airspeed stays under control. Look at a spot about fifty meters after the start of your runway and try to keep that place locked on your windshield."

She blinked. *Follow an imaginary piece of string down.* She could do that. "Right."

Ava pushed the collective lower as she stared at the white strip of sand racing toward them. The chopper turned slightly left, she touched the right pedal. It straightened again. "Oh, shikes. The sand is coming at us too fast."

"Easy does it," soothed Nick. "As you get closer, you're going to want to pull up hard on the cyclic and collective. Don't. Just a little on the collective will soften your landing. Helicopters are stronger than they look."

"We're getting really close to the sand." Ava shuddered.

"Use the pedals *gently* to keep the nose pointing at the end of the beach. Once you touch down, you'll skid along the sand. Don't forget to use your pedals to stay straight, and keep the cyclic lever steady."

"I'm going too fast."

"Don't think about your speed. You just need to be straight. Once you touch down, the sand will slow you. Then lower the collective to the floor and use the pedals to stay straight. As you come to a stop, roll the throttle to idle. You can do it, babe."

Ava clenched her teeth. "Hold on." They hit the sand with a shuddering lurch, slamming her forward against her seatbelt. The chopper momentarily slid right then back to the left. Ava tried not to slam the pedals as she struggled to keep the nose straight. "We're sk-skidding." She pushed the collective all the way down and rolled the throttle off. They rocked to a stop several meters from a wall of wet rocks.

Ava burst into tears. "We made it."

"Thank God." Nick's voice quavered. "Be careful getting out. Watch the rotor blades. We've been tracking the chopper on radar, so we know where you've landed, and medical help is on the way for Barry. We've also got a tracking device on Pearce's yacht, and we can remotely disable the propeller. I promise I'll find you, Angel."

"Okay."

"Come on," yelled Lex. "Let's go." He climbed out of the chopper.

As he slammed the rear door, Ava thought quickly as she undid her belt. She only had a few seconds. "I never stopped loving you, Nick, but don't let this ruin your life. You need to be there for Liam."

"I love you too, Angel. Don't give up, I'm coming for you."

Her door was wrenched open. "Out." Lex gripped her arm and hauled her onto the sand.

Ava fell to her knees then vomited over his shiny black shoes.

"Shit." He stalked into the shallow water and swished his feet about.

Wiping her mouth, Ava stood then glared at him. "You want to hope Barry doesn't die."

"Another loose end I don't need to worry about. No one will find the chopper for days, which will be too late for old Barry." Lex waved his gun at her. "Let's go, I've organized a little welcome aboard party for you."

An engine drew Ava's attention to the ocean where a small tender made its way toward them. Time was running out. Barry needed urgent attention. She prayed Nick would be in time. Drawing in a deep breath she wondered how she could have been so wrong about Damon?

Chapter Twenty-one

Nick looked at the people surrounding him in Broome's Control Tower. His teammates, several flight controllers and Gibbs watched him, yet the silence was deafening. They'd been listening in to Ava and Lex's conversation for several minutes before Nick spoke to Ava.

"What a cluster-fuck." He slumped back in the console chair, then dropped his face into his hands, taking a minute to calm his racing heart and get his head in order. He wanted to rip Walsh's throat out, but to keep Ava alive he had to stay focused and rational. She done everything he'd asked. She was alive and safe. For how long was another matter. The second she saw an opportunity to run, she would, which scared the crap out of Nick. He could only hope Pearce thought enough of Ava to protect her from Walsh.

Ajax whined beside him then nudged Nick's leg.

"Hey, buddy." Nick ruffled his fur then glanced under the desk to where Liam lay curled up asleep. At least he was safe. Nick drew in a deep breath then looked at Jarred and Gibbs conferring quietly beside him. "I'm going after Ava, but first we need to get Barry medical attention. If he's alive he needs to be airlifted to the coronary unit at Royal Perth Hospital ASAP."

Gibbs nodded. "You get him here and I'll have my pilots fly him to Perth in the Jet."

"Thank you."

Jarred met Nick's gaze. "I can see you've worked out a plan. Care to share?"

"Liam stays here with Simon and Ajax, where I know he's safe. Simon can track the yacht and when we're close, disable it via satellite. We take the Hawk and set down on the same beach as

Barry." *Please God he's still alive.* "Ryan and Sam fly Barry back here in the Hawk then Gibbs gets him to Perth in the jet."

Nick wiped his sweaty palms on his Kevlar suit, but kept his attention on Jarred. "I will fly Barry's chopper out to the yacht. With no lights and such an overcast night, we stand a good chance of taking them by surprise. You and Talos drop into the ocean while I land on the yacht's helideck. My arrival will cause enough commotion for you two to get on board unobserved."

"I agree with the first bit, but you are not landing on the yacht. That would be suicide." Jarred narrowed his eyes. "Do we have masks, snorkels, and fins on the Hawk?"

Talos straightened from where he'd been leaning against a window with Simon. "You bet we do, Colonel."

Jarred turned to Gibbs. "I need clearance to do what's necessary to rescue Ava?"

Gibbs grimaced. "All right, but I'd prefer you bring Walsh and Pearce in alive. I need to interrogate them. Our Immigration Minister wants to stop the illegals entering Australia. Also the AFP and our counterparts in Asia are keen to make an example of the kingpin running this smuggling operation."

Jarred hesitated. "Walsh told Ava he had two more loose ends to tie up. As he thinks we're dead and Barry's dead, then who is he referring to?"

Nick closed his eyes briefly. "Madeline and Helen Davis, Ava's partner."

Jarred stared at the ceiling briefly then looked at Gibbs. "Get an officer to check on Helen Davis. I can't see that she's a threat to Pearce, but maybe she's seen or heard something that could incriminate him. Madeline is another story. She might drive me crazy, but she's a damn thorough investigative journalist. She'll be like a bloodhound, sniffing under every stone until she brings down the people she thinks are responsible for our deaths, and Pearce knows it."

"You're right." Gibbs frowned. "I'll double the guard and head over there myself."

Nick came to his feet. "Once Pearce realizes Ava won't cross over to the dark side, he'll want to silence her, which means we need to find her fast." He cleared his throat. "Ryan should have the Hawk refueled by now. Let's do this."

The flight up the coast took fifteen long minutes, in which time Simon radioed to inform them of the yacht's position and advise them Helen wasn't at her apartment, and that the safe and shop had been cleaned out. The police also found blood on the floor and evidence a body had been dragged through it.

Nick didn't hold much hope of finding Helen. If she wasn't already shark bait, she soon would be. Another innocent person dragged into this mess. According to Simon, the yacht was heading out to sea. With the thickening cloud cover the crew shouldn't notice the Hawk, but as a precaution, Nick killed the lights as they approached the beach where Ava had landed.

He brought the Hawk down close to Barry's Bell 204, then opened his door and jumped the last few feet, sprinting to the smaller chopper. He pulled the door open and placed two fingers against the side of Barry's neck, searching for the carotid artery. Immediately he felt warm skin and then a faint pulse. His relief was short lived. Barry was unconscious and clammy.

"Come on, old mate. You can't go out this way." Nick released the belt then hoisted Barry over his shoulder, grunting under the weight as he ploughed through the soft sand back to the Hawk.

Ryan climbed through from the cockpit and grabbed the medical kit while Talos assisted Nick to pass Barry across to Sam and Jarred, who then laid him over several seats.

"Sam and I will get him onto the oxy-viva, and get an IV hooked up before we leave," called Ryan. "You get going."

"Thanks." Nick itched to do just that. He glanced at Jarred and Talos. They had removed their bulletproof vests and were busy sliding knives into sheaths and clipping waterproof gun bags to their belts. Their masks, snorkels, and fins lay on the sand beside the small chopper.

Sliding into Barry's seat, Nick fastened his belt then pulled on the headset. He could just detect Ava's soft perfume, which almost brought him undone. He had to treat this like any other mission. Stay professional; pretend he didn't know or love the target who needed extracting. That just wasn't going to happen. He would do whatever it took to save Ava. Failure wasn't an option. Once Jarred and Talos closed their doors, Nick radioed Broome Tower.

Within minutes they were flying low over the dark ocean, heading for Pearce's yacht. The plan was for Simon to remotely disable the yacht via satellite once they were within a couple of kilometers. The risk of taking the propeller out too soon might induce Pearce or Walsh to kill Ava before help arrived.

Nick flicked a glance over his shoulder. "Get ready, we're about five minutes from the drop zone. The rain is getting heavier and will help mask our approach."

"We're ready," called Jarred. "Tell Simon to hit the switch. Once we jump, you head back to Broome."

"I've decided to go in low and drop you nice and close. They won't notice with this rain and you'll conserve energy if you don't have so far to swim."

"All right. Then you get the hell out of there."

"But…"

"That's an order, Lieutenant. The Coast Guard will pick us up."

Keeping his eyes on the gauges, Nick didn't answer. No way was he leaving. He would fly out of range and wait for word from Simon. If need be, he could hit the yacht with the chopper's spotlight. The night and ocean would appear blacker outside the light, and give Jarred and Talos a better chance to get aboard safely. Once they were onboard, Nick would kill the spotlight, shrouding the yacht in darkness and give the boys the upper hand.

The tension in his body tightened as Nick flicked the radio. "Broome Tower, this is Delta Romeo Whisky. We are a couple of minutes from target. Please advise Simon to disable the yacht's propeller and give me its latest location."

"Delta Romeo Whisky, this is Broome Tower. Copy that. Putting Simon through now. Good luck."

Taking a deep breath, Nick descended to fifty feet above the ocean. "Wait for my signal." He kept his eyes on the radar altimeter. The last thing they needed was to hit the water.

"Delta Romeo Whisky, this is Simon. I've disabled the yacht but haven't detected any conversations. They must be below deck. Here's the yacht's latest co-ordinates."

Nick listened then adjusted his cyclic stick to the right. "Got it. Thanks, Sime. Drop zone, one minute." Again he looked over his shoulder. "You fellas ready?"

Talos and Jarred both nodded then undid their belts and removed their headsets. Once their masks and snorkels were on, they pulled their flippers over their wrists, then with a nod opened both back doors and eased out onto the skids. The driving rain and wind hit Nick like a blast from Antarctica. The skills these guys had always amazed him. It had been an eye-opener training and working with them over the last four and a half years. He would definitely miss them.

Somehow they got the doors shut while hanging on. Nick felt the weight shift as they jumped into the ocean. He immediately drew the cyclic stick to the left, soaring away to the west, where he intended making wide circuits of the yacht in case the boys needed him.

Ava paced the luxury cabin, her panic and nausea rising. She was a terrible sailor at the best of times, and the waves rocking the yacht weren't helping. The engines had stopped five minutes ago after a loud bang, which sent a shudder vibrating through the yacht. Could the loud bang have been Nick's team remotely disabling the propeller? She hoped so.

When Lex had dragged Ava below deck, she'd feared he'd meant to force himself on her, but instead he'd locked her in this cabin. Ten minutes later she'd watched through the porthole as a speedboat come alongside, carrying Damon Pearce, two Asian men and Helen.

Ava glanced at her friend, sitting stiffly in an armchair, fidgeting with the edge of her wide sleeve. The bruise under her eye had darkened and her lip still looked swollen. She also had a deep cut on her hand, which she'd told Ava happened when the two Asian men broke into her apartment wielding knives. They'd forced her to open the shop and then robbed it bare. Ava wished they'd left Helen behind. Bringing her onboard the yacht didn't bode well for a healthy future.

"I'm sorry you've been dragged into this, Helen, but we will be rescued. Nick and his team are tracking this yacht. They will save us."

Helen's eyes widened. "Tracking us—how?"

"By satellite. They know how to disable the propeller remotely."

"You think that clunk was the propeller being disabled?"

"I hope so, otherwise we're about to meet up with that ship Lex told me about. Can you see anything outside?"

Helen peered out the porthole. "I can't see through the heavy rain." She drew in a deep breath. "Our captors told me Nick and his friends are dead, so how could they possibly disable the propeller?"

"Nick's not dead. I just hope he gets here soon."

"We're quite safe here for the time being," mused Helen.

Ava sighed. "I heard Lex telling one of the crew to set explosives. They're planning to blow the yacht up. There won't be any trace of it or us left. We need to make contingency plans in case Nick doesn't get here in time."

Heated voices in the corridor caught Ava's attention. She ran across the cabin and pressed her ear to the locked door. "I can hear Damon demanding to know what's going on. He sounds angry." She hammered on the door. "You'll never get away with this, Damon. And if I don't get some fresh air, I'm going to be sick all over the carpet."

Heavy footsteps thundered along the corridor then she heard Damon's voice. "Ava, is that you?

Ava looked at Helen who stared at her oddly. "Of course it's me. You had your henchman kidnap me."

"I did no such thing." He rattled the handle. "Someone open this door immediately."

What the hell was going on? Ava glanced back at Helen as more male voices joined Damon outside the door. "It sounds like he didn't know I was here."

Helen lifted her hands as if bewildered and her wide sleeves slipped to her elbows. Ava's gaze caught on the twisted pearl wristlet. A one of a kind that until recently had been locked in Ava's safe. Time stood still as Ava tried and failed to come up with a plausible reason for Helen to be wearing the wristlet.

"What is it?" asked Helen. "You've gone terribly pale."

Get a grip, Ava, there has to be an explanation. "Erm, where did you get that pearl wristlet?"

Helen twisted her hand, admiring the dainty piece of jewelry. "My son gave it to me a few days ago. It's lovely, isn't it?"

"Yes." Ava ignored the commotion in the corridor and met Helen's strangely intense gaze. "Doesn't your son live in Queensland?"

"Not any more. He's been living in Broome for a while now."

A sudden chill crawled along Ava's spine. Why hadn't Helen mentioned that? Nothing made sense. The intricate filigree design on the wristlet's clasp was impossible to duplicate without having the original to copy. How had Helen's son got hold of it? Who was Helen's son?

She dragged her eyes away from Helen as a key turned in the door.

Damon strode into the luxury cabin, his eyes moving from Ava to Helen. "What's going on? I made it clear, Ava was to be left alone."

Helen shrugged. "We can't afford loose ends." She picked up a beauty case from beside her chair. "This case holds a fortune in highly sought after gems. Luckily everything stolen from my shop is insured, and the police will never suspect me of stealing from myself or you." She smirked at Ava. "When I show up battered and bruised, with a sob story of how we were both kidnapped, they'll believe I'm an innocent shopkeeper who managed to escape. In fact, I helped plan this whole operation." She laughed. "My goodness, dear, you should see your face."

Ava could not believe her ears. Helen was her friend and partner, not a criminal. "But those men punched you when they took Liam, and they cut your hand tonight, and you don't like Damon."

"Cutting my hand was my idea. We needed to leave blood on the floor. And, I had to make Liam's kidnapping believable, but you're right—I don't like Damon. It was his idea that I take you on as a partner, so you would stay in Broome. Still, it's worked out well. We now have all the media mogul's gems as well. The police will believe I am an innocent victim who escaped. You were not so fortunate."

"It was you who broke into my safe?"

Helen laughed. It wasn't a pleasant sound. "No, dear. I gave the key to my son, Lex. He robbed your safe at my request."

Damon looked stunned. "What?"

Helen shrugged. "I thought we could pin it on Nicholas Flanagan. He goes to jail, I keep the gems and you, Damon, get the girl. Barry Sanders and that other pilot knew too much, so I had Lex deal with them too."

"Lex Walsh is your son?" Ava couldn't get her head around it. "I thought you were my friend. I thought you cared about Liam and me. You meant to kill Liam and Nick?"

Helen looked at her watch. "By now it's a done deal. Kaboom. We set a trap. Lured Nick and his friends in then a devoted employee set an explosion to go off shortly after they landed. No loose ends."

"I don't believe this," muttered Damon staring at Helen. "You took Liam?"

"Get over it." Helen turned and frowned at Lex, standing in the doorway. "Nicholas Flanagan and his friends attached something to the propeller to disable it, and there's a tracker onboard. Find it, and contact the freighter. The sooner we're off this yacht the better."

"Good idea." Lex leaned out the doorway and yelled the same instructions to someone in the corridor.

Ava ducked her head in an attempt to cool her rage. Boasting that Nick and the team were alive and on their way would make things significantly worse for her. She needed to stay calm. If she knew one thing for sure, it was that Nick would rescue her, or die trying. He loved her, and it was the skills he'd acquired in the SAS that he'd need to save her.

But if I'm too calm, Helen will know something is up. She lifted her chin defiantly. "You're lying. Nick and Liam are on their way back from King Leopald Ranges and when Nick realizes I'm missing, he'll contact the police."

Damon swore. "Christ, Helen. Do you have any idea what you've done? Nicholas Flanagan is part of some special ops unit. When I agreed to our partnership, I didn't sign on for this. Tax avoidance is one thing. Kidnapping and murder is another."

Ava stared at Damon as she slowly joined the dots. "You're partners?" Her heart began to thud faster. "You're smuggling diamonds and pearls out of the country and illegal immigrants in?" Her voice rose.

"No." Damon shook his head. "We don't smuggle people. Helen arranged for me to channel a little merchandise into the Asian market. I didn't have anything to do with the robbery or Liam's kidnapping. I thought Nick was behind them."

Lex Walsh stepped through the door. "News flash. We often import big paying immigrants into Australia. I deliver them to the mainland for a cut, and in return the captain smuggles your gems into Asia. You're up to your eyeballs in it."

Fury radiated from Damon's face. "I might manipulate people to get what I want, but I've never resorted to murder or been involved in people smuggling and kidnapping. I will not be a part of this."

Lex laughed. "Where do you think your housekeeper or this

crew, or for that matter, the pearl farm and mine workers come from?"

Damon looked at Lex incredulously. "You're not serious?"

"Oh, I am, and while we're putting all our cards on the table—we have a man on his way to deal with the female journalist. A man whose authority no one will question."

Ava gasped. "Madeline's no threat to you."

"Yes, she is," said Lex. "But not for long."

As Damon ranted at Lex, Ava glowered at the woman she'd considered a business partner and friend. If Nick didn't make it in time, would he accept Helen's story? Or would he see her for what she really was? *Probably not.*

Helen stared back with smug satisfaction plastered over her face. "I did warn you months ago that getting involved with Damon was a bad idea."

Ava shook her head in dismay. Helen might think she had it all figured out, but Nick and his friends were alive and on their way. There were still two things that bothered Ava. Who was the man going after Madeline, and who was Helen planning to blame for the kidnappings, murders, and blowing up the yacht?

Helen paced to the door and stood beside Lex. "It will be light soon. We need to find out how close the freighter is. Once we've passed on this stash, we can blow up the yacht then head back to Broome in the speedboat."

Damon stared at Helen. "No one is blowing up my yacht, and you can give Ava back her gems. Then you can take the speedboat and get the hell out of here. I don't want anything more to do with either of you."

Helen huffed. "I don't take instructions from you." She took the gun Lex handed her and pointed it at Damon. "Lex and I will be leaving in the speedboat, and I'm taking all these gems, but you're staying here."

Suddenly it all clicked in Ava's mind. She'd been wondering who would get the blame. Now she knew. "There is no honor among thieves."

Damon turned to her. "I'm sorry, Ava, I never meant for this to happen."

She needed to stall. Buy them some time. "I accept that you

weren't involved in the robbery or kidnapping Liam, but did you have anything to do with the explosion at Madeline's apartment in Melbourne last night?"

His eyes widened. "No, I didn't, but it has to be connected with her secret. There are people who would go to those lengths to keep it out of the public arena."

"Who?"

"Her husband, his business partner, both their families. High profile people don't like their dirty washing dragged through the media. I warned Madeline she could be in danger. Not from me, but others who are much closer." He sighed. "Look, I fancied Madeline for a while, but after attending your exhibition in London and then speaking to you, I set the wheels in motion to get you here."

"Why?"

"Ava, I care about you."

She raised her chin defiantly. "Then help me save Madeline."

Helen shook her head. "It's too late for that, dear." She raised her arm, pointing the gun at Ava.

"No!" Damon dived as a boom blasted in Ava's ears. They went down in a crashing thud of arms and legs. Pain lanced through Ava's shoulder then warm liquid flowed into her armpit and across her chest. "Oh, God, I've been shot."

"Two for one. Not bad, Mother." Lex laughed then he and Helen left the cabin.

Gunfire erupted on the deck above, leaving Ava's ears ringing. Had Nick arrived, only too late? She'd been so worried about Liam and Nick that she hadn't considered her own death. It was so unfair. She needed to stay conscious long enough to tell Nick she didn't blame him.

More shooting, closer this time.

Damon groaned. "Ava."

She blinked then tried moving her legs and arms. Her shoulder hurt but it wasn't debilitating. Maybe she hadn't been critically wounded. Wriggling her way out from under Damon, she got up on her knees and rolled him over.

"Shikes." Bile rose in her throat at the jagged hole in his chest. She tried to stem the blood flow with her hands, but it leaked between her fingers. She glanced at her T-shirt, soaked a vivid red. The awful sickly sweet metallic smell had her heaving. Preparing herself for another bullet hole, she glanced at her shoulder.

There wasn't one. Blinking she looked around. She must have hit her shoulder on the edge of the bed. Damon had taken the bullet meant for her. He'd saved her life. Breathing through her mouth, Ava looked at him anxiously. "Damon, you're hurt really bad." She dragged a light throw off the bed and tried to pack it over the hole. Blood soaked it in seconds, which dripped onto the carpet and her jeans.

Damon's eyes fluttered open. "I didn't hurt anyone, Ava. I didn't know Lex was Helen's son. You need to escape before they kill you."

"I heard guns. Help is here. You have to hang on."

"I'm done for, lost too much blood, but you still have a chance. Run, Ava, run." His eyes rolled back in his head and his body went limp in her arms. She hadn't even realized she held him. Carefully she moved the throw. The blood had stopped pumping along with his heart.

Biting her lip, she clambered to her feet, her tears blinding her as she staggered to the open door. Wiping her eyes, Ava peeked left then right. Empty. She couldn't do anything for Damon, but she had to get off the yacht before it exploded.

There were stairs at each end. She went left toward the bow. A guttural gurgling sounded above her then an Asian man tumbled down the carpeted steps, landing at her feet.

She froze, waiting for him to move.

He couldn't. A thick-bladed knife had been thrust all the way through his neck and blood poured out of the wounds on either side.

Ava dry-retched at the gruesome sight and ran in the other direction. She raced up two flights of stairs then crawled on her hands and knees through the saloon. She was almost to the doors when her gaze fell on the pearl wristlet lying on the carpet. The intricate catch had to be fastened properly or it would come loose, so must have fallen off Helen's wrist. Quickly she stuffed it in her pocket then clambered to her feet and ran.

On the back deck she could see another Asian man shooting toward the bow. A bullet hit him right between the eyes and Ava clamped a hand over her mouth as the man fell over the side of the yacht. With the howl of the wind and waves buffeting the yacht, she didn't even hear a splash. Blood would bring sharks, and the West Australian coastline was known for some of the biggest.

Ava glanced down at her blood-soaked T-shirt and jeans. Jumping into the ocean lost its appeal. Looking up, she saw Lex raise a long tube-like object, shaped a little like a giant bullet onto his shoulder. He pointed it into the air and flicked up what appeared to be a sight. *A rocket launcher.* Her gaze rose to a small chopper off the boat's stern, and Nick's shocked eyes staring at her.

"No!" She hurled herself across the deck, sliding on the wet surface before slamming into Lex.

Through the cockpit window, she saw Nick's shoulder move as he yanked the cyclic stick to the right, trying to evade the impact, but there was nothing slow about the speed with which the missile hit, destroying the main rotor blades in a spray of shrapnel. As pieces of debris smashed into the yacht, the main body of the chopper dropped into the black ocean.

"Nick!"

Lex swung the launcher at her but caught his foot on a deck chair and stumbled. Ava ran toward the back of the upper deck. She squealed as a huge man in a black wetsuit and mask bounded up the steps. He sidestepped her then dived at Lex. They both went careening over the side of the yacht. She guessed it could be Talos, but she wasn't hanging round to find out. Someone had to save Nick.

Ava flinched as a bullet splintered the paneling beside her. She scrambled down the narrow steps to the lower deck then sprinted for the stern, to where Helen had untied the speedboat and tried to keep her balance as the yacht pitched and rolled with the swell of the ocean. The murdering cow was making a run for it.

Oh, no you don't. Ava took a running jump and slammed into Helen. The beauty case went flying as they hit the deck hard. Ava jarred her elbow, but it wasn't enough to stop the inferno of rage and devastation igniting inside her. She dragged Helen onto her knees by the front of her jumper and slapped her hard in the face. "You monster. How dare you put my baby's life in danger." Ava punched Helen, crying out as searing pain stung her knuckles.

"Christ, woman." Jarred grasped Ava around her waist, his arm encasing her like a thick cable of twisted steel. "You'll get yourself shot."

Helen scrambled to her feet then jumped into the speedboat.

"Let go of me." Ava struggled as Helen started the engine. "That murdering bitch is getting away."

"Don't waste your energy." Jarred yelled in her ear. "She's got nowhere to go. Where's Pearce?"

"Dead." Ava twisted in his arms. "Nick's been shot down."

"I know, but it wasn't a direct hit and he's done more HUET training than most chopper pilots."

"What the hell does HUET mean?"

"Helicopter underwater escape training."

As Helen took off in a wide arc, Ava stared at the ocean, praying for Nick's head to appear. Suddenly the rage inside her turned to ice as an enormous fin sliced through the water then disappeared under the yacht. Her hands shook as she clutched Jarred's arm.

"Sh...ark."

"A Great White." He pushed her behind him and raised a bulky looking rifle to his shoulder. "Talos, leave that bastard. You need to get out of the water now!"

Ava could barely drag in a breath as she watched Talos swim for the rear of the yacht. Lex was swimming in the direction of the speedboat.

A Great White. Ava clung to the rail, her gaze glued to where the chopper went down.

Nick, where are you?

CHAPTER TWENTY-TWO

Nick pushed the memory of Ava soaked in blood from chest to knees to the back of his mind. Her attempt to save him had broken Walsh's concentration enough to shift his aim. Ava had saved Nick's life. Had Talos got to Walsh in time to save her?

That wasn't Nick's only worry. With the rotor blades gone, the weight of the helicopter's engine and gearbox had turned the chopper upside down. His ears popped as the chopper sank into the black depths. He hit the spotlight, checked the mouthpiece of the small compressed air cylinder on the front of his flotation vest and braced for impact. The cabin filled quickly. His plan to get out fast took a nosedive when the first of the great whites swam through the shaft of light from the spotty, a human body clamped in its monstrous jaws. Two more sharks attacked in a feeding frenzy.

Nick purged the water from the mouthpiece of the cylinder and drew a welcome breath. The cylinder was supposedly good for eight to ten breaths, so he figured he had roughly two minutes of air if he stayed calm. But these motherfucking sharks had to be at least sixteen feet in length.

Then they were gone, but only from the light.

Holy shit. Upside down, submerged in water, surrounded by sharks, and still sinking. What else could go wrong?

The spotty flickered and died, leaving him in total blackness. *And there you have it.* Nick mentally cursed. He needed to get out now. *At least I don't have to swim through meat cleaving rotor blades. Then again the sharks could still take care of that.* Nick didn't hold much confidence in the Kevlar suit. It might be blade resistant, but those three-inch, razor sharp teeth and the strength of the jaw behind them was lethal. His flotation vest, might get him to the surface, but then what? How far away was the yacht?

It's now or never. Keeping one hand locked on the doorframe, so as not to become disoriented, Nick took another breath from the cylinder and jettisoned the door. It fell away. With his free hand, he released the seatbelt then dragged his body out of the chopper. Once free, he tugged the inflation cord on his flotation vest. He didn't try to swim, it was easier to let the vest expand and take him in the right direction. Up.

An extremely long, terrifying passage in total darkness.

Nick's lungs were bursting by the time he hit the surface and hauled in much needed air. He felt bad about Barry's chopper, but it could be worse. He'd hate to explain to the Army how he'd sent a multi-million-dollar Black Hawk to the bottom of the ocean.

By the dawn sky he could see the yacht off to his left, lit up like a beacon. Lights glowed from every porthole. Nick raised the whistle then thought better of it. Sharks could pick up some frequencies.

He could see three figures leaning over the rail at the stern, one small and two large. Ava stood between Jarred and Talos. Relief surged through Nick as he raised an arm. "Hoy."

"There he is!" It was Ava's voice. She ran to the starboard side and began waving just as a monstrous fin rose between Nick and the yacht.

That's a big shark. Nick stayed motionless, watching the fin glide through the water then sink below the waves again. "Not good."

Talos and Jarred had their guns out, but bullets wouldn't stop this monster. Nick heard an engine splutter then burst to life. It was a speed boat. "Helen?" Maybe there was hope for him yet, but why was she helping Lex into the boat? He'd take her as a hostage.

Another fin, smaller this time, but not by much, glided past Nick then circled. "Shit."

He looked for Helen, but she was making a wide arc of the yacht. "Over here, I need help." He looked for the fin and couldn't see it. Hopefully the speedboat's motor had drawn it away.

The beat of extremely big engines pulsated through his body then a panamax-sized ship emerged from the curtain of rain. By the water line, Nick could see it was fully loaded. Rising with the swell of the wave, he might as well be a grain of sand compared to the enormous ship bearing down on the speedboat.

Fuck. The ship's crew had no chance of seeing Helen. They were too close. *Christ, this is unbelievable.*

Ava's scream jerked his attention back to the yacht. She was pointing at something behind Nick. He chose not to look. If he only had seconds to live, Ava would be the last memory he took with him, and what a memory. She handed something to Jarred then yanked off her T-shirt and jeans then ran to the bow in her tiny bikini panties and bra.

Nick's bemusement turned to terror and he yelled, "Christ, no, Ava. Don't jump, you've still got blood on your body."

She didn't jump but hurled the blood stained clothing into the ocean. "Geez, what a woman." He felt a disturbance beside him then froze as the motherfucker of all sharks glided past within six feet of his shoulder, heading in a direct line for the bow of the yacht. It could probably swallow a jet ski without blinking. Nick held his breath until the shark was well clear of him, then he swam for the yacht, not stopping when he heard the continuous emergency horn on the freighter, or the chomping and crunching of fiberglass as the freighter ran over the top of the speedboat. Even if Helen and Walsh had managed to dive clear, they'd probably be dragged under the boat and thrust straight into the propellers. Nick increased his speed. Blood in the water would bring more sharks.

"Nick," roared Talos. "Catch this."

Breathing heavily, Nick stopped swimming to reach for the lifebuoy soaring toward him. Once he'd lifted his body onto it, Talos and Jarred pulled the rope as fast as they could. Ava stood beside them, hopping from foot to foot, yelling encouragement.

Nick had almost reached the yacht when Ava screamed his name. Reaching for his handgun, Nick swiveled, nearly shitting himself as he discharged six rounds into the cold, black eyes of a shark coming straight at him. More bullets slammed into it from above him as the buoy hit the back of the yacht.

This is it. Nick dropped the gun and raised his fists as he faced rows of razor sharp teeth, but before the shark could chomp on him, it was snapped up in the jaws of a Great White twice its size. Nick exhaled with relief as Jarred and Talos caught his arms and hauled him aboard the tray at the back of the yacht. "Fuck, that was close."

Ava threw her arms around him, shaking as she clung to him. "I thought..."

"I'm fine, Angel."

The ship's horn blasted again and Nick looked up to see several crewmen leaning over the railing. He wrapped his arms tightly around Ava. "Let's get you below deck, sweetheart."

"I love you." She grabbed his face and kissed him, soliciting whistles from the freighter's crew.

"I love you too." Nick had his angel back in his arms, an angel who had saved his life twice in the last ten minutes. "Come on, babe. I don't want those guys ogling you."

Jarred nudged Nick's shoulder. "Lieutenant, while you're below look for some concealable weapons. Our problems aren't over yet."

Nick's gaze shot from Jarred to the crew on the freighter who—thanks to the lightening sky—he could see held rifles. *Hell's bells. I hope we're not jumping out of the pan and into the fire.* "You got it, Colonel." Grasping Ava's hand, he towed her across the deck and through a door.

"This way," called Ava, dashing past him then around a curved wall.

Nick followed her down a set of spiral stairs then along a dimly lit corridor to a stateroom, where she hesitated and looked at Nick. "Damon was in partnership with Helen, selling gems on the black market, but he didn't have anything to do with the robbery or Liam's kidnapping." She stood back and pointed at a body lying on the floor in a pool of blood.

Nick stared at Pearce. "Who shot him?"

"Helen. She meant to shoot me, but Damon threw himself in the way." Ava's voice wobbled. "They thought they'd shot us both. Damon died saving my life."

"Helen?" Nick pulled Ava into his arms and held her tightly as his gaze fell on the hole in Damon's chest. For all the man's arrogance and self-importance, he'd done a noble thing saving Ava, but why would Helen want to kill Ava? He shook his head as the jigsaw began to fall into place. "Come on, Angel, let's find you some clothes."

Unnerved at how close Ava had come to dying, Nick opened the door opposite. He needed to stay focused. "I never figured Helen for this. She certainly fooled me."

"And me." Crossing to a huge walk-in-robe, Ava began opening drawers. "It gets worse. Lex Walsh is Helen's son, and they admitted to killing Max. They were planning to meet up with a freighter, then blow up the yacht and blame everything on Damon."

"So, was Damon involved in the people smuggling too?"

"No, just tax evasion. He was stunned when Lex said they were smuggling gems *and people*. Damon didn't have anything to do with bombing Madeline's apartment either." Ava gasped. "Oh, God. We have to get a message to Madeline. A man is on his way to kill her."

"Who?"

"I don't know. Here, put these on." She threw a T-shirt, jocks, and sweatpants still in their sealed packaging at him.

"Thanks. You have a shower and I'll dig out some clothes for Jarred and Talos. We don't want the freighter's crew to get a close look at our Kevlar suits."

"But they've already seen you."

"I know, but from a distance it looks like we're wearing wetsuits." Nick urged Ava into the bathroom. "A shower will make you feel better." He didn't mention the blood staining her pale skin or its pungent smell. From experience he knew Ava would spend ages scrubbing the blood from her body. It would take longer to scrub it from her mind. Witnessing such a gruesome death was bad enough, but to know the person dying in your arms, their blood soaking through your clothes was nightmare material. He'd been there, done that and lost a good buddy.

Once the door closed, Nick undid his knife sheath then stripped off the suit and dressed. He was rummaging through Damon's chest of drawers when Jarred and Talos entered the cabin. "I've found one handgun and a box of ammunition," Nick said, pointing to two piles of packaged clothes on the bed. "I thought you might want to get out of the Kevlar suits."

"My thoughts exactly." Jarred peeled his suit off. "The crew is in the process of lowering a lifeboat. We can't contact Simon or the Coast Guard because the yacht's radio has been smashed, but we grabbed the bugs so Simon can hear everything we say. Otherwise, we're on our own."

Talos leaned against the walk-in-robe's doorframe. "We saw Pearce's body. What happened?"

A ray of sun broke through the clouds as Nick strode over to the porthole. The ocean swell made it hard for the crew to lower the lifeboat. Satisfied he still had a little time up his sleeve, Nick told Jarred and Talos what he knew.

"We need external help." Jarred pulled on the sweatpants then reached for one of the T-shirts on the bed.

Talos was just shedding his suit when the bathroom door opened. "Stall her." Naked, he ducked into the walk-in robe and closed the door.

Dripping wet and wrapped in a towel, Ava padded across to Nick but her gaze locked on Jarred. "It's urgent you send someone to check on Madeline. Walsh said a man is on his way to deal with her."

Jarred pulled his T-shirt over his head. "Madeline's fine. We've got two police officers and Gibbs watching her."

"No, she's not fine." Ava gave Nick a beseeching look. "Walsh said no one would question this man's authority. Madeline is in grave danger."

Talos stepped out of the walk-in-robe wearing a T-shirt that strained over his massive shoulders. The sweatpants weren't a bad fit, just several inches too short. He frowned at Jarred. "Who do we know in authority that no one will question, and who has easy access to Madeline?"

"You're not suggesting Gibbs?"

"Who else?"

Jarred's jaw clenched. "It isn't Gibbs. If Simon can hear us, he'll contact Sam and Ryan. They'll keep Madeline safe." He scratched the stubble on his chin. "I don't know if Helen and Walsh survived that collision, or the sharks got them. A pity as they could have identified the man going after Madeline."

Ava gasped. "Helen said they were meeting up with a freighter." She looked toward the porthole. "Could that ship be it?"

"More than likely." Jarred grimaced. "We need a damn good reason to be aboard this yacht. Something they'll believe."

Nick nodded. "How about we're part of a research project, studying Great Whites. Our boat hit a submerged container and began to sink, which is why we grabbed our diving gear. This yacht came along and the crew rescued us."

"Hmm," murmured Talos. "What about the bits of rotor blades and debris?"

Jarred checked the porthole then turned back to them. "We tell them the crew turned on each other. One of them shot down the chopper when the pilot tried to leave. Another two escaped in the speedboat."

"What about me?" asked Ava.

Without missing a beat Jarred continued. "We found you locked in a cabin, claiming to have been kidnapped. Then we discovered the propeller wasn't working. That will be our excuse for Nick being in the water. He was trying to fix the problem."

"That's good, Colonel," said Nick. "After seeing those sharks, none of the ship's crew will check the yacht's propeller, and they would have felt the impact of hitting the speedboat."

Ava bit her lip. "Jarred, the crew saw me kiss Nick and it wasn't a kiss between strangers."

Jarred looked faintly amused. "Arh, but Nick is the person who rescued you from a locked cabin after being kidnapped. Then you almost witnessed him eaten by sharks. It was a female response to a very emotional experience."

"That works for me." She grinned at Nick. "After such an ordeal, I would look on you as my hero. So stripping to save you seemed the right thing to do, and kissing you is, as Jarred says, a female response to an emotional situation."

Nick exhaled. "Just don't leave my side."

"I will stick like glue."

Talos checked the porthole. "We don't have much time to find that stash of gems stolen from Ava. I'd wager they were bound for the black market aboard that freighter."

Ava's head shot up. "Helen had them in a beauty case." Her shoulders sagged. "By now they're at the bottom of the ocean."

"A beauty case." Jarred frowned. "You knocked a small case out of Helen's hand when you jumped on her. It must still be up on deck."

"Thank goodness. Helen was behind the robbery and Liam's kidnapping."

"So Nick said, and I gathered as much when I saw you attack her." Jarred glanced at Talos. "Make sure you leave a tracking device on this yacht so the Navy or Coast Guard can locate it. We'll take the other tracker with us so Simon can keep tabs on us."

Talos nodded. "No worries, and I'll hide that beauty case in the engine room." He dashed out of the cabin.

"Get dressed, Angel." Nick handed a bundle of clothes to Ava. They were too big, but at least they'd hide her tempting curves. As she ran back into the bathroom, Nick re-strapped his knife-sheath to his calf under the sweatpants. "They might search us, so I'll hide my knife and gun on the lifeboat."

Ava came out of the bathroom looking like a teenager in her big brother's clothes. She'd folded the sweatpants several times and pinned them.

Jarred handed her a pearl bracelet and small disc. "Stick this bug into the folds of your sweatpants until we're on board the freighter. We'll put a tracking device in there too."

Ava did as he asked then fastened the bracelet round her wrist. "I'd forgotten I gave that to you. Helen stole this from my safe. It's a good thing I remembered I had it in my pocket or it would be inside a shark now. How long will it take for help to get to us?"

Jarred shrugged. "I've no idea, but thanks to these state-of-the-art bugs, Simon now knows about the freighter. I suspect he's already contacted the Navy to see if they have a patrol boat in the area that can assist us."

"And Madeline?" Ava's voice hitched as she stared at Jarred. "Who will assist her?"

Nick noticed Jarred's fists were clenched so tight his knuckles were white. "Simon will take measures to protect her." He didn't need to add if it's not too late. The look he threw Nick said it all.

Nick checked the porthole again. "They've got the lifeboat in the water so we should get up on deck." He shoved the Kevlar suits into a deep drawer under the bed then pulled the quilt over it. "Let's hope they believe our story."

CHAPTER TWENTY-THREE

The cold breeze whipped Ava's hair across her eyes as she held onto Nick for balance. She should be freezing, especially as they were being covered in a fine mist of sea spray every time a swell hit the yacht. Damon's woolen jumper and sweatpants helped keep the chill out, but even so a trickle of sweat slithered down her spine as the lifeboat motored toward them. Up on the ship's deck she could make out eight people, but how many were in the lifeboat? The odds were not good if things went sour.

She pushed away the image of Damon's lifeless body as trepidation filled her. Would she ever hold Liam again? What lay in store?

Talos had hidden the gems somewhere in the yacht's engine room and now stood with Jarred by the stern. How they expected to take on these armed smugglers was anyone's guess. Ava could only hope the ship's crew fell for their story. That aside, leaving a yacht with no propeller might seem like a good idea, but watching the approaching lifeboat rise and drop on the swells made her tummy churn. It looked anything but fun, especially knowing there were sharks out there.

The hatch opened and two Asian men climbed out followed by a whiskered Westerner. The whiskered man threw a rope to Jarred. "Looks like a war zone. Care to explain what's going on?" The whiskered man had a broad Australian accent. When his gaze lingered on Ava's chest, she shivered and moved closer to Nick.

"I'll make a full report to your captain." Jarred tied off the rope. "But basically, one of the crew shot down a chopper before escaping in the speedboat you ran over. The yacht's propeller is broken, and there's a couple of dead bodies below."

"I see. You mind if we take a look?"

"Not at all."

While the whiskered man used his 2-way radio to speak with the captain, the two Asian men boarded the yacht and went below deck. It was a tense few minutes for Ava as she fought nausea and looked at the massive ship.

Although the dawning sky remained heavy with clouds, Ava could see the armed crew clearly. They were mostly Asian, although the captain appeared to be a Westerner. Her breath caught at the thought of being searched. Nick had stuck a handgun in the back of her waistband and strapped Talos' knife round her calf, veiled by the sweatpants.

Ava tried not to think about sharks that were longer than the lifeboat or how three ex-SAS soldiers could possibly protect her and take on twelve or more armed men. She was a shivering mess, yet Nick, Jarred, and Talos acted as if they were exactly who they were pretending to be as they chatted with a white whiskered man standing in the open hatch of the lifeboat. He introduced himself as Bob, his gaze sweeping up and down Ava. She didn't trust him.

Another Asian man sat at the steering wheel, keeping the engine running. By Ava's reckoning, ten minutes had passed when the two crewmen reappeared. They both carried sports bags stuffed with what looked like Damon's clothes and shoes. One had a smug grin as he held his arm out to the whiskered man. Outrage filled Ava as she recognized Damon's gold plated Rolex and signet ring.

"We found three dead bodies."

Bob nodded. "Anything else?"

"No, must have gone down with the speedboat."

Ava swallowed. Were they talking about the stolen gems? Her gaze returned to Damon's watch. What sort of people robbed the dead and raided their possessions?

Criminals without humanity or conscience.

The whiskered man waved her forward, but Nick stepped into the lifeboat ahead of her then turned and helped her in. Talos and Jarred followed, then the crew climbed through the hatch and closed the door. Ava was reminded of a front-loader washing machine, only the churning water was on the outside.

As they approached the massive ship, Ava's heart lodged in her throat. It was probably a good thing she hadn't eaten in hours and had already thrown up over Lex, or she'd cast her accounts again. Even with her empty stomach, bile rose in her throat as the lifeboat crested another wave and the huge ship loomed closer. How could they possibly get up there safely? And what awaited them once they were on board?

She glanced at Bob and caught him watching her again. She shuddered and sidled closer to Nick.

His hand wrapped around hers. "You okay?"

"Scared and cold." That was putting it mildly. Petrified and turning into an iceberg would be more apt. She sneaked a quick look at the whiskered Australian. He watched her too, but more with curiosity. She felt Nick's hand glide down her back and remove the handgun from her waistband. Several minutes later he had a coughing fit and leaned forward over his knees. It was a ruse enabling him to remove the knife and sheath from her calf. Ava was impressed at how deftly it was accomplished, under the watchful eye of Bob.

Ava drew in a breath, intentionally drawing Bob's attention away from Nick. "I'm worried about my son. Do you think the captain can find out if he's okay?"

Bob nodded. "Sure."

The lifeboat bumped against the ship then one of the crew opened the hatch and climbed out. Something clanged on the roof and Nick squeezed her hand. "He's connecting the pulley so they can winch us up."

"Oh."

The crewman climbed back inside then closed the hatch. Suddenly the lifeboat lurched then began to rise beside the ship. Ava clung to Nick's hand.

He smiled at her as if he wasn't the least concerned. "Don't worry, these guys know what they're doing." His fingers tightened around her hand.

Nick looked at the whiskered man. "Where are you headed?"

"Japan. We took on coal at Port Headland."

They jolted to a stop and then the hatch opened. Ava couldn't stop shaking. These men had to be part of the smuggling ring. If they killed her and Nick, what would happen to Liam? Ava tried to calm her wayward thoughts. If they died Maggie would take care of Liam, but what would losing his parents do to her son?

Nick and Talos kept her between them as they climbed out of the lifeboat. Ava glanced back but saw no sign of the gun or knife. As she climbed to the main deck of the ship, Ava noticed a large man in a crisp, fawn colored uniform. Several other men in reddish coveralls stood behind him. *This must be the captain.* His smile didn't reach his eyes and knowing what he was involved in, she shouldn't really be surprised.

"Welcome aboard. I'm Captain Claude Renner. I understand you've had a harrowing experience." He spoke with a heavy accent. Ava guessed German.

Jarred stepped forward and shook the captain's hand then introduced Nick, Talos, and her. "Captain, this young lady was kidnapped—" He paused as two men in soaking wet weather gear dumped a heavy duty net further along the deck.

Ava glanced at Nick and Talos who were also watching the men. Was the net important?

Jarred returned his attention to the captain. "We are part of a special ops team sent to Broome to uncover a human smuggling ring. This young lady was involved with one of my men four years ago. We used that relationship as cover for sending him here."

Ava couldn't help the gasp that escaped. Why had Jarred changed his story and why did his words sound so truthful? Nick squeezed her fingers and Ava swallowed her panic. Of course he was making this up. She was jumping to conclusions again.

"Smuggling?" The captain stiffened.

"Yes. I'm glad you were in the area to rescue us. The Navy and AFP are tracking the yacht and will pick it up in the next few hours. I'd be much obliged if you could radio the mainland and let them know we are on your ship before the Navy sends out a search and rescue party."

"Of course. I will attend to that straight away. In the meantime, I will have one of my men take you to the officers' mess for breakfast, then perhaps you can tell me the whole story."

"Thank you. By the way, there were two people in the speedboat that collided with your ship. You didn't see what happened to them, did you?"

"No. One of my officers spotted the boat and sounded the horn, but it was too late. We found no survivors."

Ava noted Nick and Talos hadn't so much as blinked an eyelid as they listened to the exchange. Suddenly the clouds parted and sunlight filtered across the ocean and main deck. Ava counted seven raised platforms spread out in front of her. One had helipad markings on top. She assumed they covered hulls full of coal. A clang drew her attention to a crane on the other side of the ship. It was anchored to a set of stairs being raised. Why had the crew bothered to lower the stairs when they'd used a lifeboat?

The captain glanced across the deck as the stairs clicked into place. "Were the people on the speedboat part of your team?"

Jarred shook his head. "No, they were the leaders of a smuggling ring we're after. They're also wanted in connection with several murders and two kidnappings."

Captain Renner rubbed his chin. "You understand this is most unusual. I only have your word for what has happened, so before we go up to the officers' mess, I will need to make sure none of you are carrying weapons."

"That's fair enough." Jarred turned so that his back was against a white wall, then he planted his feet several feet apart. "We are unarmed."

Ava dragged her feet as Nick urged her forward then he and Talos mimicked Jarred's stance. She guessed it made sense to protect their backs while being frisked, but what could they do against an armed crew.

It was Bob the Australian who did the frisking, and when it came to Ava's turn, she was surprised he didn't take liberties. Still, she shivered as he ran his hands up her legs, down her arms and around her waist. Four armed crewmen stood watching.

As Bob stepped back the captain looked at Ava. "Please accept my hospitality. After breakfast I will have you shown to a cabin where you can freshen up and rest."

"Thank you." Ava went to follow the captain, but Jarred stepped in front of her. Nick waved her forward then shadowed her and Talos brought up the rear, followed by Bob and another armed officer.

Ava stepped over a raised ledge and found herself in a narrow passageway. A door was open on her left and she saw two men in red overalls. They were standing in front of panels full of lights and dials. Ava returned her attention to the corridor and almost ran into Jarred who had bent to tuck in a loose shoelace. His fingers brushed against her ankle and she caught a glimpse of something black in his hand. He'd taken one of the bugs from her trouser hem. That's when she noticed the red droplets covering the floor ahead. *Blood.*

The captain half opened a door on the right and Ava realized it was a lift. Her gaze dropped to the floor where reddish streaks had been smudged across the floor. The captain closed the door. "There are too many of us to take the lift, so Bob will take you up to the officers' mess via the stairs. I will join you once I've contacted the mainland."

Ava glanced at Nick and Jarred. They didn't seem to have noticed the blood. Was that also blood in the lift? Could Helen or Lex have been rescued?

They stepped over another raised ledge into a stairwell then climbed one set of stairs before exiting into a corridor full of doors. The officers' mess was a large room at the end with views over the stern and side where Ava could see two crewmen securing the boarding ladder. One half of the room was taken up by a carpeted area with two sofas, a fridge, and widescreen television. The other side housed four dining tables set with white linen and cutlery.

The aroma of bacon cooking wafted from a galley to the left, where Ava could see two male cooks working. To her reckoning that made a crew of fourteen. How many more were on board?

Bob pulled out a chair for her and motioned for everyone to sit. "Enjoy your breakfast. I need to attend to a couple of things then I will return with the captain."

"Thank you." She wanted to talk to Nick about the blood and what she'd seen on deck, but several officers were within hearing.

Nick took the chair on her left. Talos and Jarred sat opposite with their backs to a wall. Their eyes kept gliding around the room. They seemed tense as if expecting something to happen. Her appetite vanished.

A kitchen hand still in his early teens brought out a pot of coffee and jug of milk. Then he returned with plates of eggs, bacon, and sausages. When Ava smiled at him, he blushed profusely. If this ship did indeed smuggle people, he would be arrested along with the rest of the crew, yet he was only a kid.

Ava had almost finished her coffee when Captain Renner and Bob walked in. It surprised her that all the other officers and crew were neat and tidy, whereas Bob was unshaven and his clothes crumpled as if he'd worn them to bed. He sat at the end of the table closest to her. There was something very familiar about him.

The captain sat at the other end then cleared his throat. "I've contacted the Port Authority in Broome and they're alerting the necessary people. I have been advised to continue on to our next port, where you will disembark and be returned to Australia." He looked at Ava. "Bob said you were concerned about your son. I will ask the Port Authority to check on him for you. Where is he at the moment?"

She was about to answer when Nick nudged her knee and spoke for her. "Liam is with members of our team. I'm sure he is safe."

The captain's eyes flicked to Bob before settling on Jarred. "I'm interested to know how this all came about. Why you were on a yacht with dead bodies?"

Jarred laid down his knife and fork. "We work closely with the AFP. They requested we locate a smuggling ring rumored to be operating in this area. As most of my team was focused on another operation, I sent Nick in early. He has intimate knowledge of the area and a history with Ava. They have a child together. I decided we could use that relationship to our advantage, especially as Ava is involved in the jewelry market. We did extensive research before taking the job and discovered Ava also had close ties to Damon Pearce, a man of interest."

Ava had been about to reach for a glass of water. She dropped her hand and stared at Jarred. She knew he was stretching the truth, but even so he sounded extremely believable. He met her gaze.

"I'm sorry we misled you, Ava, but it was necessary, and I think you will agree, it has brought you and Nick back together."

Nick's hand brushed her knee, a comforting touch that she desperately needed. If she hadn't seen the disbelief on Nick's face when he confronted her about Liam, she would indeed believe Jarred's story. *Wait a minute. What if it's true? Nick didn't know about Liam, but what if he really did come to Broome to search for these smugglers? No, he didn't. He came looking for me.* The worrying thought gnawed at her. One look into his eyes and she relaxed. Nick hadn't lied to her.

The captain pursed his lips. "So why was this young lady kidnapped?"

Jarred smiled. "Fortunately for us, Ava's business partner decided to rob the safe of several hundred thousand dollars in gems, which sadly are now at the bottom of the ocean. Her plan was for Nick to take the fall for the robbery, thus getting him out of the way. A mistake on her part as Nick called us immediately. That led to an intense surveillance operation. We planted a GPS tracking unit and several cutting edge listening devices on Pearce's yacht, which is how we kept track of it. The leaders of the ring kidnapped Liam, Ava and Nick's son, which was a very stupid move."

Bob narrowed his eyes. "You heard every conversation onboard the yacht?"

"Unfortunately, only the saloon was bugged." Jarred glanced around the table. "Anything said in the saloon was transmitted back to my operations center before being passed onto the AFP. After hearing the shooting, I guarantee my people will have notified the AFP. It is disappointing however, that the ringleaders died. Now we will never know their contact in Asia or how they get the illegal immigrants into Australia."

The captain looked at Ava. "Did these ringleaders say anything to you that might indicate how their operation worked?"

"The whole thing is a bit of a blur. I was stunned to discover my business partner was responsible for kidnapping my son and stealing from me. Then she tried to shoot me. I can't remember much else."

"But you will." His eyes never left her face. "In time."

"I don't know anything, Captain. I just want to go home to my son."

As the captain turned his attention back to Jarred, Ava studied him. Had he really radioed Broome's Port Authority? There was something odd about the two men's relationship. She didn't trust them, but how could she find out if Helen or Lex were on board? She had an idea but it was risky. "I do remember something."

Everyone stopped eating and looked at her.

"Damon Pearce said he had nothing to do with the people smuggling, but Helen was planning to let him take the blame." *And, now for the bombshell.* Ava took a deep breath. "She mentioned they were meeting up with a ship."

The captain nodded. "Makes sense. This is a very busy shipping lane with most of the traffic going between Australian and Asian ports."

Ava considered this information as she ate. There was a chance this was the wrong ship. She thought about the net and blood. They needed to search the ship. "Captain, I hate to impose, but I've had no sleep in the last twenty-four hours and I'm dead on my feet. May I make use of one of those cabins you spoke of?"

Nick nudged her knee again. He didn't want her taking risks. *Too bad.*

"Certainly." The captain waved the young boy over. "Yuri, are the cabins ready for our guests?"

"Yes, Captain."

"Good. We only have two spare at the moment so I hope you don't mind sharing."

Talos hadn't said a word through breakfast. He put down his mug and looked at the captain. "How many crew do you carry?"

"It varies. Anywhere between seventeen and twenty-two. At the moment we have a compliment of eighteen. They are busy with their duties, so I would appreciate it if you would remain in your cabins, or the lounge nearby while on the ship. I don't wish to lose anyone overboard."

Great. We are outnumbered and confined to barracks. Ava pushed back her chair. "I suffer sea sickness, Captain, and if I don't get fresh air occasionally I'm really ill. Could you make an exception if Nick comes with me?"

The captain's jaw tightened but then he nodded. "As long as my crew are aware you are on deck, I will allow it."

Talos also stood, towering over the table. "This is the first time I've been on a ship. Perhaps Bob could give me a tour before I catch up on some sleep?"

The captain stiffened. "Bob is busy. I will give you a tour."

Jarred pushed back his chair. "Mind if I join you?"

Ava glanced at Bob in time to see a fleeting expression of

annoyance cross his face. He definitely reminded her of someone. Was he angry that the captain had pulled rank or was it something else?

Bob caught her watching him and smiled. "While your friends are exploring the ship, I'll show you the bridge, Miss Mitchell." His smile didn't reach his eyes and again she would swear she caught a glimpse of someone familiar. Who?

"That won't be necessary." Nick rested his arm across the back of her chair. "After what Ava has been through, I think she needs to rest."

"Very well. I will see you at lunch."

Ava narrowed her eyes and watched him stroll out of the officers' mess. He'd called her Miss Mitchell. How did he know her last name? *Gotcha.*

CHAPTER TWENTY-FOUR

Talos and Jarred trailed behind Ava as Nick followed the captain out of the officers' mess. As far as he was concerned, none of the crew would get anywhere near his angel. The frisking couldn't be avoided, but he'd been within a whisper's breath of pouncing when Bob slid his hands around Ava's waist. Luckily the man had heeded the warning in Nick's eyes and drawn back. They all squeezed into the lift which had been scrubbed clean while they were eating. Jarred's little stunt in the passageway below had drawn Nick's gaze to the blood droplets. Someone who was bleeding heavily had recently come in from the main deck.

The lift took them to D-Deck where the captain turned left. "These are the cabins you will be using." He stopped between two doors, one on either side of the passageway. They were both labeled *Spare*. "The bridge is above us on the Nav-Deck. You can use the lift or stairs to get to the officers' mess for meals, which is on A-Deck. If Miss Mitchell needs fresh air, you may use the Upper-Deck exits. There are safety rules that require all external doors are locked in case of attack, so please advise one of my crew if you want to go outside."

Captain Renner pointed toward the other end of the passage. "My quarters and those of my senior officers and engineers are on this deck. You may use the guest lounge on this deck if you wish, but please don't wander. The lift will not take you down to the engine room without a key. It is out of bounds for all but my crew. Another safety requirement."

"Fair enough." Nick noticed several doors were labeled with officers' names. "Thanks, Captain. We'll catch up with you at lunch."

Nick opened a door and stood back to let Ava enter first. He caught Jarred's eye and read his message clearly. *Stay alert.*

The cabin was clean and larger than Nick expected. A double bed rested against one wall. The carpet and sofa were clean but worn. A television, bar-fridge, and cupboard took up the remaining wall space. He could see a dated ensuite through a door on the right. The ship was probably twenty or thirty years old.

Ava ran across to a porthole and opened it. "We can see the whole front of the ship from here. Look how smoothly we're cutting through the ocean. No wonder my tummy doesn't feel so bad, but I can't see any land."

Nick slid his arms around her. "I'm proud of you, Angel. Most people would have freaked by now."

"Believe me, I'm freaking. Did you notice the blood?"

"Yes."

"Do you think the crew used that boarding ladder to get someone out of the water?"

"It would have helped, but the steps don't reach sea level. It's another guard against pirate attack at sea. In a lot of working ports they chopper pilots on and off the ships. It's the port pilots who steer the ships in and out of the ports, not the ship's captain. Sometimes they use pilot boats instead of choppers. The crew then drops a specially designed rope ladder down for the pilot to climb up to the boarding ladder."

Nick drew Ava against his chest. "Having said that, a badly injured person wouldn't be able to climb a rope ladder, especially during a storm or rough seas."

"Then how would the crew get an injured person out of the water?"

"By dropping a cargo net. They're strong enough that anyone could climb up to the boarding ladder."

"A cargo net." Ava twisted and looked up at him. "I saw two men folding a really thick net."

"That's why Jarred changed his story. The men were saturated as if they'd been well and truly dunked by waves, probably as they fished someone out of the water."

Ava eyes widened. "You think the crew rescued Helen and Lex."

"Possibly. Did you see either of them dive off the speedboat before it hit the ship?"

"No. I was watching you."

"I imagine one or both of them are in a cabin. We'll need to search the ship."

"How? The crew will be watching our every move."

"We'll know more once Jarred and Talos get back. For the moment we're safe. Captain Renner and Bob are trying to decide if they've been implicated and what they should do with us."

"There are several things about Bob that bother me."

"What?"

"He called me Miss Mitchell. How does he know my last name? Also, it's like the captain defers to him, and Bob reminds me of someone."

"I got the same feeling. I bet the reason Captain Renner is giving Jarred and Talos their tour is because Bob doesn't know the workings of a ship."

"Do you believe the captain radioed Broome's Port Authority?"

"Not a chance."

"What about Jarred and Talos, will they be okay?"

Nick smiled. "They can take care of themselves. Can I borrow a couple of your bobby pins? I'm going to check out the cabins on this level. Stay here and lock the door after me. I won't be long."

Ava pulled out two long hairpins and handed them to him. "What if the others come back?"

"They'll be a while yet." He skimmed his fingers over her hip, smiling when she quivered under his touch. "I was a fool to ever let you go. You didn't believe what Jarred told the captain, did you?"

"He was very convincing, but I know you love me." She stroked his cheek. "I thought that monster shark was going to take you away from me. It was like I was being split in two. Then I saw more sharks."

"It wasn't much fun for me either. For a minute I thought you were going to sacrifice yourself to save me. That's got to be the worst ten seconds of my life." Nick lowered his head and kissed her, letting his pent up emotion free.

He smiled when she closed the remaining gap and clung to him, returning his kisses with abandon. He pulled away. "When you're safely back in your own bed, I'll show you just how much I love you."

"Good. I hold you to that, although if Simon stays over, I'll have to muffle my screams."

"Shit." Nick smacked his palm against his forehead. "The bug."

Ava looked at him in alarm. "What's wrong?"

"Simon is never going to let me forget this." Nick reached down and pulled the bug and tracker from Ava's trouser hem.

"No." She clasped a hand over her mouth.

"I'll find a place to hide these. Be back shortly." Nick poked his head out of the cabin. At least they weren't being guarded. He quickly checked the cabin opposite then moved along the passageway, knocking lightly on every cabin before using the hairpins to open each door. They were vacant but all showed signs of occupation.

The last door on the left was the captain's. Nick didn't bother knocking. The captain's quarters were twice the size of the others. The main room had a large desk, corner lounge, and coffee table. Behind that was a small dining table with two chairs and windows looking out over the front of the ship where he could see seven sealed hulls.

Nick opened a door to his left. It led into a bedroom and beyond that a bathroom. His gaze slid over the double bed, chest of drawers, and a cupboard. He closed the door and turned his attention to the desk. It held a monitor and laptop, and was covered in papers. The windows behind were curtained.

To his surprise, Captain Renner had left his computer on and the search engine open. He should shoot an email off to Simon. Nick hesitated. Their unidentified hacker could intercept the email, but Nick didn't have time to send a coded message, and it was too good an opportunity to miss. Their listening bugs were cutting edge and cost a mint, but there was always the chance they hadn't worked.

He brought up his email account then sent his fingers flying across the keys as he informed Simon what had happened. Nick requested Simon get in touch with the Navy to send a patrol boat after them. He pressed send then closed down his account. After a quick search of the drawers he stuck a bug under the desk and the tracker in a bottom drawer. Voices out in the corridor alerted Nick that he'd run out of time.

"Shit." He crossed to the door ready to knock out whoever came in.

The door opened several inches then Nick heard Ava's voice. "Excuse me, Captain. Could you show me how to turn on the television?"

"Certainly." The door closed again.

Nick waited ten seconds then opened it. The passageway was empty, so he slipped out then closed the door and strode back to their cabin.

The captain had the remote control in his hand. "After your ordeal, I thought you would welcome some sleep, Miss Mitchell."

"I wanted to see if there was any mention of the explosion in King Leopold Ranges. The smugglers tried to blow up Nick's team, along with their own people. They're getting rid of anyone who can identify them."

From the doorway, Nick noticed the captain's shoulders stiffen. "I see."

Ava yawned. "Actually, I am tired and a bit queasy. I think I will catch some sleep before lunch."

Nick gave the captain a nod then held the door open for him. "I just checked out the other spare cabin. This one definitely has a better view."

As soon as the captain left, Nick locked the door then urged Ava across the room, out of earshot. "You were supposed to stay here, but that was quick thinking. Thank you." He hugged her.

"Just call me Double-O-Seven—Jane Bond." She turned serious. "What can I do to help you?"

"Nothing. I need to know you're safe while we take care of things."

"Don't worry, I've got no intention of getting in the way."

A series of taps sounded at the door. A signal he knew well. "That's the boys." Nick opened the door.

Jarred stood in the corridor. "Did you get a chance to search this level?"

"Yep." Nick held the door wide. "There's no crew and I've planted a bug and tracker in the captain's cabin. I also sent Simon an email. With a bit of luck, a Navy patrol boat will be here within the next couple of hours."

"Don't count on it. This is an undercover operation and it will take time to get a thing like that authorized, if at all."

Talos came out of the cabin opposite and strolled in then closed the door behind him. "This is definitely the right ship. I bumped the lift buttons so that the lift stopped at every deck. There's an armed crewman standing guard on C-Deck."

Ava sat on the bed. "Which level is that?"

"One down." Nick sat beside her. "We came in on the Upper-Deck. A, B, and C are below us, and the bridge is called the Nav deck, which is right up on top."

Ava looked up at Jarred. "Did you come across any illegals?"

He shook his head. "No, but we didn't expect to. They would be dropped off before the freighter reached Port Headland. When a ship arrives in an Australian port, Customs come on board. They go through paperwork with the captain then they get the crew to stand by their cabins. Their identity is checked against their passport then the cabin is searched for drugs, booze, cigarettes, and any undeclared items. Once the cabin is given the all clear, the crewman locks it and Customs move on."

Ava looked at Nick. "So how do the illegals get into Australia?"

"We must assume the ship stops out here and Lex has been using Pearce's yacht to transfer them to the coast. They would take the gems out the same way once the ship was on its way back to Asia."

Nick glanced at Talos. "How many crew are we dealing with?"

"The captain said eighteen. We counted sixteen including the teenager. I assume there's two off duty or in the cabin with whoever is injured."

"I left a bug in the bridge," said Jarred. "We need a distraction so we can get our weapons."

Nick nodded. "The lifeboat isn't locked. Ava could fake seasickness and while I take her for a walk to the bow you can retrieve our stuff."

"Okay, do it, but take your time. While you're out walking we will secure the engine room. I noticed the ship's hospital is lockable from the outside. It might be a good place to confine any crew we come across. Let's meet back here in one hour."

Ava clasped her hands together. "I meant to tell you, I asked Damon about the explosion at Madeline's apartment. He wasn't responsible, but he suggested her husband, his business partner and both their families' might go to those lengths to keep her secret out of the public arena."

Jarred frowned. "Her husband has offered me big money to give Madeline twenty-four hour protection."

Talos opened the door. "That's a good alibi if Elliott wants her dead. Let's hope it's not too late."

They crowded into the lift then descended to the Main Deck. Nick moved out ahead of Ava then closed the door on Jarred and Talos.

An Asian officer stepped out of the Ballast Control room. "You need to go somewhere?"

"Yes, my fiancée is seasick and needs some fresh air. Captain Renner said it would be fine to walk on deck as long as we let someone know."

The officer nodded and led the way to an external door. He turned two levers then pulled the door open and waited for them to pass.

Nick held back. "Can you show us where we are allowed to walk?"

"Yes." The officer stepped over the raised ledge and led them around the central block. "You may go as far as the bow, but please stay well away from the edge. It can be slippery."

"Thank you." Ava started walking.

Nick looked about. There was a cool breeze blowing and the sun had disappeared behind the grey clouds. Playing for time, he pointed up. "They look ominous. Do you expect more bad weather?"

The officer nodded. "A little rain over the next few hours and a storm later tonight. It is nothing to worry about."

Nick stepped out where he knew they'd be in sight of the bridge. "How often do you make this trip?"

"It varies according to our destination. We go to Port Headland, Freemantle, North Queensland, and Newcastle. The distance is much longer for the east coast."

The wind whipped Ava's hair about as the last of her braid came undone. She didn't once hesitate in her steady pace toward the bow. Nick noticed the teenage boy off to one side holding a fishing line. Ava must have seen him too and changed direction to speak to him.

The officer immediately became more alert. "If you will excuse me, I must call Yuri inside. He has duties to attend to." The officer strode toward Ava and the boy.

Nick casually strolled after him. By now Jarred should have slipped out of the lift and with Talos on guard, collected their weapons from the lifeboat. Nick looked back toward the central block. He could see several faces up in the bridge watching him. He also saw Jarred duck back inside the Upper deck. *So far so good.*

The boy ran past Nick keeping his eyes downcast.

Ava strolled back with the officer. Her cheeks were pink and she was shivering, but her eyes glowed with excitement. "It's freezing out here, but at least I feel a little better. Now I might be able to get some sleep."

"You certainly need it." Nick put a protective arm around her, shielding her expressive face from the bridge as they walked back to the central block.

As the lift door closed Ava's fingernails bit into his arm. "Guess what?"

"By your face, I'd say you've discovered something important."

"Yes. I asked Yuri where Bob is at the moment and he told me *Mr. Walsh* is with the captain on the bridge. I knew Bob reminded me of someone. He must be Lex Walsh's father and that means he's Helen's ex-husband."

"He may not be an ex-husband at all. A lot of planning went into this smuggling operation. I bet the three of them are very tight."

"So what should we do?"

"I was going to leave you in the cabin, but I think you're safer with me." The lift stopped and Nick opened the door then edged out. "We'll take the stairs down to the engine room. Stay behind me and keep your eyes open."

"Okay."

Nick opened the door to the stairwell and listened. All was quiet so he stepped in and then closed the door behind Ava. "These stairs will take us down to the engine room, but it's the way most of the crew moves between decks."

She nodded, her eyes full of nervous excitement. Nick shook his head in wonder. His angel had grown balls in the last four years.

At almost a run, they descended the stairs. When they reached the lowest level Nick held up his hand and whispered, "It's going to be hot in there and the boys won't be expecting us, so stay here unless you hear someone coming down the stairs."

"All right."

Nick opened the door and was instantly hit by a blast of suffocating air. It was like stepping into a sauna. He edged forward cautiously. The last thing he wanted was to be knocked out by Talos. The man was lethal.

Nick stopped and observed the huge generators, compressors, and maze of pipes. It reminded him of a power station, only everything was condensed in the one space. He couldn't think of anything worse than working in this noise and heat. A flash of movement to his left caught his attention. It was Talos.

The big man strode over. "We've secured three crew in workshops, and one who was monitoring a control board. They're trussed up and locked in a service store-room." Perspiration coated Talos' face and neck. He passed Nick a sheathed knife then held up two heavy-duty locks. "We can use these to lock any crew on the Upper deck in the ship's hospital."

Nick quickly strapped the knife to his right calf. "Besides the Ballast and Control rooms, what else is on Upper deck?"

Talos narrowed his eyes as if thinking. "Gym, hospital, conference room, change rooms, and a couple of offices."

Jarred stepped around a massive silver tank. Like Talos, his face dripped with perspiration. He didn't look surprised to see Nick. "Hell, it's hot in here. We need to sabotage the ship before it leaves Australian waters. Any ideas?"

Nick considered. "I can cut the fuel line from the service tank to the main engine."

"Do it. Where's Ava?"

"In the stairwell. By the way, I'm pretty sure Bob is Lex Walsh's father."

"A real family affair." Jarred handed Nick a set of earmuffs. "Best if Ava stays with us."

Talos pulled the door to the stairwell open and beckoned Ava inside. She gasped as the oppressive heat hit her. Nick handed her the earmuffs. "Put these on and stay close."

Chapter Twenty-Five

Aware he had to move fast, Nick ran past the generators and up a set of grated steps. He pushed open a door to an air-conditioned control room and searched for the panel he needed. All engines work the same. Without fuel they would falter then stop. He was about to cut the feed to the main engine when a man wearing red overalls entered the room from the other side. He looked at what Nick had his hand on then threw his clipboard and leapt forward.

Nick braced himself, raised his fists, and found his center. "Let's make this quick, mate. I've got things to do."

The crewman threw a punch.

Nick dodged and came in with a right hook, then followed with an upper cut to the chin.

The man's head snapped back. He faltered, spat some blood, then charged.

Nick danced about the control room, evading the man's wild swings and throwing a jab here and there, but he didn't have time to linger. Taking a side-on stance, he kicked out his right foot and connected with the man's solar plexus, knocking him into the console where he bashed his head and dropped to the floor.

After cutting the fuel feed, Nick motioned to Ava and they retraced their steps to the exit door. Once in the stairwell, she pulled off the earmuffs and they climbed to the Upper-Deck where Nick opened the door and ducked his head out. The external doors at each end of the passage were locked, but several internal doors were open. He heard a grunt and something heavy hit the ground.

"This way." Nick stepped into the conference room as an Asian man ran from the adjoining control room. Without a second's thought, Nick lunged at the man. They crashed to the floor then Nick hit out with a quick jab. He was about to follow up with another punch when Ava hit the guy with a steel hole-punch, knocking him out.

Talos hauled another man in red overalls from the control room. "Let's lock these guys in the hospital."

They were dragging the men along the passageway when Jarred stepped out of a doorway further along. He had a guy over his shoulder in a fireman's hold.

Ava flattened herself against the wall as they passed. "How many is that?"

Talos smiled. "Ten. We found two asleep in their cabins."

Jarred opened a door toward the end of the passageway and went inside. Nick followed then helped Jarred truss their captives' hands and feet with medical tape. When the men regained consciousness, they wouldn't find it easy to get loose.

Talos shut the door then slid a lock through the housing. "The hospital has an external door on the main deck, so I need to secure that too. I'll be back in a minute." He unlocked the exit door and slipped outside.

Nick noticed Jarred looking distracted, as if he were miles away. "What's up, boss?"

"Did you mention Madeline in your email to Simon?"

"Yeah. Hopefully she's safe."

"It can't be Gibbs. Simon's checked him out and I've had it from the highest level, that's he's clean."

"But something's bothering you about him?"

"We know Gibbs has ties to Sheik Tariq Zakour Farid. If Gibbs and his sister are the sheik's children, then why isn't their father's name on their birth certificates? And why was Simon stone-walled when he tried to dig deeper?"

Ava frowned. "Maybe if Inspector Gibbs and his sister's heritage were public knowledge then their lives would be in danger. Is the sheik wealthy?"

Jarred nodded. "Beyond anything you can imagine and a very powerful man in the Middle East. He owns the island we were on and a Lear jet that Gibbs has free use of."

Talos stepped back inside the passage and locked the door. "Sorry

I took so long. I heard voices outside the Nav-Deck. I had to wait until they went inside."

Jarred opened the door to the stairwell. "Let's check A-Deck. It houses the officers' mess, galley, and crew's mess." He passed Nick the gun. "Only use it if you have to."

Again Nick kept Ava behind him. As they reached A-Deck, Jarred checked the passage then he and Talos headed to the left.

Nick took Ava's hand and ran to the right. The external doors were locked. He stopped at the officers' mess and snuck a quick look. An officer was sitting at one of the tables reading a newspaper. Nick ducked back as the teenager came out of the kitchen and placed a mug in front of the officer. Nothing was said and the boy went back into the kitchen where the sound of clanging pans and utensils could be heard.

"Stay here. If someone comes along, say you're looking for something to settle your stomach." Nick went to step forward, but Ava grabbed his arm. "Don't hurt the boy."

"I won't." He ran lightly across the officers' mess, his shoes almost soundless. He'd almost reached the officer when the man glanced over his shoulder, but by then it was too late. Nick hit him with the gun and the man slumped over the table.

A yell sounded in the kitchen and Nick sprinted to the door. He saw the teenager backed into a corner, clutching a metal tray to his chest. His eyes were wide with terror as he watched Talos and a cook threaten each other over a stainless steel bench. Each held a lethal looking blade, and by the cook's movements he knew what he was doing. Nick couldn't get a clear shot at the cook without risking the boy's life. From the crashing sounds coming from the crew's mess, Jarred also had his hands full.

"Oh, God." Ava grasped Nick's arm.

"Stay behind me." Nick beckoned to the boy again, but he'd shrunk further into the corner, paralyzed with fear.

Suddenly the cook screamed an obscenity and hurled his knife. Talos threw his body sideways, and the blade shaved past his shoulder. The cook drew another two knives from the block then jumped up on the bench. He moved incredibly fast.

Talos barely had time to snatch the tray off the boy and push him under the bench before the cook threw another knife. Talos blocked its path to his chest with the metal tray. The knife still managed to pierce the tray before dropping to the floor. Talos kicked it under the oven.

Nick shifted sideways. He couldn't get a clear shoot as Talos was now in the way.

Ava dropped to her knees at Nick's feet and shuffled forward. "Yuri, come here. We won't hurt you."

"Blast." Nick still couldn't get a shot off and now Ava was inside the kitchen. He was positioned side-on in the galley's doorway, where he could also keep an eye on the entrance to the officers' mess, which is what saved him from the bullet that smashed into the door's framework. He dropped to the floor, took aim and fired. An overweight cook cried out as he was hit in the shoulder and knocked back into the passageway. The gun lay on the floor of the officers' mess.

Nick ran over, grabbed it, then turned his attention back to the kitchen. The boy crawled toward Ava. Both were hidden from the knife-wielding cook by saucepans of all sizes under the bench.

With another scream, the cook hurled his knife at Talos then jumped off the bench, his legs and arms braced for a martial arts attack.

Talos knocked the knife away with the tray then, as if it were a Frisbee, sent it spinning at the cook. The tray hit the cook then Talos followed up with a savage roundhouse kick. The cook took the blow in his ribs then collapsed to his knees gasping for air. Talos picked up a cutting board and wacked the man over the head, knocking him out. "I hope he cooks better than he fights."

Nick rolled his eyes. "You might need to look in on Jarred. Sounds like he might need some assistance."

Talos ran through to the crews' mess on the other side of the galley.

Nick helped Ava up then looked down at the teenager. "We could use your help. It's your choice, but if you side with the rest of the crew, you'll be arrested."

"I help you because they not good men. My mother is poor and I must work to support my family."

"We need to know exactly how many crew are on board."

"Twenty, plus Mr. Walsh. He not crew, he captain's friend."

So the captain lied. Nick narrowed his eyes at the boy. "Where does Mr. Walsh board the ship and is he alone or do others get on with him?"

Yuri shrugged. "He not sail every trip, but he board when we out at sea, and he come with one, or two people. They stay in their cabins and I not allowed talk to them."

"Before we came aboard, did the crew rescue a man or woman?"

The boy nodded. "I see a man with no hair who sometimes comes on board to see the captain and Mr. Walsh. And, I see a woman with a bleeding head."

Nick looked at the boy. "Where are they now?"

"In a cabin on C-Deck."

"Can you get me some rope and is there somewhere close we can lock the crew?"

Yuri nodded. "There is supply room that the cook has keys to." He bent down and unhooked a bunch of keys from the cook's belt. "I show you."

Stepping out of the officers' mess, Nick glanced down the passageway and noticed a crumpled form in red overalls. As he watched, Jarred dragged another man out of the crew's mess. Nick bent down and checked the cook he'd shot. "He'll live, but we'd better pack this wound so he doesn't lose any more blood."

Ava ran to the nearest table and snatched up the linen cloths, then she knelt by Nick and crammed one inside the cook's shirt.

Nick tied the other tablecloth around the man's chest and shoulder.

"This is the storeroom." Yuri inserted a key in a door and opened it. "I get you rope now." He ran to the stairwell door and was gone before Nick could stop him.

"I hope we can trust him." Nick hauled the cook into the storeroom then went to get the officer he'd knocked out earlier.

He was helping Talos heave the knife-throwing cook into the storeroom when Yuri came running back with a coiled rope.

"Thanks, mate." Talos took the rope and cut it into lengths, then they tied the men securely and locked the door.

Nick passed the cook's gun to Jarred. "Yuri told me there is a crew of twenty plus Bob, so we still have a few to find."

"I help you find them," said Yuri.

Nick held up a hand, listened then smiled. "The engines have stopped."

Jarred opened the stairwell door. "Let's clear the bridge before the captain realizes he doesn't have a crew. And, don't forget we have ears up there. Anything we do or say will be analyzed later by the AFP."

They raced up the remaining steps to the Nav-Deck where Nick cautiously eased the door open. Giant windscreen wipers were swishing across the front windows. It had started to rain again.

An officer stood frowning at a panel of lights and switches. He held a two-way radio to his ear. "Captain, I don't know why the engine has stopped. I can't reach anyone in the engine or control rooms. Yes, Captain. I will try them again."

Another officer in wet weather gear stood outside the bridge. He held a massive set of binoculars to his eyes and looked out over the ocean.

Talos crept up behind the officer at the panel and slammed his fist into the man's jaw. The officer wobbled then went down like a 90-kilo pin in a bowling alley. Ignoring the light rain, Nick tapped the other officer on the shoulder then hit him with a quick jab. The man fell against the rail then shook his head and lashed out. His punch went wide, leaving him off balance and open. Nick delivered a hammer punch to the ribs followed by an upward palm to the chin. The man's eyes rolled then he dropped to his knees and face planted on the deck.

"Sorry, mate." Nick lugged the guy inside then locked the external door before helping Talos secure their captives. They dragged them into a change-room where an assortment of jackets hung on pegs.

Jarred inhaled. "That leaves one crewman, Bob, Lex, and the captain."

"And Helen." Nick glanced at Ava. He'd been worried about her witnessing so much violence, but she gave him the thumbs up. It shouldn't surprise him; she'd dealt with much worse over the last twenty-four hours. He looked around the bridge. "Where's the boy?"

Talos opened the stairwell door as an alarm sounded. "He's either snitched on us, or the captain's realized he doesn't have a crew and knows we're responsible for shutting down the engine."

"Secure the lift and stairwell doors." Jarred strode over to the navigation screens. "I can see two other ships but neither is close.

Let's hope that tracker is still working. In the meantime, we have access to a satellite phone. I'll check in with Gibbs first." He keyed in the number and waited.

"Gibbs speaking." The inspector's voice filled the bridge.

"This is Jarred Steele. I want you to arrange extra security for Madeline Shaw. Lex Walsh boasted that someone in a position of authority is intending to kill her."

"I would if I could find her. She's given the local cops the slip and disappeared. Sergeant Evans has patrols out searching for her."

"Damn woman's a journalist. What do you expect?" Jarred slammed his palm on the console. "I won't know who is after Madeline until I interrogate Lex Walsh. At the moment we're on a coal freighter that is being used to smuggle people into Australia. We've contained most of the crew, although for how long is anyone's guess. Does Simon have our location?"

"Yes, and he's picking up your chatter. He's passed everything on to the AFP, and the Department of Defense, but it seems a decision is pending. Some...bureaucrat wants to wait and see what happens. It's too expensive to divert a Naval ship to your aid."

"Fucking pencil pushers. We can't contain this crew for long. They outnumber and outgun us."

"I'm doing all I can, and Simon's been harassing everyone he knows, but at the moment you're on your own. I'll keep looking for Madeline."

"Do that." Jarred banged the phone down. "Next time the government needs our help, I'm going to charge them double." He looked around the bridge. "We need to be prepared if the crew escape and mount a counter attack."

"Lookie here." Talos lifted a sniper rifle off a desk at the back of the bridge. He weighed it then raised the scope to his eye. "This is a nice piece of equip..." He suddenly lowered the rifle, his gaze locked on the forward deck. "Colonel, we've got a problem."

Nick followed Jarred to the front windows and peered through the rain. What he saw sent shiver along his spine. "Shit."

Down on the main deck, Bob Walsh held a gun to the boy's head.

"What is it?" Ava ran over to the window and gasped. "Yuri!"

Jarred glanced at Talos. "Stay out of sight. We'll need every advantage we can get."

The 2-way on the console crackled. "Have I got your attention yet?" Bob nudged the boy closer to the edge. "This is what's going to happen. You will give yourselves up and the crew will put you in a lifeboat to make your own way back to Broome while we continue to Asia. If you don't agree I'm going to put a bullet in the kid's head. If you still refuse to surrender, there won't be any negotiations. The crew will hunt you boys down then feed you to the sharks, but we will keep the pretty lady for our amusement. I will give you ten seconds to decide. Nine. Eight. Seven. Six."

"That bastard has a death wish." Talos checked the rifle's magazine.

"Four. Three."

Jarred snatched up the 2-way and pressed the speak button. "All right, don't shoot the kid."

Bob nodded. "I knew you'd see reason."

"He's lying." Ava grasped Nick's arm. "Don't trust him. They won't let us go, we know too much."

"It'll be all right, Angel. You stay well back and get down fast when I tell you." Keeping close to the wall, Nick ran to the external door on the left and eased it open. The rain would block Bob from noticing, but Nick wasn't taking any chances.

"You have ten seconds to get in position, Talos." Jarred paced across the bridge and opened the door leading to the right wing then pressed the 2-way. "We're coming out."

Dropping to the floor, Talos wormed his way out of the bridge.

Jarred stepped out on the right wing and murmured. "I see our last crewman and the captain below us. They're both armed."

"I'll take the captain." Nick slipped his gun into the back of his sweatpants and stepped out of the bridge ahead of Ava then checked she was behind them, protected.

Jarred raised the 2-way to his mouth. "We're unarmed."

"I want to see the big fella," yelled Bob.

"He's in the cabin," said Jarred. "Suffering a bout of sea sickness."

"I need to show you how serious I am." Bob raised the gun to the boy's head.

Two shots rang out.

Chapter Twenty-six

Ava bit her fingernail as she paced the bridge. She wished she knew the number for Broome's Control Tower or Simon's cell. She needed to do something, anything to erase the image of Talos shooting Bob, or Yuri falling overboard. Jarred had shot the crewman dead and Nick had wounded Captain Renner in the leg. She had no compassion for those evil men, but she prayed Talos and Nick had rescued Yuri.

"Why are they taking so long?" She looked out the bridge window again. The cargo net was hanging over the side of the ship, but she couldn't see any movement.

Jupiter. She had to remember the codename. She'd promised Nick she wouldn't open the door unless she heard that word, and if he wasn't back within fifteen minutes, he'd told her where to hide. The thought sent a shiver through her.

Who could she call for help? Who had enough political clout to over-rule government bureaucrats? Ava stilled then looked at the phone. Did she dare?

Silly question. She picked up the phone and keyed in the personal cell number of one of the most important and influential men in Britain. After three rings it was answered, but Ava didn't give her father time to speak. "David, it's Ava, I need your help."

"Ava? What's wrong, sweetheart."

She quickly outlined what had happened and where she was. Her father's horrified exclamation warmed her heart. Leaving England after finding her real parents had been hard, especially as they were both so loving, but they deserved time together and Ava had her own dream to follow.

"Can you help us, David?"

"I'll do my best."

"Thanks. Just in case things go wrong, promise me you will look after Liam."

"You have my word. Don't do anything silly."

Ava glanced at her watch. Ten minutes had passed. She'd meant to keep her eyes on the cargo net. Had Talos and Nick rescued Yuri?

A loud knock made her jump. "I have to go, David." Ava hung up and ran to the door. "Who is it?"

She heard a male rumble but couldn't make it out. "What's the codename?"

"Open the door, Miss Mitchell. We have your boyfriend and his two mates. If you want them to live, you will give yourself up."

Ava swallowed and stepped back. Her heart raced and her breath came in short gasps as she stared at the door. Suffocating heat spread through her body, making her dizzy. Perspiration broke out on her forehead and above her lip. This couldn't be happening. Not after the way the team took out the rest of the crew. How could Lex have overpowered three incredibly fit and armed men? She didn't believe it.

Another loud rap made Ava jump. "Do you hear me, Miss Mitchell?"

She ran to the middle of the bridge and spoke as clearly as her shaking voice would allow. "Lex Walsh wants me to open the door. He claims he has the guys, but I don't believe him. I have to hide before Lex breaks into the bridge." *Hopefully Simon heard all that.* Ava ran to the change room, staying clear of the two bound men. She pulled on a long waterproof coat then covered her head with the hood.

There was no one outside the bridge, and she didn't know if Lex was still at the stairwell door, so she opened the external door to the left wing. Nick had told her where to hide, but her hands were shaking as she ran behind the bridge and began climbing the narrow ladder. The rungs were slippery and she lost her footing twice before reaching the roof of the bridge. *I am so not cut out for this.*

Panic seized every cell as she stared up at the steel structure rising above her. Ava guessed it was for radar or satellite reception. The tower had a platform about half way up, then another higher. This wasn't for the faint of heart. "I can do this."

Taking a deep breath, she began to climb, not daring to look down until she'd reached the platform and then she wished she hadn't.

"Oh, shikes." She closed her eyes and lay flat on her stomach, pretending she wasn't so very high above the ocean. At least there was a railing to stop her falling over the edge.

The waterproof jacket kept her dry, but she was soon shivering from the cool breeze. It took every ounce of courage she had to open her eyes, inch forward, and search the deck below.

It's so far down.

Ava breathed through her nausea, wishing the ship would stay still. She could see the cargo net hanging down the side of the ship. As she scanned the main deck, a strong throbbing shook the tower. The ship's engine had started. Ava squirmed a little further forward to look down over the bridge. Lex Walsh stood on a wing, talking into a 2-way. He stepped inside the bridge and a minute later his voice boomed out of a speaker causing Ava to almost jump out of her skin.

"I suggest you surrender before I lose my patience and shoot my hostage."

Ava wriggled back out of sight and bit her lip. At least Simon and the AFP were hearing everything in the bridge. She had to remain calm; Nick knew what he was doing. Ava buttoned up the jacket then curled into a ball, trying to ignore the breeze and swaying motion.

How much time passed was anyone's guess. Unbelievably, she must have dozed off, because all of sudden she was blasted out of her daydream by a mega horn that vibrated through every cell in her body. It was another ship.

"Holy mother of God." Ava's mouth dropped open as she stared at a gigantic Naval ship coming from the north. Movement below caught her attention.

It was Helen. Her head was bandaged and she wore red overalls. She climbed through a hatch into the lifeboat then shut the door. Ava frowned. There was no way Helen could escape from the Navy, so what was she up to, and who was going to lower the lifeboat?

Two small boats shot away from the Navy ship and sped toward Ava. As they got closer, she counted eight people on each. They were armed and wore camouflaged overalls, helmets, and life jackets, which she assumed were bulletproof.

Suddenly a massive chopper lifted off from the deck of the war ship then zoomed over the ocean to hover above the bow of the freighter. Six people dropped out, one after the other and slid down two thick ropes.

Ava could only stare. Was her father responsible for this?

Her legs shook as she climbed to her feet. Then holding the rail with one hand, she began waving and yelling.

"Up there," yelled a coarse voice.

Ava froze as two crewmen on the deck pointed their rifles at her. "Shikes." She fell to her stomach and covered her ears. The din of bullets hitting the steel under her was terrifying. Why were the idiots trying to kill her? They were surrounded by armed sailors. Unless she was the only witness left, and must be silenced, but that would mean.

"No, Nick's fine." She squeezed her eyes closed. "He has to be."

The shooting stopped and Ava crawled to the edge to see what was happening. The two men in overalls were splayed out on the deck. They weren't moving. One sailor ran to a crane and switched it on, lowering the boarding ladder for the incoming boats. The rest of the sailors separated, taking cover behind the raised coal hull covers.

Ava watched in fascination as they set up their rifles on miniature tripods. She eased onto her back. The sun was breaking through the clouds. She closed her eyes and let the warm rays chase away her chills. At the moment she had nothing better to do, nor did she want the Navy sailors mistaking her for a bad guy.

Nick signaled Yuri to stay still and quiet then edged around a large valve in the engine room, searching for movement. After rescuing the boy, they'd had no choice but to bring him with them. They'd checked the ship's hospital first and found their captives still locked inside. The crew on A-Deck was also still locked in the supply storeroom, but the guys from the engine room must have got loose to start the engine again.

Through the thickened glass of the control room, Nick could see two crewmen with swollen faces arguing. Right on cue, Talos stepped up beside them and smashed their heads together then stood back as they dropped to the floor.

"Come on, Yuri." Nick sprinted up the grated steps and into the control room. He turned off the fuel feeds and shut down the engine for a second time. A ship's horn blasted, vibrating through the hull of the coal ship. "There it is again, Talos. It has to be another ship. They're probably wondering why we were stopped."

"I'll lock these two up and look after the boy." Talos grabbed each of the crewmen by their collars. "You check if Jarred has found Lex and Helen yet."

Nick gave a nod. "Since hearing Lex demand our surrender, I've been worried about Ava."

"You head to the bridge and I'll work my way there. Be careful, I'm sure I heard shooting a while ago."

Nick gave Talos the thumbs up and bounded up the stairwell. At C-Deck he met Jarred on his way down. "Did you find them, Boss?"

"No, but we have a Frigate off the stern, and I saw six sailors drop out of a Seahawk. They were shooting at someone but I couldn't see who."

"I need to check on Ava." Nick pulled out his gun and ran up the stairwell. He burst into the bridge with his finger on the trigger, ready to fire at the slightest movement, but the bridge was empty. He could see the war ship off the stern and armed sailors moving along the deck of the coal ship toward the central block.

The bureaucrat must have changed his mind.

Nick ran out onto the wing and looked up. There was no sign of Ava, but Lex Walsh was on the roof of the bridge. He took a pot shot at Nick then yelled. "Call them off or your girlfriend dies." He began climbing the tower.

"Fuck." Nick shoved his gun in the back of his sweatpants and scaled the ladder. Once on the roof, he sprang onto the tower's ladder and climbed almost at a run. Below he could see a sizable force of armed sailors converging on the central block and external stairs.

Lex was almost to the platform, breathing hard.

Nick couldn't tell if Ava was up there or not, but he increased his speed and lunged, grasping Lex's ankle as he clambered onto the platform.

Lex lost his balance and fell to his knees, losing the gun over the side. He kicked Nick in the shoulder then scrambled to his feet. As

Nick bounded onto the platform a sense of relief flooded him. Ava wasn't there. He shifted sideways away from the ladder and looked Lex Walsh in the eyes. "This is for Barry." Nick smashed his fist into the bastard's nose.

Crack.

Lex bellowed. "I'm going to kill you, then throw your girlfriend to the sharks." He lunged at Nick, slamming him against the railing.

Nick shoved Lex away and glanced up. Could Ava be on the platform above?

They traded several punches then Nick hit Lex hard in the stomach, knocking him on his backside. "You're finished, Walsh. The Navy will escort you and your mother back to Broome to face smuggling and murder charges."

"Not all is lost. Your mate Barry is dead and so is the journalist."

"Barry is alive and on his way to Perth." Nick thought quickly. He needed the name of the man sent to kill Madeline. "As for your hit man, he dropped you right in the shit. How do you think the Navy got here so fast?"

Walsh sneered. "Never trust a cop, no matter how high up the ladder he is. I should have topped him first." Lex scrambled to his feet, pulled a knife, and charged again.

Nick caught hold of a vertical bar and swung his body off the platform, then back over the railing. He landed behind Lex then kicked him hard in the kidney, knocking him down. "You're going away for a long time, Walsh, along with your mother and the cop. What did you say his name is?"

"I didn't." Lex waved the knife in front of Nick. "I'd rather die than go back to jail, but first I'm gunna kill you." He lunged.

So is it Gibbs or not? Nick kicked out with his foot, forcing Lex to take a step back. A yellow raincoat dropped from above, covering Lex's head and shoulders, blinding him. Nick moved fast, catching a bar again to launch his body through the air. He kicked out hard, hitting Lex in the chest and sending him backward off the platform.

Lex screamed, his arms flailing as he fell to the deck far below. His landing wasn't pretty. There was no doubt in Nick's mind that Lex Walsh died on impact.

Nick looked up and locked gazes with his emerald-eyed angel, clinging to a steel ladder on the side of the tower. "Hi, babe, what are you doing up there?"

"Oh, you know, terrorizing myself."

"You want to come down?"

"My hands are pretty much glued to the steel, so you might have to come up."

Nick checked the main deck and got a wave from one of the Navy officers. He could see Jarred and Talos speaking with several others, so he swung out on the ladder and climbed up until he had Ava between his chest and the ladder. "Okay, Angel. Step down one rung at a time and we'll take a break at the roof of the bridge."

They descended slowly then, once on the roof, Ava turned into his arms. She was shaking so violently he could hear her teeth chattering. "That's the most harrowing experience I've ever faced. When I saw Lex coming up the ladder, I crawled across the platform then climbed the ladder on the other side. I knew if I stayed there I'd be in your way, but I was so terrified he'd stab you. It took me ages to get the raincoat off."

"It's over, Angel." Nick shook his head. "I didn't expect a war ship to come after us. I thought the government was leaving us to our own devices."

Ava cringed. "After you left the bridge, I rang my father on the satellite phone. I think he was going to contact our Prime Minister."

Nick laughed. "I bet that went down well. Even so, the Prime Minister couldn't manage this at such short notice."

She stretched up and kissed him. "Thank you for saving me."

"It's what I do." Nick frowned. "Sorry, it's what I used to do. This is officially my last mission for Steele Intelligence. From now on it's flying tourists round the Kimberley and being with my wife and son."

"Wife?"

"Yeah, unless you're planning on marrying some other guy."

"No. You're the only guy for me. I love you, my darling." She stroked his face. "But I've got a better idea. Why don't we move to Sydney? I love working with pearls, but I find it way too hot here. You can do things with your mates, and keep your job with Steele Intelligence."

Nick blinked. "I thought you didn't want me to do this sort of work?"

"I didn't, but it's who you are. I have no right to take that away from you. Just promise me you'll be careful and won't get killed."

"I promise to do my best. I love you, babe." He leaned forward and kissed the tip of her nose. "Let's get off this roof so I can kiss you properly. By the way, dropping that raincoat on Walsh was ingenious."

"Thank you." She shuddered. "I couldn't let him kill you."

"Not a chance, Angel."

CHAPTER TWENTY-SEVEN

Exhaustion swamped Ava as she made her way down to the wing where Jarred and Talos were waiting with several armed sailors. Ava gave Jarred and Talos a hug then turned into Nick's arms. "Did you save Yuri?"

"Yes."

The distinctive *whop, whop, whop* off an incoming chopper had them all looking to the southwest.

"That's a Black Hawk." Jarred led the way down the external stairs to the main deck then they all ran along the deck, past the sailors who were marshaling the freighter's crew to the boarding ladder ready for transfer to the war ship.

Ava and Nick reached the helipad as the Black Hawk came to rest on the raised dais. The rear door opened and Simon jumped down then lifted Liam to the ground.

Ava clutched her chest. "Oh, Nick, look." She held out her arms and caught Liam as he jumped off the dais. She kissed and hugged him then swung him round and round.

"Mummy, I'm dizzy."

Nick strolled over and wrapped his arms around both of them. "Hey, buddy. What are you doing here?"

"Daddy." Liam launched himself at Nick. "I come to save you."

"Maddy!" Jarred's voice carried across the deck.

Ava looked toward the Black Hawk where Sam was helping Madeline out. She looked as if she'd been dragged through a blackberry bush on a windy night in the middle of a storm. Her hair was wet and tangled. The jeans Ava had lent her were torn at the knees and stained with mud. She was soaked.

As soon as Maddy spotted Ava, she gave a wan smile. "I'm glad to see you're all still in one piece. I've been so worried."

Jarred gave her his hand and helped her off the dais. "Are you okay?"

Her face crumpled then with a hiccup she buried her face against his chest. "I thought you were dead."

"I'm not that easy to kill." Jarred closed his arms around her. "What the hell happened to you?"

Sam jumped off the dais. "Madeline's had a very busy night. If not for her quick thinking, she wouldn't be with us."

Madeline sniffed. "I had a bad feeling, so I turned off the lights and watched the street from Ava's bedroom window. A car drove into the driveway and the constable guarding me wandered over as if he knew the driver. The man shot him with a silencer then dragged him around the side of the house. I climbed out the window and ran."

Madeline looked up at Jarred. "It was too dark to identify him, but I thought if I could make it to the police station everything would be all right. Then the same car came speeding up behind me. I ran across a park, but he followed me, so I jumped fences and stayed in the shadows until I reached the police station. I ran into Zac Gibbs coming out."

Jarred narrowed his eyes. "Go on."

"There was a Sergeant Evans with him. The sergeant told Zac he'd look after me, but Zac said that wasn't happening. Then the Sergeant pulled a gun, but Zac was quicker. He shot the sergeant. I panicked and ran."

"So Gibbs is corrupt?" Talos' hands clenched, reminding Ava that Talos didn't trust the Inspector.

Sam grinned at Talos. "Gibbs is not corrupt. After he wounded Sergeant Evans, Gibbs called for assistance then caught up with Madeline. After a bit of a struggle he brought her to the Control Tower. Sergeant Evans has been on the AFP's watch list for a while and as soon as the sergeant pulled his gun, Gibbs figured he was the man sent to kill Madeline."

Simon interrupted. "Then we heard a frigate was on her way to help you so decided we'd join the party. Where are the Walshes?"

Talos turned his thumb down. "Bob and Lex are dead and Helen has disappeared. She may have jumped overboard after I shot Bob."

"No, she didn't." Ava pointed to the orange lifeboat high above them. "I saw her climb into that boat."

Nick grimaced. "I bet she's the brains behind the outfit. At least we have one of the gang to hand over to the AFP."

"This is a big boat, Daddy?" Liam craned his neck. "Did you get the Neanderals?

"We sure did, buddy."

Ava glanced at Madeline. She looked dead to the world with her eyes closed and head resting against Jarred's shoulder. He didn't seem to notice that he was gently stroking Madeline's back as he stared up at the lifeboat.

"I'll tell the Navy guys where to find Helen," called Talos, striding toward the central block as another group of sailors boarded the ship.

"Who are they?" asked Ava.

Nick stepped up on the dais and held out his hand. "The engineers and officers who will bring this ship back to port." He looked at Sam. "I see Ryan flew the Hawk here, so I guess you were acting as second pilot."

Sam chuckled. "Yes. Not that I would have been much help in a crisis."

"At least you know how to fly a chopper, but I won't tell the Army if you don't."

Ava linked fingers with Nick then they climbed onto the dais and ambled over to the Black Hawk. She scrambled in and sat expecting Nick to join her.

He placed Liam beside her then smiled. "By law, there's supposed to be two pilots up front, so I better do my duty. The Army would have a fit if they knew Ryan flew out here without another qualified Black Hawk pilot." He buckled Liam then stood aside to let the others in. "It's almost over, babe."

Simon sat beside Ava then Jarred took a seat facing. Madeline sat beside Jarred and once she was buckled in she leaned her head against his shoulder.

Ava hid her grin as Jarred's eyebrow rose. "Are you quite comfortable?"

Madeline sighed. "I'm tired and I'm cold, so deal with it."

Jarred huffed. "I'm happy you're alive, but you're a pain in the butt, Madeline."

"It takes one to know one, chief." She closed her eyes and snuggled closer. "I'm happy you're alive too."

Ava glanced at Liam, who was wide-awake and smiling at her. "We love Daddy, don't we Mummy?"

"Yes, munchkin, very much."

Talos jogged over and leapt in. "Righto, let's hit the road. We've got a Black Hawk chopper to finish painting for Liam and then I want to get home to my girls."

Ava closed her eyes and leaned against Simon. She was aware of Sam climbing aboard and the door sliding closed, then someone putting a headset on her, but the effort to open her eyes was beyond her.

Ryan's voice brought her out of her dozy state. "For a while there I wasn't sure you'd make it, Nick."

Nick's laugh warmed her soul. "I've got too much to live for, mate. I've got my angel back and a great little boy. How's Barry?"

"A medical team flew with him to Perth then he was rushed into surgery. He came through with flying colors and should be back to normal in a couple of months."

"It's time he retired."

"I think he's hoping you'll buy the business."

"Nope. After talking to Ava, I'm not leaving. You guys are stuck with me."

"Yes." Ryan cheered. "That's the best news I've heard all week."

"Me too. Welcome back," called Talos.

Ava opened her eyes to see Jarred watching her. He smiled. "I'm glad you came around. I was prepared to play every trick in the book to keep my team together."

She returned his smile. "We'll need somewhere to live until we find our own place, Jarred. I hear you have a beautiful big home on Sydney Harbour."

He sighed. "Great, you're going to fit right in with Kallie and Jane."

"And me," murmured Madeline. "I plan to move to Sydney, so I can help you out with research and stuff."

Jarred groaned. "That's all I need. Ryan, Simon, stay single or I swear I will sack you. I can't handle any more bossy women interfering in my men's lives."

Simon laughed. "My mother and sisters have tried to get me

shackled for years. Believe me, Colonel. I have no intention of becoming henpecked like my father."

"Famous last words. I'd watch your back, Sime." Nick chuckled. "Let's get this bird in the air, Ryan."

Ava relaxed as the Black Hawk lifted off the deck. She must have slept because it seemed no sooner had she closed her eyes then they were landing in front of Barry's hangar.

As Simon helped her out of the chopper a man with fair hair and blue eyes strode toward them. "Who is that?"

Simon glanced over his shoulder but didn't answer. Instead he turned to Jarred who held a sleeping Maddy in his arms. "We have company, boss."

Jarred stiffened. "About fucking time he showed some interest in his wife."

Ava couldn't believe how rigid Jarred had become. His jaw was like granite and a pulse throbbed in his neck.

Talos shook his head. "I know Elliott does a lot of good in Vietnam, but Madeline is his wife. She deserves better than this two-bit marriage."

Jarred looked at Maddy asleep in his arms. "We don't always get what we want."

She opened her eyes, yawned, then blinked at Jarred. "What can't you have?"

His stance hadn't softened but his lips curved. "Your husband has arrived. Better late than never, I suppose."

Madeline made no move to get out of Jarred's arms as the man approached. "Elliott, what are you doing here?"

"You said you wanted to talk face-to-face, so here I am."

Ava studied Elliot. He was handsome and had kind eyes. His smile widened. "I see Jarred has everything under control as usual, although I don't think I've ever seen you this scruffy, Mads."

Ava flinched at the coldness in Jarred's eyes as he glowered at Elliott Shaw. "A bomb detonated in your wife's apartment last night. This morning she narrowly escaped another attempt on her life. Bloody hell, Elliott, you're not taking this seriously. Madeline's life is in danger."

"Sorry, old man. I do appreciate how grave things are. That's why I want you to provide Madeline with twenty-four hour protection. She's safer with you than anyone else."

Madeline wriggled until Jarred set her down then she smiled at her husband. "What are you doing here? I thought you had a meeting in Sydney."

"You're more important. If it's any consolation, the police in Melbourne said your closet and safe survived the explosion. At least you don't have to replace your clothing or jewelry. And, you're still alive. That's a bonus."

"Yes." Madeline kissed Elliot's cheek as she hugged him. "Once the insurance money comes through, I intend to buy a place in Sydney." She took his hand and turned to Ava. "I'd like to introduce you to a new friend of mine. Ava is an amazingly gifted jewelry designer. She made my opera pearls, which I'm delighted to say is in my safe. Ava this is my husband, Elliott."

"Hello, Ava. It's lovely to meet you. You're the third girlfriend Madeline has made since joining forces with Jarred."

What a strange thing to say. Ava flicked a glance at Jarred's set face.

"Hello." She shook Elliot's hand, more confused than ever. The way he and Maddy interacted showed warmth, but a kiss on the cheek after more than a month apart didn't sit right with Ava. Where was the chemistry? Then again she'd grown up in a house with two stiff and distant people. So who knew?

Ava figured Elliott couldn't possibly have missed the chilliness being radiated at him from the other men. Yet he continued to smile openly and speak as if they were the best buddies in the world. "Oh, by the way, Zac Gibbs said he'd catch up with you all tomorrow, once he's finished interviewing the people you apprehended."

"What about Yuri?" asked Talos. "Did Inspector Gibbs mention a boy?"

"Yes. Zac said once the boy gives his statement, he'll be flown home."

"Good."

Nick climbed out of the chopper's cockpit and strode over. He barely nodded at Elliott before taking Ava in his arms and kissing her. It was a kiss between lovers, a kiss of passion and promise. She loved it.

He finally raised his head, then tucked her against his side and looked at Elliott Shaw. "About time you turned up. What are your plans for Madeline?"

Elliott raised an eyebrow. "Zac has given us clearance to fly to Melbourne this afternoon. Once we've sorted the apartment, we'll head to Sydney."

Simon huffed, drawing all eyes. "What Nick is asking, Elliott, is how do you plan to keep Madeline safe?"

"Hire you guys of course."

"We're not babysitters." The hostility in Jarred's voice sent shivers down Ava's spine.

Madeline turned on Jarred, her stunning blue eyes sparking with outrage. "I'm not a baby, Chief. I am a woman, capable of taking care of myself."

"You're a loose cannon in need of a keeper." A seductive smile stole across Jarred's face. "If you were mine, I'd keep you so busy, you wouldn't have time to gallivant about the world risking your life."

Madeline gasped. "Why you egotistical moron. I need more than a quick roll in the sack to keep me fulfilled."

"That's not what I meant, but let me assure you, Pocahontas, a roll in the hay with me would never be quick."

She blushed profusely, seemingly lost for words.

A spluttered cough did nothing to hide Elliott Shaw's amusement. "I see relations between you two are as volatile as ever. Maybe more time together would remedy that. Who knows, you might even become fond of each other."

Ava's mouth dropped as she stared at Madeline's husband. He had to be blind, and completely insensitive not to notice the friction between Jarred and Madeline. They were like active wires; the arcing sparks threatening to engulf them in flames.

With a sigh, Madeline stepped forward and hugged Ava. "I'm so happy we've become friends. Once I get things sorted, I'll ring you."

"I'd like that."

"On that note, we're out of here." Nick took a sleepy Liam out of Sam's arms. "I'm taking my family home. Stay safe, Madeline. I'll catch the rest of you tomorrow."

Ava gave them a wave as Nick caught her other hand. Once they were out of earshot he grinned. "I need some sleep, then we should practice our baby making skills."

Ava laughed. "We do make beautiful babies."

"That we do, Angel."

Chapter Twenty-eight

Nick stood with Ryan in the gardens of Vaucluse House overlooking Sydney Harbour and tried not to look at his watch. It wasn't often he suited up like a penguin, and the desire to loosen his tie was growing.

Six weeks had passed since their close call on the coal ship. In that time, the Navy had recovered Ava's gems from the yacht and Ava had finished the media mogul's order. Helen Davis had been sentenced to life, along with Sergeant Evans. The coal ship's crew had also been charged and jailed. Nick had helped Ava pack up her business then move to Sydney. Much to everyone's surprise, Jarred insisted they stay at his place while looking for a home of their own. Something Jarred soon regretted, as Kallie, Jane, and Madeline descended regularly to help plan the wedding.

The closer the wedding got, the more excited Ava became. Nick, on the other hand, had been nervous of meeting her father, the prominent English politician. It had been wasted energy as David had instantly put Nick at ease, and they'd since had a game of golf together. Nick had met Maggie five years ago, and wondered how he'd missed the similarities between her and Ava.

After a lot of thought, Ava sent Hector and Shirley Mitchell an invitation to the wedding, but they'd declined. As far as Nick was concerned it was no loss. Now it was D-Day. The sun was shining and a gentle breeze drifted off the harbor. Ava had wanted a garden wedding and Mother Nature had turned on a perfect April afternoon.

Friends and family had been arriving for the last thirty minutes and were sitting about chatting and laughing. Nick nodded at the two senior Army officers in the front row. Paul and Steve were identical twins. They'd come to see him several weeks ago. Neither had married and one of them was his father. It didn't matter which, they were both great guys and made it clear they wanted a relationship with him, as did their parents. Nick smiled at the elderly man and woman. Nice people he looked forward to spending time with.

Simon gave Nick a wave from where he stood with Inspector Gibbs, who had brought his sister, Safiya with him. The rest of the guests were made up of Jarred, Talos, Jane, Sam, Kallie, and Barry.

Ryan nudged Nick. "Do you remember me telling you I'd spied a tasty morsel on the Fijian Island?"

"Yes. Let me guess, she's the young woman with Gibbs? His sister I believe."

"His sister?" Ryan looked toward the dark-eyed beauty. "Well that changes things."

Nick observed the young woman's gaze drift over the guests then fix on Ryan, her spontaneous smile lighting her whole face. He also noticed the scowl Gibbs directed at Ryan. "I wouldn't go there, mate."

Ryan chuckled. "Gibbs can't watch her all afternoon, and I only want to steal one kiss."

Jarred ambled over and raised an eyebrow. "You're not having second thoughts are you, Nick?"

"No, why?"

"The way you keep looking about, I wondered if you were planning to do a runner."

Nick laughed. "I'm anxious to see my bride arrive."

"Then I'll let you in on a secret. The wedding party are inside Vaucluse House and have been there since before you arrived."

"Arh, in that case I can relax."

Simon left Gibbs and strolled over. "The inspector just told me something very interesting."

"What's that?" asked Nick.

"After my request for the Navy to intercept the coal ship was refused, some unknown person hacked into the Joint Operations Command's computer system, then released an order for that Frigate to change course and go to your aid."

Nick frowned. "You're kidding."

"Nope. The defense force and Government are shitting themselves. Whoever this hacker is, he's got balls and talent. The directive was routed all over the world, but originated from Port Stephens where the trail has gone cold."

Nick stared at Simon. "Why would this hacker want to help us?"

"I've no idea, but it has to be the same person who has been shadowing my emails. I believe he or she intercepted Nick's email asking for help. When my request was denied, the hacker decided to do us a favor."

"That's weird," said Ryan.

"It gets weirder." Simon passed Jarred a sheet of paper. "This was pushed under my parents' front door yesterday. It's a classified, government document detailing a secret summit. I checked with a friend who works for Australia's Secret Intelligence Office. Off the record, he told me the summit is by invitation only, and the computer scientists attending will be representing our government, major banks, the Defence Force and Secret Intelligence Service."

Jarred rubbed his chin. "All that brain power in one location. You think our hacker will be there?"

"Gibbs certainly does. If the hacker can redirect a war ship, what else is he or she willing to do?" Simon shook his head. "I'm concerned this may relate to a software program I helped Professor Cortez design. It was a government-funded project to fight cyber fraud. In the wrong hands, the potential ramifications are mind-blowing."

"When is this summit?" asked Nick.

"Gibbs thinks sometime toward the end of the month. Oh, and he asked me to tell you everything is set for tomorrow. What's that about?"

Nick chuckled. "Gibbs asked me and Ava to accompany his sister to Fiji. And, in return, Gibbs is providing us with free air travel aboard the Lear Jet, and a two week honeymoon on the island."

"No kidding. What about Liam?" asked Ryan.

"Maggie and David are taking him to the Gold Coast where I dare say they intend to indulge his every wish."

Jarred's lips twitched. "Too late to run; it looks like your bride is coming."

As Jarred and Simon took their seats, Nick turned to face the short aisle between two rows of white seats. Beyond the seated guests lay an expanse of grass then the historical Vaucluse House, and one small boy holding a toy Black Hawk helicopter.

A familiar melody drifted across the lawn and Nick recognized the song he and Ava had slow-danced to many times, which more often than not led to love making.

Liam walked purposely toward Nick, wearing a miniature black suit and huge smile as he held the chopper out in front.

Ryan nudged Nick. "Check out what's hanging under the chopper."

Nick gaze dropped to a white satin ribbon swinging from side to side with the weight of the two wedding bands attached to its end. "That's clever." Nick winked at Liam as he took his place beside Ryan.

Next came Madeline, wearing a cobalt blue, three quarter length gown. She looked stunning, leaving him baffled how Elliott could bear to be apart from her.

Nick's attention was seized by the vision of a fiery angel in a long cream gown. His bride was breathtakingly beautiful. She wore a delicate tiara of pearls set amongst her red curls that had been caught up except for one thick spiral. Her parents walked on either side, looking as proud as punch, but Ava glowed as she glided across the grass.

Nick's gaze shifted to the dainty pearl earrings then a solitary pearl teardrop sitting above the tantalizing glimpse of cleavage. The fitted bodice shimmered with hundreds of lustrous pearls, which led Nick's eyes to the sheer fabric falling from below the bodice to the ground.

Maggie and David stepped away then Ava gave him a glorious smile, her love radiating from her eyes, making them shine brighter than any jewel. "Hello, my darling."

"Hello, Angel." Nick picked up her left hand and kissed the inside of her wrist. "You look beautiful."

"Thank you. You're looking very handsome." She squeezed his fingers and whispered, "I need to tell you something."

Nick chuckled. "A prerequisite to becoming a Black Hawk pilot is being able to count." He winked at her. "I'm predicting a special delivery a week or two before Christmas."

"I'm well aware you can count, my darling, however what I want to tell you is, we are expecting two special deliveries."

The air left Nick's lungs. "Twins?"

She nodded as tears filled her eyes

Nick swallowed the lump in his throat. "We're having twins?"

"Yes. I was going to tell you later, but my mother came with me to the medical center. She can't keep the grin off her face, so it won't stay a secret long."

"I thought you were taking Liam for his immunization."

"Yes, but I decided I'd have a quick check up."

Nick's gaze slid over Ava's parents, and his newfound family. All six were smiling broadly, so happy to be part of his and Ava's big day.

He swallowed and gave them a nod. As a starving, neglected, and angry teenager, Nick had never dreamed he'd have so much love and support around him. He'd spent years fighting for respect, wishing he'd had a decent family. Now he had that and so much more.

Nick swiped the moisture gathering at the corners of his eyes then looked at his bride. "You've brought so much happiness to my life, Angel."

"We are two halves of a whole, my darling."

"True. It's a good thing we've bought a house with a big garden." Nick squeezed his bride's hand and turned to the celebrant who had been waiting patiently. "Make this angel my wife, so I can spend the rest of my life in heaven."

Epilogue

Two hours north of Sydney Harbour lay the popular holiday destination of Nelson Bay in Port Stephens. There wasn't a cloud in the sky as a catamaran cruised out of d'Albora Marina, sending gentle ripples to buffet the hulls of the other boats. The cat had been moored at this stunning location for the past two years. Now, due to one determined young lady, it was vital the owner relocate.

He'd been involved in the field of computer science, cyber fraud, and online espionage for most of his adult life. Now he was a hacker using a unique soft ware program that could over-ride any computer system in the world. As such, its worth was invaluable.

The program's existence had come at great personal loss. In the wrong hands, it could potentially throw Wall Street into chaos, bankrupt entire countries, fund terrorist organizations, and start wars.

He'd manipulated the program to infiltrate the emails and computer of Simon Hawk who worked for Steele Intelligence and Personal Security Services. An interesting experience shadowing a man who regularly accessed confidential information from secure databases. This came as no surprise to the hacker, but was Simon Hawke up to the challenge ahead?

The hacker glanced at the file beside him on the fly bridge. He had a personal dossier on each of the six men working for Steele Intelligence. The contracts they accepted were undercover and often dangerous, yet with the resolution of each job, no mention was made of these men or their involvement on any media platforms.

The hacker concentrated on steering his cat through Nelson Bay, escorted by a small pod of dolphins as he headed for open sea. With the Amethyst Code now operational and an innocent young woman's life on the line, it was paramount Simon Hawke and his friends join the game.

And so it begins.

About the Author

Erin Moira O'Hara grew up in the Blue Mountains of Australia, with a garden backing onto native bushland, hidden caves and fabulous lookouts. Weekends were spent exploring, climbing trees and creating secret bases. Her love of reading began with visits to the local library, where she became absorbed in a world of intrigue, fantasy and action-packed adventures. The moment Erin read her first romance; she recognised the importance of finding the right man to share her life. She now lives with him close to the largest saltwater lake in Australia. Their home overlooks bushland and is surrounded by an abundance of bird life and an ever-growing garden.

Erin's writing encompasses everything she loves—intrigue, suspense, passion and romance.

If you would like to know more, please visit:
http://www.erinmoiraohara.com

www.ingramcontent.com/pod-product-compliance
Lightning Source LLC
Chambersburg PA
CBHW031944110726
47902CB00001B/291